A Mother's Trust

Also by Dilly Court

Mermaids Singing
The Dollmaker's Daughters
Tilly True
The Best of Sisters
The Cockney Sparrow
A Mother's Courage
The Constant Heart
A Mother's Promise
The Cockney Angel
A Mother's Wish
The Ragged Heiress
A Mother's Secret
Cinderella Sister

Dilly Court

A Mother's Trust

arrow books

Published by Arrow Books 2011

2 4 6 8 10 9 7 5 3 1

First published in Great Britain in 2011 by
Arrow Books
Random House, 20 Vauxhall Bridge Road,
London SW1V 2SA

www.randomhouse.co.uk

Addresses for companies within The Random House Group Limited can be found at:
www.randomhouse.co.uk/offices.htm

The Random House Group Limited Reg. No. 954009

A CIP catalogue record for this book
is available from the British Library

ISBN 9780099562535

The Random House Group Limited supports The Forest Stewardship Council (FSC®),
the leading international forest certification organisation. Our books carrying
the FSC label are printed on FSC® certified paper. FSC is the only forest
certification scheme endorsed by the leading environmental organisations,
including Greenpeace. Our paper procurement policy can be found at
www.randomhouse.co.uk/environment

Typeset in Palatino by Palimpsest Book Production Limited,
Falkirk, Stirlingshire
Printed and bound by CPI Group (UK) Ltd, Croydon CR0 4YY

For Sara and Grace

Chapter One

Saffron Hill, Clerkenwell, 1877

The darkness surrounding the table was heavy with the spirits of the departed, or so it seemed to Phoebe, who was hiding in a cupboard watching the proceedings through a knothole in the door panel.

A single candle created a pool of light in the centre of the green chenille tablecloth on which rested the hands of the nervous participants in the séance, their fingers touching and their heartbeats palpable in the eerie silence.

'Is there anyone there?' Annie Giamatti's voice rang out loud and clear. 'Are there any spirit people who would like to speak to me?'

Phoebe waited for her mother's cue which meant she must tug the piece of string dangling in front of her face. It was attached to a length of gauze that had been smeared with fish scales to make it appear phosphorescent and concealed in a gaudily painted vase on the sideboard. It was hot and stuffy in the cupboard and she had a sudden urge to sneeze. She wrinkled her nose, holding her breath until the moment passed.

A low throaty moan from Annie was the pre-arranged signal and Phoebe pulled the cord with the expertise of long practice. If she tugged too hard the material would fly up to the ceiling and might get caught on one of the cup hooks that held it in position. If she did not exert enough pressure it would hang limply like a chemise on a washing line and the game would be up.

'I see a spirit manifesting itself,' Annie droned in a monotone. 'Come closer, friend, and speak to us.'

A muffled scream followed by excited gasps and whispers passing between the three women at the table indicated that the apparition had created the desired effect.

'Is that you, Henry?'

Phoebe recognised the voice of Mrs Fowler, widow of the late Henry Fowler, cobbler and notorious skin-flint. She sounded frightened but filled with hope.

'It's me, ducks.' Annie's tones deepened into her interpretation of a male voice.

'Are you happy where you are now, Henry?'

'Very happy, Ethel.'

'Are you in heaven or the other place, Henry?'

'I'm all right, Ethel, but I have to leave you now . . .' Annie's voice trailed off as if the tortured spirit of poor Henry was being dragged back to limbo.

'Don't go yet, ducks,' Ethel pleaded. 'Tell me where you kept your cash. I got to pay the bills and I'm down to me last farthing.'

Phoebe held her breath, hoping that her mother remembered Henry Fowler's boast that he kept his money hidden in a place where Ethel would never think to look. It had taken several pints of brown ale to loosen his tongue in the public bar of the Three Bells, but Annie had come home laughing fit to bust, and a little swipey herself. 'The crafty old codger hid

2

his gold sovs in his peg leg, Phoebe. He hollowed out the wood and dropped them in one by one. Would you credit it?'

Annie exhaled three shuddering breaths. 'I'm fading fast.'

'Tell her, you mean old goat.' This time the voice belonged to Ethel's sister, Minnie Sykes, a large woman with fists like hams who, widowed at an early age, had taken on the profession of rat catcher. It was fabled from Saffron Hill to Bleeding Heart Yard that she killed the vermin by biting off their heads. Phoebe was convinced that it was no lie. She gave the string a gentle tug, hoping to distract Minnie's attention for long enough to allow her mother to finish the séance before things turned ugly.

'Tell me, Henry, please. You got no use for money where you are. For the love of God think of your dear ones left to struggle on alone.' Ethel ended on a sob, which might have been more convincing if Phoebe did not have first hand knowledge of the dear ones left to struggle on their own. Henry had fathered three sons, all of them raw-boned and burly, and a daughter, Dolly who was a bit simple. The brothers worked at the metropolitan railway terminus, doing jobs that required brawn and no brains. It was said that by the time they reached the door of the family hovel in Bleeding Heart Yard on a Friday night they had already squandered their weekly wages on strong drink and loose women. Phoebe peered anxiously through the knothole.

'Please, Henry,' Ethel cried, wringing her hands. 'For the sake of our boys tell me.'

'Me wooden leg,' Annie murmured. 'You'll find it there. Don't let them layabouts have it, though, and pay Annie Giamatti double what she asks.'

Ethel leapt to her feet. 'Gawd save us. I told Dolly to use it for kindling. We got to get home double quick, Minnie.'

'Trust the old miser to do something bloody silly like that.' Minnie rose from her seat. She glanced down at the small woman cowering on a stool beside her. 'Get up, you silly bitch. The dead can't hurt you.'

'I seen his ghost. It'll come to us in the night and suck the life blood from us.'

Minnie caught her a resounding clout around the ear. 'Shut up, Biddy. Get out of that door and run to Bleeding Heart Yard as fast as your skinny little legs will carry you. Stop that stupid girl from lighting the fire with Henry's wooden leg or it'll be the worse for all of us and you in particular.'

Biddy let out a low wail and made for the door.

Phoebe grasped the latch on the cupboard door with fingers that shook a little. She was always nervous when things did not go entirely to plan. How Ma kept herself calm under such circumstances she did not know, but from her vantage point she saw her mother snap upright, coming out of her trance with amazing speed. She leapt to her feet and moved swiftly to bar their exit. 'Not so fast, Mrs Fowler. There's a matter of my fee. A shilling, if you please. Although I do believe that the late departed Mr Fowler said you ought to pay me double for revealing his secret.'

Ethel attempted to shove her out of the way but

Annie was used to such tricks and she stood her ground. 'My fee, if you please, or even if you don't. You ain't leaving here until you cough up, lady.'

Minnie advanced on her like a warship with all guns primed and ready. 'You'll get out of the way, Annie Giamatti, if you know what's good for you.'

Ethel put her hand in her pocket and took out some coins which she thrust at Annie. 'Here's tuppence. I got no more until I find Henry's money.'

Minnie grasped Annie by her throat and for a moment Phoebe thought that her mother's thin neck might snap like a twig. She was about to rush out from her hiding place and go to her assistance when the door burst open. Fabio Giamatti strode into the parlour, filling the small room with his presence. 'What's up, Annie? Are these women giving you trouble?'

'It's all right, Father-in-law. Mrs Fowler was just about to cough up the reddy.'

Phoebe's grandfather stood with his arms akimbo. He might be all of sixty-five but he was muscular and fit from years of working in the ice cream trade, lifting the blocks of ice that he purchased from the depot to say nothing of handling heavy milk churns. His hair had once been black as jet, although Phoebe could only vaguely remember him in those days, but now it was streaked with silver as if an artist had tinted it with a paintbrush. As light flooded the room from the passageway, Phoebe could see his heavy features contorted in a fierce scowl. He did not have to say anything more. Minnie Sykes was no match for Fabio Giamatti and Ethel was patently terrified. She tipped the contents of her purse into Annie's outstretched hand, and swearing beneath her breath she scuttled from the room, closely followed by Minnie who was dragging Biddy by the scruff of her neck. 'Get a move on, Ethel,' she roared. 'If that brainless fool's burned the thing I'll throw her on the fire after it.'

Phoebe opened the door and stepped out of the cupboard, wiping the perspiration from her forehead on the back of her hand. 'Did she pay up in full, Ma?'

Annie studied the coins, frowning. 'A penny short, but for a moment I thought I was a goner. That Minnie is a fierce woman.'

Fabio went to pull back the curtains and light filtered through the grimy windowpanes to reveal a room crowded with large, ornately carved mahogany furniture upholstered in red plush. The mantelshelf was crowded with bric-a-brac, as were the shelves in the recesses on either side of the chimney breast. The walls were hung with poorly executed watercolours of scenes of the Italian lakes, brought back from trips to the mother country by the Giamattis, who purchased them in their native Stresa on the shores of Lake Maggiore. A distant relative fancied himself as an artist and sold his work to tourists and members of his family who were disposed to encourage him in his chosen career, although Phoebe fancied that he must be quite poor if that was his only source of income.

'When are you going to stop this nonsense, Annie? Why you no find something more suited to the widow of my sainted eldest son?' Fabio shook his head, sending a pitying glance in Phoebe's direction. 'The poor bambina. What sort of life is it for her? Eh? What man will want to marry the daughter of a woman who speaks to the dead?'

Annie shrugged her shoulders as she pocketed the money. 'Phoebe isn't a child. She'll be twenty next birthday, and I don't have to listen to this sort of talk. I get enough of it from Mamma Giamatti. If your sainted Paulo had not got himself into a fight with one of the high mob he might be here today to look after his wife and daughter.' With a toss of her flaxen curls, Annie stalked out of the room. Her high-heeled boots made tip-tapping sounds on the tiled floor of the passage leading to the front door. Phoebe heard it slam behind her mother as she stormed out of the house.

'Are you all right, cara?' Fabio asked, frowning. 'You look pale.'

'I'm fine, Nonno.' Phoebe sat down on the chair recently vacated by Ethel Sykes. Only now she realised that her knees were trembling. Her grandfather was right. Minnie Fowler was not the sort of woman to cross, and if he had not arrived on the scene at that moment matters might have got completely out of hand. Ma was playing a dangerous game when she took on the denizens of the back alleys and courts in Clerkenwell, not to mention the members of the street gangs with whom she consorted in the pubs. Ma was a good woman at heart, but she had a weakness for strong drink. Right now she would be heading for the Three Bells or some other public house with the money from the séance in her purse. It would not remain there long. Annie would roll home the worse for liquor and fall into a drunken stupor in the room they shared at the top of the house, and Phoebe would be left to do her mother's chores as well as her own. Grandmother Giamatti was a hard taskmistress. She ruled the house in Saffron Hill with a rod of iron. Her two remaining sons, Lorenzo and Julio, were big muscular men who, like their father before them, earned their living making and selling ice cream on the streets of London, but they were patently in awe of their indomitable mother.

Fabio pulled up a chair and sat down beside her. 'You should not allow your mamma to ruin your life, Phoebe. I keep her under my roof for the sake of my dead son and for your sake too, but not for hers. It is a bad thing that she does. She no more speaks to the dead than I am the king of England.' He patted Phoebe's hands as they lay clasped on her lap. 'You're a good girl. Find yourself a worthy man. Get married and have lots of bambini. That is a woman's real destiny, my flower.'

Phoebe smiled and squeezed his fingers. 'Perhaps, Nonno. But not yet.'

'Gino would make a good husband, and he is very fond of you.'

'And I like him, but not enough to spend the rest of my life with him.' Rising to her feet, she smoothed the worried lines from his forehead with the tip of her forefinger and dropped a kiss on the top of his silver-streaked hair. He smelt of cream and melted sugar, lemon zest and strawberries; all the good things that went into Giamatti's ice cream and water ices. Not for him were the cheap tricks used by some of their neighbours, who used cochineal to colour water and called it raspberry ice, or milk diluted with water and even worse water coloured with chalk to manufacture the product they sold as penny licks. Fresh unadulterated milk, eggs and sugar were the ingredients of Giamatti's ice cream. Crushed raspberries or strawberries bought in Covent Garden market with the dew still on them were used to make the refreshing water ices for which people queued on days when the heat in the city would fell an ox.

Phoebe was proud to be a part of a family with a long tradition of honest trading, but she could not abandon her emotionally fragile mother to the fate that must befall a woman with a weakness for strong drink. She gave her grandfather an affectionate hug. She loved every line and wrinkle, and the craggy contour of his face that had the strength of a lion and the gentleness of a lamb. She would do nothing to hurt him, but she must make her own way in the world and that did not include marrying Gino Argento or any of the young Italian men she knew who were involved in the ice cream trade in Saffron Hill. 'I must go and find Ma before she spends the whole shilling on gin or she'll be dead drunk by nightfall.'

He patted her hand. 'Go, then. But think about what I said, cara. It will soon be autumn and Mamma and I will be heading south to Italy for the winter months with Lorenzo and Julio. I want you to come with us, little one. Leave Annie to look after herself, I beg of you.'

'I'll think about it, Nonno.' Phoebe hurried from the

room before he had a chance to press her further on the subject. It came up every year at the end of the summer season, when those families in the community who had made a handsome profit from their labours and saved every penny of it set off for their homeland to spend the winter. Each year since she was considered old enough to have an opinion of her own, Phoebe had chosen to remain in London with her mother. Sometimes it was tempting to escape from the mud and filth of the city and head for the sweet clean air of the Italian mountains and lakes, but to leave her mother to cope alone would be like abandoning a small child to her fate. In the close-knit Italian community, blonde, blue-eyed Annie was still a foreigner despite having married into an old-established family, and Saffron Hill, belying its colourful rural-sounding name, was in reality a mean street lined with a higgledy-piggledy mixture of overcrowded tenements, pubs and small dirty shops selling everything from milk to articles lifted from the pockets of the unwary by street urchins. Phoebe could speak the language of her father's family like a native, but Annie still stumbled over the words and pronunciation, especially when her brain was addled with jigger gin.

It was to the Three Bells that Phoebe hurried, making her way through the piles of rotting vegetables, horse dung and drifts of straw that covered the cobblestones. She was used to the stench of overflowing sewers and the putrid flotsam washed up on the banks of the Thames at high tide, but today it was hot and clouds of bluebottles feasted on the detritus. She held a handkerchief soaked in some of her grandmother's lavender cologne to her nose as she stepped over a dead rat in the gutter. Overhead a couple of carrion crows circled hopefully, waiting their chance to alight in the busy street and tear at the rotting flesh.

'Phoebe, wait for me.'

Recognising Gino's voice, Phoebe stopped, turning her head to look at him in surprise. 'Gino. What are you doing here? I thought you would be out selling hokey-pokey.'

He grinned, displaying a row of even white teeth. 'Sold out, cara. It's a hot day and I got nothing left to sell, so I come looking for my bella Phoebe.'

'That's nice, Gino. But I can't stop.' She continued walking at a brisk pace but he fell into step beside her, seemingly regardless of the fact that he was trampling ankle-deep through rubbish.

'It's your mamma, again, isn't it? What has she done this time, cara? Is it an angry wife or a cheated client who chases her?'

'Neither.' Phoebe stopped outside the pub door. 'She has money.'

He pulled a face. 'Not for long, eh?'

'No.' Phoebe pushed the door open, grimacing as a gust of hot smoky air billowed out of the taproom. She stepped inside, peering through the haze of tobacco smoke, but it was the sound of her mother's laughter that directed her to a corner of the ingle nook where she found Annie seated beside a rotund gentleman dressed in sombre black with a white stock at his neck over which his several chins wobbled when he chuckled. His chubby fingers, mottled like pink pork sausages, toyed with the buttons on Annie's cotton blouse.

'It's time to go home, Ma,' Phoebe said firmly.

Annie looked up at her and her eyes widened, but the smile remained fixed on her face. She lifted her glass to her lips in a defiant gesture and drained its contents in one gulp. 'Go away. Can't you see I'm busy?'

Phoebe squared her thin shoulders. 'You're wanted at home, Ma. I'd like you to come now.'

Annie's companion cleared his throat. 'You heard what your mother said, young lady. Show some respect for your elders and do as she bids you.'

Phoebe recognised him as Amos Snape, a clerk who worked at Nicholson's Distillery in St John Street. She had seen him in her mother's company on several occasions, and although he was preferable to some of Annie's other gentlemen friends he had a somewhat dubious reputation and it was rumoured that his late wife's death was not as accidental as he claimed. Annie might think she was subtly gleaning details about his domestic affairs in order to lure him into a mock séance, but Phoebe suspected that Amos had designs on her mother that did not include paying a penny or twopence in order to contact his dear departed; in fact the very reverse was probably true. If it were at all possible for the dead to speak, Nellie Snape might have something to say that would wipe the smile off her husband's face forever. If she closed her eyes, Phoebe could visualise a hangman's noose dangling over his head. She did not need a crystal ball to predict Snape's future, and from the lascivious gleam in his small piggy eyes when he glanced at the swell of Annie's breast, she could tell that his intentions were far from honourable. The large glass of gin that stood untouched as yet next to the tot that her mother had just consumed was evidence enough of his desire to get Ma swipey. Not that Annie needed much encouragement. Phoebe leaned closer. 'Come along, Ma. Please.'

Annie giggled, shaking her head. 'I done me bit this morning, love. Give a girl the chance to have some fun.'

Phoebe was about to insist when Gino laid his hand on her shoulder. She glanced up into his face and he winked at her before turning his full attention on Amos. 'I don't want to worry you, cully. But I think I see your boss walking down the street in this direction. Maybe he looks for you, maybe not. It's a mystery. Yes?'

Amos leapt to his feet, his prominent belly straining against the buttons on his waistcoat. 'Are you certain? Or are you spinning me a tale, you stupid macaroni.'

Gino held his hands palm upwards with an expressive shrug of his shoulders. 'Do you want to take a chance on it, signore? I maybe a stupid macaroni, but I ain't the one who'll look foolish when his boss finds him in the pub.'

'Get out of my way, Eyetie.'

With a bow and a smile, Gino moved aside. 'Signore.'

Amos shot him a malevolent glance as he barged past and hurried out into the street.

'What did you do that for?' Annie demanded angrily. 'We was just having a bit of a giggle, and I was close to finding out how poor Nellie come to a sticky end.'

Phoebe helped her mother to her feet. 'Never mind that now, Ma. Let's go home, shall we?'

'What are you grinning at?' Annie said, glaring at Gino. 'You should be at work, young man.'

Gino shook his head. 'I've sold my share of hokey-pokey for today, Signora Giamatti.'

'That's as maybe, but my girl has things to do. You'll have Mamma Giamatti to deal with if you keep Phoebe from her chores.' Annie picked up the glass of gin and downed it in one swallow. She gave a sigh of satisfaction. 'That was good Hollands, none of your jigger gin for Amos; I'll say that for him. But thanks to you two I'll have me work cut out now to persuade him to contact his dear Nellie.' She tossed her head, eyeing Phoebe defiantly. 'I ain't coming, girl. So don't look at me like that.' Her expression changed on an instant from sullen to one of delight.

Realising that she had lost her mother's attention, Phoebe turned her head and her heart sank as she realised who it was that had wrought the change in her mother's mood. Burly costermongers and porters from the nearby markets moved swiftly out of his path as Rogue Paxman crossed the floor to join them. Phoebe glanced anxiously at the man who was known to be the leader of a notorious mob. If her father had not become embroiled in their nefarious doings he might still be alive this day. She felt suffocated by his presence and when she swallowed there was a bitter taste

14

in her mouth, but to her horror she realised that her mother was smiling a welcome to the man who had brought tragedy to their family. 'Mother,' Phoebe said in a low voice. 'Come with me, please.'

'Oh, Lord, don't be such a spoilsport,' Annie said without looking at her. 'I think Rogue wants a word or two with me.'

Gino made a move towards Annie, as if to protect her, but Paxman, still smiling, barred his way. 'Excuse us, mate.' There was a hidden threat in his words, and Phoebe was alarmed to see his hands fisted at his side. Rogue Paxman was not a man to take no for an answer. His shrewd sea-green eyes set beneath straight fair eyebrows and a thatch of corn-gold hair were at odds with his powerful physique and the strong set of his jaw. He stood a good head and shoulders taller than Gino and he was not the sort of man with whom any sane person would pick a quarrel. Sending a pleading look to her mother, Phoebe clutched Gino's arm. 'I think we'd best leave now. Come along, Ma.'

Annie shook her head. 'I'll be along when I'm ready, ducks. Right now I've got business with Rogue. Private business.' She tapped the side of her nose, winking at Paxman as she resumed her seat. She held up her empty glass. 'A glass of Hollands would go down a treat.'

He took it from her with slight inclination of his head. 'I'm happy to oblige, ma'am.' With a smile directed at Phoebe he made his way to the bar.

She turned on her mother, bending down to speak in an urgent undertone. 'Ma, have you lost your senses?

15

Rogue Paxman is a villain. Pa might be here now if he hadn't got mixed up with the mobs. Don't have anything to do with him, I beg of you.'

Annie gave her a tipsy smile. 'Don't fuss, girl. I'm not a muggins. I can think for myself. Rogue and his brother Ned have money. I ain't going to live in Mamma Giamatti's attic for the rest of me life. At last I can see a way out for you and me, Phoebe. I'm sick of the smell of bloody ice cream and that Italian woman telling me what to do. I'm tired of pretending to conjure up spirits when the only one that interests me comes in a stone bottle. The Paxmans owe us, and they're our ticket out of Saffron Hill.'

Phoebe glanced anxiously over her shoulder. She could see Paxman making his way back to the table. 'The only place he'll lead us to is the cemetery, Ma. He's nothing but trouble and his brother is even worse.'

Annie threw back her head and laughed. 'Got your own crystal ball now, have you, ducks?' She looked up at Paxman as he passed her a fresh drink. 'Ta, Rogue. Come and sit beside me and we'll have a nice cosy chat. My girl's just leaving.'

Phoebe hesitated, meeting his amused gaze with a stubborn tilt of her chin. She hated this man with a passion, and his worthless brother too. It was rumoured that the Paxman family had been involved in criminal activities for generations, and they lived in some style in a large house overlooking Charterhouse Gardens. Rogue had been born to the life and although there was a degree of respect for his gang locally, this was tempered by fear. The only thing that could be said of

16

the Paxman mob was that they kept the other high mobs at bay. Their rule was absolute and their code was law to those who lived by it. Phoebe had heard her grandfather complaining that if the police had as much control of the streets as the Paxman brothers, this part of London would be a safer place. Phoebe could not agree. The law was there to protect honest citizens, and must be upheld without resorting to the bullying tactics adopted by the Paxmans. That's what her father had taught her and she clung to that belief.

Refusing to return Paxman's ironic smile, she felt anger roil in her belly. She would not see her mother tread the path that had led to the death of her beloved Paulo. Phoebe knew that the men her mother flirted with meant nothing to her, and her addiction to strong drink was a feeble attempt to escape from the hope-lessness of her situation. Ma might be weak, but she was a good woman at heart. Of that Phoebe was certain. She snatched the glass from her mother's hand. 'No, Ma. You've had enough.'

Paxman sat astride a chair, and his eyes mocked her. 'Isn't that up to your mother, Miss Giamatti?'

Phoebe knew that he was laughing at her and this only added to her sense of anger and frustration. 'Mind your own business, Rogue Paxman. I'm taking my mother home. She's not well.'

Annie had paled visibly and Gino was plucking nervously at Phoebe's sleeve. 'Come, cara,' he whis-pered. 'This is not good.'

'Sensible chap,' Paxman said lazily. 'Take the little tigress home where she belongs.'

Annie made a grab for the glass, but Phoebe held it out of her reach. 'No, Ma. You'll make yourself ill again.'

Two bright spots of colour stood out on Annie's cheeks. 'I'm your mother, Phoebe. You'll do as I say. Give me my drink.'

'Yes, don't be a silly girl,' Paxman said, grinning. 'Go home and play with your dolls, or polish your crystal ball.'

Taking a deep breath, Phoebe tossed back the gin with a defiant flick of her wrist, but the unaccustomed spirit caught the back of her throat and she coughed and spluttered as she struggled for breath. Tears ran down her cheeks and someone was slapping her on the back. A handkerchief was thrust into her hands and she mopped her streaming eyes.

'That will teach you not to do stupid things,' Paxman said, chuckling.

Realising that it was his hanky that she held in her hand, Phoebe thrust it back at him. 'Leave me alone.'

'Come now,' Gino urged, eyeing Paxman nervously. 'This is no place for you, Phoebe.'

'Quite right, Gino, my boy.' Paxman nodded in approval. 'Take her away from here.'

Phoebe drew herself up to her full height. 'Go away, Gino. This has nothing to do with you.' Ignoring his muttered protests, she reached out again to her mother. 'Please come home, Ma.' She blinked as the room seemed to tilt sideways, or perhaps it was her head that was spinning. She could not work out which, but the gin was certainly having an effect. 'Please, Ma,' she added faintly.

Annie rose unsteadily to her feet. 'You stupid girl. Get out of here.' She raised her hand as if to slap Phoebe's face but the blow never landed. Annie's knees buckled and she slipped silently to the ground.

Paxman stood up. 'What a pair you are,' he said dispassionately.

Phoebe's senses were still dulled from the after-effects of swallowing strong spirits on an empty stomach, and she gazed down at her mother in disbelief. She had seen Ma swipey on many occasions but never insensible. 'Are you all right, Ma?'

'I'll get help,' Gino said, backing away through the interested crowd of onlookers.

'Don't bother.' Paxman bent down to scoop Annie up in his arms as if she weighed no more than a feather pillow. 'Let's get this woman home where she belongs.'

Phoebe's head was beginning to ache and she was in no condition to argue. She followed him as he carried Annie out of the pub and down the street towards the Giamattis' tall, narrow house, wedged in between a shop selling milk and a hay merchant. Gino had run on ahead despite Phoebe's pleas for him to stop. She saw her grandfather emerge from the house and she could tell by the way his bushy eyebrows met over the bridge of his nose and the scowl on his face that there was going to be trouble.

Fabio stepped into the street, rolling up his sleeves. 'What is all this?'

'It's nothing, Nonno,' Phoebe said hastily. 'Ma fainted. That's all.'

Fabio leaned closer to her. 'Have you been drinking?'

'No. Well, yes. But I can explain.'

Fabio caught her a blow round the head that sent Phoebe spinning across the cobblestones and she landed in a heap on the doorstep, clutching her sore ear. 'What have I told you about liquor? It's the way of the devil, my girl.'

Paxman thrust Annie's limp body into Fabio's arms. 'And I'm supposed to be the villain round here. I've never hit a woman, old man. Take this one and keep her safe.' He strode across to lift Phoebe to her feet. 'Are you all right?'

She nodded, pulling away from him. 'I don't need your help.'

He shrugged his shoulders. 'Tell Annie to keep away from Ned,' he said in a low voice. 'That's what I was going to say to her. Your mother plays a dangerous game, Phoebe. She doesn't know what she is getting into. Take her to Italy in the autumn if you can, but if you value her life, then make certain she keeps away from my brother and that bastard, Amos Snape.'

Chapter Two

Inside the house, Fabio carried Annie up three flights of stairs to the attic room she shared with Phoebe. He laid her down on the iron bedstead, straightening his back and running his hand through his hair as he met Phoebe's reproachful gaze. 'I'm sorry, cara. That's the first time I've ever raised my hand to you and it will be the last, but I can't bear the thought that you will turn out like her.' He looked down at Annie's prostrate form, shaking his head. 'Strong drink isn't the answer.'

'I know,' Phoebe said softly. 'It's all right, Nonno. I only drank the hateful stuff so that Ma wouldn't. I had to do something to get her away from that brute. I hate him and his whole family.'

Fabio reached out and took her in his arms, hugging her to his broad chest. His apron was spattered with cream and smelt of vanilla. 'I would rather cut off my hand than hurt you, little one. You must come home to Stresa with us in September. I cannot leave you here with your mamma and her ghosts. It's not good for you.'

'Maybe. We'll see, Nonno.'

He backed towards the doorway, ducking his head as he left the room. 'Think about it, cara.'

Alone with her mother, Phoebe perched on the

edge of the bed. Blue bruise-like shadows underlined Annie's eyes and her skin had a sickly translucent sheen. She stirred and her eyelids fluttered. She gazed dazedly at Phoebe. 'What happened?'

'You fainted, Ma. Went out like a light in the pub.'

Annie attempted to sit up, but fell back against the pillows with a groan. 'Fetch me a bowl. I feel sick.'

Phoebe held her mother's head as she retched into the washbowl and she cleaned her up afterwards, mopping her face and hands with a damp cloth as if Annie were a small child. 'Are you feeling better now, Ma?'

'A bit, ta.'

'This ain't the first time you've been poorly like this. I know because I heard you outside in the privy. Should I fetch the doctor?'

Annie's pale lips curved in a wry smile and she lay back, closing her eyes. 'It's nothing the quack can help with, Phoebe. So much for seeing into the future and hearing heavenly voices; the angels was all on holiday when I prayed for it not to be true.'

'Ma?' Phoebe took her mother's cold hand and chafed it. 'Are you ill? Have you got a fever?'

Annie's blue eyes opened and tears trickled down her cheeks. 'I wasn't sure until today, ducks. I thought at thirty-six I was too old to get caught like this.'

'You can't be! Surely not?'

Annie pulled her hand free and laid it on her belly. 'It's Ned's. I don't know if I love or hate the bugger.'

'Ned Paxman?' Phoebe released her mother's hand as if the touch of her skin burned her own flesh. 'No, Ma. You didn't. Not with him.'

Sighing, Annie shrugged her shoulders. 'He's a good-looking cove, and he makes me laugh. There's precious little of that around here.'

'But it was through him that Pa got killed by the Smithfield mob.'

'They was in it together. It wasn't Ned's fault.'

'But you went with him, Ma. How could you do such a thing?'

'Ned isn't all bad, Phoebe. I know I'm too old for the likes of him, but the others was just flirtations. Leading them on was more business than pleasure, but it was different with Ned.'

'And do you think he'd stand by you?'

'It was just a bit of a lark for him. I knew that all along, but I couldn't help meself. He made me feel like I used to when I was a girl in Stepney.'

Phoebe slipped off the bed to pace the floor. 'If Nonno, Julio and Lorenzo find out about this there'll be trouble you can't even begin to imagine, Ma. If the Camorra gets involved there'll be murder and mayhem.'

Annie curled up on her side, wrapping her arms around her knees. 'What will they do to me and my baby?'

Phoebe froze, closing her eyes in an attempt to shut out the pictures of bloodlust and revenge flashing before them in quick succession. 'They mustn't find out. I don't know what we'll do but I'll think of something.' She moved to the bed and sat down beside her mother. 'How far gone are you?'

'I don't know. Two or three months. I'm not sure.'

'It's the middle of July. In six weeks or so the family will be leaving for Italy.' Phoebe did a quick calculation in her head. 'The baby should be due early in the New Year, and the family won't return until April.'

'We can't hide a baby from them, Phoebe. They'll find out sooner or later.'

Brushing her mother's damp hair back from her forehead, Phoebe forced her lips into a smile. 'We'll sort something out, Ma. In the meantime you mustn't let on, not to anyone, and you mustn't see him again. I want you to promise me that, because I hate to think what will happen if the Paxmans find out you're carrying Ned's child. It's not just the baby's life at stake here, Ma. You'd be in danger yourself.' Phoebe cocked her head on one side as she heard the faint sound of her grandmother's voice calling to her. She moved swiftly to open the door. 'Coming, Nonna.' She paused on the threshold. 'Get some rest, Ma. I'll tell Nonna that you've got your monthly and you're feeling bad.'

'She's never liked me,' Annie murmured sleepily. 'No one was ever going to be good enough for her precious Paulo.'

Closing the door, Phoebe hurried downstairs to join her grandmother in the kitchen where she was preparing the evening meal of boiled cabbage, bacon and macaroni, the staple diet of the more frugal Italian families who saved every penny they could to fund their eventual return to their native land. Maria Giamatti glanced up from chopping fat bacon to give her granddaughter a sceptical look. 'She's drunk again.'

'No, it's not that, Nonna. Ma's not feeling too well.'

Phoebe picked up a cleaver and began shredding a huge head of cabbage. 'It's the usual thing.'

'In my day young girls did not mention such a topic, and we certainly did not take to our beds. I always said she was no good for my poor Paulo.' Maria seized a clove of garlic and smashed it with the heel of her hand. 'A few months in Stresa will put a stop to her wandering off to the pub whenever she feels like it.'

'Yes, Nonna.' Phoebe had learned long ago not to argue with her grandmother. Maria's word was law in the Giamatti household.

'And there will be no more nonsense about you staying in London with your mamma,' Maria added, pointing the knife at Phoebe. 'If you had come home with us last winter you would have been promised to Gino and preparing for your wedding by now. You are a grown woman, Phoebe. Soon you will be on the shelf; an old maid. I was married when I was fifteen and had Paulo the next year, and it was the same for your mamma. Soon you will be too old to have babies. I bet you no see that in your mamma's crystal ball.'

'But I don't love Gino.' The protest was drawn from Phoebe's lips before she could stop herself. She knew it was useless to argue with her grandmother but the discovery of her mother's pregnancy had unnerved her.

Maria threw the chopped bacon into a large pan on the range and tossed in a couple of cloves of garlic. 'You think I loved Fabio when I married him? No, but I did as my family wished and love came later. Your mamma has filled your head with silly thoughts.'

'She loved my father.'

'And now my boy is dead. He would not have got himself mixed up with the high mobs if she hadn't kept on at him to move out of this house and get a home of their own. She was never satisfied; she always wanted more and more. If Lorenzo and Julio marry good Italian girls they will be content to live in the family home.'

Phoebe cut out the hard core of the cabbage with a flick of the knife. It was on the tip of her tongue to say that maybe the reason for her two uncles remaining single was that their romances ended abruptly when their prospective brides were introduced to their future mother-in-law. But beneath the blustery temperament and belligerent attitude Phoebe knew that her grandmother possessed a kind heart, although it was well hidden. Maria considered that any outward display of affection was a sure sign of weakness, and rarely allowed the tender side of her nature to come to the fore. Phoebe had realised long ago that it could not have been easy for a girl from the mountains of northern Italy to leave her home and make a life for herself and her family in the sooty, crime-ridden East End of London. It had taken courage and fortitude to endure the rigours of setting up a business in competition with all the other immigrant families, many of whom came from the region of Calabria and would undoubtedly have been brigands in their time. Although mostly reformed and turned into respectable citizens, the element of barbarism lurked beneath the surface and the odd revenge killing was not unknown, especially amongst the immigrants from the area where the 'Ndrangheta was a powerful force.

'Gino is a good boy,' Maria said, continuing the conversation despite Phoebe's failure to respond. 'He comes from a respectable family. He'll make a good husband and father.'

'Yes, Nonna. I've finished chopping the cabbage. What else would you like me to do?'

'I would like you to go for a walk with Gino after supper. Every evening he comes to the door and asks you out, and each time you make some excuse. I say give him a chance, Phoebe. I don't know what you're waiting for, but you no get a knight in shining armour in Clerkenwell.'

The rays of the setting sun turned the River Thames into a stream of molten lava as it flowed past Pigs Quay on the ebb tide. A cloud of smoke and fumes from the city gas works hung in the still warm air like a feather mattress suspended above the chimney tops. The sky was streaked blood red and purple and heat rose from the cobblestones, making each step that Phoebe took feel as though she were walking on hot coals. There was an eerie stillness as the ships, barges, wherries and lighters had moored for the night and their crews had either gone home or disappeared into the many pubs dotted along the river's edge. The setting might have been romantic had it not been for the putrid odours arising from the mud and the general city stench of sewage and rubbish left to rot at the roadside, but Phoebe was not in the mood to listen to

Gino's sweet talk. Her mind had been elsewhere all through the evening meal and even now, with Gino holding her hand, she could think of nothing but the desperate situation brought about by her mother's affair with a notorious gangster.

'You haven't heard a word I've said.' Gino took both her hands in his and squeezed them gently.

'I'm sorry.' She met his anxious gaze with an apologetic smile. 'I'm just a bit worried about Ma. You saw how poorly she was today.'

'I saw only that she was drunk. You can't live your life for your mamma. She thinks only of herself.'

Gazing down at the water, Phoebe shuddered as a body floated past, face down with his arms outstretched as if the corpse was flying towards the sea. Gino released her hands and placed his arm around her shoulders. 'Don't look, cara. It's a common enough sight but not one you should see.'

Phoebe dashed her hand across her eyes. 'Poor man. What dreadful misfortune could have made him take his own life?'

'He might simply have fallen overboard and drowned, or perhaps he was dead drunk.'

'It's such a sad ending for anyone. He must have a family somewhere who will miss him and mourn for him. Perhaps he has a wife and children waiting for him at home.'

'Don't think about it, Phoebe. He could just as easily be a bad man who will be missed by no one.'

'Even so, he looks so lonely floating out to sea on the tide.'

'The river police will fish him out and take the corpse to the dead house. He will be taken care of.' Gino turned her to face him, laying the tip of his finger on her lips. 'Forget the unfortunate one, cara. I didn't bring you here to make you sad.'

The sincerity in his eyes and the gentleness in his voice was balm to Phoebe's troubled mind. She smiled. 'You're a good friend, Gino.'

'I want to be more than that. You know how I feel about you.'

She shook her head. 'Please don't say any more. I don't want to hurt your feelings but this isn't the right time.'

'Why not? Why won't you let me speak about what is in my heart?'

'There are things you don't know, Gino. Things that I cannot tell anyone, not even you.'

'You can trust me, cara. I would lay down my life for you. Marry me, Phoebe. Be my wife and let me take care of you forever.'

She had known for months that he was trying to pluck up the courage to propose. Thus far she had managed to evade the issue, but a moment's lapse of concentration, combined with the upset of seeing a drowned man floating downriver had made her drop her guard. Now she must face the consequences and give him his answer. Looking into his eyes, she saw both hope and fear. She felt his body tremble as he let his arm fall to his side. They were standing only inches apart but she was certain she could hear his heartbeats. 'I'm very fond of you, Gino. You're my dearest friend, but I can't marry you.'

29

Why? His lips formed the word but no sound came from them other than a sigh.

'Because I'm not right for you. I'm not sure I could ever marry anyone, especially now.'

He grasped her by the shoulders, giving her a gentle shake. 'Why? I deserve to know why you reject me. Our families expect us to marry. I can support a wife and children. You would want for nothing.'

'There are reasons, Gino. There is a secret that is someone else's and I cannot tell anyone, not even you.'

He was silent for a moment, gazing abstractedly across to the opposite bank. Slowly, he turned his head to look her in the eyes. 'It's to do with your mother, isn't it? And it has some connection with the Paxman gang.'

Startled by his acute perception, Phoebe had no ready response. She looked away. 'I can't say any more.'

'You must. If it is what I think it is then it concerns you too. Annie has been seen with Ned Paxman. It's common knowledge. It doesn't take much imagination to guess what the outcome of that might be.'

The need to unburden herself was almost too great to bear, and Gino had come perilously close to the truth. She nodded her head. 'I only found out today. She's carrying his child. You know what will happen if the family find out.'

'Vendetta,' Gino said, frowning.

'That's what makes me afraid,' Phoebe said, clutching his hands. 'Even though my grandfather and my uncles have nothing to do with the Camorra, I fear that they will call upon those who have connections.'

'Undoubtedly, that's what would happen.'

30

'It was bad enough that my father was killed by the high mob, but if they find out that Ma has betrayed them with Ned, I daren't even think about what they would do to her and to the child.'

'How far gone is she?'

Phoebe felt the blood rush to her cheeks. It was unseemly to be discussing pregnancy with a member of the opposite sex, even one who was as well known to her as Gino, but this was not the time for false modesty. 'She's not certain. Two months, maybe more.'

'She might stand a chance then if she remains in London when the family return to Italy for the winter.'

'That's what I think, and I will stay with her, but we have to keep it from those who can't afford to travel to their villages. You know how people love to gossip.'

Gino's lips curved into a smile. 'I do, but there will still be the problem of the child. Your mamma will have to find someone to take it in.'

The cold hard logic of this hit Phoebe with a force she could not have anticipated. For all the disgrace and the fact that her half-brother or sister would be related to the Paxmans, she realised how hard it would be to see her own flesh and blood given away to strangers. She could not begin to imagine how her mother would feel in such dire circumstances. 'We'll meet that problem when it arises,' she said slowly. 'But I can trust you not to say anything, can't I? You will promise me not to repeat this to a soul?'

Gino wrapped his arms around her. 'I promise, cara. But I fear for both of you if this should come out.'

'And you understand why I cannot marry you?'

His eyes darkened. 'No, but I think you care for me a little.'

'I care for you a lot, and maybe when this is all over . . .'

'What are you saying, Phoebe? Is that a yes?'

She managed a wobbly smile. 'It's a maybe.'

He drew her into his arms and kissed her tenderly but without passion. It was, she realised, a promise of things to come. He smiled into her eyes as he released her. 'I will not press you for your answer until I return from Italy. I must go, you do know that, don't you?'

She nodded her head. 'Of course. Your father would expect it of you.'

'And it would make it easier for you to stay here in London with your mamma if everyone thought that we had an understanding.'

Phoebe eyed him warily. 'What are you suggesting, Gino?'

'I think we should tell your family that you and I are betrothed.' He took a small gold signet ring from his little finger. 'Wear this and it will protect you from the gossiping tongues. It will make your grandmother happy too, I think. And I will rest easy knowing that you are safe from the attentions of those who are left behind.'

'I don't know,' Phoebe said slowly. 'I haven't said I would marry you, Gino.'

'I understand, and if the answer is no when I return, then so be it. I love you, Phoebe, and I want to protect you in any way I can. Of course I would much rather you came to Italy with the rest of us, but I understand that you cannot leave your mamma.'

'No, I can't. She wouldn't know what to do on her own.'

Gino's lips tightened, but there was sympathy and understanding in his eyes. 'I think your grandmother might be more easily persuaded to let you stay in London if she thinks you are soon to be a married woman.'

'You would do all this for me?' It was a question that she hardly dared ask.

'And more.' He kissed her again and this time there was no doubting the strength of his feelings. She gave herself up to the heady delight of a passionate embrace. It was wonderful to feel loved and needed for herself alone, and she returned his kisses with increasing fervour. He was young and strong and until this moment she had not realised the depth of his feelings for her. It was an intoxicating mixture.

The sun had set by the time they set off on the walk home from Pigs Quay. Saffron Hill was bathed in deep purple shadows. The bustle of the ice cream trade was stilled as the early risers had gone to their beds, but the night-time denizens of the courts and alleyways were making their appearance. Prostitutes lingered on street corners and the sounds of revelry emanated from the open pub doors. Ragged street urchins importuned the men who frequented the drinking houses, and feral cats and dogs sniffed about in the gutters for anything remotely edible.

As she entered the house Phoebe turned to say a last goodnight to Gino but he followed her inside. 'We will tell them together, cara.'

Her courage had failed her at the last minute and

she would have willingly sent him away, but even as she tugged at the ring it would not come off her finger. He raised her hand to his lips and kissed it. 'It's a sign. Don't be afraid, Phoebe. I will never let any harm come to you.' Still holding her hand, Gino followed the sound of voices to the parlour, where they found the family assembled. The only person missing was Annie.

'Gino?' Fabio rose from his chair. 'This is late for a social call.'

Lorenzo tossed the butt of his cigarillo into the empty grate. 'He looks like a man big with news.'

Julio leapt to his feet and slapped Gino on the back. 'I knew it. He's plucked up the courage to ask our little Phoebe to marry him. It's true, isn't it?'

Phoebe glanced nervously at her grandfather, but he was smiling, and her grandmother, who had been piling empty coffee cups onto a tray, stopped what she was doing to throw her arms around Gino. 'It is true; I can see it in your eyes. I am pleased for you.' She turned to Phoebe, wagging her finger. 'And you were so coy when I brought up the subject of marriage today. You must have known all along that you would accept this young man. I say shame on you for teasing your nonna in such a way.'

Still speechless, Phoebe suffered hugs and kisses from her grandmother and her uncles. She looked to Gino for help but he was conversing earnestly with her grandfather.

'I should have come to you first, Signor Giamatti,' Gino said humbly. 'Since Phoebe has no father now, I ask for your permission to marry your granddaughter.'

Fabio kissed him on both cheeks. 'You have it with my blessing, Gino. I couldn't wish for a better husband for my precious pearl.'

Phoebe glanced down at the ring on her fourth finger. Suddenly the voices of her family faded away and she closed her eyes. She could see the small cottage on the banks of Lake Maggiore where the family would soon return to harvest the vegetable crops they had planted the previous spring. All summer long these would have been tended by relatives living nearby and the returning emigrants would be greeted with feasting and dancing late into the night. Several families in Saffron Hill, including the Argentos, originated from the same area, but others had come from as far away as Naples and beyond. The vision in her head was misty at first, but as it cleared she could see that the sun was shining on the blue waters of the lake. Then as if a grey veil had been drawn over the familiar scene, the sky darkened and wind whipped the glassy surface into waves like the sea. She could hear a bell tolling and a feeling of dread made her tremble as a funeral procession wended its way along the village street.

'Are you all right, cara?'

She opened her eyes and found herself looking into Gino's concerned face. 'Yes. I'm sorry. It's been a long day and I'm tired.'

He raised her hand to his lips. 'I will leave you now, cara mia. Tomorrow we will talk again.'

'More than talk by the looks of things,' Julio said, grinning.

His mother shot him a warning glance. 'That's

enough of that, Julio. This is a serious moment in a young woman's life. You should set a good example.'

'I'm sorry, Mamma.' Julio exchanged meaningful looks with his elder brother but even this was not lost on their mother.

'That goes for you too, Lorenzo,' she said sternly. 'You are thirty-five years old and should have been married a long time ago. I should have grandchildren at my knee, not two overgrown louts like you.'

'I'm going to my bed,' Lorenzo said, heading for the doorway. 'How does it feel to be man of the moment, Gino? I suppose you realise that from now on Julio's and my lives are going to be hell?' He winked, jerking his head in his mother's direction as he stepped into the hallway.

Maria bristled visibly. 'I saw that, Lorenzo. You should show some respect for your mamma.'

Julio hurried to her side, brushing her cheek with a kiss. 'Don't be hard on him, Mamma. It's not his fault that no woman will look at his ugly face.' He followed his brother out of the room and Phoebe could hear them laughing as they made their way upstairs to the room they had shared since they were boys.

'I'll see you out, Gino.' She hurried him from the parlour before her grandmother could let loose a torrent of angry words that would be forgotten as soon as they had left her lips. She knew from experience that Nonna's outbursts were like volcanic eruptions but they were usually short-lived, and Nonno was the best person to deal with his wife's fiery temperament.

Gino hesitated on the doorstep, seemingly unwilling to be parted from her. 'What was wrong just now?' he asked gently. 'You went so pale I thought you might faint. What was it that upset you?'

Phoebe forced her lips into a smile. She had never told anyone about the premonitions that forced themselves into her mind's eye, blotting out the present and foretelling future events with terrifying accuracy. She was afraid to admit, even to herself, that she had the power of second sight. It was, she told herself, simply an overactive imagination that had been encouraged by her mother's dabbling in the supernatural. 'It was nothing, Gino. I'm tired, that's all. Anyway, you must go. You have to be up at four like my uncles and Nonno.' She brushed his cheek with a kiss. 'Goodnight, and thank you.'

'I would do anything for you.' With a last tender smile, Gino walked off in the direction of his home not far down the street.

Phoebe closed the door and leaned against it. She was trembling from head to foot. The vision that had forced itself upon her was still fresh in her mind. She had not seen into the coffin, but she knew for certain that it was not the body of the dead man she had witnessed floating face down in the murky waters of the Thames. The hairs stood up on the back of her neck and she was suddenly cold as ice, even though it was a warm evening. She fell to her knees, covering her face with her hands. 'Take it away,' she whispered. 'Please take this dreadful vision from me.'

Chapter Three

Saffron Hill festered beneath a relentless summer sun. The pavements and cobbled streets retained the heat of the day so that even in the middle of the night they were warm to the touch. The air was rank with the odour of rotting meat and animal excrement. The night soil collectors, although used to noxious smells, wore neckerchiefs tied over their faces in a vain attempt to filter out the worst of the stench. But the hot weather was good for trade and the ice cream men could not keep up with the demand for water ices and penny licks. The ice imported from Norway was stored in deep wells beneath the merchants' premises, but by the middle of August supplies were running low. Even so, Fabio was a happy man. He boasted that they had doubled their takings from last year and there would be more profit to come. He might even delay their return to Italy if the heat wave continued into September. Phoebe prayed for rain.

Annie was unwell. She no longer frequented the pub and she said that the thought of drinking alcohol made her feel nauseous. It was left to Phoebe to do the detective work when a would-be client booked a séance, or lodged a request for Annie to gaze into her crystal ball and reveal what the future held for them.

There was no shortage of people with a penny or two to spare for such information, but Annie seemed to have lost her enthusiasm for her work. She spent most of her time lying on her bed, complaining about the heat which made it impossible for her to sleep at night. When questioned by the family, Phoebe blamed her mother's indisposition on the weather, which her grandmother accepted with a shrug of her ample shoulders. 'What do you expect from a fair-haired slip of a thing who would be blown away by a puff of wind? If my Paulo had married a girl from home she would have been plump and strong and borne him many children.'

Phoebe had heard it all before and she took comfort from the fact that her grandmother's sharp eyes had not spotted the slight thickening of Annie's waistline, or her frequent trips to the privy in the back yard when she suffered prolonged bouts of morning sickness. Fabio and his sons were too involved in their booming business to take any notice of an ailing woman, and even if they had observed a change in Annie, Phoebe was certain that they would simply put it down to an aggravation of nerves. If Julio and Lorenzo had been married men they might have recognised the signs, but their days started at four in the morning and ended when they arrived home at seven in the evening. They were not much interested in what went on in the house unless, of course, there was some disaster in the kitchen which meant that they did not get their dinner on time.

Left to her own devices, Phoebe managed to keep her mother's clients happy. She had spent so many years watching, listening and learning Annie's technique that conducting a séance was second nature to her. She had discovered a natural aptitude for her work, and she had an almost uncanny knack of giving comfort to the bereaved. It was almost as if the dear departed really were passing on messages to their loved ones, but Phoebe did not allow herself to dwell on the fact that she might have genuine psychic powers. She put her success with the crystal ball down to the fact that she had known most of her clients for as long as she could remember. She had either grown up with them or had played in the streets with their children. She knew their histories and she was convinced that hopes and dreams differed very little from person to person. Always ready to lend a sympathetic ear to other people's troubles, she often found herself in the position of counsellor and confidante. It was a heavy burden to bear, especially when she had worries of her own.

The one good thing that had come from Annie being laid low by her pregnancy was that she had seen nothing of Ned Paxman. He had not come near the house, although that was no surprise to Phoebe. The Paxmans were not inclined to mix with the locals. Unlike some gangs that extorted protection money from the traders in their stamping ground, it was said that the Paxmans limited their criminal activities to areas away from Clerkenwell, although no one to Phoebe's knowledge had ever defined exactly how they operated. The respectable Italian families would have nothing to do with anyone who belonged to or was associated with the notorious street gangs. Phoebe had been painfully aware that her mother was playing a dangerous game when she began a liaison with Ned. She suspected that he would have been pleased enough to take advantage of anything that Annie had to offer, but he could get what he wanted from any number of young women who were blinded by his undeniable good looks and ill-gotten wealth.

Her suspicions were confirmed one morning at the end of August when she saw him coming out of the Three Bells pub with a dollymop on his arm. The girl was obviously a maidservant on her day off and she was extremely drunk. Phoebe had been tempted to draw her aside and warn her about the consequences of allowing a man like Ned Paxman to lead her astray, but she knew her words would be wasted. The girl, who was very young and quite probably inexperienced in the ways of the world, was teetering on the brink of disaster. If she became pregnant she would be sacked from her job and disowned by her family. It was a common enough tale, and, like the other unfortunate women who suffered this fate, she would end up on the streets. Her child, if it lived, would either be placed in the care of a baby farmer or grow up doomed to a life of crime and poverty. Phoebe saw the whole sad story acted out like a play before her eyes. She turned away and almost bumped into a familiar figure. He doffed his slightly battered top hat and bowed to her.

'It's Phoebe, isn't it? I never forget a face, particularly one who looks like a painting of the Madonna.'

'Rogue Paxman.' His name dripped off her tongue like acid.

'Don't look so surprised,' he said, smiling. 'I have seen one or two great works of art in my time.'

'I don't doubt it. I expect you've seen a great many things in the fine houses that you've burgled.' She knew she should have ignored him, but she wanted to wipe the smug smile off his face. He was a bad man and his brother had all but destroyed her mother's life. She knew that Ma was also at fault, but Ned Paxman had fathered a child without a thought for its future and it was probably not the first or the last.

Paxman's eyes danced with amusement. 'The little Madonna has claws like a cat. You intrigue me, Phoebe Giamatti. You are not a bit like your mother.'

'Let me pass,' Phoebe said stiffly as he barred her way.

'Just one thing I'd like to put straight, Madonna. I don't burgle houses, and as it happens I enjoy looking at paintings in the National Gallery when I am not otherwise occupied.'

She met his gaze without responding to his smile, even though it was more disarming than she could have imagined. 'I'm not interested in what you do. You and your brother are gangsters. I don't want anything to do with you.'

'You are very unlike your mother, then. She was happy to consort with my brother, but I haven't seen her around for quite a while. Could it be they had a lovers' tiff?'

He was laughing at her, she was certain of that. He reminded her of a tiger playing with his prey before killing and eating it. 'My mother doesn't want anything to do with him. She's been working hard.'

'Really?' Paxman leaned against the doorpost of a milk shop. 'That's not what I heard. According to the local gossips, Annie has taken to her bed. Could it be she is suffering from a broken heart? I did warn her about Ned. I'm afraid he's rather a bad boy when it comes to the ladies, but I would have thought her crystal ball might have told her that.'

'Good day,' Phoebe said stiffly. 'I have better things to do than to exchange gossip with you, Mr Paxman.'

'Roger,' he called after her. 'Rogue is just a nickname.'

Phoebe walked on with her head held high. She knew that he was teasing her and she resented his attitude to both her and her mother. He was a common criminal and his brother was even worse. It was a sobering thought that the child her mother was carrying would be related by blood to such low people. She had been tempted to throw that fact in Paxman's face, but some sixth sense had warned her against such an action. Rogue Paxman might have his own ideas regarding the child's future. The thought of her half-brother or sister being raised by criminals sent Phoebe's blood running cold through her veins.

'Oy, Phoebe.'

She stopped and turned her head to see Biddy O'Flaherty scurrying towards her with her skirts bunched up around her knees and her cheeks flushed from heat and exertion. 'What's the matter, Biddy?'

'Young Dolly's been taken queer. I can't find Minnie and I dunno what to do.'

Phoebe hesitated. She did not want to get mixed up

with the Fowler family or the denizens of Bleeding Heart Yard who were a rough lot. It was rumoured that the Clancys and the O'Donnells had joined one of the high mobs that were the sworn enemies of the Paxmans. It did not take a crystal ball to foresee trouble looming.

Biddy grabbed her by the hand. 'Please come. She don't move and I ain't sure she's breathing. She could be dead for all I know. Ethel will kill me if any harm's come to the girl, and if she don't skin me alive, Minnie will. I was supposed to be keeping an eye on young Dolly but I was hanging out the washing. I only left her for a moment.'

Phoebe hooked her wicker basket over her arm. Beneath the butter muslin there were three plums and a slice of gingerbread. It was the latest food for which her mother craved. Annie had begged her to keep it a secret from Nonna, who would immediately put two and two together and make quattro. 'All right,' she said reluctantly. 'But you really should find Ethel. It's her daughter after all.'

Biddy hurried back the way she had just come, dragging Phoebe by the hand. 'Dolly always was a bit soft in the head, but she's been a sight worse since the beating Ethel gave her for burning Henry's wooden leg.'

Phoebe had to run to keep up with her. 'She didn't find the gold coins then?'

'How did you know about that?' Biddy shot her a suspicious glance over her shoulder. 'I thought your ma was like one of them priests what listens to confessions of the papists. Sorry, if you are one of them, being half Eyetie and all.'

Phoebe let this pass. 'It's common knowledge since Ethel made such a song and dance about it. But I'm sorry if Dolly took the blame. It really wasn't her fault, and anyway surely the fire wouldn't have been hot enough to melt gold?'

Breathless but seemingly determined to keep up the conversation, Biddy paused for a moment, holding her side. 'Stitch,' she muttered. 'Got a bloody stitch in me side. There was gold, several guineas so I heard tell. Not that Dolly could ever get a story straight, but like the fool she is she run out into the yard yelling her head off that she'd found gold. She never saw who took the money but by the time we got there they was miles away. Ethel clubbed the poor cow round the head with what was left of the stump. Knocked her out cold she did.'

'We'd best hurry then.' Putting her mother's delicate condition and her cravings to the back of her mind, Phoebe broke into a run. It was not far to Bleeding Heart Yard and the Fowlers lived in one small room behind the cobbler's shop where Henry had plied his trade. There was a new man working there now. He was tiny, with a cruelly misshapen body and a hunchback that made the poor man look as though he was permanently bent over his last. He barely looked up from hammering hobnails into a boot as they hurried past his open door, making their way along the narrow passage towards the back of the building. Their footsteps echoed on the bare floorboards and Phoebe almost lost her balance as she skidded on a large piece of plaster which had fallen off the wall leaving the laths exposed like the ribs of a skeleton. The heat was intense and the smell of stale beer and rotting cabbage mingled with the stench of urine and unwashed bodies. It grew steadily worse as they reached the Fowlers' lodgings.

'What'll I do if she's croaked?' Biddy muttered. 'I'll have to move south of the river.'

Phoebe was too anxious about Dolly to worry about what might happen to Biddy, and she opened the door peering nervously inside the room. With one small window as the only means of ventilation, which was covered in grime both inside and out, the Fowlers lived in a permanent twilight. She could just make out a figure slumped on the floor by the empty grate. Dolly Fowler was not quite fifteen but she had the body of a ten-year-old child. Phoebe went to kneel at her side. She held her hand close to Dolly's mouth and felt a faint whisper of a breath. 'She's not dead,' she said, breathing a sigh of relief. 'Go and find her mother. I'll stay with her. She'll need a doctor too, or else we'll have to get her to the hospital.'

'She'll kill me. She'll do for me, she will.' Still mumbling beneath her breath Biddy retreated.

Phoebe turned Dolly onto her back and cushioned her head on her lap, stroking the matted mouse-brown hair back from the unconscious girl's forehead. 'Speak to me, Dolly. It's Phoebe Giamatti. I've come to help you.'

Dolly's eyelids fluttered and opened briefly before

closing again. Phoebe chafed her cold hands. 'Come on now, my girl. This won't do at all.' She spoke firmly, hoping that, used as Dolly was to obeying orders, she might respond to authority but to no avail. Phoebe untied her apron and made a pillow of it which she laid beneath Dolly's head. She rose to her feet and went in search of water and a reasonably clean cup or mug. It was difficult to make out anything in the semi-darkness, but she could see that the table in the centre of the room was littered with dirty crockery. Flies buzzed inside an empty jug, feasting off the remains of milk that had turned sour and coated the bottom in a thick gelatinous mess. She had hoped there might be some water or even a bottle of small beer so that she could wet poor Dolly's lips, but there was nothing. She did not want to leave her, but Dolly was deathly pale and her breathing thready. Perhaps she had suffered some kind of fit, or maybe she had simply fallen and hit her head on the hearthstone. Whatever ailed her it was obvious that she needed prompt attention. Phoebe waited for a little longer but Biddy had not returned and, in desperation, she went in search of help. There seemed little point in requesting assistance from the cobbler, who resolutely turned his back on her as she went past his window, and the rest of the house seemed deserted.

As soon as she put a foot outside the building the heat hit her with such force that she gasped for breath. The air was thick with dust and the yard was deserted except for a few ragged children playing blind man's buff, seemingly oblivious to the oppressive weather.

Picking up her skirts, Phoebe ran towards the steps taking two at a time. In Charles Street, she stopped to look around, hoping to find someone who might help, but the passers-by were mostly women on their way to market with baskets slung over their arms and a few old men poking about in the rubbish in search of something to eat. A clerk from the law courts hurried past, refusing to stop and listen to her plea for help, and she experienced the same indifference from a carter and a drayman delivering beer to a nearby pub. Shielding her eyes against the sunlight she hoped to see Minnie or Ethel hurrying towards her, but it seemed there was no one who would give her the time of day let alone offer to help in an emergency. There was no point in returning to Saffron Hill as all the men, including her grandfather, were out peddling their ice cream to the hot and thirsty public.

There was nothing for it but to brave the taproom of the nearest pub. She opened the door and went inside. Heads turned and bewhiskered faces eyed her curiously. She was well aware that no decent woman would put her foot in this establishment but she had seen the angel of death hovering above Dolly's inert form. She peered through the veil of tobacco smoke looking for someone with a kind face, but too late she realised that she had stumbled into a meeting of the Leather Lane mob. She knew one or two of them by sight and they were criminals of the worst order. She backed towards the door, avoiding the clutching hands of a man with a livid scar running down the left side of his face.

'Don't go, sweetheart,' he said with a throaty chuckle. 'Stay and chat for a while.'

She turned and ran out into the street, closing her ears to the sound of raucous laughter that followed her. She hailed a passing hansom cab and when it did not look as though it would stop she leapt into the road, waving her arms. Swearing volubly, the cabby drew his startled horse to a sudden halt. 'Get out of the way, you silly bitch. D'you want to get killed?'

The occupant of the cab opened the half-doors. 'Phoebe Giamatti?' Paxman stared at her in disbelief. 'What's wrong?'

Despite the fact that it was Rogue who was staring at her with his brows knitted together in a frown, he was the first person to have noticed her distress. 'There's a badly injured child in Bleeding Heart Yard,' she said breathlessly. 'I need to get her to hospital. Will you help me?'

He leaned down, holding out his hand. 'Get in.' He hauled her onto the seat beside him. 'Bleeding Heart Yard, cabby.'

'Make up your bloody mind.' The cabby flicked his whip and urged his horse to a trot.

'I'll ignore that remark,' Paxman said, relaxing against the stained leather squabs. 'Since you gave the poor fellow the fright of his life just now.'

'Thank you.' Phoebe stared straight ahead. It took all her self-control to be civil to him.

'For what? I haven't done anything yet.'

She could tell by the tone of his voice that he was

laughing at her but still she refused to look at him. 'The girl has had an accident. She's barely breathing.'

'And I suppose you want me to go into some dirty hovel and touch this creature who is no doubt alive with vermin.'

'She's likely to die if she doesn't get urgent medical treatment.' This time she did turn her head to give him a straight look. 'But if you're too much a gent to get your hands dirty I'll thank you for the lift and find someone else to help.' She reached up to tap on the window. 'Stop here, please, cabby.'

She prepared to leap from the vehicle as it drew to a halt but Paxman caught her by the arm, holding her in an iron grip. 'Don't be a fool. You'll break your neck if you're not careful and then it will be you who ends up in hospital.' With the ease of an athlete, he sprang from his seat and before she had time to protest he lifted her to the ground. 'Wait here, cabby.'

Phoebe ran on ahead, racing down the steps into Bleeding Heart Yard. She could hear his footsteps close behind her and his presence, even though he was the last person on earth she would have asked for help, was oddly comforting. The children scattered before them, regrouping in doorways to watch suspiciously as Phoebe and Paxman entered the house. They were still there when Paxman re-emerged carrying Dolly in his arms. Phoebe collared the eldest and most intelligent-looking boy. 'I want you to tell Mrs Fowler that we've taken Dolly to St Bartholomew's hospital. Can you remember that?'

He nodded and his eyes widened as she thrust a halfpenny into his hand.

'Good boy. Don't forget to tell her. It's very important.' She watched the boy scuttle off clutching the money as though afraid she might change her mind and take it back. Life is strange, she thought, as she followed Paxman who was holding Dolly in his arms as though she were a baby. Here was the notorious gang leader, carrying Dolly as carefully and tenderly as a father with an injured child. If she had not seen it with her own eyes she would not have believed it possible that a man with such a fearsome reputation could have shown such compassion for a stranger. She climbed up to sit beside him as he cradled the insensible Dolly.

'Don't look at me like that,' he said with a wry smile. 'I'm not an ogre, but in my line of business I have to be tough. That doesn't mean I'm totally without feeling.'

Refusing to be cajoled by his studied charm, Phoebe concentrated her attention on Dolly. 'She's very pale.'

'She's half starved. She weighs almost nothing. Who's responsible for this child?'

'She lives with her mother, Ethel Fowler, the cobbler's widow.'

'That explains it. Old Fowler was a miser and his wife's a harpy.'

Phoebe could not contain her curiosity. 'How do you know them?'

'I wear boots that need to be mended, just like any man. And old Fowler fancied his chances on the gaming tables. Our paths crossed once or twice.'

Phoebe shot him a covert glance beneath her lashes. His profile was straight and strong, reminiscent of some of the marble statues she had seen once on a visit to Milan when she was a child. He looked up suddenly, as if sensing her close scrutiny, and she averted her face. She would not give him the satisfaction of thinking that she was at all interested in a person of his low calling. She smothered a sigh of relief as the cab drew up outside the hospital.

Paxman carried Dolly into the reception area and immediately commanded the attention of a young nurse who almost fell over herself in her attempts to please him. Cynically aware that he was exercising his considerable charm in order to get his own way, Phoebe followed them into a small cubicle, but she was immediately ousted by a senior nurse who appeared as if from nowhere and ordered her to take a seat in the waiting area. She perched on the edge of the hard wooden bench and was joined a few minutes later by Paxman, who sat down beside her.

'Thank you, but there's no need for you to stay,' she said stiffly. She felt even more ill at ease in his company now that the immediate crisis was past, and she became aware that they were attracting curious stares from the patients waiting to be seen.

'I agree.' He rose to his feet. 'I could serve young Dolly better if I went to find that mother of hers. Not that I think Ethel Fowler would be a ministering angel and her rat-catcher sister is even worse, but the child needs to have someone present who is responsible for her welfare.'

Phoebe opened her mouth to protest, but he forestalled her with a smile.

'She's lucky to have you, of course, but when all is said and done I think you have enough on your hands looking after your own mother.'

Phoebe's heart gave an uncomfortable flick against her ribs. 'There's nothing wrong with Ma,' she said quickly. Too quickly, she realised when she met his intent gaze. This was a man who was nobody's fool.

'I didn't say there was. I hope she's not pining for my errant brother. He seems to have that effect on women.'

'I wouldn't know about that.' She turned her head away, unwilling to be subjected to his intense scrutiny for a moment longer than necessary. 'Hadn't you better be going? I can manage here, ta very much.' She looked up, startled, as he took her hand and laid a silver half-crown on her palm, closing her fingers over the coin. 'What's that for?'

'I imagine that you'll need to pay for the girl's treatment, and I doubt if Mrs Fowler would be willing to cough up the reddy. Old Henry wasn't the only skinflint in that family.' He picked up his top hat and set it on his head at a jaunty angle. 'Goodbye, Phoebe. I hope we don't meet again under such dire circumstances.'

'I hope we don't meet at all,' Phoebe murmured to his retreating back, but not loud enough for him to hear. After all, he had been more than kind to Dolly. Perhaps his heart was not as black as people made out, but his fearsome reputation could not have been earned by doing good deeds. She settled down to wait for someone to come and tell her what was happening to Dolly. Minutes later a young nurse glided up to her like a grey and white swan.

'Did you come with Miss Fowler?'

Phoebe nodded her head. Her throat constricted with fear as she studied the nurse's face for a glimmer of hope. 'Yes, I did.'

'Are you her sister perhaps?'

'No, just a friend, but her mother's been sent for. She should be here any minute now.'

'The doctor wants to perform an operation on Miss Fowler. It needs to be done very soon.'

'What operation? What's wrong with her?'

A glimmer of a smile curved the nurse's lips and her brown eyes softened. 'You mustn't worry, miss. We'll do everything to make your friend well again, but we do need a parent or guardian to agree to the treatment.'

'I'm sure Mrs Fowler is on her way.' The words had barely left Phoebe's lips when there was a disturbance at the main entrance. Raised voices preceded Ethel and her sister Minnie as they stormed up the aisle between the wooden benches.

'There she is, Ethel,' Minnie screeched, pointing her finger at Phoebe. 'There's the interfering little wretch that stole our Dolly away.'

'I'll have you for this,' Ethel muttered breathlessly. 'What right had you to take my child from her home? And what d'you mean by sending that villain Rogue Paxman to find me? It'll be the talk of every tavern from here to Shoreditch.'

The young nurse stepped forward. 'Please keep your voice down, ma'am. This is a hospital and there are sick people to consider.'

'Oh, an 'orspital is it? I'd never have knowed it, you silly bitch. Where's me daughter? I'm taking her home.'

'Yes, we want Dolly and we're leaving now,' Minnie added, rolling up her sleeves.

'What's all this noise?' A doctor in a white coat had come up behind them unnoticed.

The nurse blushed rosily. 'I'm so sorry, Dr Murchison. These ladies are a bit upset.'

'A bit upset, you potty tart?' Ethel took a deep breath that inflated her already large bosom to alarming proportions. 'My daughter's been kidnapped, doctor. You're a party to a criminal act.'

Phoebe laid her hand on Ethel's arm. 'Please, Mrs Fowler. This isn't helping Dolly. She's very poorly. She needs an operation.'

'What?' Ethel screamed. 'Are you trying to extort money from me, doctor? Because if you are I ain't having it. I'm a poor woman. The rumours about the gold was false and anyway it was all pinched because of that stupid little cow.'

'Yes, me sister had to whack her good and hard for burning the wooden leg and then letting a bloody thief pinch the gold.' Minnie flexed her muscles, glaring at the doctor.

'I think Dolly must have fallen and hit her head again this morning,' Phoebe added hastily. 'I found her in a heap on the floor by the hearthstone. That's where she lay.'

Dr Murchison folded his arms across his chest, his pale eyebrows drawn into a knot over the bridge of his large nose. 'I've heard enough. You, ma'am,' he jerked his head in Ethel's direction, 'would be up before the beak on a charge of child cruelty if I thought it would stick. Your daughter has a fractured skull and needs urgent medical intervention in order to save her life. Now, do you agree to allow the procedure to go ahead, or do you want to risk a charge of murder being brought against you?'

Chapter Four

'Murder?' Ethel paled visibly and then appeared to recover, bristling like a turkeycock. 'Who says so? A sawbones like you? I don't have to believe you, cully.'

'Hush, please,' the nurse said urgently. 'You're upsetting the other patients, Mrs Fowler.'

'Perhaps you'd best send for a constable, nurse,' Dr Murchison said, glowering. 'I haven't time to stand here and argue with this person.'

'Here, who are you calling a person?' Minnie advanced on him with a belligerent set to her jaw.

Eyeing Minnie nervously, Phoebe noticed for the first time that she had whiskers growing out of her chin like a man. This confirmed her long-held suspicion that Minnie Sykes was only half female. She held her breath, hardly daring to intervene in case she made matters worse. It was a stand-off now; a battle of wills between the doctor and the two sisters.

'Well, ma'am. Make up your mind,' Dr Murchison said icily. 'Do I send for the police or will you agree to the life-saving operation on your child.'

'She's no child,' Ethel said, brazen to the last. 'She's all but fifteen. Old enough to be wed, so she's no longer my responsibility. Chop her head off for all I care, but don't send her back to me. I never want to see the

57

simpleton again. Come, Minnie. We know where we're not wanted.'

'I'll take that as a yes, then.' Dr Murchison turned to the nurse. 'Make Miss Fowler ready for the operating theatre, please. There's no time to lose.'

He was about to walk away but Phoebe caught him by his coat tail. 'Doctor, one moment if you please.'

He turned his head to give her an appraising glance. 'Yes, but hurry.'

'Who will pay for Dolly's operation? I've half a crown I can give you now.'

His stern features relaxed a little. 'That will be a matter for the ward clerk to sort out later. We do have some charitable beds and maybe we can utilise one of those for Dolly since her mother seems to have washed her hands of the poor creature.'

'Will she die, doctor?'

He hesitated. 'I won't lie to you, Miss er . . .'

'Phoebe Giamatti. I'm just a friend.'

'And a good one too, if I may say so. Well, Miss Giamatti, I'll do my very best. The outcome is in the hands of a higher authority.'

Phoebe sank down onto the hard wooden seat. She knew Dolly only a little, but she had been touched by the sorry conditions in which she found the girl, and even more so by the knowledge that her wretched mother had disowned her. She could not imagine her own mother doing anything so cruel and callous. Ma might be many things, but she had always been kind and loving. A little too loving perhaps when it came to the opposite sex, but that was just Ma. It was in her nature to give and it seemed that it was in Mrs Fowler's nature to take. Phoebe settled down to wait for the outcome of the procedure in theatre. She knew that Nonna would be angry with her for being away so long, and that Ma would be fretting for the fancies that her appetite craved, but they would have to wait. She sat upright against the rigid panel at the back of the bench, praying that Dolly would survive the operation.

She must have drifted off into an uneasy doze as suddenly she realised that someone was shaking her gently by the shoulder. Phoebe opened her eyes with a start and found herself looking up into the smiling face of the young nurse.

'The procedure was successful, miss. Dolly has come round from the anaesthetic and you may see her if you wish.'

Phoebe swallowed hard as tears of relief threatened to choke her. She rose slowly to her feet, stretching her cramped limbs. 'Thank you, nurse.'

'Come this way.'

Following the nurse through long corridors that smelt strongly of carbolic, Phoebe was faced with a new problem. Dolly had survived but now she was as good as orphaned. Unless Mrs Fowler changed her mind, and from what Phoebe knew of her she deemed this unlikely, Dolly had no home and she was unfit for most types of work. She would end up on the streets or in the workhouse. Her future looked bleak indeed.

The nurse led her into a long ward lined on either side with regimented rows of iron beds with starched white sheets and glassy coverlets drawn up to the chins of the patients, most of whom lay motionless, either sleeping or staring vacantly at the ceiling. Dolly was in a bed furthest from the door. Her head was swathed in bandages and her eyes were closed. She was deathly pale and Phoebe turned anxiously to the nurse. 'Is she going to be all right?'

The nurse pulled up a chair, motioning Phoebe to take a seat. 'She's still suffering the effects of the anaesthetic but if you talk to her she might respond.' She waited until Phoebe had settled herself before drawing the curtains round the bed. 'I'll bring you a cup of tea, miss. You've had a long wait.' She withdrew, leaving Phoebe alone with the unconscious girl.

'Dolly.' Phoebe leaned closer to the bed. 'It's me, Phoebe. Can you hear me?'

She was rewarded by a flicker of Dolly's eyelids and a slight movement of her pale lips. Encouraged, Phoebe moved a little nearer. 'You gave us a nasty fright, young Dolly. But you're all fixed up now, and soon you'll be your old self again.'

Dolly opened her eyes, focusing on Phoebe's face with obvious difficulty. 'Ma?'

'No, dear. It's Phoebe. You probably don't remember me, but I used to keep you amused sometimes when your ma came to my house to have her fortune told.'

'Ice cream,' Dolly murmured sleepily. 'Hokey-pokey; penny licks.'

Encouraged, Phoebe smiled. 'That's right. I used to give you ice cream when Nonna wasn't looking. You like ice cream, don't you, Dolly?'

'I do.' Dolly closed her eyes and drifted off to sleep with a gentle smile curving her full lips.

Once again, Phoebe blinked away tears. Whatever the surgeons had done, they had brought Dolly back to life again. She sniffed and searched in her skirt pocket for a hanky. Nonna always insisted that Phoebe should have a clean hanky in her pocket and wear freshly laundered undergarments, just in case. Quite what that case might be Phoebe had only a vague notion, but she thought it might have something to do with street accidents, such as being run over by a brewer's dray, or falling beneath the wheels of a hansom cab and ending up in hospital. Or in Dolly's case, simply falling to the floor and hitting your head on a sharp object, if that was how she had received her near fatal injury. Phoebe suspected that Dolly might have been beaten by her mother or had been flung across the room in a fit of temper, which would account for the severity of her wound. The truth of what had occurred in that dreadful room might never be known. Ethel would never admit to any wrongdoing and Dolly was unlikely to remember the exact course of events leading to her accident.

Phoebe looked up as the nurse drew back the curtain and handed her a steaming mug of tea. 'There you are, miss. Drink that and it'll bring the colour back to your cheeks. You'd gone quite pale back there. I thought we might have to find a bed for you.'

Phoebe accepted the tea gratefully. 'Ta, nurse. I was feeling a bit queasy, but I'm fine now, and Dolly has spoken to me. She remembered ice cream. Perhaps I could bring her in some. Would that be allowed?'

'I don't see why not, miss. But I suggest you go when you've drunk your tea. She needs plenty of rest and quiet.'

'But she will be all right, won't she?'

'It's too early to tell and anyway you'd need the doctor's opinion, not mine. But she's come this far, so I think it's a good sign.'

Phoebe returned to the hospital whenever she could get away from the house and her interminable chores. Each time she visited Dolly she took a small basket lined with cabbage leaves and packed with ice in which she placed a bowl of Nonno's vanilla ice cream. It was worth all the trouble to see the smile on Dolly's face. She was recovering well, but the question of where she would go when discharged from hospital was looming large in Phoebe's mind. Neither Mrs Fowler nor Minnie Sykes had been near the ward, and Dr Murchison did not bother to disguise the contempt he felt for Dolly's family when he told Phoebe that she would soon be well enough to leave hospital. Phoebe did not need her mother's crystal ball to tell her that Dolly would not be welcomed at home. So far she had kept the reason for her daily visits to Bart's from the family. Her mother had barely noticed her absences, living as she was in a self-centred world of her own, and fretting daily because Ned had made no attempt to contact her. 'He doesn't love me,' she moaned when Phoebe showed concern for her. 'He was pleased enough to have his way with me but he don't care for me, not one bit.' She turned her face to the wall, refusing to say another word.

There had been nothing that Phoebe could say or do which would make any difference or penetrate the wall of misery that her mother had built around herself, and there was no one at home in whom she could confide. Her grandfather was fully occupied making vast quantities of ice cream and water ices to supply the public's needs, and somehow she did not think her grandmother would be very sympathetic to Dolly's plight.

In the end it was Gino who discovered the truth by following her one evening when she went to the hospital. He was outside, leaning against the wall and smoking a cheroot, when she emerged from the main entrance. He tossed the butt into the gutter and fell into step beside her. 'So, are you going to tell me what's going on, cara? I thought we had no secrets from each other.'

'It's not really a secret, Gino.'

'Then why do you come here every day? You aren't sick, are you?'

She slipped her hand through the crook of his arm, giving it a squeeze. 'No, of course not. It's not me, it's Dolly Fowler. She had a bad fall and needed an operation.'

He threw back his head and laughed. 'That's a relief. I thought you were either dying of consumption or you had fallen in love with a handsome doctor.'

'You are silly, Gino. Why didn't you ask me outright? And why did you feel the need to follow me? It was wrong of you.'

He shrugged his shoulders. 'I love you, Phoebe. I

know you don't feel the same way about me and that our engagement is in name only, but I never know what's going on in your head. Sometimes you seem very far away from me.'

She stopped, turning to face him squarely. 'You are so good to me, Gino. I appreciate everything you're doing for me and for Ma. Without your help I would never have managed to persuade Nonno to let me stay in London.'

'And what will happen when your mother is delivered of the child? What will you say to your grandparents when they return to London next spring?'

'I don't know. That's Ma's problem, not mine. All I know is that I have to protect her from the Paxman gang and from my uncles. They believe in vendetta and I know that Julio has friends in the Camorra, and possibly the 'Ndrangheta too. Nonno doesn't know about it and he would be furious if he found out, and I don't want my family torn apart by Ma's affair with Ned Paxman.' Phoebe stopped to draw breath, looking over her shoulder in case anyone might have overheard her anxious words. The gangs had spies everywhere. There was no one you could trust implicitly. Spies were rewarded by their masters and punished by those whom they betrayed. The dead houses on the banks of the Thames were filled with corpses fished out of the water by the river police or the lightermen.

In answer, Gino drew her roughly into his arms, pressing her back against the cold glass of a bookshop window. His mouth sought hers and his tongue parted her lips, caressing, tasting and consuming her with a sudden release of pent-up passion. His body was hard against hers and she could taste the smoky fragrance of the cigar on his breath. She struggled at first but the sweet sensations racing through her blood made her go weak at the knees. Needy for love and understanding, she slid her arms around his neck, allowing him to take her weight as she gave herself up to the pleasure of a close embrace from a man who loved her with all his heart. A small voice in her head warned her that this was unfair, but his ardour had awakened something deep inside her that craved to be satisfied. It was Gino who eventually drew away just far enough to gaze into her face. His eyes were glazed with desire and his full lips were parted as if he were about to kiss her again.

She let her arms fall to her sides. 'We should get home, Gino.'

'You do love me, cara. You wouldn't kiss me like that if you had no feeling for me.'

'I don't want to give you false hope.'

He stroked her neck with the tips of his fingers. 'But you could love me. I know it.'

'There's too much going on in my head. With Ma in such a state and having to keep her condition a secret from Nonna, I can't think about my own feelings. You must give me time, Gino.'

He brushed her hair back from her face, dropping a kiss on the tip of her nose. 'I'll give you all the time you want, my beloved Phoebe.' He raised her hand to his lips, kissing the gold ring. 'It's going to be a long winter for me without you, but in the spring I hope you'll have made up your mind.'

'I will. I promise you that I will.' She straightened her blouse, tucking it into the waistband of her navy blue serge skirt. 'Now, let's go home. If Nonna is in a good mood perhaps she'll ask you to stay for supper.'

'He's a fine boy,' Maria said, ladling boiled cabbage onto the macaroni and bacon. 'You'll be well cared for when you marry Gino. I don't know why you can't come with us and marry him right away. I could have a great-grandchild on my knee by next summer if only you would see sense. You shouldn't give up your young life for that mother of yours.'

Phoebe smiled. She knew better than to argue with Nonna. 'Shall I take this one up to Ma?'

Maria's brow darkened. 'She can come downstairs and eat with the family. I'm getting tired of her vapours. She's done nothing but lie in bed all day. I think I could stand her going to the pub and coming home tipsy better than this pretence of being ill. She should get up and do a day's work. I'm the slave round here, working my fingers to the bone while she swoons and playacts.'

Phoebe was struck with a sudden brilliant idea. She put the plate down. 'Nonna, I think I have the solution. As I'm doing Ma's readings and the table tipping and everything, I can't help you as much as I used to, but I know a young girl who might just suit. She is a willing worker and will do as she's told.'

'Who is this you talk about? I can't afford to pay a servant.'

'It's Dolly Fowler. You know, Ethel's girl.'

66

Maria curled her lip. 'I know Ethel. She's a nasty woman.'

'And she's thrown poor Dolly out of the house. She beat her black and blue and put the poor girl in hospital.'

'I heard that the girl is a simpleton anyway, and I don't need another sickly person to look after. Besides which, I don't want Ethel Fowler banging on my door and causing trouble.'

'She won't do that, Nonna. She doesn't want anything to do with Dolly.'

'And I told you, one invalid in the house is quite enough.'

'Dolly is getting better all the time and she's in desperate need of somewhere to stay.'

'I don't know. We'll be going to Italy soon. What will we do with her then?'

'She can stay here with me and Ma. She can help me with the séances until Ma is well enough to take over again.' Phoebe could see that her grandmother was weakening and she gave her a hug. 'You are a generous woman, Nonna. You wouldn't want to see a young girl put in the workhouse for want of a charitable deed, would you?'

Maria shook her head. 'You could charm the birds from the trees when you put your mind to it. You remind me so much of my poor Paulo. If only he had kept away from the high mob he would be here today. He loved his mamma. He wouldn't see me put upon by others.'

'So you'll give Dolly a chance then, Nonna?'

'Did I say so? I don't remember agreeing with you.'

Phoebe kissed her grandmother's leathery cheek. 'But you will, dear Nonna. You will do this for me and I'll love you forever and ever.'

Pink in the face and smiling, Maria pushed her away. 'You bad girl. When did I ever deny you anything?'

Phoebe blew her a kiss. 'Thank you, Nonna. You're an angel.'

'I hope that isn't one of your predictions, cara. I'm not ready to join my ancestors in heaven just yet.' She picked up the ladle she had dropped when Phoebe hugged her. 'Now go and get your mamma. I want her sitting at the table with the family or she gets no food tonight.'

'Yes, Nonna. I'm going now.'

Annie had reluctantly agreed to come downstairs for supper, but she ate little and said even less although Gino did his best to draw her into conversation. As usual, Julio and Lorenzo ate in silence, wolfing their food with evident enjoyment even though it was the same meal that their mother placed on the table every evening. Thrift was the keyword in the Giamatti family, and as Fabio was always telling them, it was through these strict economies that they could afford to winter in Italy. When they had finished eating, he left the room and returned moments later to proudly display a new fowling piece that he had purchased in one of the most reputable gunsmiths in London.

'That doesn't look like it was cheap, Papa,' Lorenzo

said, winking at his brother. 'Not much economy there, I don't think.'

'It will save money,' Fabio replied calmly. 'We will eat well when we return home in two weeks' time.' He passed the weapon to Lorenzo for his approval. 'You boys can use my old guns and we will go up into the mountains and shoot game birds for the table.' He glanced at his wife, grinning. 'That is if Maria has not forgotten how to cook such delicacies.'

She tossed her head. 'I'm the best cook in the whole of Lombardy and you know it, Fabio. We work hard here so that we can live like kings at home. I can't wait to get on that boat which will take us away from this fog-bound island.' She rose from the table and began collecting the dirty crockery. 'Come, Phoebe, you can help.' She shot a withering look at Annie. 'I suppose you're too tired now to do anything useful.'

Annie smiled weakly. 'I'll do what I can, Mamma.'

Fabio took his gun from Julio and polished the stock with his sleeve. 'I must put you to bed, my little one. We will have a fine time hunting, you and I.'

Julio pushed back his chair, grinning. 'I'm going outside for a game of morra. Are you coming with me, Gino? As I recall you won last time.'

'I can beat you whenever I choose,' Gino said, puffing out his chest. He stood up, leaning over to catch Phoebe by the hand as she started to clear the table. 'You don't mind, do you, cara?'

She smiled. 'Of course not, Gino. Go ahead and beat my uncles.'

'You don't ask her, Gino,' Lorenzo said lazily. 'You

tell the little woman what you intend to do, or you just do it and let her find out the hard way.'

Julio slipped his arm around Gino's shoulders. 'You have to start married life on the right foot, amico.'

'You would know all about that, of course, Julio,' Phoebe said lightly. 'Having been a bachelor for all your twenty-eight years, you are the expert.'

Julio tossed a crust of bread at her. 'You are not too old to put over my knee.'

'Children, that's enough.' Maria picked up a pile of plates and headed for the scullery. 'You are supposed to be her uncles, not her brothers. It's about time you boys grew up into men and had families of your own. And you, Gino,' she jerked her head in his direction. 'Try to persuade my little Phoebe to come to Italy with us. I would like to see you both married in the church by the lake this year, while the leaves are still on the trees.'

Holding her hand to her forehead, Annie moved towards the door. 'All this talk makes me dizzy. I'm going to lie down, Phoebe. You can help Nonna with the dishes, can't you?'

'Yes, Ma. Of course.' Phoebe shot a wary glance at her grandmother, hoping that she would not make a fuss, but Maria merely shrugged her shoulders and cast her eyes heavenwards.

With a conspiratorial wink in Phoebe's direction, Gino took Julio by the arm. 'Come then, amico. I challenge you and Lorenzo to a game of morra. Let's see who's the better player.'

A diversion had been created and Phoebe seized the

opportunity to hurry her mother from the room. 'Go to bed, Ma. I'll bring you up a cup of tea later, but now I'd best help Nonna and keep her happy.'

Annie gave her a weary smile. 'You're a good girl, Phoebe. I don't know what I'd have done without you these past weeks.' She made her way towards the staircase, moving slowly as if each step was an effort. Phoebe felt the hairs on the back of her neck prickle. It was surely not right for a woman to be as tired and listless so early in pregnancy. She shivered, but the feeling passed quickly and a sharp summons from her grandmother brought her back to the present. She must keep up the charade for another two weeks, and then she could concentrate on caring for her mother without fear of revealing her condition to the family. But for now her most pressing problem was how to break the news to Nonna that Dolly was to be allowed out of hospital the following day, and she had promised to collect her.

Next morning, Phoebe conducted a table tipping session for the wives of two of the ice cream sellers. The bereaved sisters wanted to be certain that their dear departed mother, having suffered a long and painful last illness, was well and happy on the other side. They confessed that their husbands had no knowledge of what they proposed to do and that they would disapprove strongly of such a heathen practice. Phoebe assured them that what happened in the darkened room was as safe as the confessional in church. When the table began to rock, seemingly of its own accord, their anxious questions were answered by mysterious

71

taps on the floor. Phoebe had no idea how this process worked, but the fact was that it did, and her clients left in a much happier frame of mind than when they had arrived. Satisfied that she had done her best for them, she pocketed the money, intending to use it for the cab fare when she brought Dolly home from the hospital.

The moment she left the house she was assailed by doubts. Phoebe was well aware that Ethel Fowler had no intention of taking care of her daughter, but she felt that she had to make certain. She did not want to fall foul of the law and give the cunning Fowler family the opportunity to say that Dolly had been kidnapped. They were an unscrupulous lot, and might demand money by way of compensation. She could not allow that to happen, but it was with a degree of trepidation that she returned to Bleeding Heart Yard. She had no idea if she would find Ethel at home, but as luck would have it she caught her just as she was about to leave the house.

'What d'you want?' Ethel demanded, glaring at her with narrowed eyes. 'If you've come to ask me to take that ungrateful wretch back you're in for a disappointment.'

Phoebe drew back a pace. The smell of sour spirits mixed with unwashed body odour was almost over-powering. Ethel's eyes were bloodshot and the hair escaping from beneath a grubby mobcap was matted, with lice clinging to several of the grey strands. Phoebe shook her head. 'Not exactly, Mrs Fowler. But she is going to be discharged from hospital today and I thought you should know. She is your daughter after all.'

'She's a grown woman now and not my responsibility. The stupid little cow refused the best offer she's ever likely to get so I've washed me hands of her. She can go out and earn her own living.'

'So you don't care what happens to her?'

Ethel moved a step closer, her lips drawn back in a snarl, exposing decayed and broken teeth which put Phoebe in mind of a row of tumbledown cottages. 'That's right, missy. I don't care. She lost me a small fortune and I don't care if I never sets eyes on her again.'

'And that's your last word, is it?'

'Me very last, so sling yer hook.'

Phoebe walked away, torn between feelings of relief and sorrow. She was relieved that there would be no repercussions from the Fowlers if she took Dolly home with her, but she was deeply distressed by Ethel's uncaring attitude towards her daughter. She wondered how she was going to tell Dolly that her mother had abandoned her.

When she arrived in the ward she found her sitting on a chair beside the neatly made up bed. She was fully dressed, and apart from the bandages which covered her head she looked surprisingly alert. She smiled and flushed with pleasure when she saw Phoebe. 'Have you brought me some ice cream?'

The nurse who had been on duty when Dolly was admitted came bustling up to them. 'Good morning, miss. Have you come to take my patient home?'

Phoebe nodded. 'Yes, if she wishes to come with me.'

'I don't want to go to Ma's,' Dolly said with her bottom lip trembling. 'Don't send me back there.'

'No, I won't do that.' Phoebe held out her hand. 'I'm taking you home with me. We'll look after you.'

'And can I have ice cream again?'

'You shall have all you can eat.' Phoebe turned to the nurse. 'Thank you for all you've done for her.'

'It's all in a day's work, miss.' The nurse drew her aside. 'But she'll need to rest and mustn't do anything too strenuous until she's fully recovered. What I mean to say is that she shouldn't be put to work for several weeks yet.'

'I understand, and I'll take good care of her.'

'I'm sure you will, miss. You've got a kind face. I'd say she's a lucky girl to have a friend like you.'

Phoebe took Dolly by the hand and led her out of the ward and through the maze of corridors to the main entrance.

'Me legs is a bit like jelly, miss,' Dolly murmured, leaning heavily on Phoebe's arm. 'I don't think I can walk very far.'

Phoebe helped her to a chair by the door. 'You won't have to walk anywhere. I'm going outside to hail a cab.'

'What? Me riding in one of them hansom cabs?' Dolly's pale blue eyes lit up and her lips curved into an excited smile. 'I ain't never rode in a cab afore, miss. And can I have ice cream as soon as we gets to your castle?'

Phoebe smiled. 'Of course you can, but it's hardly a

castle. It's just a house in Saffron Hill and it's not grand.'

'It will be a castle to me, miss.'

Outside the hospital, Phoebe was lucky enough to catch the eye of a cabby who had just dropped off a fare. She asked him to wait while she went to fetch Dolly, and she was just about to help her into the cab when a loud voice behind them made her turn with a start. She found herself looking into the irate face of Amos Snape.

'Where d'you think you're taking that girl?' he demanded angrily.

Cowering, Dolly uttered a cry of distress. 'Don't let him take me, miss. I won't go with him, no matter what Ma says.'

'What has this got to do with you, Mr Snape?' Phoebe slipped her arm around Dolly's trembling shoulders. 'How do you know this child?'

'She ain't a child,' Snape said through gritted teeth. 'I paid her mother good money for her and got nothing for it.'

'How dare you speak like that in front of a young person?' Thoroughly incensed, Phoebe faced him fearlessly. 'You were trying to get off with my mother the last time I saw you, Mr Snape. If your intentions towards this girl are what I think, then shame on you.'

'Mind your own bloody business, you interfering trull.' Snape made a grab for Dolly but Phoebe stepped in between them.

'She's just come out of hospital. Can't you see that she's been injured, you stupid man?'

Snape abandoned his attempt to grab Dolly, who was now clinging to the wheel of the hansom cab as if her life depended upon it. He seized Phoebe round the neck, shaking her like a terrier with a rat. 'I paid for her services and I'm entitled to my money's worth. The simpleton is only good for one thing and that's what I bought.'

She could hardly breathe. A red mist blotted out Snape's florid face. She was within seconds of losing consciousness when suddenly the pressure was relieved and Snape went spinning onto the cobblestones.

Chapter Five

Dazed and gasping for breath, Phoebe found herself being supported by strong arms.

'You're Annie's daughter.' It was a bald statement of fact, spoken without rancour or emotion. Ned Paxman set her back on her feet, eyeing her curiously. 'You want to keep away from the likes of him.' He aimed a savage kick at Amos, who was kneeling on the cobblestones clutching his corpulent belly. The blow caught him on his flank and he let out a howl of pain and rage.

'I'll have the law on you, Paxman.' Shaking his fist, Amos moved out of reach, shuffling on his knees through the piles of straw and horse dung that covered the cobblestones.

Dolly started to giggle but she covered her mouth with her hands when Amos lurched to his feet and turned. 'You won't find it so funny when I get you home, my girl.'

Dolly cowered away from him, her eyes wide with fear. 'No, I ain't going with you, mister. You can't make me.'

'No, he can't,' Phoebe said, moving to her side. 'You're coming home with me, as promised.'

'I've paid for her,' Amos snarled. 'Either she comes with me or she gives me back my money.'

Ned took a step towards him. He did not have to fist his hands in order to look menacing. His dark eyebrows were lowered in a frown and his mouth was set in a hard line. 'It seems to me that it's Ethel Fowler you should be dealing with, Snape. She took your money so you get it from her, if you can. Now clear off before I really lose me temper.'

Straightening his rumpled clothing, Amos shot him a withering glance as he backed away. 'I'll remember this, Paxman. You see if I don't.'

'I'm shaking in my shoes, cully.'

Amos hunched his shoulders and walked away, limping slightly and casting a malicious glance over his shoulder at Dolly, who was clinging to Phoebe's hand as if she would never let go.

Ned fixed his attention once again on Phoebe. 'So where's your ma then, girl? I've been waiting for her to come and see me. Has she found another bloke?'

Phoebe shook her head. 'No. Nothing like that. She's been ill.'

'What's wrong with her? She was well enough last time we was together.'

'Smallpox,' Phoebe said in desperation. 'She's over the worst but she don't want to be seen in public.' She touched her cheek as if to indicate an unsightly blemish left by the disease.

'Perhaps I'll call on her sometime.'

'No.' The word slipped out before she had time to think, but she realised immediately that she had said the wrong thing. The stubborn set of Ned's jaw made him look disturbingly like his elder brother. 'I mean, not yet,' she said hastily. 'Ma wouldn't want anyone to risk catching the disease, especially you, Mr Paxman. She speaks very highly of you.'

His lips curved into a pleased smile. 'So she should. We were good together and to tell the truth I quite miss her. She made me laugh, and we had a lot in common.'

The cabby, who had been watching the scene with some enjoyment, thumped his hand on the cab roof. 'If you're hiring me then get inside, ladies. I'm losing money all the time I'm stuck here listening to your chit-chat.'

Ned tossed a coin at him. 'That'll cover your costs, cully. I ain't quite finished speaking to the young lady.'

The cabby tipped his hat. 'All right and tight, mister. No offence meant.'

'I must get Dolly home,' Phoebe said, assisting her frightened charge into the cab. 'I'll be sure to pass on your good wishes to Ma.'

Ned caught her by the arm. 'Tell her to come to the Three Bells as soon as she's feeling fit. If she don't turn up soon I'll be knocking on your door. I know where you live.'

Cold fingers of panic clutched at Phoebe's belly. Ma was beginning to show. So far she had managed to conceal her thickening waistline, but when the family had left for Italy it was going to be difficult to keep her condition a secret. 'Ma is thinking of going to Italy for the winter,' she said in desperation. 'Nonna is getting older and she needs a younger woman to help in the house.'

Ned threw back his head and laughed. 'Well, she's

not going to get that from my Annie. She's either up for a good time or else she's summoning up spirits. Those that don't talk to her go straight down her throat. I never met a girl who could hold her liquor like Annie Giamatti. Tell her I miss her.' He seized Phoebe round the waist without giving her a chance to protest and lifted her bodily into the cab. 'Drive on, cabby.' He stepped aside as the vehicle moved slowly forward.

Phoebe heaved a sigh of relief as the cabby urged his horse to a smart trot, putting a safe distance between them and Ned Paxman, but she realised that the respite was only temporary. She had not credited him with having genuine feelings for her mother, but now she could see that she had been mistaken. He might only think of Annie Giamatti in terms related to his own selfish pleasure, but he did appear to have a genuine concern for her welfare. What, she wondered, would he do if he found out that he was to become a father? Once again the more pressing problem raised its ugly head. What would the Giamattis do if they discovered that their beloved Paulo's widow was carrying a criminal's child? A muffled sob broke through her train of thought and she turned to Dolly with a feeling of guilt. 'Are you all right, Dolly?'

'That nasty man, miss. He can't come and get me, can he? I never said I'd go with him. Honest.'

Phoebe patted her hand. 'Of course not. You mustn't give him a second thought. No one is going to make you do anything that you don't want to. You're going to be safe in Saffron Hill. I'm going to look after you.'

* * *

Maria looked up from kneading the pasta dough. She pointed a floury finger at Dolly's bandaged head. 'What happened to her?'

Phoebe slipped a protective arm around Dolly's shoulders. 'I told you, Nonna. Dolly had to have an operation after the accident.'

'They cut off me hair, missis,' Dolly said plaintively. 'Can I have some ice cream now?'

Maria angled her head. 'Is she a bit simple?'

Embarrassed by her grandmother's forthrightness, Phoebe shook her head. 'She's not recovered fully, but the doctors say she will in time. I promised her some ice cream.'

'Hokey-pokey,' Dolly said hopefully. 'A penny lick.'

Maria thumped the dough with her fists. 'You've taken on something there, Phoebe. Go and see your grandfather. He's in the cellar making up another batch of the stuff. I can't abide it myself, but the boys can't keep up with demand in this hot weather.'

'It's all right with you if Dolly stays, then?' Phoebe needed to have her grandmother's approval. Her word was law and if she took against poor Dolly nothing would make her change her mind. 'She'll help around the house.'

'I like scrubbing floors,' Dolly murmured dreamily. 'I'd rather do that than let him fumble me tits.'

'What?' Maria's eyes opened wide. 'What did she say?'

Phoebe grabbed Dolly's hand. 'She's a bit confused, Nonna.' She tapped her head, indicating the site where Dolly had been injured, and made a hasty retreat

81

before her grandmother could start asking awkward questions. As soon as they were out of earshot, she stopped. 'It's best not to mention Amos Snape and men like him in front of my family. It would make them very angry to think that someone would take advantage of a girl like you.'

Dolly's eyes clouded and her bottom lip trembled. 'Did I say something wrong?'

'No, but try to remember what I just told you. Now we'll go downstairs to the cellar and see if Nonno has some ice cream ready.'

'I'm going to like it here,' Dolly said happily. 'I could eat ice cream all day, and all night too if it come to that.'

Phoebe noted with pleasure that her grandfather and Dolly were almost instantly on the best of terms. Fabio was delighted to find someone who would willingly spend the day tasting the ice cream and giving him her honest opinion. Dolly appeared to have the palate of a wine connoisseur when it came to sampling each batch of strawberry, vanilla or chocolate ice cream. Fabio was experimenting with many different flavours which he hoped one day to sell all year round. It was his ambition to have a café similar to that established by Carlo Gatti, where he would sell ice cream, pastries and good coffee in an attempt to wean the English from their addiction to tea. Fabio took Dolly under his wing, teaching her the rudiments of making the confection she loved, and in return she cleaned the cellar room and scoured the milk churns. She was kept busy all day, although he allowed her to rest as soon as she grew tired. This left Phoebe free to look after her mother and to continue her séances in the front parlour. Sometimes, when she felt well enough, Annie conducted the sessions, but more often than not she took to her bed, complaining of the heat and fretting because Ned had not made any attempt to see her. Phoebe had refrained from mentioning her meeting with him or the fact that he had shown concern for her mother's health. She was only too aware that a mere mention of his name might encourage her mother to seek him out. It did not take much imagination to foresee the disastrous consequences of *that* meeting.

The heat wave continued throughout August and into September. Fabio put off their departure date several times. The demand for ice cream and water ices continued and the family were making too much money to give up until the weather broke and the autumn gales and rain put an end to their trade. The days were growing shorter and the evenings and early mornings cooler, and with this subtle change in the weather Annie's health began to improve. Phoebe knew that it was only a matter of time before her grandmother guessed the truth, and her mother's secret would become public knowledge. The shame and bitter recriminations would be almost impossible to bear.

Annie was already threatening to tell Ned. She seemed convinced that he would do the right thing and make an honest woman of her. Phoebe tried to tell her that this was wishful thinking, but Annie refused to listen. Instead, she hitched the top hoop on her crinoline cage a little higher and laced her stays as tightly as possible while still allowing herself to breathe. Phoebe caught her one day just as she was about to set off towards Wilderness Row. She knew instinctively that her mother was heading for the Paxmans' house and that she must stop her, but Annie slapped her restraining hand away with a petulant frown. 'Leave me be. You don't tell me where I can go and who I see. It's my business.'

Phoebe glanced anxiously over her shoulder. They were attracting the attention of a group of Italian women who were chatting to each other on the street corner. 'Ma, keep your voice down. Gino's mother is watching us and she's with that Tartaglia woman. You know how she gossips.'

'I don't care. I have to see him, Phoebe. You must understand that.'

'It would be fatal, Ma. He only wants one thing and it isn't marriage. At best he'll deny that it's his, and at worst,' Phoebe shuddered. 'It doesn't bear thinking about.'

'He loves me. He'll marry me and I can get away from the Giamattis forever.'

'Please don't do this.'

Annie's lips curved in a smile. 'You worry too much, my little one. I've seen eternal happiness in the crystal ball. I'll have a strong and healthy son and Ned will be proud of us both.'

There was a feverish gleam in her mother's eyes and suddenly Phoebe was more than afraid. A cold shiver ran down her spine and she clutched her mother's hand. 'Forget him, please. Come inside out of this heat.'

'Don't be daft, girl.' Annie pulled away from her and almost bumped into Amos Snape, who had appeared suddenly like an evil genie from a lamp.

Phoebe held her breath. This was something she had not anticipated. She drew herself up to her full height, ready to defend her mother and Dolly from his unwelcome advances. The only trouble was that Annie did not seem at all displeased to see him. She bridled coquettishly. 'Amos, love. I ain't seen you for weeks.'

His scowl melted into a fawning grin. 'Where've you been, Annie? I missed our little chats at the pub.'

'Oh, I don't go there no more, ducks. I've been a bit poorly but I'm well now and I made up me mind not to frequent them common taverns, although I could manage a bite to eat in a chop house, if you was to offer.'

Amos proffered his arm. 'Of course, my angel. It's me dinner time anyway, and I'm famished.' He led her away, casting a triumphant look in Phoebe's direction.

She could do nothing other than watch them sauntering down the street arm in arm, but at least Amos's arrival had diverted her mother's attention from Ned Paxman, even if it was only a temporary distraction. There were times when she despaired of her wayward parent and this was one of them. Why her mother could not see that Amos was a hateful person Phoebe was at a loss to understand. She could only hope that they did not bump into Ned, or anyone who would tell him that they had seen Annie Giamatti looking unscarred by the dreaded smallpox, if not in the pink of health.

Phoebe went indoors to set up the room for a table tipping session. One thing was certain and that was her need to earn enough money to keep them through the winter. She had Dolly to think of now, and Ma was not in the first flush of youth. She would be almost thirty-seven when she gave birth after a gap of almost twenty years. There would be expenses involving a midwife and possibly a doctor if there were complications.

That evening, she shared her anxieties with Gino. They had gone for a stroll down to the river in the hope of catching a breath of air on Blackfriars Bridge, regardless of the stench emanating from the polluted waters of the Thames. It was hot and sultry with the threat of a thunderstorm hanging over the city in a sulphurous cloud. The river snaked sluggishly between the wharves on either bank and the ships tied up alongside bobbed up and down on the incoming tide.

'What is it that bothers you tonight?' Gino asked gently, laying his hand on Phoebe's as it rested on the railings. 'Is it your mamma?'

She stared down into the curdled tea-coloured waters. 'I can't seem to make her understand the need for absolute secrecy. Today she went off with Snape as if she had not a care in the world. She wants to see Ned Paxman and confront him with the news that he's to become a father. I've tried to tell her that it would be a terrible mistake, but she won't listen.'

'My poor Phoebe. Why don't you leave her and come

with us to Italy? She's a grown woman and she made this problem for herself. It shouldn't be for you to get her out of this mess.'

Phoebe managed a weak smile. 'Sometimes I think that Ma is more of a child than Dolly.'

'Leave them together, cara. They can look after each other. Marry me and let me take care of you.'

There was no doubting the sincerity in his voice or the tender expression in his eyes, but to abandon her mother and Dolly was unthinkable, and Phoebe could not commit herself to such a promise. She shook her head. 'You are a good man, Gino. But I must do what I have to do.'

He toyed with the ring on her finger, but his gaze did not waver from her face. 'You will give me your answer in the spring when I return?'

She nodded her head. 'I will.'

'And there is nothing I can say to make you change your mind and come with us to Stresa?'

'Nothing. I'm sorry, Gino.'

As he drew her into his arms the sky darkened and a flash of forked lightning preceded an ear-splitting crack of thunder. Huge spots of rain the size of half-pennies began to fall from a leaden sky and they ran for shelter. By the time they reached the gatehouse of Bridewell Hospital they were both soaked to the skin, but the rain was warm and they were laughing. Gino put his arm around Phoebe, wiping the raindrops from her cheeks with the tip of his forefinger. 'You are beautiful, my Phoebe. You could have stepped from a painting by one of the great Renaissance masters.'

'You say such lovely things, Gino.'

'But you don't believe me?'

She stretched her arms out into the pouring rain. 'I think you see me as others don't, and I know I looked like a drowned rat, but thank you anyway.'

He caught her by the hands and danced her out of their place of shelter into the rain-soaked street. Splashing through deep puddles, he whirled her round in a wild tarantella singing a snatch of 'Champagne Charlie Is My Name' in a rich tenor voice. Phoebe was giggling too much to hear the sound of booted feet racing towards them and it was not until they were surrounded by rough-looking men carrying clubs and sticks that she realised they were in the centre of a pitched battle between two rival gangs. A huge thunderclap almost deafened her and there was a momentary lull in the men's advance, but another flash of lightning revealed stark, ferocious faces and narrowed glinting eyes. Gino caught her round the waist and half carried, half dragged her to the relative safety of the hospital gatehouse. They stood, arms entwined as the blows started to fall in a vicious attack. Phoebe could feel his heart thudding against her breast and he held her so close that they seemed to be breathing as one.

She buried her face against his shoulder in an attempt to shut out the shouts and the sound of wood cracking skulls and breaking limbs. Cries of pain and swearing were drowned out by the thunder of hobnails and the shattering of glass as missiles were thrown, breaking windows all round. Taking a furtive peek she saw bodies littering the street, bloodstained and writhing in agony. She did not hear the man who lurched into the gatehouse until it was too late to avoid him as he barged into them. He fell unconscious at their feet. Gino slipped his arm around her waist. 'We must get away from here,' he whispered as another man stuck his head round the corner and poked the inert body with a stick. He did not seem to see them and he threw himself back into the fray. Stepping over the crumpled figure, Gino helped Phoebe into the street and holding her hand he began to edge along the wall in an attempt to get away from the brawling mass. They had only managed to get a few feet when one of the gang spotted them, and with a whoop that sounded like an ancient battle cry he felled Gino with a single swipe of his huge fist. 'Take that, Eyetie bastard. Go back home where you belong.'

'Gino!' Phoebe fell to her knees cradling his head on her lap, but their attacker caught her by the hair and yanked her to her feet. 'What's this then, pretty? What sort of man allows his bit of muslin to follow him into a scrap? You don't want to knock around with foreign coves. I'd take better care of you, sweetheart.' He closed his large hand over her left breast and pushed his face so close to hers that his foul breath enveloped her in a stinking miasma of stale beer and rotten teeth. His grip tightened on her hair until she thought that every last one would be pulled from her head, and then just as suddenly as he had appeared he released her and sank silently to his knees.

'I might have guessed it was you, Phoebe Giamatti.'

Rogue Paxman stuck his boot in the middle of the man's back so that he fell flat on his face in the mud. 'This is getting to be a habit. What in hell's name are you doing here?' He fended off a body that came flying towards him, sending the semi-conscious man crashing against the wall where he crumpled to the ground, bent over like a hairpin, as if taking a nap.

Ignoring Paxman, Phoebe knelt at Gino's side. He was regaining consciousness and she wiped his face with her hanky. She looked up at Paxman who was staring down at her with a look of disbelief. 'This is all your fault,' she cried angrily. 'You and your gang make the streets unsafe for decent folk.'

Her words were drowned out by the blast of police whistles. Paxman bent down and caught Gino by the lapels of shirt, heaving him to a standing position. 'You must be mad bringing a girl to this place after dark. Take her home or you'll have me to deal with.' He jerked Phoebe to her feet and thrust her hand into Gino's. 'Go now. Take the side street and shelter in St Bride's church until this is over.' He shoved them unceremoniously towards the entrance to Bride Lane, and then he was gone.

Dazed and leaning heavily on Phoebe, Gino allowed her to lead him to the safety of the church where he rested in the doorway until he was able to stand unaided.

'Are you all right, Gino?' she asked anxiously.

He nodded, rubbing his sore head. 'That was Rogue Paxman. How do you know him?'

'I wouldn't say I know him,' she countered, glancing around to make sure that they had not been followed.

'I try to keep away from both the Paxman brothers. They're nothing but trouble.'

'I don't like it. They're bad men and I can't bear to think of you left alone in London while they roam free.' Gino wrapped his arms around her and she could feel him trembling.

'I'll be all right,' she whispered, planting a kiss on his cold cheek. 'You mustn't worry about me, Gino. I won't have anything to do with the Paxmans. It'll be Ma and me and Dolly. We'll live quietly like three church mice.' She giggled as the clock in the tower struck ten. 'That must be a sign. We've someone up there looking after us, so you can rest easy.'

He stroked her wet hair back from her forehead. 'I'd die if anything was to happen to you, cara.'

'We'll both die of lung fever if we don't get home and change out of these wet things. And I'll have to explain to Nonna why I've stayed out so late with you, or she'll take Nonno's new fowling piece and walk us both down the aisle.'

'Maybe that would be the best thing for both of us.' Gino rubbed his sore head. 'Come. It sounds as though the police have done their work. I'll take you home.'

Luckily for Phoebe there was no one about when she crept into the house. She could hear the rumble of men's voices coming from the dining room and she could only guess that her grandfather and uncles were talking business. There was no sign of her grandmother and that in itself was a relief. She tiptoed upstairs to the top floor bedroom where she found Dolly asleep on the truckle bed by the window, but to her horror her mother's bed was empty. She stood shivering in the doorway, uncertain as to what she ought to do next. Perhaps Ma had felt unwell and had gone to the privy in the back yard. She hoped so, but she had to make certain. Surely Ma would not be so silly as to go out drinking. Not in her condition.

Without stopping to change out of her wet clothes, Phoebe retraced her steps and went outside into the dark yard where the privy and pump were situated. The storm had abated but now a steady drizzle was falling from the dark skies. She opened the privy door but the only occupant was a large spider sitting in the middle of its web. Her heart sank. She was used to her mother's gallivanting in normal times, but this was different. In her delicate condition and in this dreadful weather she would be taking a terrible risk. The streets were always unsafe after dark, but doubly so on a night when the gangs were at war with each other. She hesitated, standing in the rain regardless of her own personal discomfort. She knew she had no choice other than to try to find her mother and bring her home.

The Three Bells was all but deserted. The Smithfield gang members were otherwise engaged, and Phoebe suspected that they had fled south of the river in order to escape from the police. They would slink back to their dens in the courts and alleyways next day, but for now they were absent from their customary meeting place. Charlie, the potman, eyed her warily. 'Get on home, ducks. You'll catch your death. There ain't no one here to entertain you tonight.'

Phoebe chose to ignore the implied insult, insinuating that she was on the game. 'Have you seen Annie?'

'Would that be Iron Leg Annie, or Cross-eyed Annie, or . . .'

'Annie Giamatti.'

'Oh, Spooky Annie. Yes, I seen her an hour or so ago. Gone off with that Snape fellow from the distillery. A bit swipey she was or she might have thought twice about keeping company with the likes of him.'

'You don't know where he lives, I suppose?'

'I knows everything about everyone what drinks in this pub. And one thing I'll tell you for nothing is that Ned Paxman won't be too pleased if he ever finds out his moll is carrying on behind his back.' Charlie made a cutting motion, swiping his finger across his throat.

Phoebe clutched his arm. 'Never mind that. Where does Snape hang out?'

'Turk's Head Yard, love. Mind you, it's not the sort of place I'd recommend to a young person like you. I'd leave her to come home on her own, if you know what I mean.'

'Ta, Charlie.' Phoebe left him still muttering about the dangers of the area where Snape had lodgings, but she ignored his warning and ran out into the rain to continue searching for her mother.

Turk's Head Yard was situated opposite the railway line at the junction of Turnmill Street and Cowcross Street. It was the sort of place where it was barely safe to venture in broad daylight, let alone in the dark. The torrential rain had gone a little way to wash the detritus from the streets, although the surface drains were blocked with rubbish and overflowed, forming gushing torrents of filthy water to soak the unwary pedestrian's feet as they crossed the road. Phoebe was past caring. She could not have been colder or wetter if she had gone for a swim in the Thames. She plucked up all her courage and entered the narrow court. She was instantly aware of shadowy figures moving silently between the closely packed buildings. A man lurched out of a house either drunk or under the influence of opium and she shrank away from him, but he appeared to be too far gone to even notice her. A ragged child was curled up in the doorway of a pawnshop with a mongrel dog wrapped around his feet like a living muff. The dog opened an eye and growled deep in its throat as Phoebe hurried past.

She had no idea which of the dilapidated buildings housed the rooms rented by Snape and only now she realised the futility of her mission, but just as she was about to give up and return home, she saw a white figure weaving from one side of the narrow alley to the other, her long hair flowing about her shoulders and her bare feet moving soundlessly over the wet cobblestones. 'Ma?' Phoebe could hardly believe her eyes. She forced her aching limbs to move and was just in time to catch Annie as she collapsed in her arms.

Chapter Six

The smell of sour blue ruin on her mother's breath
was oddly comforting. At least it went some way to
explain her semi-conscious state. Supporting Annie's
weight, Phoebe managed to get her to the main road,
where a quick examination in the light of a street lamp
reassured her that there were no obvious physical
injuries. Annie's mutterings made little sense, but that
could be down to the amount of alcohol she had
obviously imbibed, and the fact that she was wet and
chilled to the bone. It was not far to the Giamattis'
house, and exerting the last ounce of her flagging
energy Phoebe helped her mother up the stairs to the
top floor.

In the safety of their room, Phoebe helped her out
of her wet things and into a cotton nightgown. 'What
happened tonight, Ma?' she demanded as she dried
Annie's wet hair with a towel. 'Did he hurt you?'

Annie shook her head. 'I think I killed him.'

'What?'

'It was all fun and games to begin with.' Annie raised
her hand to her brow. 'My head aches something
chronic. Get me a seltzer, love.'

'All in good time. Tell me what went on in Snape's
lodgings.'

Annie appeared to sober up as she recalled the events that had led up to her flight from Turk's Head Yard. 'We was having a drink and a giggle, and then he got a bit too familiar. I told him to lay off 'cos I wasn't that sort of woman, but the bastard was all over me in a trice. I picked up the nearest thing, which happened to be the gin bottle. I cracked him over the head with it and ran. I never even stopped to put on me shoes and they was me best pair.'

Phoebe glanced at the bare boards by her mother's bed, frowning. 'Your shoes are still here, Ma.'

Annie stifled a giggle. 'Crikey. I must've taken yours, ducks. I was in a bit of a hurry to get out before Mamma Giamatti realised I'd gone.'

'Oh, Ma. What am I going to do with you?'

'The coppers will be after me.' Annie's voice rose on a note of panic. 'You've got to hide me, Phoebe.'

Dolly stirred and moaned as she turned over in her narrow bed and Phoebe laid a finger on her lips. 'Hush, Ma. You'll wake her. We don't want Dolly blabbing about this to anyone who'll listen.'

Annie clutched her stomach, her eyes widening. 'He's moving about. Ned's son's a lively one. He's going to be just like his pa.'

The mere mention of Ned's name sent a cold shiver running down Phoebe's spine. She pulled back the covers and pressed her mother onto the bed. 'You must rest, Ma. I'll take care of everything.'

Reluctantly, Annie swung her legs onto the mattress and pulled up the coverlet. 'You got to find out if Snape's alive or dead. If I've killed the beast I'll have no choice but to go to Italy with the family. Maybe the whole damn business will have blown over by next spring.'

'Yes, Ma. Everything will be all right. You mustn't worry.' Phoebe picked up the candlestick and made for the door. Snape was a poor apology for a man but murder was a hanging offence, and she had to be certain that he had survived. 'Can you remember Snape's address, Ma?'

Annie raised herself on her elbow. 'It's number ten and his room's on the ground floor at the back of the house. But you're not thinking of going there now, are you?'

'I know what I'm doing, Ma. Go to sleep now and don't worry.' Phoebe let herself out of the room, closing the door softly behind her.

The storm had passed, leaving the streets muddy and pockmarked with deep puddles. Phoebe's clothes were almost dry by the time she reached Turk's Head Yard, and a distant church clock chimed out the witching hour. She found the house wedged in between what appeared to be a brothel and an undertaker's premises. The front door was hanging on one hinge as though an impatient person had at one point forced it open. She went inside, feeling her way along the damp walls to the rear of the building. A sour smell of damp rot and fungus pervaded the atmosphere, which was thick with dust, and strands of cobweb clutched at her hair. At the end of the corridor a faint sliver of light revealed that the door had been left ajar. Trembling, but determined to discover Snape's fate, she opened it further, peering inside the room. In the flickering light of a single candle she could see Snape slumped in a chair. The bare boards surrounding him were covered in broken glass. A strong smell of jigger gin bore witness to Annie's statement, and an upturned chair showed signs of a brief struggle.

Tiptoeing across the floor with her heart hammering against her ribs and her mouth dry with fear, Phoebe picked her way through the shards of glass to get near enough to Snape in order to reassure herself that he was still breathing. In fact he was snoring, and although she could see a reddened lump on the back of his balding head, he was obviously very much alive. Her hand flew to her mouth as she stifled a sob of pure relief. She had not believed that a woman as slight as her mother could fell a man the size of an ox, but she had heard of people with thin skulls for whom the slightest bump had proved fatal. Snape was patently not in that category. She bent down to retrieve the shoes that her mother had abandoned in her haste to escape, and she left Snape to sleep off the effects of the copious amounts of alcohol he must have consumed. He would doubtless have a bad headache in the morning, but with luck he would not remember too much of the previous night's events. She made her way home without further incident. The increased police presence on the streets after the skirmish between the rival gangs had cleared the area, if only temporarily, of those who might have waylaid a lone woman. Even so it was with a sigh of relief that she let herself into the house. In a few short hours her grandfather and uncles would be up and going about the daily routine of collecting ice and making the ice cream for the last time that season. In a couple of days the family would leave for Italy and Ma's secret would be safe.

The family left as planned, but not without a last concerted effort to persuade Phoebe to accompany them to their winter home. Gino was the most persistent of all, and she had to be firm to the point of stubbornness in her refusal, but now she had the excuse of looking after Dolly, who wept copiously every time anyone suggested that Phoebe might leave her. Maria had, somewhat reluctantly, formed a bond with Dolly. Her maternal instincts had been roused by the girl with the body of a woman and the mind of a child. Dolly's operation wound was healing but she presented an odd sight now that the bandages had been removed, with patches of fair hair sprouting out of a shaven head. The local children made fun of her and took it in turns to try to pluck the cotton mobcap from her head in order to get a better look at her bald pate. If Maria was witness to any of this taunting she chased them off with a broomstick, but Phoebe did her best to keep Dolly at her side. She allowed her to sit in on the table tipping sessions and was priming her to take part in the séances that would be a necessity if they were to support themselves through a long hard winter.

Annie had kept to her room after her ill-judged outing and her attack on Snape. Despite Phoebe's continued reassurance, she was convinced that she had committed a murder or at least done him irreparable damage. She lived in constant fear of the police and each time she heard a knock on the door she would hide beneath the bedclothes. Phoebe was certain that Snape would not have reported the assault to the authorities, and she was prepared to deny that her mother had ever left the premises should he arrive and demand compensation for a cracked skull. It was not until the day after the family departed that Snape finally made an appearance in Saffron Hill. Phoebe answered the door and was barely surprised to see him standing on the pavement outside.

'What can I do for you, Mr Snape?'

'You can stop acting the innocent, missy. You know very well why I'm here. I want to see Annie.'

'She's unwell. She can't see anyone.'

'Another attack of the smallpox, I suppose.'

Phoebe clenched her fists behind her back. Snape could only have heard that tale from Ned Paxman. What if he had boasted of seducing Annie in Ned's presence? The very thought of it made her blood run cold. She forced herself to appear calm. 'I don't know what you're talking about.'

He put his foot over the threshold. 'I want to see Annie.' He took off his top hat and rubbed the back of his head. 'She crowned me with a bottle, the little harlot. But as I've always said, I like a woman with spirit.' He pushed past Phoebe and there was nothing she could do to stop him as he headed for the parlour.

With the male members of the family on their way to Italy there was no one left to protect them. She hurried after him. 'I'm not doing any fortune telling or séances this morning, Mr Snape.' Catching sight of Dolly peering out of the kitchen, Phoebe placed her finger on her lips, but she need not have worried. Dolly had seen Snape and she was obviously scared out of her wits. She dodged back into the room and shut the door. Breathing a sigh of relief, Phoebe followed him into the parlour. 'What do you want?'

'All right, missy. I'm a direct man. I'll come straight to the point. I want to know if your trull of a mother is going to name me as the father of her bastard.'

This was the last thing she had expected. Phoebe stared at him in astonishment. 'I don't understand.'

'I know a full belly when I feel one, so don't try to pretend that it ain't so. I got a position to keep up at work and I don't want a cheap little moll like Annie Giamatti making trouble for me.'

'You're mistaken, mister.'

'Then it's Paxman's,' Snape said with a smug grin. 'I thought as much. Now get your crystal ball out, love. Tell me how much it's worth to keep my mouth shut.'

She was trembling and her palms were damp with perspiration, but she was not going to let him see that she was afraid. 'Get out of my house.'

Snape struck a pose. 'You can't make me do anything, Phoebe, my love. I got the upper hand and I want recompense for a sore head and a bottle of good spirit. I could have given the slut blue ruin but I gave her the real thing.'

'And I expect you filched that from the distillery,' Phoebe said angrily. 'Don't come here making threats, mister. I've got friends who will sort you out if you don't leave us alone.'

'All the Eyeties who stayed behind are out asphalting the roads now the season's over. Amos Snape don't scare so easily, miss. So do I go to Paxman and tell him that Annie Giamatti is carrying his little mistake, or do I get what I want?'

'What is it you want?'

'I want Dolly Fowler. She's bought and paid for. Give me the simpleton and we'll say no more about any of this. I can be as silent as the grave if it's worth my while.'

'Get out of my house.' Phoebe's voice rose to a scream. 'You disgusting man. Go away before I call the police.'

Snape curled his lip. 'Go on then, love. Call the cops and I'll report your ma for common assault and attempted murder.' He touched the back of his head as if to demonstrate a point.

'You can't see Dolly,' Phoebe said in desperation. 'She's not here. She went to Italy with my grandparents.'

Snape's expression froze into one of disbelief. 'You're lying.'

'I wouldn't be so stupid. You'd find me out sooner or later.'

His hand shot out and he caught her by the wrist. 'That's right. I would, and if you're telling lies it'll be the worse for you and that mother of yours.'

'Search the house then if you don't believe me.' Phoebe knew she was taking a chance by inviting him to see for himself, but she judged it worth the risk if it bought her some time. She met his suspicious gaze with what she hoped was an air of innocence.

He released her with a grunt of disgust. 'I've got to get back to work, but if I find out you've tricked me . . .' He stormed out of the room, leaving the sentence hanging like a threat over Phoebe's head.

She sank down on the nearest chair as her knees buckled beneath her. She knew that this was not the end of the story as far as Snape was concerned. He was capable of anything when it came to satisfying his perverted lust for a helpless creature like Dolly, whose own mother had been prepared to sell her into sexual slavery. She jumped as she heard the front door slam behind him. At least they were safe for the time being, but for how long? As the strength returned to her lower limbs, she stood up and paced the floor. The crystal ball set in the middle of the table was catching the light as the sun filtered through the window. If she had a genuine ability to foretell future events she might know what to do next, but it was all trickery and pantomime. She turned at the sound of footsteps and met Dolly's anxious gaze.

'It was me he wanted, wasn't it?' Dolly's face was pale as milk and her blue eyes were magnified by tears. 'You won't let him take me, will you?'

Phoebe hurried to her side, taking her cold hands in a firm clasp. 'Never. You're part of our family now. I'll keep you safe, so you mustn't worry.'

'But he might come back. Ma sold me to Mr Snape. I belongs to him.'

'No. You don't and you mustn't think like that. You're a free person, Dolly. No one can sell you and no one can buy you. It's as simple as that.'

Dolly's lips trembled. 'But he thinks it's so. He'll lie in wait for me like a cat catching a bird and he'll pounce.'

Phoebe squeezed her hands gently. 'We've got to get away from here. I don't know where we'll go, but I'll think of something.'

'You're clever, miss,' Dolly whispered. 'You'll save me from the cat-man.'

'I will, I promise. But you must stay indoors today. Keep out of sight. We must make Snape think that you've gone to Italy with my family.'

'I'm good at hiding,' Dolly said, brightening visibly. 'I used to hide from Ma when she was on the rampage. She beat me with Pa's wooden leg. That's how she hurt me head.'

'I know, dear. But that's all in the past.' Phoebe gave her a reassuring hug. 'Now I want you to go back to the kitchen and make us all a lovely cup of tea. I'm going upstairs to talk to Ma.'

'I can make tea.'

'Of course you can. I'll only be gone for a few minutes, so don't open the door to anyone. Remember you're hiding.'

Dolly nodded emphatically and hurried from the room repeating over and over again, 'I mustn't open the door to anyone.'

Phoebe hesitated for a moment, staring at the crystal ball for inspiration. Matters had come to a head now and she must make the right decision. They could not stay in Saffron Hill; that was becoming increasingly clear. They must leave soon and preferably under the cover of darkness. She must get Ma and Dolly to a place of safety. She stroked the cold glass with the tips of her fingers, closing her eyes and hoping for an answer. She could hear the waves lapping on the shingle as if she were standing on Bridewell Wharf watching the incoming tide. She opened her eyes and the sound faded away. Perhaps she had imagined the fresh saltiness carried on the breeze that had momentarily fanned her cheeks. It was all in her mind, she decided, moving towards the doorway. She did not believe in the power of the crystal ball. It was all a sham. She hurried from the room and made her way upstairs.

She found her mother huddled up beneath the coverlet staring blankly at the wall. Suddenly her patience snapped. 'Ma, this is ridiculous. You must get up.'

Slowly, Annie turned her head to stare at her daughter. 'Why? Give me one good reason why I shouldn't just lie here and die.'

'Because we're in terrible trouble, Ma. I need you to help me.'

Annie shook her head. 'I can't help anyone, ducks. Snape will have me arrested and I'll probably die in prison with my unborn babe.'

With a swift movement, Phoebe snatched the covers off the bed. 'Stop it, Ma. Get up this instant and stop feeling sorry for yourself.'

Annie stared at her in amazement. 'Don't speak to me like that, Phoebe. I'm still your mother.'

'Then start acting like it. You've got the baby to think of now and if we don't get away from here Snape has threatened to tell Ned Paxman that it's his.'

Annie snapped upright, clutching her nightgown to her swollen breasts. 'Snape doesn't know about the child.'

'He's not stupid, Ma. He saw the state you're in and he guessed the rest. Now he's after Dolly as he can't get what he wants from you. What have you to say to that?'

Tears spilled from Annie's eyes and she buried her face in her hands. 'Don't speak to me in that tone of voice, Phoebe. It's not my fault.'

'Then I don't know whose fault it is, Ma. I've been patient with you all this time and I've told lies to protect you, but we can't go on this way. Can you imagine what will happen if Paxman wants to acknowledge the baby as his? The family would disown you at the very best, or it could start a war between the gangs and the Camorra. The Thames would run with blood because of you.'

'No. It's not true. You're just saying these things to frighten me.'

'I'm saying them because they're true. We've got to leave this place tonight or first thing in the morning at the very latest. God knows where we'll go or how we'll live, but if we stay here we might all die. Do you understand me now, Ma?' She hesitated, looking over her shoulder as someone tapped on the door, and Dolly peered nervously into the room. 'Come in, love. It's going to be all right. Don't look so scared.'

'You was shouting and it's my fault.' Dolly entered, carrying a tray of tea which she thrust into Phoebe's hands. 'I should go back to Ma. I'm causing you nothing but grief.'

Phoebe placed the tray on the washstand, shaking her head. 'You're not to blame, Dolly. And we're going to go somewhere nice.' She paused, closing her eyes as once again the scent of brine and fresh air filled her nostrils. 'We're going to the seaside.'

'Have you lost your mind, Phoebe?' Annie stared at her in horror. 'To the seaside?'

Phoebe smiled. 'I know it's a lot of nonsense, but the crystal ball showed me the way.'

Dolly picked up a cup of tea and handed it to Annie. 'I never seen the sea, but I heard people talk about it.'

'I did have an elderly aunt and her spinster daughter, who lived in Brighton,' Annie said, sipping her tea thoughtfully. 'My cousin Judy and me kept in touch for a while, but the old lady could by dead for all I know. All my family die young.'

'Brighton it is then.' With more certainty than she was feeling, Phoebe lifted a cup of tea to her lips. 'Best pack what you need for the journey. We're leaving in the morning before the rest of the street wakes up.'

They caught the first train from Victoria next morning. Their escape from Saffron Hill had gone unnoticed in the dark and they had caught a horse-drawn omnibus which took them directly to the station. Dolly had been subdued when they left the house but once settled on the hard wooden seats in the third class compartment of the train she became as excited as a small child on Christmas Eve. Annie was less enthusiastic and although she said little, Phoebe knew that her mother still believed that Ned would have married her had he known about the child. It had taken all her powers of persuasion to get her this far. Until they were safely on the train Phoebe had been afraid that her mother might suddenly make a bolt for it and return to Saffron Hill and the man she loved, but at least now she could relax a little and pray that Aunt Egeria still lived in the house on West Parade that Annie remembered as a child.

The house was at the end of a Georgian terrace. It had seen better days. Phoebe stood on the pavement, staring up at the crumbling white stucco and the rusty wrought-iron balconies. The end wall bulged slightly as though it was about to dive into the sea taking the whole terrace for a morning dip. The smell of boiling cabbage wafted up from the basement next door, mingled with a hint of fish that was not at its freshest. Annie dropped her carpet bag on the ground with a stifled groan. 'It wasn't like this when I last came here. I remember it as being all white and lovely, like a rich person's house. Inside there was red carpet and a statue of a blackamoor standing at the foot of the staircase holding up a lamp. Aunt Egeria wore lavender silk gowns in the afternoon and her maid brought us tea in dainty cups with primroses and bluebells painted on them.'

'I expect she's dead,' Dolly said in a sombre tone. 'Old people die. Kittens die too. I had one once but it died when I cuddled it, and it was all floppy.'

Phoebe gave her hand a sympathetic squeeze. 'Never mind, dear. I'm sure it went straight to heaven.'

'And the dog I used to give scraps to died as well,' Dolly continued soulfully. 'And I once found a dead pigeon in the privy.'

'If you don't shut up I'll scream,' Annie said with feeling. 'We've come all this way on a wild goose chase and all because Phoebe took it into her head that she can foretell the future. That's my talent, not yours, my girl. I wish you'd mind your own business sometimes. I've left everything I care about in London to come to this.' She gesticulated dramatically and burst into tears.

Phoebe released Dolly's hand to pat her mother gently on the shoulder. 'You're tired, Ma. There's only one way to find out if your aunt is still alive. I'll knock on the door and ask.' She left them standing disconsolately on the pavement while she climbed the stone steps leading up to the front door which was in sad need of a lick of paint. The lion's head doorknocker might well be made of brass but it was green with verdigris and blackened by exposure to the elements. She raised it twice and let it fall, cocking her head on one side and listening to the echo. She waited for a while and then knocked again. This time she could hear shuffling footsteps coming towards the front door. It opened with a grinding sound and she found herself looking into the face of a tired-looking woman who could have been any age between thirty and fifty.

'We're full. Can't you read the sign?' The woman pointed to a piece of cardboard stuck in the front window bearing the legend *No Vacancies*. She was about to close the door when Phoebe put her foot over the threshold.

'Does Mrs Egeria Edwards still live here?'

'She's dead. Died ten year ago. Now push off.'

'She was my mother's aunt,' Phoebe said hastily. 'Did you know her?'

'I should know the old battleaxe. I'm Judy Edwards, her daughter, and we're still full. No rooms to let, especially for poor relations.'

Before Phoebe had a chance to speak Annie had her foot on the bottom step. 'Here, you. I heard that and we ain't poor. We've got money to pay for bed and board. You was always a stuck-up, spiteful little cow. Moody Judy I used to call you when we was younger and I see you ain't changed much.'

'And neither have you.' Judy gave her a speculative glance. 'Any fool can see that you're in the family way, and no wedding ring, I'll bet.'

'I'm a respectable widow woman for your information, Judy Edwards,' Annie said, holding up her left hand to demonstrate the narrow gold band. 'I don't see no wedding ring on *your* finger. Obviously no one wanted to marry a sour-faced old maid like you.'

Phoebe sent a warning glance to her mother. 'Please don't fight. This isn't getting us anywhere.'

'She started it,' Annie said darkly. 'She always did, and I'd get into trouble from Aunt Egeria. She never liked me.'

Judy stood with arms akimbo, eyeing her cousin with obvious distaste. 'Then you must be desperate to come looking for her now. You never showed much interest in Ma while she was alive. You never come to the door with calves' foot jelly nor a bunch of grapes when she was struck down by illness. The last time you put pen to paper you was living the high life in London with the Eyeties, and travelling to Italy for the winter while we froze to death down here on the coast.'

'We'd best leave, Ma.' Phoebe could see that Dolly was distressed by this spirited encounter and she was feeling far from happy herself. 'We won't trouble you any longer, Miss Edwards. I'm sorry that your ma passed away, it must be hard for a woman on her own.' To her intense surprise, Judy's dark eyes filled with tears.

'You ain't like your ma and that's for certain.' She blew her nose on a scrap of tattered cotton that she took from her apron pocket. 'Looks like rain. You'd best come inside. You can have a cup of tea and a bite to eat. Never let it be said that Judy Edwards is a mean woman or that she bears a grudge.'

'Not much,' Annie muttered.

Hoping that Judy had not heard this last remark, Phoebe managed a smile. 'That's very kind of you. We've been travelling since before dawn and I'm sure that Ma and Dolly could do with a sit down. We'll move on as soon as they're rested and perhaps you could direct us to a cheap lodging house.'

'Never mind that now,' Judy said, stepping aside

and ushering them in. 'Straight along the corridor and downstairs to the kitchen. Leave your bags in the hall.'

Phoebe hesitated at the foot of the steep staircase as a pale-faced girl leaned over the banisters. Dark curls framed an oval face and her large brown eyes were fringed with thick lashes. She smiled but her expression changed as Judy pushed Phoebe aside and mounted the first step, rolling up her sleeves as if she meant business. 'I can see you, Rose Jackson. You and your old man owe three weeks' rent. I want it by suppertime or you can look for digs elsewhere.' She shook her fist as Rose disappeared from view. 'I should have known better than to take entertainers, they're a fly-by-night lot.' She glared at Phoebe. 'Well, go on then. What are you waiting for? And remember, girl. This is only temporary. Don't go running away with the idea that Judy Edwards is a soft mark.'

Chapter Seven

With an exasperated tut-tutting sound Judy went on ahead, still mumbling beneath her breath. The passage-way was dark and narrow with doors leading off on either side, but these were firmly closed. A staircase at the end of the corridor led down to a large basement kitchen with a flagstone floor and a blackleaded range which took up at least half the space along one wall. A fire burned in the grate and a large black kettle bubbled cheerily on the hob. Pots and pans hung from the low beamed ceiling and a scrubbed pine table with benches on either side stretched almost the complete length of the room. The remnants of a meal lay where they had been abandoned and the stone sink was piled high with dirty dishes. Judy, it seemed, was not a very efficient housekeeper.

Annie looked around with her lips pursed and Phoebe knew instinctively that her mother was about to say something scathing. 'This is very kind of you, Cousin Judy,' she said quickly, before Annie could open her mouth.

'Being too kind is my greatest failing,' Judy said gloomily. 'People take advantage of my good nature.' She set about making a pot of tea. 'Sit down, for good-ness' sake. You're making the place untidy.'

Annie made a point of dusting the bench before she took a seat, but Dolly flopped down on the floor, spreading her legs wide so that she looked like a rag doll that a bored child had discarded. 'I'm tired,' she said, leaning back against the brick wall and closing her eyes.

'Is she always like this?' Judy demanded, warming the pot with hot water from the kettle. 'Not all there?'

'Dolly's had a hard time,' Phoebe said, leaping to her defence. 'She had an operation on her head.'

'That accounts for it.' Judy finished making the tea and left it to brew while she searched for cups on a dresser crammed with oddments of china, household ledgers, broken ornaments and candle stubs stuck onto saucers and pot lids. 'Who is she anyway? Not one of yours by the looks of her, Annie.'

'Certainly not.' Annie bridled visibly. 'Anyone would think I was a woman of easy virtue if they listened to you, Moody.'

Unabashed, Judy poured the tea. 'So who's the father of this one? I don't see a husband hanging on your coat tails.'

'It's a long story,' Phoebe said without giving her mother a chance to launch into an account of her affair with a much younger man who just happened to belong to a notorious street gang. 'If we might have something to eat, please, cousin? I can pay.'

Judy eyed her suspiciously. 'So if you ain't broke how is it that you came here looking for lodgings? What's going on?' She turned to Annie. 'What happened to your old man? And why aren't you off to Italy, as normal?'

Annie choked into her teacup. 'Paulo's dead. He was killed by the high mob ten years ago.'

'So the nipper isn't his then? Ma would be spinning in her grave if she could see you now. She always said you'd come to a sticky end.'

'That's cruel, Judy, even for you. But then you was always spiteful.'

Judy cleared a space on the table with a sweep of her arm and began slicing a loaf of bread. 'I speak as I find. So are you going to tell me the truth or do I have to guess?'

Annie covered her eyes with her hand. 'I can't. It's too painful.'

'Then I will.' Phoebe launched into an explanation making it as brief as possible, interrupted by occasional snores from Dolly, who had fallen asleep on the floor.

Judy listened attentively while she buttered the bread and carved slices from a leg of boiled mutton. 'So you're running away then? I guessed as much.'

'Just until the baby is born,' Phoebe said, eyeing the food and realising that she was extremely hungry. 'We need to find somewhere to stay until the New Year. Then we'll return to London.'

'With a baby in tow.' Judy raised her eyebrows. 'No one will think it strange, of course.'

'I'll tell Ned,' Annie said, snatching the plate that Judy offered her. 'When he sees our child he'll do the right thing by me.'

'You always was soft in the head, girl.' Judy took a plate over to Dolly and prodded her with the toe of her boot. 'Wake up, sleeping beauty.'

Dolly opened her eyes. 'I was dreaming about dinner.'

'Well here it is. You can earn your keep by helping Phoebe do the washing up when you've eaten.'

'Ta, miss.' Dolly snatched the plate and began cramming bread and meat into her mouth.

Judy took a seat in a Windsor chair by the range. 'Well now. You're all in a pretty pickle, I must say. How do you propose to support yourselves during the long winter months?'

'I'm a clairvoyant.' Annie said proudly. 'I do séances and table tipping. I read the crystal ball and tell people their fortunes.'

'And no one's ever found you out as a cheat and a liar?'

Annie almost choked on a mouthful of cold lamb. 'That's not fair, Judy. I can see into the future and I do get messages from the other side.'

'It's a pity you didn't foresee that little complication, isn't it?' Judy said, staring at Annie's swollen belly.

'He's not a complication,' Annie cried angrily. 'My son will be the best thing that's ever happened to me.' She shot an apologetic glance at Phoebe. 'Next to you, of course, ducks. You're a good girl and I dunno what I'd have done without you.'

Phoebe put her empty plate down on the table. 'Ta for the food, Cousin Judy. I'll do the dishes and then we'll be on our way. We need to find somewhere to stay before dark, and the nights are drawing in.'

Judy shrugged her thin shoulders. 'There's no hurry. Tell the truth I'm enjoying the diversion. For years I slaved away running this lodging house for Ma, and looked after her while she was ill. Now it's nice to see other people in a worse state than myself. I might even let you stay for a few days, if you don't mind sharing the attic room with the spiders and mice.'

Dolly clambered to her feet. 'I don't mind spiders and I once had a pet mouse. He used to come out at night and keep me company when the others was asleep, but he died. Everything dies in the end.'

'We won't think about that now,' Phoebe said, giving her an encouraging smile. 'Let's get this mess cleared away and then perhaps Cousin Judy would show us where we can put our things.'

'Like I said before, it's only temporary, so don't get ideas about staying here for the winter.' Judy rose to her feet and unhooked a bunch of keys from a nail in a beam over her head. She handed it to Phoebe. 'It's the door opposite the stairs on the top floor. And call me Judy. I'm your ma's cousin for my sins, not yours, and we won't go into the second cousin business. Just Judy will do nicely.'

'It's very good of you, Judy.' Annie made an attempt to rise but sank back onto the bench with a sigh. 'If I might go to our room I'd like to rest awhile. I get very tired these days and we've had a long journey.'

Judy eyed her askance. 'Rest now then, but don't think you're going to get away with lazing about when there's work to do. I earn my living by taking in lodgers. They're entertainers for the most part, although some of them take other jobs in the winter. There's not much call for Punch and Judy on the beach in November.'

'Punch and Judy.' Dolly stared at her open-mouthed. 'Does he punch you, miss? I wouldn't let him stay here if I was you.'

Judy turned to Phoebe, frowning. 'Take her with you. I've no patience with simpletons, and to save the poor soul racking what's left of her brains we'll call it the Punch and Jessie show. It's an embarrassment having my name plastered all over the seafront in summer. I wish the old girl had called me anything but Judy.'

'Come along, Dolly.' Phoebe reached out to take her hand. 'Let's go upstairs to see the spiders and mice. You might find a pet amongst them.'

As they left the room, Dolly glanced over her shoulder at Judy. 'She don't have no bruises, Phoebe. If he punches her he does it so they won't show. That's what Ma did to me until she forgot herself.'

'For God's sake stop babbling, Dolly.' Annie turned on her with an exasperated sigh. 'You're making my head spin with your idiotic prattle.'

'I ain't an idiot,' Dolly whispered in Phoebe's ear. 'Am I?'

Phoebe gave her a hug. 'Ma's in a delicate condition and she's worn out. You take one of her bags and I'll take the other. Let's see what Judy's attic has to offer.'

The room was long and low-ceilinged with a window in the roof that when prised open overlooked the sea. The rain-washed slates glistened as a pale sun forced its way between the dark clouds and glinted in golden lights off the pebbles as the ebb tide licked the shore.

Until today Phoebe had only seen the sea when they crossed the Channel on the packet boat, and then she had marvelled at its vast expanse and the power of the foam-flecked waves. Listening now, in the quiet at the top of the house, the sound of the waves on the foreshore was like music to her ears, with only the mournful cries of the seagulls wheeling overhead and the occasional rumble of a horse-drawn vehicle to break the hypnotic rhythm. After the noisy hubbub of London it seemed like paradise. She had loved the great blue lakes in northern Italy but there was something endless and timeless about the sea. When she stood on the busy wharves overlooking the river she could imagine the muddy waters of the Thames flowing into the North Sea, and being cleansed by inclusion in the vast body of salt water.

'Here, shut that bloody window, I'll catch me death of cold.'

Her mother's voice broke into her reverie and Phoebe did as she was told, but even though the grimy window-panes shut out the sea and sky, she knew they were still there.

'This is disgusting,' Annie said, prodding the straw palliasse with her foot. 'I'm not sleeping on the floor for anyone. I suppose Judy thinks this is funny.'

Phoebe glanced round the room, which was just an open space beneath the rafters. There were signs that it had been used recently, but the previous occupants had not bothered to make their quarters habitable. Perhaps maidservants had slept up here in bygone days when the family had money, but the cobwebs and bare floorboards bore testament to the fact that this part of the house had been neglected for a very long time. Annie sneezed as a cloud of dust rose up like a spectre from the bedding. 'It's nothing that a bit of elbow grease won't cure, Ma,' Phoebe said hopefully. 'We'll take the palliasses down to the yard and I'll give them a good beating.'

'They're probably running with fleas and lice. I'm used to a feather bed.' Annie sat down on a spindly chair which wobbled dangerously, one leg appearing to be shorter than the others. 'I'd sooner sleep on the beach than up here.'

Phoebe went to her side and slipped her arm around her mother's shoulders. 'You're exhausted, Ma. We'll make ourselves as comfortable as possible for tonight and then in the morning I'll go out and find somewhere else for us to stay. It's just one night and it will offend Judy if we don't accept her offer.'

'Bah!' Annie almost spat the word at her. 'Judy is a bitch. She always was and she's not changed. No doubt she's thoroughly enjoying the sight of me in my present condition and with no man to protect me. She was always jealous of me. I won't stay where I'm not wanted. We're leaving first thing in the morning, and that's that.'

Next morning at breakfast Phoebe came face to face with Judy's lodgers. Annie had remained in bed, saying that she was unwell and refusing to take even a cup of weak tea, but Dolly was eager to meet their fellow residents. She perched on the end of the bench munching toast as she listened to the introductions being made by Judy, who was in charge of the enormous brown china teapot and named each person as she refilled their cups. The first to greet them was a large man with a flaming red beard and a bald pate, which made his head look as though it had been put on upside down. He half rose from his seat. 'Good morning, ladies. I am Herbert Jackson, entertainer and puppeteer.' He motioned Phoebe to sit down and squeezed onto the bench beside her. 'I give the Punch and . . .' Receiving a fierce look from Judy he corrected himself. 'I give the Punch and the person we do not name in this house shows on the beach.'

'With my help, Poppa,' Rose said chirpily. 'Don't forget me.' She smiled at Phoebe and reached across the table to shake her hand. 'I'm the one who gets the bookings and takes the money from the audience. I'm the business brains, aren't I, Poppa?'

'You are, my pet.' Herbert smiled indulgently. 'My little Rose is my right hand, so to speak. When her mother passed on she took over my management and saved me from sinking into a life of drink and debt.'

'Ma ran off with the theatre manager in Bournemouth,' Rose said, her smile fading. 'They went to Blackpool and that was the last we heard of them, but we manage well enough on our own.'

'We do, my dove.' Herbert turned to a small man with mutton-chop whiskers and a waxed moustache who had nudged him in the ribs. 'What is it, Fred, old chap?'

'My introduction, cully. Don't forget the supporting acts.'

Herbert inclined his head. 'Of course. I'm sorry, I was forgetting my manners. Miss Giamatti, may I introduce Fred Jones, also known as Armando Janos, who is by profession a world famous sword swallower and juggler.'

Fred smiled modestly. 'That is true, but out of season I clean windows. My former act as a high wire walker gave me a head for heights, until I fell and broke my leg in three places. I'm a martyr to rheumatism, Miss Giamatti, but I can still climb a ladder, although it gets harder each winter.'

Phoebe smiled and nodded but was prevented from responding by the woman seated next to Rose on the opposite side of the table. 'And I am Madame Galina Lavrovna. I trained at the Imperial Ballet School in St Petersburg and performed for the crown heads of Europe.'

'That was several lifetimes ago, love.'

All heads turned to the small woman seated at the far end of the table. She looked round with a pained expression on her wizened features. 'I only speak the truth.'

Madame Galina subsided into her double chins, blushing furiously. 'That was cruel, Augusta, even by your standards. I was the toast of St Petersburg for a whole season.'

'And now you are burnt toast, love.' Augusta winked at Phoebe, mouthing the words 'she drinks'.

'That's not fair, Gussie. Everyone likes a drop of something warming in the winter to keep out the cold.' Madame Galina cast an appealing glance at Phoebe.

'I daresay you like a tot of buttered rum punch on a bitter winter's night, don't you, love?'

'Well, I er . . .' Phoebe looked to Herbert for help but he shook his head. 'Sometimes, Madame,' she said, not wanting to hurt the woman's feelings. 'But I'd love to hear about the Russian ballet when you have time.'

'Oh, she's got time, love,' Gussie said, reaching for another slice of toast. 'Her ladyship works behind the bar in a pub. How have the mighty fallen.'

Madame Galina subsided in a flood of tears, covering her face with a large white handkerchief.

'That was unkind, Gussie,' Rose said in an undertone. 'Why do you always have to upset her?'

'Because now I've got a chance to get my own back and I enjoy it.'

'What do you do now, Miss Augusta?' Phoebe asked in an attempt to steer the conversation away from the unfortunate Galina.

Gussie squinted short-sightedly at her. 'Ho, I see someone's got manners round here. Well, young lady, I'll tell you what I do. I spend my days making bonnets for rich women with more money than taste. I could still have my job in the theatre if it wasn't for Madame's weakness for grog. The dreadful addiction to strong drink lost her every booking she ever had.'

'I don't know why you stay with her then, Augusta,' Judy said, refilling her cup with yet more tea. 'Why don't you move on?'

Madame Galina blew her nose loudly. 'I'm still here,' she muttered. 'I heard everything you said, you bitch, Gussie.'

Ignoring her quivering friend, Gussie turned her attention to Judy. 'I pay me rent, don't I? I don't owe you nothing, Judy Edwards.'

'That's true, but you give us all earache with your continual sniping at poor Galina. Leave her alone, I say. Or find some other digs.' Judy slammed the teapot down on the table. 'I'm sick of listening to you carping day in, day out. It's your choice, Augusta. I could fill your room ten times over without any bother.'

Dolly, who had been silently absorbing this interchange from the beginning whilst munching toast and jam, suddenly burst into tears. 'Please don't shout at each other.'

Phoebe put her arm around Dolly's shoulders. 'She's a bit sensitive since the operation.'

'Operation?' It was said in a chorus as all eyes turned to Dolly, the differences between Augusta and Galina apparently forgotten.

Dolly pulled off her mobcap to reveal her shaven head and the livid scar on the side of her skull. 'They cut me brain. I'm a phenomenon, whatever that means. The doctors told me so.'

'Wonderful,' Herbert cried enthusiastically. 'She would make an excellent side show. People would pay good money to see a phenomenon.'

'Dolly's not for show,' Phoebe said hastily. 'She's still on the road to recovery and needs rest.'

'We all have to make a living, love.' Herbert tugged at his beard and for a moment Phoebe thought it might be glued on, but it remained firmly in place. 'If it's good enough for my Rose, it should be considered suitable for young Dolly.'

Phoebe realised then that she had touched on a tender spot. She laid her hand on his arm. 'I'm sorry. No offence meant, Mr Jackson.'

'None taken, I'm sure.' Rose leapt to her feet. 'Come on, Poppa. We've got to get to the theatre.'

'Are you performing there?' Phoebe seized the opportunity to steer the conversation to safer ground.

'We understudy the actors,' Rose said gravely. 'But mostly we're front of house.'

'That sounds exciting.' Phoebe looked to Herbert for confirmation but he appeared to have taken umbrage and he stood up abruptly, tipping up the bench so that Dolly slid to the floor in a flurry of petticoats and peals of laughter. This broke the ice and everyone joined in, even Herbert. He was moved to smile graciously at Phoebe. 'If you are looking for work I might be able to find you something at the theatre, even if it's selling programmes or clearing up after the performance.'

'Thank you. That's very kind of you, but I was planning to continue the work I've been doing with Ma in London.'

'Don't tell me she's got you telling fortunes and conducting sham séances?' Judy impaled a slice of bread on the tines of a toasting fork with unnecessary force.

'It's not entirely make believe,' Phoebe said mildly. 'I know some of it's a put up job, but not all. There are times when I believe that Ma really can see into the future, and sometimes it happens to me too.'

'You have the gift then?' Fred was suddenly alert. 'You could make a fortune on the seafront in summer.'

Rose and her father were halfway to the door but Herbert stopped and turned to stare at Phoebe. 'Have you ever done your act on stage?'

'It's not an act, Mr Jackson.'

He shrugged his shoulders. 'It's all the same thing, dearie. Conjuring, magic, illusion or foretelling the future is all an act. We have our resident illusionist and magician Caspar Collins and his assistant, the lovely Hyacinth, but you never know when she might need an understudy. Visit the theatre as I suggested, and we might find something for you.'

'Thank you, I will.'

Herbert seized Rose by the hand. 'Come along, my pet. We have no time to waste.' He swept her out of the room as if they were exiting the stage.

'Well, that's an offer you can't refuse,' Judy said firmly. 'You can't stay here or anywhere for nothing and you'll have to support your mother since she's decided to play the invalid. Annie should have trodden the boards. I've always said so.' She began clearing the table, rattling the cutlery and slamming the plates together. 'Make yourself useful, Dolly. Get up off the floor and stop giggling. You can wash up.'

Madame Galina and Gussie left their seats and headed for the doorway, jostling each other for position. 'I was first,' Madame said crossly.

'You always push in, you big booby.'

'Shut up.'

'I won't shut up, Galina. You started it.' Augusta

gave her a shove that sent the fat woman stumbling through the doorway.

'Are they always like this?' Phoebe asked in a low voice.

'Always.'

'But why do they stay together if they hate each other?'

Judy carried a pile of dirty crockery to the stone sink and slid it into the cold greasy water. 'Bring the kettle, Dolly. You'll need some hot water to wash up in.'

'What went wrong between them?' Phoebe was struggling to understand the relationship between the one-time prima ballerina and her dresser.

'What do I care?' Judy returned to the table to finish clearing away the breakfast things. 'They pay their rent and that's all that matters to me.' She made another trip to the sink. 'You can finish up here before you go to the theatre. I assume you'll take Herbert up on his generous offer.'

Phoebe nodded. 'Yes, I will.'

'Good. Because I want a week's rent in advance and the moment you fall behind, you and my sainted cousin and the simpleton are out of my house.' Judy watched as Dolly walked slowly towards the sink carrying the kettle of hot water. 'If that girl moves any slower she'll be walking backwards. I'm going to market but I want to find this kitchen spotless by the time I get back.' She snatched her bonnet and shawl from a peg behind the door, and hooking a wicker basket over her arm she left them with only Fred for company. He seemed to have escaped her eagle eye and was squatting quietly at the end of the table finishing off his breakfast with apparent difficulty. Phoebe could not help noticing that he had only a few teeth left in his head and was rolling the toast round and round in his mouth before gulping it down. She would not be surprised if he suffered from the most appalling indigestion. She went to take his empty plate but he caught her by the wrist, peering up into her face. 'I can tell you everything,' he said in a stage whisper.

'About what, Mr Jones?'

'About Gertrude, for that's Galina's real name, and her friend Augusta.'

'I'm not sure that's a good idea.'

'It was a man.' Fred shook his head sagely. 'It always is, if you ask me, ducks. They both fell in love with the dance master, a Russian fellow with an unpronounceable name. Anyway, he was engaged to Augusta, who must have been quite a pretty plum before she shrivelled up into a prune, but Gertie fancied him too.'

Phoebe shifted uncomfortably from one foot to the other. 'It really isn't any business of mine. Perhaps some things are best forgotten.'

Fred shook his head. 'You wanted to know why they don't get on and I'm telling you. The wedding was arranged but then Gertie announces that she's in the family way and he's the father. He, being a soft fool, marries Gertie and jilts poor Gussie. She takes a knife to him and stabs him in the breadbasket, although luckily it's not fatal.'

'How terrible.' Phoebe felt almost sorry for Augusta,

who had been driven to a crime of passion. 'What happened then?'

'Gussie being the ballerina's dresser knows a thing or two and she tells the Russian that Gertie was never in the family way and he's been had good and proper. He confronts Gertie with the truth and she panics and gives him a mighty shove which sends him over the balcony in the theatre, so now the poor chap really is dead and the two women have to flee the country or face arrest for murder and attempted murder.'

'Why have they stayed together then? If they hate each other it seems like madness.'

'Gussie says that in the beginning it was because they didn't trust each other. Both of them thought the other one would shop her to the police, and then it became a habit. After years of struggling to make a living they're like Siamese twins, joined at the hip never to be parted. You get used to them, ducks. They don't mean half of what they say.'

'You're a very wise man, Mr Jones.'

'Fred, love. Call me Fred.' He rose stiffly to his feet. 'Best get on or I won't earn nothing today.' He limped from the kitchen, dragging his gammy leg in an awkward gait. Phoebe could not imagine how he managed to do his job as a window cleaner, but it was obvious that Judy would have little sympathy for anyone who was unable to pay their way. She fingered the leather pouch tucked in the pocket of her skirt in which she kept the money that they must live off until she could start earning. It was considerably lighter after taking out their cab fares and the cost of the railway journey. She would have to give Judy something on account, since Ma was not in a fit state to move on, and at this rate their cash would soon dwindle to nothing. The stark reality of their situation was only just beginning to dawn on her.

Chapter Eight

Later that morning Phoebe arrived at the theatre in New Road, slightly damp from the sea mist that had engulfed the town and feeling rather bedraggled as she entered the imposing building. She was greeted by Rose, who emerged from the box office with a cheerful smile on her pretty face. 'I'm glad you came, Phoebe. Poppa will be too.'

Phoebe suspected that this was a polite lie, but her admiration for Rose's irrepressible good humour grew moment by moment. 'I'm very grateful to both of you. I'm sure it's quite difficult finding work here in the winter.'

'It is, but we've been here for as long as I can remember. Poppa and Mamma were a double act in the old days.'

'Really? What did they do?'

'Acrobatic dancing. Poppa used to hurl Mamma into the air and catch her. They were a huge success. They even performed at the Theatre Royal in Drury Lane.'

'Amazing,' Phoebe said sincerely. She could not visualise Herbert Jackson as anything other than a portly middle-aged man. 'Are there any jobs going, Rose? I really don't mind what I do, and it's only temporary.'

'You won't be staying in Brighton then?' Rose's mouth drooped at the corners and her eyes dulled.

'Just for the winter. It's a long story.'

Rose brightened visibly. 'I've got plenty of time. There's not much to be done this morning. Come and sit in the auditorium and tell me everything.'

Seated at the back of the stalls, Phoebe breathed in the odour of stale cigar smoke and the fug created by warm bodies in an enclosed space. She could almost smell the excitement that last night's audience had felt as they watched the show. The gilded decor and red plush upholstery put her in mind of a sumptuous palace of entertainment. The velvet curtains were pulled back to reveal the empty stage which seemed to be bathed in suspense, waiting for the next act to come on. She was so enthralled with the ambience that she was finding it hard to concentrate on responding to Rose's eager questions about life in London.

'Do go on,' Rose said earnestly. 'Tell me why you didn't go to Italy for the winter. I would have thought a change of air would do your mother a power of good, especially in her delicate condition.'

Phoebe had no intention of shaming her mother by allowing the paternity of her unborn child to become common knowledge. As far as the rest of the world was concerned, Annie Giamatti was a tragic widow who was not well enough to accompany the family to Italy and had come to the coast for her health. Phoebe did not mention the Paxman gang or the fact that her own father had died due to his involvement with the high mob many years ago. She managed to tell the

132

sorry tale without actually lying, and she could see from the sympathetic look in her eyes that Rose believed every word she said. Feeling slightly guilty, but also relieved that there would be no further awkward questions, Phoebe shot a sideways glance at her new friend. 'So do you think Mr Jackson could find work for me? I could start right away.'

Rose stood up, waving to her father who had just walked on stage carrying a broom. 'There's no need to do that today, Poppa. Look who's come to help out.' She dragged Phoebe to her feet and propelled her down the aisle towards the stage. 'Phoebe says she'd be glad to do anything as long as it's paid work and it's legal.' She trilled with laughter and her father smiled benignly.

'You see the humour in everything, petal. You are a bright ray of sunshine in a dark and dreary world.'

Rose climbed the steps onto the stage and took the broom from her father's hands. She beckoned to Phoebe. 'Come on up. You can start here and work your way back through the dressing rooms. The performers are an untidy lot so you'll have your work cut out to clean up after them, but it's a start. When you've done that there's the auditorium to sweep out and ashtrays to empty. I'm sure there's enough work to keep you busy, and luckily there's no matinee today so you don't have to rush.'

'I think it's time we stopped for some light refreshment,' Herbert said as Phoebe mounted the stage. 'You look a bit bedraggled, if you don't mind me saying so, my dear. A nice cup of tea will set you up for the rest of the day, and Rose will pop out to the bakery on the corner. We usually have something to eat at about this time each morning. I'm not denigrating our landlady's breakfasts but a couple of slices of toast don't constitute the sort of meal that a fellow needs to get through until noon.' He put his hand in his pocket and took out a threepenny bit which he pressed in Rose's hand. 'Some gingerbread or perhaps a meat pie would go down well, my love. We have to keep our strength up.'

Phoebe set to work with a will but she soon discovered that it would have taken a small army of charwomen to get the building to Herbert's exacting standard of cleanliness. He kept her supplied with tea and cake, but by six o'clock that evening she was completely exhausted and her hands were raw, her back ached and she could hardly put one foot in front of the other as she walked home with Rose. Herbert had taken himself off to the nearest pub on the slender pretext of promoting the show that was taking place that week. Rose did not seem to mind that her parent was spending their hard-earned money, although Phoebe was beginning to realise that only one of them actually did any work and it was not Herbert. Charming he might be, generous he was definitely, but when it came to doing anything that resembled hard labour, Herbert Jackson was never to be found. She suspected from the hint of alcohol on his breath when he returned from an errand earlier on that he had already stopped off for a drink.

'Poppa's an artiste,' Rose explained as they battled against a boisterous wind laced with salt spray that tugged at their bonnets and shawls. 'You should just

134

see the faces of the children when Mr Punch beats Judy with a stick. I think that he pretends it's Miss Edwards when she's been in a particularly bad mood, although I don't mean to offend you, and please don't repeat that to anyone.'

'I won't,' Phoebe promised breathlessly as she attempted to keep up with Rose. In the gathering dusk the sea had taken on the colour of the leaden sky with a charcoal line denoting the horizon. White horses tipped the waves and she could taste salt on her lips. If she had not been so tired she might have enjoyed the spectacle. As it was she could barely climb the steps to the house and it was left to Rose to knock on the door.

It was opened by Dolly, and Phoebe was immediately struck by the sudden change in her appearance. Her hair seemed to have grown miraculously, and hung about her face in corkscrew ringlets. 'It's pretty, ain't it?' she cried joyously, tugging at a golden strand. 'Miss Judy found it in a sea chest she keeps in her room. One of them theatricals left it when she done a moonlight flit.'

Stepping over the threshold, Phoebe realised that Dolly was wearing a wig; a rather well made and expensive-looking hairpiece to boot. 'It's very pretty.'

'It's the same colour as me natural hair. Now I can go out and not feel that everyone is staring at me.' She reached out her hand and grabbed Rose by the sleeve. 'Come in and shut the door. It's nearly suppertime and Miss Judy has made boiled salt cod and I cut up the cabbage. I been a good girl all day. She'll tell you that for sure.'

Rose closed the door, shutting out the damp night air. 'You've done well then, Dolly. It takes a certain sort of person to get on with Miss Judy, so good for you.'

Dolly preened herself, puffing out her chest. 'She never hit me. Not even once.'

'I should think not.' Although Phoebe was only too well aware of the torments Dolly had suffered at her mother's hands, she could not help but be shocked by such unwarranted violence to someone as childlike as Dolly. She slipped her arm around her shoulders and gave her a hug. 'No one will lay a finger on you while I'm around.'

'You're freezing cold,' Dolly said in a motherly tone. 'Go and sit by the fire. You too, Miss Rose. I'll make a pot of tea. I'm good at that, Miss Judy said so.' She started for the kitchen but paused at the foot of the stairs. 'I kept an eye on Annie, like you said. But she won't eat nothing and she ain't got off her bed all day.'

'I'll go up and see her now.' Phoebe took off her damp shawl and bonnet and handed them to Dolly. 'Don't worry. I'll take over now.'

The bedroom was in darkness apart from a pale square of night sky revealed through the window-panes. Phoebe could just make out the humped shape of her mother beneath the coverlet. She made her way to the washstand and struck a vesta, lighting the stub of a candle that Judy had given them the previous evening. 'Are you awake, Ma?'

'Leave me alone.'

Phoebe moved swiftly to the bedside and pulled

back the covers. 'This won't do, Ma. You've got to get up. You can't stay in bed until the baby's born.'

'I'm going to die,' Annie moaned. 'I've nothing left to live for.'

'That's wicked talk. If you don't care for me, think of the child. You say you love Ned, well prove it.'

Annie turned her head to peer up at her daughter. 'How? He don't want to know me.'

'He certainly won't want to know a woman who behaves like an invalid when there's nothing wrong with her. Women have babies all the time and they don't take to their beds.'

'You're cruel, you are, Phoebe. You know how delicate I am.'

'You'll fade away if you don't eat and you'll kill the baby. Is that what you want, Ma?'

'I'd like a drop of gin. You've got money, Phoebe. Go down to the pub and buy a bottle, then I'll think about getting up.'

'I'll do no such thing. Get up now and put your clothes on. You're coming down to supper if I have to carry you.'

Annie curled up in a ball, pulling the sheet up to her chin. 'You wouldn't.'

'Yes, I would.' Phoebe tweaked the sheet from her mother's fingers. 'And I want you to meet Mr Jackson who works at the Theatre Royal. He might even have a job for you if you speak nicely to him.'

Annie raised herself on her elbow. 'What sort of job?'

'I don't know. You'd have to ask him that, but you won't find out by lying in bed. Maybe you could tell fortunes on stage, or contact the dear departed of people in the audience.'

'I can't really talk to the dead, Phoebe.'

'I know that, Ma. But it never stopped you in the past. We've got to pay our way, and then you'll need someone to look after the child when it's born. That will cost money too.'

This made Annie sit bolt upright. 'What do you mean?'

'You won't be able to take the baby back to London, Ma.'

'I hadn't thought that far, Phoebe.' Annie rose slowly from the bed. 'I can't give Ned's child away.'

'And do you think he would want to marry you? Think hard before you answer.'

Annie shook her head. 'I'm not stupid, Phoebe. I know he was just having a good time and using me. It's not an easy thing for a woman to admit.'

Phoebe took her mother's hand and held it in a firm grasp. 'We've got several months yet, Ma. We'll think of something, but in the meantime you've got to look after yourself, and that means coming downstairs now and having something to eat. Judy's not the best cook in the world, but it's food and I'm starving.'

Phoebe had the satisfaction of seeing her mother eat some of the boiled salt cod that Judy put on the table and she toyed with the cabbage, but managed to eat a slice of bread and dripping. Both Herbert and Fred seemed kindly disposed towards Annie, but then as Phoebe had observed on numerous occasions men always had a soft spot for her mother. The women, apart from Rose and Dolly, were less welcoming, but no one said anything that was likely to upset or offend Annie. Altogether the meal was a great success and Judy forbore to make any cutting remarks, which was a relief to Phoebe. Herbert showed a keen interest in Annie's psychic powers and invited her to visit the theatre where she might meet Caspar, the illusionist. But it was not until almost a week later that Annie felt strong enough to undertake the walk to New Road.

The first thing Phoebe knew of her mother's arrival was when Rose brought her into the auditorium. 'There, Annie,' Rose said, waving to attract Phoebe's attention. 'You can see how hard your daughter works. We've never had such a good cleaner.'

'Cleaning?' Annie's voice rose to a crescendo. 'My Phoebe is working as a cleaner?'

Phoebe put down her broom and hurried to join them. 'Yes, Ma. I told you that I worked here.'

'But you didn't say you were mopping floors and sweeping up the debris left by the audience. I thought you had a nice clean job in the box office or you were assisting the magician.'

Phoebe glanced nervously at Caspar Collins who was on stage rehearsing a new act with the support of the lovely Hyacinth, who looked distinctly bored. 'No, Ma,' she whispered. 'As you can see, Mr Collins has an assistant.'

Annie stared at Hyacinth, who was studying her fingernails as if they were the most interesting things in the world, while her partner frowned over an illusion that he was trying to perfect. 'She's nothing but

139

a dollymop,' Annie said, picking up her skirts and heading for the stage.

'What's she doing?' Rose said anxiously. 'She mustn't upset Caspar. He's world class, Phoebe. We're lucky to have him in the show. He's had offers from every theatre in the south of England and he's ever so handsome and clever.'

'Ma, come back.' Phoebe started after her, but she was too late. Annie mounted the stage.

'Oy, you, Mr conjuror chappie. I want a word in your shell-like.'

'Oh, no.' Phoebe clamped her hand to her mouth as Caspar Collins stopped what he was doing to stare at the person who had had the temerity to interrupt his work. 'Ma, come down off the stage, please.'

Annie shot her a sideways glance, which was enough to convince Phoebe that she was wasting her time. Ma might act soft and gentle when it suited her, but she was a regular virago when her temper was roused. Phoebe could tell by Caspar's withdrawn expression that he was not amused. Then out of the corner of her eye she saw Herbert advancing on them. She sighed. Ma had done it again. Just when things were beginning to work out Annie Giamatti had done her worst. She held her breath, waiting for Caspar to speak. She studied his classic profile which could have been copied from an ancient Greek coin, and she had to agree with Rose. Caspar Collins was a handsome man. Even in her anxious state, she could not help but admire the set of his broad shoulders and his undoubted air of distinction. His dark hair was sleeked back from a widow's peak but his winged eyebrows were knotted together in an ominous frown. His well-moulded mouth was drawn into a tight line of disapproval as he looked down at Annie, who was berating both him and his assistant.

'Call yourselves performers,' she cried angrily. 'Look at her, Mr Caspar. She's more interested in how she looks than learning her job. Why don't you get yourself a girl who knows what she's doing? Someone with brains and a bit of class.'

'Who are you?' Hyacinth demanded. 'You can't talk about me like that, you interfering old hag.'

'Old hag?' Annie's pale skin flushed crimson. 'You've got a nerve, lady. I'm well known in London's psychic circles.' She held up her hand, giving Herbert a warning look as he hurried to her side. Phoebe's heart sank as she realised that he was accompanied by the theatre manager, who was wearing a black swallow-tail coat which, she thought, gave him the appearance of a butler in one of the toffs' houses she had seen in London. She bit her lip, hoping that Herbert would stop Ma from making things even worse, but Annie shook off his restraining hand. 'I will say my piece, gentlemen,' she continued unabashed.

Caspar angled his head and Phoebe was surprised to note that his dark eyes were now alive with amusement. 'Let her speak. I don't often meet my critics face to face on stage.'

'That's right, you don't.' Annie adopted a more moderate tone. 'And I ain't criticising you, mister. As far as I can see you've got a good act, but she's letting

141

you down.' She jerked her head in Hyacinth's direction. 'D'you want the men in the audience to ogle that silly little moll? And d'you want their wives to walk out because they've taken offence at their men's behaviour?'

Hyacinth bridled. 'Are you going to let her say things like that about me, Caspar?'

'Leave this to me, Hyacinth. Take some time in your dressing room to compose yourself. I'll call you when I need you.'

'Well, I never did!' She flounced off the stage, muttering beneath her breath.

Seemingly unmoved, Caspar turned his attention to Annie. 'I'm interested in your comments, Mrs . . .'

'Giamatti,' Annie said graciously. 'You might have heard of me in psychic circles.'

Before Caspar had a chance to respond, the theatre manager stepped in between Annie and Herbert. He bowed from the waist. 'Madam, I am Marcus White, manager of this theatre. I must ask you to leave the stage and allow Mr Collins to continue with the rehearsal.'

'Yes, Annie, love. You should do as Mr White says.' Herbert proffered his arm. 'Allow me to escort you.'

Annie laid her hand on his sleeve with a seraphic smile. 'I've said what I had to say.' She allowed him to lead her to the top of the steps but she paused, turning to give Caspar a long look. 'You should have my daughter as your assistant. She's helped me with more séances than you've had hot dinners, young man. Get rid of the trollop and hire a true professional.'

She pointed to Phoebe, who was clutching her broom handle and wishing that the floor would open up and swallow her. 'That's my little Phoebe.'

'Come, my dear. I think it's time for our morning tea,' Herbert said tactfully as he helped Annie down the steps. 'I have a particularly tasty seed cake in my office. Rose, put the kettle on.'

Phoebe shot an apologetic smile in Caspar's direction. 'Sorry,' she murmured. 'Ma is very outspoken. She meant no offence.' She backed away but he beckoned to her and she hesitated. 'Yes?'

'Come onto the stage, Miss Giamatti. Let me take a closer look at you.'

'You've got top billing, Caspar.' Marcus lowered his voice. 'We're booked solid all week. Don't do anything rash.'

'I know what I'm doing,' Caspar said calmly. 'Come closer, Miss Giamatti. I won't bite.'

With a flick of his coat tails Marcus descended the steps, shooting a warning glance at Phoebe as he walked past her. 'You're not paid to stand around. Get on with your work, girl.'

'Yes, sir.' Phoebe went back to sweeping the floor but Caspar seemed unwilling to allow the matter to rest there. He vaulted off the stage to bar her way.

'I want to talk to you, Miss Giamatti. Put the brush down, please, and take a seat.'

She glanced nervously at the wings in case Marcus White was spying on them but he was nowhere in sight. She perched on the edge of a seat in the front row. 'You mustn't take any notice of Ma,' she said anxiously. 'She means well but she shouldn't have spoken out against your Miss Hyacinth. She's very pretty.'

'I agree.' Caspar sat down beside her, resting his hands on his knees. 'But your mother's right in one way and wrong in another.'

Intrigued, and also fascinated by his deep velvety voice, Phoebe found herself staring into his eyes. 'I don't follow, sir.'

He smiled. 'Hyacinth's beauty is her only asset, and it is sometimes a distraction, but she uses it to her own advantage and not mine. She has would-be suitors queuing up at the stage door in the hope of catching a glimpse of her. She has dreams of finding a rich husband amongst her admirers, and I'm afraid her attention often wanders.'

'That's all very well, sir, but it's got nothing to do with me.' Phoebe rose to her feet. 'I must get on or I'll lose my job.'

'I was going to offer you another one, more rewarding and much less unpleasant than cleaning the auditorium.'

'I know you were.' Phoebe moved aside as he stood up. His presence was oddly disturbing and she had an inexplicable sense of foreboding. 'I couldn't take Miss Hyacinth's place. It wouldn't be fair on her. She can't help being beautiful.'

'Which is true, but I don't think she will be with me for long.'

'That's her choice, sir.'

'I see you're a woman who knows her own mind,

Miss Giamatti. We will have this conversation again very soon, I'm sure.'

Phoebe picked up the broom, and moved away from the stage. She worked quickly, trying to make herself inconspicuous as Caspar's assistant returned to continue the rehearsal. Phoebe could tell by the looks Hyacinth was giving her that, through no fault of her own, she had made an enemy that morning. She could feel the waves of resentment emanating from the stage, and she felt almost sorry for Hyacinth.

At midday Phoebe went to the green room, where Rose was waiting for her with their midday meal of tea and pork pie. 'Your ma certainly knows how to put the cat amongst the pigeons,' Rose said, chuckling as she filled Phoebe's cup. 'Mr White was furious with her and Hyacinth was incandescent with rage. She's used to being the main attraction as far as the gentlemen are concerned.'

Phoebe swallowed a mouthful of hot tea which made her eyes water. 'I know that, and I'm truly sorry. I don't want Hyacinth's job, and I couldn't work with Caspar. He seems to see right through me. It's as if he can read my thoughts.'

'Does he now?' Rose pulled a face. 'He doesn't do that to me, although I wish he did. Caspar doesn't give me a second glance. Maybe you two are meant to get together.'

Phoebe shook her head vehemently. 'Not likely. I expect he's a big fraud just like all the rest of us. Ma can't see further than the end of her nose, let alone into the future.'

'Well, love, I don't want to worry you, but earlier on I overheard a conversation between Annie and Poppa. They were talking about setting up a fortune-telling stall in the foyer. I thought you ought to know.'

Phoebe's appetite deserted her and she pushed the plate of pork pie aside. 'She mustn't even think of working, not in her condition.'

'Plenty of women do, Phoebe. They work until they drop the baby and get up next day to carry on. Not everyone can afford the luxury of a lying-in period.'

'Ma's not in the best of health. She's delicate.'

'She got herself in this mess. I'm sorry, but Dolly let the cat out of the bag. Gussie got the truth out of her and now everyone knows.'

Phoebe shrugged her shoulders. She should have seen this coming. 'She doesn't know the half of it. If my family find out who the father is there'll be terrible trouble.'

'It's her problem, not yours. You seem to spend all your time looking after your ma, when it should be the other way round.'

'I'll talk to her tonight,' Phoebe said, stirring her tea vigorously. 'I'll make her see sense.'

'Hmm,' Rose said doubtfully. 'Better you than me. I mean,' she added hastily, 'I could lecture Poppa all day and all night and he wouldn't take any notice of what I said. I have to be very tactful when I handle him, if you know what I mean.'

Phoebe knew only too well. She had had twenty years' experience of living with her mother and for the last decade she had helped create the illusion that Ma could contact the spirits of those who had passed on. She did not hold out much hope that her mother would listen to good advice, and when she took the opportunity that evening to broach the subject she was proved correct. As usual, Ma would go her own sweet way.

Herbert had apparently used his influence with Marcus White and Annie was granted permission to open up a fortune-telling booth in the foyer of the theatre one hour before the matinee performances were due to start, and for one hour at the end of each show. A mutually acceptable rent was agreed and Herbert made use of his many contacts in the town to procure a tent-like structure that was just big enough to seat Annie at a table and accommodate one client at a time.

Phoebe had done her best to make her mother see sense, but it seemed that everyone in the lodging house, including Judy, thought that it was an excellent scheme, and after an encouraging start the project proved to be more successful than anyone could have imagined. The theatre was filled to capacity for each show and Annie's takings increased daily. Phoebe had to be relieved of some of the cleaning work in order to act as cashier and to make sure that the queues were orderly. She was happy to help her mother but she was wary when Marcus suggested that Annie could work some additional sessions before the evening shows. Annie had no such qualms and readily agreed to his proposal. The only person who seemed unhappy with this, apart from Phoebe, was Caspar. Annie, he said was invading his territory with her supposed mystic powers. Now there was ill-feeling simmering beneath the surface between him and Annie as well as Hyacinth's open antagonism towards Phoebe. This was something that Phoebe had learned to live with. She ignored Hyacinth and she avoided Caspar.

As the weeks went by the town was held in winter's icy grip. The pavements were filmed with ice and the bare branches of the trees were tipped each morning with hoar frost. Bitter winds blew in from the east and Phoebe's concerns were for her mother's fragile health. It was no longer possible to disguise her condition, even under the flowing robes that she wore when she was seated in her small booth at the theatre. She was becoming increasingly exhausted after each session and one evening in the middle of December, when the weather had been particularly harsh, Annie collapsed on her way to the theatre. Luckily Phoebe was with her and Fred had accompanied them as he had a complimentary ticket for the latest production. The variety show had been temporarily superseded by a repertory company performing *Maria Marten*, or *The Murder in the Red Barn*, and to Phoebe's intense relief, Caspar and Hyacinth had a booking in Bournemouth, although they were due to return to Brighton in the New Year when the pantomime season ended. Fred caught Annie as she fell, but his legs buckled beneath her weight and he crumpled to his knees still supporting her in his arms.

'What is it, Ma?' Phoebe cried, raising her voice in order to be heard against the wind shrieking in from the sea. 'Is it the baby?'

Annie's eyelids fluttered and she clutched at Fred's lapels. 'I dunno. I come over all funny.'

Clutching her cloak around her as the wind attempted to rip it from her slender frame, Phoebe looked round in desperation. It was obvious that her mother could walk no further and Fred was not strong enough to carry her. She waved frantically at a passing hackney carriage but it sped past with its occupants staring curiously from the window. Otherwise the street was deserted and they were halfway between the theatre and home.

'She's swooned again, Phoebe,' Fred said urgently. 'I can't get her to her feet like this.'

Cold sleety rain was beating in Phoebe's face and soon they would all be soaked to the skin. She knelt down beside her mother, slapping her pale cheeks in an attempt to bring her round. After what seemed like an eternity but could not have been more than a minute or two, Annie opened her eyes, staring at her dazedly. 'What happened?'

'You fainted, Ma. We've got to get you home. D'you think you could walk if Fred and me help you?'

Fred struggled to his feet. 'If we both take an arm we might be able to lift her, Phoebe.'

'You'll have to help us, Ma.' Phoebe hooked her mother's arm around her shoulders and Fred supported her on the other side. Together they managed to raise Annie to a standing position. 'Well done, Ma. Now take small steps and you'll soon be home in the warm.'

'But the booth, Phoebe. I can't let my clients down. They depend on me and we need the money.'

'Let's worry about that when we've got you home safe.'

Annie stood still, refusing to move. 'No, Phoebe. If we let Marcus down he'll find someone else to do my job, especially as I've made such a success of it. We'll need all the money we can get to make a fresh start. I'm not giving up my child for anyone – not the Giamattis nor the Paxmans.'

'What's she on about?' Fred glanced anxiously at Phoebe.

She shook her head. 'She has fancies. It's her condition.'

'Don't talk about me like I wasn't here,' Annie said angrily. 'I'm not out of my head.'

'You need to rest, Ma. You've been overdoing it.'

'I'm going to the theatre.' Annie broke free from them but she staggered and it took their combined efforts to keep her from falling to the ground.

Clutching her mother in a firm grip, Phoebe heard the sound of horse's hooves and glancing over her shoulder she saw a hackney carriage approaching from the town centre. She waved frantically and it drew to a halt at the kerb. 'Get in, Ma, and no arguments. Fred will take you home and I'll go on to the theatre. I can fill in for you tonight.'

'Are you sure?'

'Quite sure, Ma.'

Annie allowed Fred to help her into the cab, but as he attempted to climb in beside her she shook her head. 'Go with my girl. I'll be all right on me own.'

Phoebe knew it was useless to argue any further. It

was only a short carriage ride to the lodging house and it was Madame Galina's evening off from working behind the bar in the Crown and Anchor. Although neither Galina, Judy nor Gussie had personal experience of childbirth, Phoebe knew that Ma was in safe hands. Judy promised to send for the doctor if it became necessary, and Phoebe was content to leave her wayward parent in their care. She linked arms with Fred and headed off towards the town centre.

When she arrived at the theatre, Marcus and Herbert were initially sceptical of her ability to take over the fortune-telling stall, but Phoebe was adamant that she could fill her mother's place without losing the clientele that Annie had built up amongst the dedicated theatregoers. After a brief discussion they agreed to give her a chance, and with help from Rose she transformed her appearance into that of a gypsy fortune teller. She settled inside the small booth to deal with the steady stream of people eager to know what the future held. She had learned the patter from her mother along with the tricks of the trade that Annie used in order to elicit personal information from the punters. Having gained their confidence, Annie would launch into predictions of good fortune or romantic encounters with handsome strangers. Phoebe followed this example to the letter, although she found it disturbing when she saw shadows of ill health or bereavement lurking in the background. These came unbidden into her mind but she was too well trained to pass on forebodings of gloom. There was enough poverty and disease already in their grim world. Even in the comparatively healthy seaside resort, death stalked young and old with equal tenacity. The end was inevitable, but what Phoebe sold was the hope of something better in the interim.

She was exhausted by the time she had seen the last person in the queue. She stepped outside to warm congratulations from Marcus. He patted her on the shoulder. 'Well done, Phoebe. I didn't know you had it in you.'

She managed a tired smile. 'I started young, Mr White.'

'That I can see, but you were obviously an apt pupil. I listened in to some of your readings and I was impressed.' He slipped his arm around her shoulders. 'I think we can talk business, my dear. It's obvious that Annie is close to her time and cannot continue much longer. I'm offering the job to you. What d'you say, Phoebe?'

'I say yes, Mr White.'

'Call me Marcus, my dear.'

Chapter Nine

Phoebe worked hard at perfecting her act, for that was what she considered the fortune-telling booth to be. It was a piece of fun; an entertainment preceding the main event and not to be taken seriously. She enjoyed seeing the patrons leave with smiles on their faces, and as the weeks went by she began to recognise the regulars. She looked forward to hearing the details of their lives, which they were only too pleased to share with her. It seemed that by giving them the hope of better things to come their attitude to the daily trials that beset them had become more positive. She could not explain this, but she was happy if she had been able in some small way to be of help to the people who were fast becoming her friends.

Although she enjoyed her new status, she could not afford to relinquish her cleaning job. She tried at first to do both but Marcus, being an astute businessman, saw his profits growing and insisted on hiring a woman to take over the more onerous tasks of scrubbing the floors and polishing the brass handrails. Phoebe still swept, dusted and tidied the dressing rooms, wiping greasepaint off the mirrors and face powder from the table tops. The repertory company was notoriously untidy, leaving fish and chip wrappers, empty beer bottles and soggy fag-ends in unexpected places. Phoebe had come across an odd shoe that had been used as an ashtray for hand-rolled cigarettes and cigar butts. Somewhere in the theatre there must be a man searching in vain for his lost footwear. She could picture the frustrated owner hopping from one dressing room to another, but it was never claimed.

The time passed quickly and Christmas was approaching, not that there was much festive spirit in the lodging house. Judy, it seemed, did not hold with celebrating the season of goodwill, or if she did she managed to hide her feelings beneath a veil of contempt for fools who spent their money on lavish meals, presents and entertainments. Phoebe suspected that Christmas dinner was to be the usual boiled ox head or cod served with cabbage and potatoes. She had never complained about the meals that were served up with monotonous regularity, but she was worried by her mother's lack of appetite and the fact that despite her enlarging belly she was pale, thin and listless. Phoebe knew that Annie missed working in the theatre and that she hated being confined to the house. Dolly was happy to keep her company and wait on her hand and foot, but Annie was easily bored and made it plain that she missed the bright lights and the adulation she received from the public.

One night when Phoebe arrived home late she was horrified to find her mother prostrate on her bed, snoring loudly and smelling strongly of gin, while Dolly slept as peacefully as a child in her truckle bed. Phoebe attempted to wake her mother, but Annie was too far gone in drink to open her eyes, and next morning it was apparent from Herbert's demeanour that he too was suffering from the after-effects of a heavy session in the pub.

Madame Galina took Phoebe aside. 'My dear girl, I think there is something you should know about your mamma and him.' She jerked her head in Herbert's direction. 'They've become regulars in the saloon bar at the Crown and Anchor. Now I like a drop of brandy every now and again as I'm sure you know, but your mamma should not be drinking in her condition. She will kill herself and the child.'

'Thank you, Madame,' Phoebe said in a low voice. 'I'll speak to Ma when she wakes up, and I'll tell Herbert Jackson what I think of him too.'

Madame Galina laid a warning hand on Phoebe's arm. 'Be careful. He's not a man to cross. He may seem like a good fellow, but when he's drunk he's a bad man. Little Rose knows this and she tries to keep him on the straight and narrow, but give him hard liquor and you must watch out.'

'He looks sorry for himself this morning.'

'A bear with a sore head is the term, I think.' Madame smiled ruefully. 'I've been there myself, little one. Best leave him until the headache wears off and he puts on his cheerful face.'

'What are you two whispering about?' Gussie demanded, rising from the breakfast table. 'It's rude, you know.'

'Mind your own business, you stupid woman.' Madame waved her away with an imperious hand.

'Keep your place, Gussie Watts. I was having a private word with my little friend.'

Gussie's small features knotted into a scowl. 'Don't believe a word the old fraud says, Phoebe. She always was a troublemaker.'

'Will you two shut up?' Herbert stood up, glowering at them. 'My head aches. I need some seltzer and there's none in the cupboard. Someone has stolen my seltzer.'

'Rubbish.' Madame Galina tossed her head. 'You've used it all up, you old soak.'

'It takes one to know one,' Herbert snapped back at her. 'I'll use another drinking establishment in future.'

'Good. You're no longer welcome in the Crown and Anchor.'

'Who says so?' Herbert moved towards her with his chin outthrust. 'You're just a barmaid, Galina Lavrovna.'

'I'll have you know that I was famous in Russia.'

'Well we've only got your word for that, you fat old faggot.'

Madame bristled visibly and for a moment Phoebe thought she was going to hit Herbert, but she was forestalled by Rose who had entered the kitchen un-noticed. 'Poppa. I never thought I'd hear you speak so harshly to someone who's been kindness itself to you and me.'

'A serpent's tooth,' Herbert declared dramatically. 'An ungrateful child.'

Rose hurried to his side, and clutched his arm, her eyes wide with fear. 'Please don't get yourself in a state. You'll make yourself ill.'

'Leave me alone, you snake in the grass.' He pushed

her aside and she stumbled against the table, knocking the teapot onto the floor. Hot tea spilt on her arm and stained her skirts. She cried out in pain and Phoebe hurried to her side, taking Rose gently by the hand and examining the injured limb.

'She's scalded her wrist.'

'Put butter on it.' Gussie reached for the dish, frowning when she saw that it was empty. 'Who ate the last of the butter?'

'Never mind that now.' Judy had been supervising Dolly, who was stirring a saucepan of porridge seemingly oblivious to the disharmony amongst her fellow lodgers, but the sight of Rose in distress galvanised Judy into action. She rushed forward to cover the scalded wrist with a clean cloth. 'Sit down, girl. You've gone white as a sheet. Dolly, make sure the porridge doesn't burn and stop snivelling. Rose will be all right.' She glanced at Phoebe who was hovering anxiously at her side. 'Make yourself useful and fetch a mop.'

'I never meant to hurt her,' Herbert mumbled, putting a safe distance between himself and Judy.

She turned on him with her lips pulled back in a snarl. 'Jackson, you're a disgrace. I've warned you before about your boozing and the evils of strong drink. Now you've hurt your daughter and I hope you're ashamed of yourself.'

Herbert cringed visibly. 'I'm sorry, Rose, love. I dunno what came over me.'

She looked up at him with tears in her eyes. 'Yes you do, Poppa. You're always like this when you've had a bellyful of gin.' She glanced at Phoebe, shaking

157

her head. 'I tried to talk your ma out of going with him, but she wouldn't listen.'

Phoebe put the mop aside and patted her on the shoulder. 'It's not your fault, and to be fair to your pa it's not entirely his either. My ma is easily led, but I'm begging you, Mr Jackson. Please don't take her to the pub again.'

'Bloody women,' Herbert muttered, heading for the doorway. 'Always grumbling about something. I feel poorly but I don't get any sympathy. I'm going for a lie down.' He stomped out of the room, slamming the door behind him.

'You mustn't take any notice of Poppa,' Rose said, wincing as Judy applied a generous amount of baking soda to the afflicted limb.

'Fetch my medicine chest from the front parlour.' Judy addressed Gussie who was watching the procedure with interest. 'I have some bandages ready made for just such an event.'

Gussie opened her mouth as if to argue and then appeared to think better of it. With a mumbled response, she hurried from the room.

'You should have been a nurse, Judy,' Phoebe said sincerely. 'I wouldn't have known what to do.'

'Pity you've left your crystal ball at the theatre, isn't it?' Judy spoke severely but her thin lips curved into a pleased smile. 'I do have a talent for curing ills, but I can't do anything for Annie or for that father of yours, Rose. Their ailments are inflicted by themselves and they should be ashamed for allowing the demon drink to rule their sad lives.'

Phoebe shifted uncomfortably from one foot to the other. What Judy said was harsh but true and there was no denying it. She moved to the dresser and picked up a cup and saucer. 'I'll take some tea up for Ma, and I'll have a few words to say to her.'

'Let me take it,' Dolly said, abandoning the saucepan, but receiving a stern look from Judy she resumed stirring the porridge. 'Poor Annie's sick,' she murmured. 'Poor Annie.'

'I'll speak to Poppa when he's himself again,' Rose said slowly. 'I'm sure he wouldn't want any harm to come to Annie or her baby. He'll be very ashamed when he realises what he's done.'

'Never mind Annie. She can look after herself.' Judy went to relieve Dolly of her task. 'Go and get yourself a bowl, child. You've earned your breakfast.'

Gussie reappeared carrying a small beechwood box which she placed on the table in front of Rose. 'I thought better of your pa. He's a different person when he's been on the booze.'

Judy pushed her aside. 'Never mind that now, Augusta. Isn't it time you left for work? You'll be in trouble with that snooty woman who owns the hat shop if you're late again. Fred left on his rounds a good half-hour ago.'

Gussie glanced at the clock on the wall with a gasp of dismay, and grabbing her bonnet and shawl from the peg behind the door she raced out of the room as if the devil were on her heels.

'It never fails to amaze me how that woman keeps her job,' Judy said, shaking her head as she opened

159

the medicine chest. Selecting a roll of gauze bandage and a piece of lint she placed the dressing on Rose's arm. 'Hold still, girl. I can't work if you wriggle about.'

Phoebe took the opportunity to fill a teacup and escape from the room, leaving Madame Galina and Dolly to watch Judy bandaging the afflicted limb as if it were the most interesting thing they had ever seen.

Upstairs in the attic room Phoebe found her mother lying in bed with her hand covering her eyes.

'Is that you, Phoebe? I have such a headache. I'm feeling quite unwell this morning.'

'I'm not surprised, Ma, and quite honestly it serves you right.' Phoebe placed the cup and saucer on the washstand. 'Whatever possessed you to go out drinking?'

'Don't scold me. I was bored and lonely. I miss London and I miss Ned. I want to go home, Phoebe. I want to tell him I love him and I'm going to have his child. Please take me back to Saffron Hill. I'll die if I have to remain here any longer. I'll die.'

It had taken all Phoebe's powers of persuasion to prevent her mother from leaving the house and heading for the railway station, despite the fact that she had very little money in her purse and nothing on which to live when she reached her destination. Annie had managed to convince herself that Ned Paxman would welcome her with open arms, and that there would be wedding bells before the spring. Phoebe remained sceptical but she listened patiently and eventually managed to persuade Annie that a long journey undertaken in the harsh winter weather would endanger her health and the child's. It would be better to wait until she had regained her former vitality, not to mention her figure, before attempting a reunion with Ned. In the end it was vanity that won the day, and a single glance at her bloated and pallid face in the mirror was enough to make Annie realise that her daughter was talking sense. Reluctantly, she agreed to stay indoors and rest.

Herbert, when he recovered from his hangover, was apparently a changed man. He promised Rose that he would eschew drink forever, and he went so far as to provide a large goose for Christmas dinner together with a plum pudding and a large bag of chestnuts. Following his example and not to be outdone, Fred arrived home on Christmas Eve with a basket filled with oranges, lemons and apples. From a poacher's pocket in his overcoat he produced a bottle of brandy and one of claret, which he explained were to make brandy butter and a warming punch on Christmas morning. Even Judy allowed herself to unbend a little, and to Phoebe's astonishment Madame Galina and Gussie seemed to have declared a truce for the festive season, or for the next twenty-four hours at least. They were positively effusive in their compliments to each other and radiated good will to everyone else. Dolly was as excited as a five-year-old and quite overcome with emotion when on Christmas morning Judy presented her with an embroidered handkerchief. Madame Galina gave her a string of blue glass beads, and Rose added a small bottle of eau de Cologne to Dolly's growing collection of presents. Phoebe had bought a picture book in a second-hand shop in town, which she told Dolly was from her and Annie. It was painfully obvious that Dolly had never received a Christmas present in her life, and she sat with her gifts cradled in her lap, rocking to and fro and cooing over them.

Annie had raised herself from her bed and Phoebe was delighted to see her mother taking an interest in the proceedings at breakfast. She was even more impressed when Annie volunteered to peel the potatoes while Judy prepared the bird for the oven. Madame Galina, Gussie, Rose and Fred went off to church, leaving Herbert to make a jug of punch, adding slices of fruit and a bottle of lemonade, which they sampled on their return, while Judy, Dolly and Phoebe served the food.

The festive meal was eaten in the rather austere splendour of Judy's dining room, where a large mahogany table was surrounded by ornately carved and rather fearsome-looking chairs. The wallpaper was heavily patterned with flowers and hung with sombre prints of highland cattle and stags at bay. A black marble clock shaped like a Roman temple sat on the mantelshelf flanked by two grinning pot dogs and sepia-tinted daguerreotypes of a grim-faced man with mutton-chop whiskers and a woman with a mouth like a steel trap and piercing eyes. Phoebe could only assume that they must be Judy's parents. The sight of them oppressed her at first but she realised quickly that this room was Judy's pride and joy, and that it was an honour for her lodgers to be allowed to enter its hallowed portals.

A fire had been lit in the grate although the chimney smoked a little, causing tiny flakes of soot to shower down on the white tablecloth like black snow. These were brushed off immediately by Gussie and the resulting smudges had to be concealed beneath swags of ivy torn from the back wall of the house. The best china was brought out for the occasion and Judy stood at the head of the table to carve the magnificent bird. Apple sauce was served with the goose and roast potatoes with lashings of gravy, and the inevitable boiled cabbage, but even this tasted delicious to Phoebe. It was, she thought, the first decent meal she had had since Nonna left for Italy.

After the last crumb of plum pudding and brandy butter had been scraped off the plates, eaten and digested, Herbert's punch was drunk in a succession of toasts to each and every one in the room. Then Fred suggested that they might play parlour games, but Judy rose from the table saying that it would be more to the point if he helped with the washing up. Shamed into subservience, he began clearing the table and Herbert leapt to his feet declaring that he was not a man to sit back and be waited on when there was work to be done. Rose had a fit of the giggles when she saw her father with Judy's calico apron straining at its strings as he tied it around his large belly and rolled up his sleeves in preparation to wash the pots and pans. In the end everyone lent a hand, and when the kitchen was restored to its former pristine state they retired to Judy's front parlour where a fire burned brightly and candles had been lit. This was another honour rarely bestowed upon the lodgers, as Rose said in an aside to Phoebe, and Judy unbent enough to allow Fred to conduct parlour games of charades, forfeits and similes. They roasted the chestnuts on a coal shovel and ended the evening with cocoa, although Phoebe rather suspected that Herbert and Fred laced theirs with the remainder of the brandy.

Altogether it was a happy occasion, and Phoebe was delighted to see her mother smiling and looking like her old self again, but she could see a shadow hanging over them. She could not shake off the nagging worry as to how the baby would be received by the family when they returned from Italy. She could imagine their horrified reaction when they discovered who had fathered Annie's bastard child, and this was not Phoebe's only problem. She was painfully aware that she would have to give Gino his answer when they were reunited in the spring. She realised with a pang of regret that she had barely given him a thought since the day they parted. Surely that was not a good basis for marriage. She wished she could confide in someone but the only person to whom she could talk was Rose, and she had her own problems.

It had come to Phoebe's notice on several occasions that Rose was not immune to the charms of a certain illusionist and conjuror. She blushed whenever his name was mentioned, and Phoebe had seen the way she looked at him when she thought she was unobserved. Her heart went out to her friend, but she thought she could do better than a man who was patently in love with himself. Caspar Collins was arrogant and full of his own self-importance. Phoebe did not like him at all, and she was not looking forward to his return in the middle of January when the pantomime season ended. Her poor opinion of him was not helped when he appeared a day earlier than expected and announced quite casually that Hyacinth had left him to marry a man who owned a glue factory in Bow. He was, Caspar said, old enough to be her father, and it went without saying that the gentleman in question was well-to-do. Rose giggled almost hysterically when she heard this but was stricken with an attack of hiccups which rendered her speechless. She retreated hastily to the sanctity of her small office, leaving Phoebe to deal with a puzzled Caspar. 'What is funny about Hyacinth leaving me in the lurch?' he demanded, eyeing Phoebe suspiciously.

She controlled her own desire to giggle, clutching her hands tightly behind her back and digging her fingernails into her palms. She had not laughed so much since Christmas Day when Fred was attempting to mime Spring-heeled Jack and tripped over a footstool falling onto Madame Galina's lap. She took a deep breath. 'I think it was the mention of the glue factory, Mr Collins.'

He shrugged his shoulders. 'The fellow smelt of boiling bones, which was quite disgusting, but then Hyacinth was and is a little gold-digger. I hope she's happy with her mansion in Bow and her elderly husband, but the wretched girl has left me without an assistant and I'm top of the bill next week.'

'I'm sorry,' Phoebe murmured, backing away towards the fortune-telling booth where her costume was stored in readiness for the matinee performance. 'I'm sure you'll find someone suitable.'

'That's easier said than done.' Caspar fixed her with his hypnotic gaze. 'You are doing well, I hear. You have second sight, perhaps?'

'No, certainly not.' Phoebe was horrified at the thought. 'It's all patter. I learned it from my mother.'

'Maybe,' he said doubtfully. 'But I sense an aura about you, Phoebe. I did from the very first time we met and I offered to take you as my assistant.'

'Hyacinth was working for you then. It wasn't a very nice thing to do.'

He shrugged his shoulders. 'I knew she would be off at the first opportunity, but the offer still holds. You have unfathomed depths. I think we could work well together.'

'I'm very flattered, sir.' Phoebe lifted the flap ready to slip into the booth. Her heart was pounding uncomfortably and she would have liked to put as much distance between them as possible, but she had work to do. 'Excuse me. I must get changed now.'

He moved slowly towards her, holding her with his eyes. 'We will talk later. Perhaps you would have supper with me after tonight's performance?'

'I don't think so. I have to get home. My mother . . .'

'Is a grown woman and perfectly able to look after herself for an extra hour or two. We will have dinner together, you and I, Phoebe Giamatti. I won't take no for an answer. When the show ends tonight I'll be waiting outside the theatre in a cab. I'll expect you to join me. After all, you have nothing to lose and much to gain.' With a flourish of his scarlet-lined opera cloak he stepped out into the street, pausing to set his top hat at an angle on his head.

Phoebe sank down on the stool inside the booth. She was inexplicably breathless as if she had been running. She laid her hand on the cool crystal ball and closed her eyes. She could see Caspar's coldly handsome face. He was standing a little way from her and his sapphire blue eyes drew her inexorably towards him. He opened his arms and she walked into them as if drawn by an invisible cord. The crystal was suddenly white hot. It burned her fingers and she withdrew her hand, leaping to her feet and sending the stool tumbling to the ground.

'Phoebe, whatever is the matter?' Rose stuck her head into the booth, her face puckered with concern. 'Where's Caspar?'

'He left a few minutes ago.' Phoebe bent down to pick up the stool. 'Are you all right now?'

'I was going to ask you the same question. Did he say something to upset you?'

'Not really. He asked me to help him in his act, that's all.'

'Lucky you. I wish he'd ask me. I'd do anything for him.'

'Then why don't you tell him so? I'm sure you'd make a much better assistant than me, and anyway we won't be here much longer. Ma's time is near, a few weeks at the most, and when the baby is born we'll be heading back to London.'

Rose's mouth dropped at the corners. 'I know, and I wish you could stay here forever. I've never had the chance to make friends my own age and I'm very fond of you, Phoebe.'

'You should have a life of your own, Rose. You do everything for your father but you ought to think of yourself for once.'

'He needs me. I know he behaves badly when he's had too much to drink, but the rest of the time he's a lamb and I couldn't leave him to fend for himself.'

'I think he could manage very well without you, and one day you'll get married and your father will have to take second place to your husband and children.'

'He's like a child himself, Phoebe. I think he'll always be with me.'

'Then that's all the more reason for you to be more independent. Speak to Caspar this evening.'

Rose looked baffled. 'He's not due to perform his act until Monday.'

'He asked me out to supper after the show tonight. Just to discuss business, you understand,' Phoebe added hastily. 'There's nothing romantic between us, I promise you, Rose.'

'Maybe not on your part, but I think he fancies you.'

'No. Not at all. He's cold as stone. I doubt if he has a heart, and if he has it's in the shape of a money bag. All he thinks about is his career and his wretched act.' Phoebe angled her head, gazing at Rose as an idea struck her. 'You go in my place. I don't want to have supper with Caspar and it would give you a chance to be alone with him.'

The colour drained from Rose's cheeks. 'I couldn't. I mean, if he wanted to take me to supper he would have asked me and not you.'

'Perhaps he needs a little push in the right direction.

You and I are about the same height. You could take my place when he calls for me this evening. With the hood of your cloak pulled over your bonnet it would hide your face and it will be dark inside the cab. He won't discover the deception until you are in the restaurant. Even then I doubt if he would want to create a scene.'

Rose clasped her hands together, the doubtful look fading from her eyes only to be replaced by a mischievous sparkle. 'Do you think I could get away with it?'

'Of course, or I wouldn't have suggested it.'

'Then I'll do it, Phoebe.'

Herbert had left the theatre early. Phoebe suspected that he had gone to the pub, but on this occasion she was grateful for his absence, and as long as her mother was not involved in the drinking session she really did not care what happened to Rose's wayward parent. Rose was nervous about the deception but Phoebe was confident that all would be well. She was convinced that Caspar would be flattered by her friend's sincere admiration for him and her desire to help him further his career. Rose was young, pretty and intelligent. She was also hard-working and loyal, which might prove difficult if her father objected to her working for Caspar, but Phoebe could only hope that Herbert would put Rose first for once and allow her to have a life of her own. She gave Rose an encouraging hug and watched through the glass door until she was safely inside the waiting carriage. Peeping through the flap she gave a sigh of relief when it drove off; so far so good. She went back to counting the evening's takings, and when she had deducted the rent for the booth and set it aside for Marcus, she placed the remaining coins in a leather pouch together with the rest of the week's profits, which would cover the cost of their bed and board. She secured it round her waist where it would be almost impossible for a pickpocket to touch it without her realising what was happening. Having been brought up in the stews of London's East End she was only too well aware of the dangers lurking round every dark corner, and even though Brighton was on the whole a safer place to live than Saffron Hill, she was always on her guard.

Having waited until the conveyance carrying Caspar and Rose had turned the corner at the end of the street, Phoebe set off for home, but she had not gone further than a few yards when she heard the rumble of carriage wheels and the sound of horse's hooves on the cobble-stones behind her. She stopped, waiting to cross the road to the seafront, but to her surprise the cab drew to a halt in front of her and Caspar leaned out of the window. 'Get in.'

She stared at him, nonplussed by the curt order. 'No, thank you. I'm going home.'

Rose's anguished face appeared over Caspar's shoulder. 'Please don't argue, Phoebe. Just get in. It's all gone horribly wrong.'

Chapter Ten

Reluctantly Phoebe climbed into the carriage and sat beside Rose, who was trembling and tears were flowing down her pale cheeks. 'What's the matter?' Phoebe demanded anxiously. 'What has he said to you?'

Caspar leaned back against the squabs, banging the roof of the cab with his ebony cane. 'Drive on, cabby.'

'No, wait.' Phoebe stuck her head out of the window. 'Please, just wait a moment.'

'I got a living to make, miss.' The cabby blew on his gloved hands. 'Don't make no money standing still.'

'Just give me a minute. The gentleman will pay.' Phoebe sat back in her seat, glaring at Caspar. 'What have you done to upset Rose like this?'

He shrugged his shoulders. 'Nothing, other than to tell her the truth. I'm not interested in the daughter of a drunken failure. I don't want my act spoiled by association with the likes of Jackson. I wanted to take you out to supper, Phoebe. I have matters to discuss with you alone, and I don't enjoy being taken for a fool.'

'Let me out of the cab,' Rose said on a sob. 'I wish I'd never agreed to do this. It was a terrible mistake.'

'Now there I must agree with you,' Caspar said with a tight little smile. 'You are free to go, Miss Jackson.

But Phoebe promised to accompany me to dine and I'm keeping her to it.'

Phoebe thrust the carriage door open. 'Get out, Rose, and wait for me. I have a few choice words to say to Mr Collins.'

'Just come away now.' Rose leapt from the cab, landing on the damp pavement in a flurry of petticoats. 'Come on, Phoebe.'

'Leave now and you'll regret that you behaved in such a stupid fashion,' Caspar said in a low voice. 'Work with me and I can promise you a better life than you've ever dreamed of.'

'I wouldn't work with you if my life depended on it, Caspar Collins. How dare you treat poor Rose like this when all she ever wanted was your good opinion? What sort of man are you?'

He leaned towards her so that their faces were close. His eyes glittered with malice. 'The sort of man who is dangerous to cross. I never forget a slight, however small. You'll be sorry for trying to make a fool of me.'

'You don't frighten me. I grew up in an area run by the high mob, and they would make short work of a toff like you.' Turning her back on him, Phoebe stepped down to join Rose. She would not let Caspar see that she was trembling from head to foot, although it was more from anger than fear. She was furious with him and angry with herself for putting Rose in such an invidious position. She slipped her arm around Rose's shoulders. 'I'm so sorry. This was all my fault.'

Rose watched the cab disappearing into the darkness. She shook her head, smiling ruefully. 'No. I'm as much to blame. I didn't have to go along with your idea. It serves me right for being such a simpleton.'

'You weren't to know what he was like. Neither of us saw through him.' Phoebe glanced up at the sky. The clouds had merged into a dark mass and large spots of sleety rain had begun to fall. 'Let's hail the next cab and treat ourselves to a ride home. I did rather well in the booth tonight.' She patted her waist but there was no comforting jingle of coins. She opened her cloak searching for the pouch but it had gone. 'He's nothing but a bloody thief,' she exclaimed angrily. 'Would you believe it, Rose? That toff is on the dip. He's bagged my whole week's takings. That's the rent money gone. How will I explain that to Judy?'

'We'll tell Marcus. He's a fair man. He'll make Caspar give it back.'

'It'll be our word against Caspar's. He's top of the bill, Rose. I don't think Marcus will want to offend his best act. I'm only there on sufferance, and if you and your pa lose your jobs at the theatre you'll be hard pressed to find work to keep you until summer.'

'What will you do?' Rose pulled her hood up as the sleet turned to hail. 'Let's hurry home. We won't do any good by standing here and catching our death of cold.'

'You're right.' Phoebe linked arms with her and they started to battle their way against the storm. 'I've got a bit put aside for Ma and the baby, but I'll have to use that until I can find a way to make Caspar give me back my money.'

'You could agree to work for him, I suppose.' Rose

shot her a sideways glance, wrinkling her nose as hard pellets of ice slapped her face. 'That's what he really wants.'

Phoebe eyed her thoughtfully. 'That's not as daft as it sounds. Perhaps I ought to play Mr Collins at his own game, for the time being anyway. Just until Ma gives birth and then we've got to return to London. Maybe by seeming to let him win I can get back what belongs to me and put him in his place for good.'

'You seem to have dropped this in the cab,' Caspar said, smiling and holding up the missing leather pouch.

'Yes, thank you. I thought I'd lost it.' Phoebe resisted the temptation to snatch it from him. She had swallowed her pride and had come into the theatre earlier than normal in order to tell Caspar that she had changed her mind, and would be delighted to accept his offer. To make matters worse he seemed to have anticipated her change of heart and was unsurprised by her decision, but he was at his most charming and it was almost impossible to believe that this was the same man who had threatened her with ruin just a few hours previously.

He pressed the pouch into her hands. 'When we perform together we will make more than this in one performance. You and I will conquer the whole country and that will be just the beginning.'

Doubtful and feeling slightly sick, Phoebe took the purse from him. Their fingers touched and she felt a tingle run down her spine. Despite the fact that she knew his charming smile was a veneer, she could see why Rose had fallen for this man. Looking into his deep blue eyes she felt herself weakening. She could imagine his well moulded lips caressing hers and those long, tapering fingers stroking her skin. She clutched the money bag tightly in her hands, dragging her gaze away with difficulty. She must not allow him to hypnotise her into becoming his devoted slave. 'I'll give my purse to Rose for safe keeping,' she murmured, moving to the edge of the stage where the steps led down into the auditorium.

'Of course,' he said evenly. 'We'll begin rehearsals as soon as you return. I have a new illusion that will stun the audience, but it will take time to perfect. We have until Monday. Do you think you are up to it, Phoebe Giamatti?'

'I hope so, but I still have my work to do in the theatre.'

He shook his head. 'I've already spoken to Marcus. You work for me now.'

'But the fortune-telling booth . . .'

'Is being dismantled as we speak.'

Phoebe could see that to argue would be useless. She must keep up the fiction that she was happy to work for the great Caspar, but it would not be for long. She turned and ran down the steps not daring to look back at him although she could feel his gaze upon her.

Rose was pacing the floor in the foyer when Phoebe found her. 'What did he say?' Rose demanded anxiously. 'Did he mention me? I'll die if he tells Poppa what I did last night.'

'Stop worrying.' Phoebe handed her the pouch. 'It's

all settled and he gave me back my money. He won't breathe a word to Herbert because it would reflect badly on him. I'm learning more about Caspar every moment I'm with him.'

Rose took the money into the office and locked it in a drawer. 'I still wish I was in your place.'

'You can't mean that.'

'Oh, but I do. There's something about Caspar that draws me to him, no matter what he says or does. I can't help it, Phoebe. Do you think I'm very silly?'

'No, of course not. We can't always choose the person we love.' Phoebe closed her eyes in an attempt to conjure up Gino's face, but to her dismay it was Rogue Paxman whose image filled her mind. She blinked hard in an attempt to banish the vision.

'You're so wise,' Rose said happily. 'I wish I were more like you.'

'No you don't. You're perfect just as you are.' Phoebe looked round as two stage hands appeared from the door which led to the dressing rooms and began taking down the striped tent that served as a fortune-telling booth.

'Marcus told them to do it,' Rose said sympathetically. 'I'm sorry.'

Phoebe shrugged her shoulders. 'It makes sense, I suppose. I'll just have to do as Caspar says for a while. It's going to be hard, but at least it takes care of Ma and the baby. They're the most important thing just now.'

It was harder than Phoebe had thought possible. Caspar was a perfectionist and a brutal taskmaster.

They rehearsed the act late into the night, taking the stage when the performance ended and carrying on into the small hours of the morning until Phoebe was so exhausted that she could barely stand. They began again early next morning and continued throughout the weekend and into Monday, which was to be their opening night. Marcus had been so confident of their success that he had been moved to give complimentary tickets to everyone in the lodging house, and they were ensconced in a private box. Annie insisted on accompanying them, although she had been unwell for several days, but she said that nothing would keep her from seeing her daughter triumph on the professional stage. Phoebe was less certain and she was extremely nervous. Never one to seek the limelight, she had to pluck up every ounce of courage in order to go out on the stage in her scanty costume which the dressmaker had run up, working day and night to sew on hundreds of spangles and sequins.

Caspar was ice cool and imperturbable. He commanded the audience with the confidence of a great general addressing his troops. It was impossible to remain unimpressed by his magnificent stage presence and Phoebe fell under his spell as did every other person in the auditorium. She moved seamlessly from one magic trick to another and when it came to the part she dreaded most, which involved levitating her whole body from a table beneath the cover of a velvet cloth, she almost fainted with fright. 'I can't do it, Caspar,' she whispered. 'It won't work.'

He looked deeply into her eyes. 'Yes, it will. Don't

be afraid, Phoebe.' He held out his arms. 'Allow your-self to fall. You will float, you will fly. Trust me.'

The hiss of the gas and the heat of the limelight made her dizzy. She collapsed into his arms and he lifted her onto the table, which had been constructed especially for the act. His voice was soft and melodic; the words made little sense but she closed her eyes and gave herself up to his will. She was lighter than air. She was rising like a feather in the wind. She could hear the waves beating on the shore, or was it the thunderous sound of applause?

'Get up, Phoebe.'

She opened her eyes and saw Caspar holding out his hand. His smile said it all. The audience rose to their feet stamping, clapping, whistling and calling for more.

'We've done it, my love,' Caspar whispered in her ear. 'You're mine now, Phoebe. You belong to me.'

She was too dazed to respond. Perhaps she had dreamt the whole thing, but the reaction of the theatre crowd was real enough and they took five curtain calls before they were finally allowed off stage.

In the wings Annie was waiting to hug her daughter with tears running down her cheeks. 'You were wonderful, ducks. I'm so proud of you.' She drew back, gazing at Phoebe's skin-tight costume with a short skirt that revealed her shapely legs clad in pink silk tights. 'But Nonna would have a fit if she saw you looking like that, and as for your grandfather . . .' Annie leaned closer to whisper in Phoebe's ear. 'He would shoot Caspar with his fowling piece.' She tapped the side of her nose and smiled. 'But what the eye doesn't see, the heart doesn't grieve, my dear girl. I am really happy for you.'

Almost overnight, Phoebe found herself something of a celebrity. Dolly could not stop prattling about her amazing performance and she told anyone who would listen that her best friend could rise up in the air like a dandelion clock on the breeze. Phoebe tried to explain that it was just an illusion but Dolly looked at her with awe and was convinced that it was true magic.

Caspar was pleased, although he said very little and insisted that they work even harder to perfect the act and bring in new ideas. Marcus had booked them both for two more weeks and Caspar was eager to take the act to London, but this was not what Phoebe wanted. February would be over by the time they finished their contract with Marcus, and Annie was getting close to her time. Despite the thrill of seeing her daughter make a success of her unexpected new career, Annie's health was giving cause for concern. Her hands and feet were swollen and she was barely able to drag her heavy body up the stairs to bed at night. Judy was concerned enough to send for the doctor, who simply advised Annie to rest.

'I could have told her that and saved myself a florin,' Judy said crossly next morning at breakfast. 'You will need to help look after your mother, Phoebe. I've still got this house to run and I'm not a midwife. I know nothing about delivering babies and to tell the truth I can't stand the nasty smelly little things that cry all the time.'

'I'll do everything I can,' Phoebe promised. 'And I'll make Ma stay in bed. Dolly won't mind taking her food up to her, I'm sure.'

'No. I'll look after Annie,' Dolly said solemnly. 'She's been kind to me and I love her. I love you too, Phoebe, and Miss Judy too. I love all of you. You're my family.'

Judy cleared her throat noisily. 'Stuff and nonsense, girl. Get on with you and take a cup of tea and some toast upstairs to Annie.' She rose from the table. 'I suppose you're off to the theatre soon, Phoebe?'

'Yes, I'm afraid so. Caspar has an idea for a new act.'

'Humph,' Judy said with an expressive wave of her hands. 'You're his slave, Phoebe. Be very careful. I don't trust that man.'

'Oh, he's not so bad when you get to know him,' Phoebe said, rising from the table and slipping on the new mantle that Caspar had insisted on buying for her. The bonnet had been an afterthought but with an emerald-green ostrich feather and satin bows it exactly matched the colour of the mantle and had been too pretty to resist.

'You shouldn't accept presents from him,' Judy said, frowning. 'He'll get the wrong idea and think you're a loose woman.'

'Nonsense. He knows I'm not like that.' Phoebe fastened the tiny fabric-covered buttons before putting on the bonnet. It was the first pretty thing she had ever had that had not been second hand or come from a stall in Petticoat Lane or Rosemary market. Caspar had an eye for fashion and perfect taste. It was part of the act that his assistant should look good at all times, he had said when he paid the bill.

'Well, beware. That's all I can say.' Judy pursed her lips. 'If Madame Galina were here she'd say the same thing. Only she's still fast asleep and Augusta has gone to work, otherwise they'd back me up. I'm telling you, Phoebe. No good will come out of this business if you let him get too close. He'll think he owns you. I've seen it all before.'

Phoebe opened her mouth to argue but decided against it. She must not be late. Caspar hated unpunctuality. She picked up the new reticule that just happened to have been on sale in Gussie's shop when they had purchased the bonnet. She was about to leave the room when Dolly burst through the door, red in the face and hysterical. 'Come quick. It's Annie. There's something really wrong with her.'

Phoebe stood by her mother's graveside barely able to believe that she would never see her again. The baby stirred in her arms as a fluttering of snow fell from a featherbed sky. She covered her brother's tiny red face with the lacy shawl that Gussie had crocheted for him. Everyone from the theatre had made time to attend the funeral, except for Caspar who had gone to London to see the producer of a show at the Grecian theatre in Shoreditch, where he hoped to secure a future booking. If he had been sympathetic to Phoebe's loss he hid it well, greeting Annie's early demise with his customary cynicism. His casual remark that Phoebe might be able to contact her mother on the other side and prove once and for all whether or not such things were possible had upset her, but she had expected little else from a man with no heart. In complete contrast, Marcus had been kindness itself. He had even paid for the oak coffin with brass handles that would have been far too expensive for Phoebe or Judy to even consider. He stood beside them now, his large presence comforting and reassuring in a world which for Phoebe had been turned upside down and inside out.

'Come, Phoebe,' he said gently. 'Let's get you and the infant inside the church. There's nothing more to be done here.'

She gazed up at him blankly. For a moment she had forgotten that the vicar had agreed to baptise the baby immediately after the interment. Suddenly her feet seemed too heavy to lift and she was frozen to the spot. She looked to Judy for help.

Clad from head to foot in black like a skinny crow, Judy moved swiftly to her side, taking the baby from her arms. 'Marcus is right. It's over now, Phoebe. She's at peace and no one can harm her ever again. We have to think of the living now.'

Marcus nodded in agreement. 'We must look after the little one.' He pulled a face as the baby opened his mouth and began to mewl like a kitten. 'Let's get him somewhere warmer.'

Without waiting for Phoebe to respond, Judy marched off towards the church. The rest of the mourners followed slowly, their heads bent against the east wind that tore at their veils and bonnet ribbons and sent Fred's bowler hat skimming across the graveyard. He raced after it, putting Phoebe in mind of a monkey puppet with his arms and legs flying out in all directions. If she had not been so sad she might have laughed.

The interior of the church was little warmer than outside but at least they were sheltered from the gathering force of the snowstorm. Dolly slipped her hand into Phoebe's, gulping back the sobs that shook her whole body. Madame Galina and Gussie stood side by side, united for once in their sympathy for the bereaved. Next to them was Herbert, clasping his top hat in one hand and holding on to Rose with the other as if afraid to let her go. She smiled up at him and squeezed his arm gently, but Phoebe noticed that her eyes, like Dolly's, were red-rimmed as if she had spent the night crying. Strangely, Phoebe thought, she had not been able to alleviate the pain of grief that lodged like an icicle in her heart by the shedding of warm tears. Nor had she been able to vent the anger she felt at the loss of her mother's life, which had ebbed away on a crimson tide. Annie had slipped from life silently, peacefully and without protest, whispering so softly that Phoebe had to put her ear close to her mother's lips. 'Name him Edward. Take care of him for me, Phoebe.'

Judy placed the squalling infant back into Phoebe's arms. 'I have no talent for babies,' she murmured. 'He's your responsibility now.'

Although she had acknowledged this fact to herself in the long watches of the night, now in cold daylight Phoebe gazed at her brother's face and the full impact

183

of Judy's words stunned her into silence. She was holding a baby that was of her blood but not her own, and he would be dependent on her for many years to come. It was a terrifying prospect.

The vicar began the ceremony, taking the baby from Phoebe as he performed the baptism. The small scrap of humanity held in the vicar's arms was now purple in the face with indignation as the cold holy water trickled down his forehead. His pink mouth was open wide like a baby bird soliciting food from its parents and his protests echoed round the vaulted ceiling of the church.

Madame Galina touched Phoebe's arm. 'He's crying the devil out, my dear. It's a good sign.' She stepped aside as the vicar handed the crying baby back to Phoebe and the ceremony came to a rather abrupt end.

'He's ready for a feed,' Gussie murmured as they walked down the aisle to congregate in the porch. 'I can't stand all that wailing. He's giving me a headache. Where's that wretched wet nurse?'

Judy sent her a scornful look. 'You'd hardly expect to find her here, now would you? I told her to wait at the house. We'd best get the young man home as soon as possible, Phoebe.'

'My carriage is outside,' Marcus said, having thanked the vicar and given what appeared to be a substantial donation to the collection. 'I can take you, Judy, as well as Phoebe and the baby, and young Dolly too as she's just a little one, but I'm afraid there won't be room for anyone else.'

Fred stepped forward. 'I'll go and find a cab to take the ladies back to the house.'

'I have to go back to the shop,' Gussie said sulkily. 'Mrs Hopkins was reluctant to give me time off as it is.'

'And I'm doing a midday shift at the pub.' Madame Galina wrapped her cloak around her ample frame.

'I'll take you two ladies then,' Herbert said eagerly. 'Rose can go with Fred. I'll follow on when I've seen Madame safely to her place of employment.'

'You will come straight home then, won't you, Poppa?' Rose clutched his arm, her eyes filled with concern. 'We have to be at the theatre this afternoon.'

Herbert flicked her hand away as if it were an annoying insect. 'I'm well aware of my responsibilities, thank you, Rose. I'll be at the theatre at two o'clock, as usual.'

'I'll expect you to be sober,' Marcus said in a low voice. 'I've had to warn you about your drinking on more than one occasion, Herbert. If you let me down again I'm afraid I'll have to let you go.'

Phoebe stood, rocking the baby gently until his cries subsided and he slept. She gazed down at his wrinkled face, thinking that he looked more like an old man than a newborn baby. The moment of panic that she had experienced in the church had faded into nothingness. All she knew was that she loved him unreservedly and the poor little fellow had neither a mother nor a father. Even if she told him the truth, she doubted whether Ned Paxman would welcome parenthood. She looked out into the swirling mass of snow falling like feathers from a burst pillow, realising that this was the beginning of a long journey. She was solely responsible for the baby. She would have to look after him until he was able to take care of himself, and most difficult of all, she would have to keep the secret of his parentage from her family and the Paxmans. Just how she was going to accomplish this was, at the moment, quite beyond her comprehension. At least Gino knew and he would help her, of that she was certain. She must settle down and write to him and to her grandparents, breaking the news of Annie's death, but without revealing the fact that she had died in childbirth. It was not going to be easy.

'Come along, Phoebe,' Judy said impatiently. 'Let's get the infant home before he wakes up and starts bawling again. I really can't stand the noise.'

'I'm coming.' Phoebe pulled her cloak around the baby and headed out into the snow, but during the short carriage ride home her mind was occupied with thoughts of the immediate future. She could stay on in Brighton for a few weeks yet, but then she would have to return to Saffron Hill and open up the house before the family's return from Italy. It would be hard to leave her friends, especially Rose. She had grown fond of Cousin Judy despite her irascible temperament and thrifty, not to say stingy, ways. And then there was Caspar. He would not be best pleased when she told him that she would be leaving his employ. She pushed the thought to the back of her mind as Edward opened his blue eyes and began to whimper. He had, she thought with a sudden sense of panic,

Ned Paxman's eyes. Both he and his brother Rogue had eyes the colour of the sea that changed according to their mood. Sometimes they were bright blue like the sky and at others green like the trough of a wave or moody grey like the ocean on a stormy day. The Giamattis, including herself, were all dark-haired and dark-eyed. Edward's eyes would always give him away.

'We're here,' Marcus said, leaning over to open the carriage door. 'We'll soon have the young man fed and comfortable again.' He climbed out onto the pavement and helped Judy down first and then Dolly. He held out his arms to take the baby. 'This is a new experience for an old bachelor like myself,' he said, smiling as he tucked Edward into the crook of his arm. 'I think I would have made a good father.'

Phoebe gathered her skirts around her and alighted from the carriage. 'There's still time, Marcus. I've never been able to understand why a man like you has escaped marriage for so long.'

'Phoebe, don't be impertinent.' Judy shot her a withering glance as she mounted the steps to unlock the front door. 'Take no notice of her, Marcus.'

Dolly hesitated, screwing her face up as the snow-flakes tickled her nose. She put her head on one side, gazing intently at Marcus. 'I think you should marry Miss Judy. She's much nicer when you're around.'

'I heard that, you stupid girl.' Judy poked her head out of the door, scowling. 'Go and put the kettle on, and see if that lazy trollop has fallen asleep again. I'm still not sure that a woman like her should be taking care of my cousin's child.' She whisked into the house and Dolly bounded up the steps after her, with Phoebe following close behind Marcus and the baby, who was working up to a crescendo of howling.

'You mustn't take any notice of Dolly,' Phoebe said, leaning all her weight on the door in order to close it as a sudden gust of wind sent a powdering of snow into the entrance hall. 'She says whatever comes into her head.'

Marcus handed the squalling baby to her. 'I'm forty-three, and a confirmed bachelor, although sometimes I do regret my unmarried state.'

'Perhaps it's time to think again,' Phoebe said, hitching Edward over her shoulder as she slipped off her damp cloak and hung it on the hallstand. 'Come into the kitchen and have a cup of tea and a slice of Judy's seed cake; it's the best you'll ever taste.'

'I'd like to, but I must get back to the theatre. I have a man coming to see me about the play we're putting on in two weeks' time.' Marcus paused, eyeing Phoebe with a worried frown. 'You didn't know?'

'I thought Caspar was booked until the end of February.'

'In the present circumstances I thought it best not to mention that Caspar and I had a slight difference of opinion. He decided that he wanted to move on sooner than planned.'

Phoebe stared at him in dismay. 'He didn't say anything to me.'

Marcus cleared his throat. 'He probably didn't want to add to your troubles, my dear. Maybe the man has some human feelings after all.'

The baby had started to cry and Phoebe patted his back in an attempt to soothe him. She had been so involved in caring for him and coping with the grief of her mother's sudden death that she had given little or no thought to Caspar or his plans for the future. She frowned thoughtfully. 'It explains why he took the sudden decision to go to London.'

'He's an ambitious man, Phoebe, but I'm sure he still wants you to work with him.'

'I never intended to make it a permanent arrangement, but I was hoping to have work for another few weeks. This has put me in a really difficult position.'

Chapter Eleven

'I'm sure we can come to some arrangement,' Marcus said gently. 'Judy is a good woman and she won't throw you out just because you can't pay the rent, and I could find you a few hours' paid work at the theatre, if that would help.' He opened the front door. 'I really must go now. Perhaps you'd be kind enough to make my apologies to Miss Judy.' He let himself out of the house, but the door had barely closed before it opened again to admit Rose and Fred.

'Why are you standing here in the cold hallway?' Rose demanded anxiously. 'Are you all right, Phoebe?'

'Yes, thank you, Rose. But Edward is hungry. I'd better go and find the wet nurse. She's probably fallen asleep again in front of the range. I don't think she can afford a fire where she lives.' Phoebe hurried off in the direction of the kitchen, where she found Judy soundly berating the unfortunate woman who had just recently given birth to a baby that had survived for only a few days. 'What's the matter?' Phoebe demanded anxiously.

Judy eyed the squalling baby with distaste. 'Can't you shut him up? I can't hear myself think with that noise.'

'He's hungry.' Phoebe approached the wet nurse, wondering if they had done the right thing by hiring a woman who was so obviously down on her luck.

190

'Are you feeling up to looking after my little brother, Mrs Oakes?'

Judy snatched Edward from Phoebe's arms and plumped him down on the wet nurse's lap. 'Now do what you're paid for, Ivy Oakes and we'll say no more about the slice of bread and jam you pilfered from the larder, but it will come out of your wage.'

'Ta, missis,' Ivy murmured, undoing her filthy, tattered blouse and exposing an engorged, blue-veined breast. 'I'm sorry about the grub, but I hadn't had a bite to eat since yesterday.'

Judy wrinkled her nose and turned away as Edward latched hungrily onto the swollen nipple. 'You can have a cup of tea when he's had his fill, Mrs Oakes.'

'Thank you kindly, ma'am.'

Dolly moved to sit by Ivy's side. 'I seen Ma feeding me younger brothers and sisters, but then she put them to the bottle with a teaspoon of gin in it. That made them sleep all right.'

'That's enough of that sort of talk,' Judy said sharply. 'Give Phoebe a cup of tea with a spoonful of sugar in it, and one for Mrs Oakes, without sugar. I can't afford to lavish luxuries on the whole of Brighton.' Taking a hanky from her pocket, she blew her nose loudly. 'I've just buried my cousin. Who, I wonder, will mourn for me when my time comes?'

Fred had been sitting quietly at the table sipping a mug of tea but he looked up at this and his moustache drooped at the corners. 'We'd all be there, Miss Judy. You've got friends and admirers in this town, you ought to know that.'

Judy held her handkerchief to her eyes. 'I know what they say about me. They call me Miss Vinegar-face in the town, even though they know nothing about my personal circumstances.'

Fred twirled his moustache nervously. 'You're a brick, Miss Judy. You never go on about it when I'm late with my rent, and there was a time when you let me work it off by cleaning the windows and scrubbing the front steps.'

'I haven't had much to make me smile.' Judy said, nodding in agreement. 'Heaven knows, I stayed at home to care for my invalid mother until she died. I've had my admirers, but Mamma always put a stop to any gentleman wishing to call on me.'

Dolly frowned thoughtfully. 'That ain't fair. I'm sure Mr Marcus would like to come to tea every now and then.'

'Hush, Dolly.' Phoebe cast an anxious glance at Judy in case Dolly had gone too far, but she seemed wrapped in her own thoughts.

'Now my cousin has gone too.' Judy sighed. 'I'm all alone in the world.'

Phoebe was sympathetic but she had heard enough. 'That's nonsense, Judy. Marcus was just saying what a fine woman you are and how sorry he is that he's remained a bachelor all these years. If you can't see that the man is infatuated with you then you're either blind or stupid. I've lost my mum and I loved her.' A sob rose to her throat and she fled from the room, unable to control the flood of tears that suddenly engulfed her. She ran upstairs to the room she had shared with her mother and Dolly and flung herself down on Annie's empty bed. The pillow still smelt of her mother's favourite lavender cologne and she closed her eyes tightly, but now she had given way she could not stop crying. She wept for her mother and for her orphaned brother. She wept for her lost youth spent hiding in dark cupboards while her mother conducted mock séances. She wept for the fact that she must leave the people she had come to love as friends and return to an uncertain life in London. She wept for herself, knowing that she must honour her promise to marry Gino, a man she did not love. Perhaps she would never know true love. At least Ma had loved Ned with all her wayward heart, and had given him a son to prove it. Perhaps Ma had been the lucky one.

Caspar was late arriving at the theatre that evening, and, as Phoebe had feared, this put him in a foul mood. Although he was too much of a professional to allow it to spoil their act he was surly when off stage, and if he noticed that she was not quite herself he said nothing that might offer her comfort in a time of deep mourning. She was fast losing patience with him and when he turned on her backstage and berated her for her lacklustre performance she retaliated angrily. 'How dare you speak to me like that, Caspar? You're the one who's to blame if the audience didn't enjoy themselves as they might have done had you been in a better temper.'

He grasped her by the shoulders, his fingers digging painfully into her flesh. 'So the little worm has turned, has she? The woman with the countenance of a medieval princess has spirit after all.'

She wrenched free from his painful grip. 'Don't mock me. I've just buried my mother and I think that's reason enough for my not being on top form, but you . . .' She took a deep breath. 'You have no excuse, Caspar Collins. Or did the theatre manager in London turn you down? Weren't you good enough for his seedy palace of varieties?'

For a moment she thought he was going to strike her but it was obvious that he was struggling to maintain his iron self-control, which was normally colder than the blocks of ice that Nonno hauled from the importer's ice cellars every morning in summer. She met his fierce gaze with a defiant lift of her chin, but to her astonishment instead of berating her he drew her roughly to him and covered her mouth with his in a long, hard kiss that was fraught with passion but without a hint of tenderness. Phoebe could not have been more shocked had he struck her across the face. He released her as suddenly as he had taken her into his arms and he walked away, leaving her staring after him in stunned silence. He had never shown the slightest interest in her as a woman, and she could not begin to imagine what had prompted his actions unless it had been to prove his mastery over her. She rubbed her mouth with the back of her hand, but the taste of him seemed indelibly printed on her lips. The hardness of his athletic body against hers had been oddly exciting, if she were to be honest with herself. She pushed the thought to the far recesses of her mind. He had insulted her and made it impossible for them to continue working together. She followed him to his dressing room.

When he did not respond to her rap on the door she opened it and stormed into the tiny room, barely larger than a cupboard. He was sitting between racks of props and costumes, staring into the dressing-table mirror. Strewn before him were sticks of greasepaint lying in drifts of face powder and the air was thick with the cloying scent of stage makeup and sweat. He did not turn his head but as she moved closer she could see his face reflected in the mirror. He was watching her warily, his features as still as a marble statue and his eyes diamond cold.

'How dare you treat me this way?' The words came out in an explosion of pent-up emotion.

Holding her gaze he remained motionless. She tapped him on the shoulder. 'Look at me when I'm talking to you, Caspar. What possessed you to insult me in such a way? Haven't I worked hard for you these past weeks? I've done everything you asked of me and more.'

This time he did turn his head slowly. His expression was carefully controlled. 'I was rejected by an oaf who calls himself a theatre manager.' He rose to his feet sweeping the higgledy-piggledy collection of items from the top of the table with his hand. They fell in a colourful heap on the floor and were buried beneath a fine mist of powder. 'That peasant had the impertinence to call me a conjuror. He hasn't even seen my act and he dismissed me as if I were a nobody.'

He bowed his head and Phoebe's anger dissolved

in a moment of pity. He looked for an instant like a naughty child caught in the act of stealing jam tarts hot from the oven, not for reasons of acute hunger but because the temptation was too great for him. Instinctively she put her arms around him and held him. He laid his head on her shoulder and for a brief moment they clung together like shipwrecked mariners on a lonely atoll without hope of being saved. 'You mustn't take it to heart,' Phoebe said softly. 'You are a great illusionist but he wasn't to know that.'

Slowly, as if ashamed of his moment of weakness, Caspar drew away from her, running his hand through his mane of dark hair. 'I'm sorry, Phoebe. I apologise for my behaviour. It won't happen again. Now leave me, please. I'll see you in the morning for rehearsal of a new illusion I want to perfect before we leave this abysmal place. Don't be late.'

She opened her mouth to tell him that he had made it impossible for her to continue working with him, but somehow she had not the heart to add to his woes. She saw him suddenly not as a tyrant but as a man unused to failure who was, probably for the first time in his life, having to swallow the bitter pill of rejection. She felt nothing but pity for him, and she left the dressing room without saying another word. But there were still big decisions that had to be made, and February was drawing rapidly to a damp and rainy close.

The snow had melted, turning first to dirty slush on the pavements and then filling the gutters to over-flowing with muddy water. It was almost impossible to get to the theatre without being sprayed by the wheels of passing vehicles, and the grey skies seemed to cast gloom over everyone. The show was due to close at the end of the month and Caspar had not managed to achieve a future booking. Phoebe was still plucking up the courage to tell him that she would be leaving for London at the beginning of March. She had saved as much as she could after paying rent to Judy and the small amount of money that Ivy Oakes demanded for nursing the baby. The remainder of her wages would help see them through the coming weeks until the family returned to England, but she would still have to supplement their income with a few séances. Quite how she would explain Edward's arrival to her family was still a matter of deep concern to her, and it was discussed at length in the house. Madame Galina was convinced that little Teddy, as he had become known, ought to be adopted by a well-to-do family who could give him a solid upbringing and a good education. Herbert was of the opinion that there were suitable institutions for infants born on the wrong side of the blanket, but Gussie disagreed. She had been raised in an orphanage and she was vehement in her condemnation of such establishments. Fred sided with Madame, saying that the child's best interests would be served if he remained in Brighton where Judy could keep an eye on his progress. Judy did not seem too keen on this suggestion. 'I am not maternally inclined,' she said firmly. 'He should go to London with his sister.'

'Come, come, my dear lady.' Fred's eyes were filled

with admiration as he gazed at her. 'You are a woman above reproach who understands the meaning of the word duty. Your conscience would not allow you to neglect a helpless infant, especially one related to you.'

Judy curled her lip and changed the subject to demand his overdue rent.

Phoebe listened politely but she had no intention of abandoning her responsibilities. She loved Teddy unreservedly and for good or ill she would stand by him for the rest of her life, no matter what other people said. Rose agreed with her wholeheartedly although Dolly appeared to be slightly put out by the attention the baby was receiving. She had become quiet and withdrawn since Annie died, and made no secret of the fact that she resented Ivy's presence in the house, day and night. With a husband who had mysteriously disappeared from the scene before she gave birth to their child, and no family of her own, Ivy was only too glad to be fed and housed. She asked for little and faded into the shadows when her services were not required, but she had proved to be a good nursemaid and lavished the affection she might have given to her own baby on Teddy. Phoebe felt quite safe leaving him in her care when she was at the theatre, but she had still not told Caspar about the baby, and he had never mentioned her mother's tragic demise. Caspar, she decided, lived in a self-centred world of his own. His act was the reason for his existence and the people around him were only important if they were some way involved in the illusory world he inhabited. Phoebe played her part to the best of her ability, but after his sudden and unexpected embrace, she was careful not to be alone with him.

'You have to tell him that you're leaving him,' Rose said on the penultimate evening of the show as Phoebe was putting on her stage makeup. 'He told me that he's got a booking in Bournemouth starting next week.'

'He hasn't said anything to me.' Phoebe patted her face with a powder puff. 'As far as I know he's still looking.'

'You've been avoiding him off stage. You've made that obvious to everyone. Has he upset you in some way, Phoebe? I thought you two got on quite well, even though he is a difficult man.'   .

'No. You're imagining things, Rose. I have to hurry home every day because of Teddy, you know that.'

'Yes.' Rose eyed her doubtfully. 'I suppose so. But you must say something. You can't just walk out of the theatre tomorrow night and not tell him that you're off to London next day.'

Phoebe patted her hand. 'Stop worrying. I'll do it in my own good time. He'll find someone else to fill my place. After all, it didn't take him long to hire me after Hyacinth left to marry her rich gentleman friend. I doubt if he'll raise an eyebrow when I tell him.' She spoke with more confidence than she was feeling, and although she intended to break the news to Caspar that evening after the performance ended, she lost her nerve and left the theatre before he had had time to change out of his magician's robes.

It had been a difficult few days at home. Dolly and Ivy had clashed openly for the first time and Dolly had thrown herself down on the kitchen floor, flailing her arms and legs and howling like a frustrated two-year-old in a tantrum. Phoebe had been powerless to stop her but Judy had yanked Dolly to her feet and slapped her face just hard enough to bring her back to her senses. Then to Phoebe's amazement Judy had wrapped her arms around Dolly and given her a hug, smoothing her tumbled blonde curls and speaking to her in gentle tones quite different from her habitual brusque manner.

Ivy snatched up the squalling baby and backed away to sit in a chair at the far end of the kitchen, unbuttoning her now spotlessly clean blouse to reveal an engorged breast. Latching on greedily, Teddy was silenced instantly, apart from the occasional muffled hiccup. Ivy sat quietly suckling him, watching Judy wide-eyed. 'It weren't my fault, Miss Phoebe,' she muttered. 'I only said I was looking forward to seeing London. I ain't never been no further than Hove, and that were only once.'

Dolly lifted her head from Judy's shoulder. 'I don't want to go back there. Ma will get me for sure, and I don't like her.' She pointed at Ivy and burst into fresh floods of tears.

Judy met Phoebe's anxious gaze, shaking her head. 'You'll have to take Ivy with you for Teddy's sake, but Dolly could stay here with me, for the time being anyway. She's a great help in the house, and if that mother of hers decided to claim her there wouldn't be much you could do to stop her taking Dolly back, and selling her to the highest bidder.'

Phoebe looked from one to the other. She was fond of Dolly, but Teddy must come first. 'What do you say to that, Dolly? Would you like to stay with Judy?'

Dolly brightened visibly. 'Yes, please.'

That settled, Phoebe knew that she must tell Caspar at the end of the evening performance. She had put it off repeatedly, but when the time came she waited until after the final curtain when everyone filed off the stage. The tumblers had invited everyone to go to the pub for a farewell drink, but Caspar had refused in his usual curt manner. He went straight to his dressing room and closed the door. Phoebe followed him. Standing outside she took a deep breath, knocked and went in.

He had taken off his velvet, star-spangled robe and was hanging it over the back of a chair. His vivid stage makeup was at odds with the white silk evening shirt which he had unbuttoned almost to his waist. 'Yes?' His tone was cold and his eyes disturbingly blank.

Phoebe clasped her hands tightly behind her back. 'I'm leaving for London tomorrow.' She tried to sound positive but she was suddenly nervous. 'I'm sorry, Caspar. I can't work with you any more.'

'Why not? Is there someone else? Have you had a better offer?' He took a step towards her, his eyes glittering dangerously. 'Who is he?'

'No. You don't understand. My family – I . . .'

'You're not leaving me.' It was a statement of fact rather than a question, and before she had a chance to move away he seized her in his arms. 'You won't get away from me so easily.' With one savage swipe of his hand he ripped her sequined costume, burying his face between her breasts. His mouth was hot on her flesh, his teeth grazed her nipples, and before she had a chance to scream for help he pinned her against the door, covering her lips with brutal kisses. 'You'll never leave me,' he whispered. 'You belong to me alone. I'll never let you go.' His hands raked her flesh as he tore away the remaining gaudy trappings of a magician's assistant. She struggled frantically but he silenced her cries with his tongue, half suffocating her with the weight of his body against hers. She kicked out with her feet but this only seemed to excite him more. His strength seemed like that of a madman intent on satisfying his lust. In desperation she bit his lip, drawing blood. Uttering an oath he clamped his hand to the afflicted part of his face and Phoebe opened her mouth to scream, but even before the sound escaped her lips there was a loud knocking on the door.

'Are you coming to the pub, old man?' Herbert's voice rang out loud and clear, echoing round the dressing room.

An angel's chorus could not have sounded sweeter to Phoebe's ears. 'Herbert, save me.' She gave Caspar a hefty shove, catching him momentarily off guard, and she kicked him on the shin, causing him to stagger backwards. She wrenched the door open and fell into Herbert's arms.

'My God, Phoebe. What has he done to you?' He lifted her off her feet and set her down in the narrow corridor. At that moment, Caspar emerged from the room, glowering at him as if he were about to commit

202

murder. 'Marcus,' Herbert roared. 'Come here. You're needed.'

'What is it, Poppa?' Rose came running towards them. She stopped, staring at Phoebe in horror. 'My God, Phoebe. What happened to you? Are you hurt?'

'Take her to her dressing room, Rose.' Herbert gave Phoebe a gentle push into his daughter's arms. 'We'll deal with this.' He glanced over his shoulder as Marcus approached them with a worried look on his face.

Clutching her torn costume to cover her naked breasts, Phoebe allowed Rose to lead her to the dressing room where she collapsed onto a wooden chair in front of the dressing table. She caught sight of her reflection in the mirror and found herself staring at a face covered in a mask of smudged greasepaint, both hers and Caspar's. Her neck and breasts were striped black and silver, with smudges of red from his lips. She shuddered and turned away, reaching for a towel. 'Fetch me some water, please,' she whispered. 'I want to wash this away.' Her hands shook as she scrubbed at her flesh as if trying to scrape away all trace of what had just occurred.

'Yes, of course. I'll be back in a jiffy.' Rose whisked out of the room, returning a few minutes later with a jug of hot water and a piece of soap. She smiled grimly as she lathered the sponge. 'This is his fine soap. Only the best for Caspar, the old devil. He didn't hurt you, did he, Phoebe? I can't believe he would lay a finger on you for all his arrogance and ill temper.'

'I'm not hurt.' Phoebe took the sponge from her and scrubbed her face and neck until all traces of makeup were gone. 'He frightened me, Rose. He kissed me and

I really think he would have raped me if your pa hadn't turned up in the nick of time.'

Rose shuddered. 'To think that I fancied him once.'

'I shouldn't have agreed to work with him. I was stupid.'

'No, I won't have that, Phoebe. He's a bad man who preys on women.'

'It's just as well I'd planned to leave tomorrow.' Phoebe scrubbed at her lips with the cloth. 'I never want to see him again, ever.'

'I don't want you to go away, but you'll be safe from him in London. It's a big place and he'll never find you there.'

'I don't want anybody to tell him where I'm going. He said he'd never let me go, Rose. He acted like a madman.'

Rose handed her a towel. 'You'll be gone first thing in the morning, and I've heard that he's going to Bournemouth later in the day. He must have assumed that you would go with him. You've had a lucky escape, if you ask me.'

The house in Saffron Hill smelt of mouse droppings and stale garlic with just a hint of the lavender and beeswax polish that Nonna lavished on the furniture and floorboards. It had been a tiring journey after an emotional parting from Judy, Dolly and the rest of the lodgers, whom Phoebe had come to look upon as family rather than just friends. Most upsetting of all was leaving Rose and they had been in tears as they promised lifelong friendship.

As Phoebe went round opening windows even though it was cold and rainy outside, she could not help comparing the dilapidated house, jostling for position amongst even less well kept buildings in a street that had never seen better days, with Judy's establishment. Its spacious, if old-fashioned rooms were admittedly on the shabby side, but the seafront location made up for what the house lacked in splendour. She knew she would miss the fresh salt air and the rhythmic sound of the waves on the pebbles which had lulled her to sleep at night. Outside in Saffron Hill she could hear the rumble of cartwheels and the clatter of horses' hooves muffled by the mud and detritus that littered the cobblestones. The raucous cries of pedlars, street sellers were almost drowned out by the loud guffaws and shouts of drunks coming from the pub on the corner. The high-pitched voices of the ragged urchins begging for coppers or screeching in pain as the bigger boys walloped those smaller and weaker than themselves were even harder to bear. Teddy would not be allowed to run riot like them, she thought as she attempted to get a fire going in the range. She glanced over her shoulder at Ivy, who was huddled in a chair with Teddy clasped in her arms as though she was afraid to put him down in this alien environment.

'Is this the first time you've been to London, Ivy?' Phoebe sat back on her haunches to wait for the kindling to splutter into flames.

'Yes'm.' Ivy's eyes were round and her sallow face pale. 'I think I want to go home.'

'And so you shall,' Phoebe said, thinking fast. She

must humour Ivy as she could not hope to find another wet nurse at such short notice and Teddy seemed to be doing well in her care. 'As soon as my brother is able to take cow's milk I'll put you on the first train to Brighton with your fare paid, and money in your purse. Is that a bargain?'

'I suppose so, ma'am.' Ivy glanced round the kitchen as if expecting cutthroats to be lurking in each dark corner. 'This is a big house for just us.'

'My family will return from Italy in less than a month,' Phoebe said, working the bellows energetically. 'It's really quite cramped when we're all here together.' She smiled to herself at the thought of seeing her grandparents again. She was even looking forward to seeing her volatile uncles after months of separation. She wondered if they would bring wives home with them this time. Nonno was always telling them that it was high time they married and continued the Giamatti line. She rose to her feet, satisfied that there would soon be a good blaze, and she picked up the soot-blackened kettle. 'Come outside with me, Ivy. I'll show you where to find the pump and the privy. You'll need both while you're staying here.' She led the way out through the scullery and into the back yard.

Ivy looked up at the high walls of the surrounding buildings and she wrinkled her nose. 'It smells something terrible here.'

'You'll get used to it.' Phoebe took Teddy from her, placing the kettle in Ivy's hand. 'There, I'm sure you know how to work a pump. You'll feel better about things when you've had a nice hot cup of tea and something to eat. Judy packed some food for us, so we'll be fine until tomorrow when I'll take you to the market and show you where to get the best bargains.'

'I don't ever have to go out on me own, do I? I'm scared of this horrible place.' Ivy pumped the handle too hard, spilling water over her shoes. 'Oh Gawd, now I'm all wet. I can't be doing with this. It's like trying to piss into a thimble. At home we had a well and a bucket.'

'It just takes a bit of practice,' Phoebe said, trying hard to be patient. She forced her lips into a smile. 'Never mind, you'll soon dry out by the fire. There should be enough water in the kettle now. Let's go inside.'

Ivy cast an anxious glance around the yard filled with barrels, buckets, a zinc bath and Nonno's handcart in which he collected the ice. She shuddered. 'I bet London rats are as big as dogs.'

'Not quite.' Phoebe shooed her indoors, wondering silently how she was going to cope with a simple country woman who was scared of her own shadow and patently terrified by everything in the city. She shivered as a cold wind whipped between the buildings and she covered Teddy with her shawl as she hurried into the comparative warmth of the house. Even more pressing was the problem she held in her arms. She adored Teddy, but how she was going to present him to her family was a constant worry. Time was running out and she would have to think of something.

Chapter Twelve

In the days that followed Phoebe began to regret bringing Ivy to London. She was too afraid to go out to market on her own and had to sleep in the same room as Phoebe at night, fearing that she would be murdered in her bed if she slept alone. Ivy had a fit of hysteria when Phoebe told her that she planned to hold a séance, and when she attempted to explain the proceedings to her, Ivy ran away and hid in the broom cupboard for several hours until hunger won and she crept into the kitchen as if expecting to see a ghost. It was fortunate perhaps that Phoebe had not found any would-be clients in their first couple of weeks, but the money was running low and one morning, having left Ivy to look after the baby, she set off for the market with her basket over her arm. She had food to purchase but she hoped that she might meet some of her mother's regular patrons.

She bought vegetables in Farringdon market as well as flour and eggs, deciding that she would attempt to make pasta as she had seen Nonna do on countless occasions. It was cheap and nourishing and she hoped that it was easy. She was busy choosing apples when she was suddenly aware of someone standing very close to her. She looked up into the blue-green eyes of

Rogue Paxman. He doffed his hat, smiling. 'Miss Giamatti. This is a pleasant surprise.'

She recovered quickly. He must not suspect that she had anything to hide. 'I might say the same, Mr Paxman. This is the last place I would expect to see you.'

He picked up an apple and bit into it. It was an oddly youthful and unselfconscious action that belied the hint of arrogance in his stance. She turned away as if intent on selecting the best fruit, and she willed him to move on before he started asking questions. If he mentioned her mother she was afraid she would burst into tears. She had put a brave face on her loss but inwardly her feelings were raw, and she was still in the first painful stage of grief.

'I often come to market,' he said, tossing a coin to the stallholder. 'I'll take a pound of apples, but serve the young lady first.'

'You're very polite all of a sudden.' Phoebe cast him a sideways glance, her curiosity aroused. 'And I can't believe that you're here just to buy apples. That's not what you do.'

He angled his head. 'And what do you think it is that I do to occupy my time, apart of course from the criminal activities that men like me carry out under cover of darkness.'

'That'll be tuppence ha'penny, miss.' The stallholder held out his hand.

She had very little money left but the cabbage, potatoes and carrots would make a nourishing soup even though she could not afford a beef bone to enhance the flavour. She put the apples back on the pile.

'Allow me.' Paxman scooped the fruit onto the scales and paid for them. Then, much to her embarrassment, he placed them in her basket.

'No, really. I can't accept.' She tried to give them back but he shook his head.

'Take them as a small gift for Annie then. We haven't seen her around for months, so we thought you must both have gone to Italy with the family. I'm sure my brother misses her company.'

Shaking her head she hurried off, and fighting back tears she pushed through the crowd of women at the entrance to the market. She had only gone a few paces along Stonecutter Street when Paxman caught up with her. 'What did I say to upset you? It wasn't my intention to make you cry.'

'I'm not crying,' she muttered, dashing away the tears with her hand. 'I had something in my eye.'

He drew her to a halt. 'My brother is genuinely fond of Annie. He was quite put out when she disappeared without a word.'

She bowed her head, unable to speak. Paxman took her by the arm and guided her across the street to a coffee house frequented by the market traders. The interior was dark and steamy, with a strong smell of roasted coffee beans mingling with tobacco smoke. The occasional fall of burning soot sizzled as it hit the live coals in the fire basket, sending out a shower of sparks like a miniature firework display. The small-paned windows were veiled in condensation and the

210

booths were packed with men drinking tea and coffee, their voices a constant hum accompanied by the clink of spoons as they stirred sugar into their beverages. Paxman approached a table close to the fireplace. A man dressed in a green-tinged black suit with leather patches at the elbows and a stiff white collar was already seated at the table, but at the sight of Rogue Paxman hovering over him, he drained his cup and scrambled to his feet. 'Just going, sir.' He made a grab for his bowler hat and rammed it on his head, nodding to Phoebe as he headed for the street door.

'Take a seat, Miss Giamatti.' Coming from Paxman's lips it was more of an order than an invitation. Phoebe sank down on the wooden settle and fumbled in her reticule in search of the hanky that Judy had given her for Christmas, which was identical to the ones she had presented to Dolly, Madame and Gussie. Phoebe blew her nose and wiped her eyes as she struggled to regain an outward show of composure, but when she looked up Paxman had gone and she was alone at the table. She could see him at the counter, talking to the serving girl. She weighed up her chances of escaping, but decided against such an action as it would only arouse his curiosity further. By the time he returned with the coffee she had worked out how much of the truth she would tell him.

He set a cup in front of her and took a seat opposite. 'Now perhaps you would like to tell me what's wrong.'

'Nothing,' she said stoutly. 'At least nothing that concerns you, Mr Paxman.'

'I think we know each other well enough to dispense

with the formalities, Phoebe. My name is Roger, as you know, although Rogue will do as I told you once before.'

'My mother died of lung disease in Brighton.' The words came out in a rush and she had the grim satisfaction of seeing him flinch.

His smile faded. 'I'm sorry. I liked Annie, and my brother will take it quite badly. Whatever you've heard of us, Phoebe, we are not the villains some people make us out to be.'

'You're not clergymen either.' She met his intense gaze steadily. 'I know your reputation, Rogue. You offer protection from the high mob to shopkeepers and small businesses for a fee that most of them can ill afford. You make money out of other people's misfortune.'

'Not at all. We keep the peace. We protect those who are loyal to us and give no quarter to our enemies. Is that so wrong?'

She shrugged her shoulders. 'The police think it is.'

He acknowledged this barb with a reluctant smile. 'We have inside knowledge that they don't possess. You could say we're doing a public service.'

She sipped the coffee. It was the best she had tasted since Nonna left London. 'Why are you bothering with me? What I do can be of no interest to you.'

'Tell me why you and your mother fled to Brighton. One day you were here; the next you'd gone. Ned came looking for Annie and found the house locked and shuttered.'

This was the time to give him just enough of the

truth to keep him satisfied. 'My mother thought she'd killed Snape. She was foolish enough to go to his rooms and he tried to seduce her. She hit him over the head and she ran away. We were afraid that the police would come after her so we went to our cousin in Brighton.'

Paxman threw back his head and laughed. 'It would take more than a little scrap like Annie to finish off a bastard like Snape. I can assure you that he's alive and still as annoying as ever. That man has a skin as thick as an elephant's.'

'It's not funny,' Phoebe whispered as she realised that people were staring at them. 'He could have set the police on her.'

'So she escaped from the clutches of the law. Don't you think that puts you both on the same side as us miscreants?'

Phoebe rose to her feet. 'I'm glad you think it's funny. I must be going now.'

He caught her by the hand. 'I'm truly sorry to hear about Annie.' He stood up, reaching for his top hat. 'Allow me to walk you home.'

She said nothing until they were outside in the street and when he offered her his arm she shook her head. 'No, thank you. I can manage to find my way back to Saffron Hill. I won't trouble you further.' She started walking but to her consternation he fell into step beside her.

'You need funds. I saw how you handled what little money you had in your purse. I realise that without Annie you must be struggling.'

Phoebe stopped, meeting his eyes with a steady gaze.

'There's no need to concern yourself. My family and my fiancé will be returning home in a couple of weeks. I have enough to live on, and even if I didn't I'm perfectly capable of earning an honest living.'

'Your fiancé?' He seized her left hand, staring at the gold signet ring which she had placed on her middle finger for safe keeping. 'I see no engagement ring.'

She snatched her hand free. 'I don't see that it's any business of yours, Rogue Paxman. Gino and I are unofficially engaged and will be married quite soon.'

'He's a lucky fellow, but if I were him I wouldn't have gone off and left my woman to fend for herself all winter.' He put his hand in his pocket and pulled out a gold sovereign which he tucked into her reticule before she had a chance to protest. 'That is a loan to tide you over until your family returns. Gino can repay me then, and you need not feel obliged to me as I'll charge him interest.'

Phoebe struggled with the strings on her reticule in an attempt to retrieve the coin and return it to him, but he walked off before she could extricate it from the folds of her hanky. 'Stop,' she called, hurrying after him. 'I don't want your money.' She glared at a group of young street arabs who were openly mocking her. 'Stop, please.'

He paused, looking over his shoulder. 'Call it a fee then. I'll book your services for ten o'clock tomorrow morning. Good day to you, Phoebe.'

She could hardly break into a run without losing face and the filthy, ragged urchins were crowding round her shouting taunts. Holding her head high, she quickened her pace and hurried homeward. She could not believe that he was serious about attending a séance and she put his request out of her mind as she concentrated on the more important task of feeding her small family. Ivy barely knew how to boil water to make tea, and it transpired that she had rarely eaten anything other than bread and scrape with a morsel of cheese on special occasions. She came from a large impecunious family and her father, an itinerant farm labourer, struggled to provide for his brood of fifteen children. How they managed to live in a one up, one down cob cottage on the outskirts of Brighton was a mystery to Phoebe, but having listened to Ivy talking about her parents and siblings she could understand a little better her natural desire to return to the place she knew and loved. Her common law husband had gone away to sea as soon as he knew that she was in the family way and had not been seen or heard of since. Poor Ivy, Phoebe thought as she rolled out her first attempt at pasta dough, life had dealt her a rotten hand and losing her baby must have been the cruellest blow. She must be more patient with her and make allowances when she refused to go out alone or even venture upstairs to the top floor in the dark unless Phoebe lit her way with a candle. She must not expect her to help in the séances, and she must hope that Ivy's milk would not dry up until Teddy was old enough to be weaned.

The pasta was a moderate success, although Phoebe was not sure what her grandmother would have made of her efforts. The vegetable soup was edible, if rather bland, and she wished that she had paid more attention to Nonna's use of herbs and spices in her cooking. Ivy ate ravenously, as if every mouthful was to be her last, and try as she might Phoebe could not convince her that there would be more to come later. At least Ivy was uncritical and if the soup lacked flavour she did not complain. With the gold sovereign tucked away in Nonna's housekeeping jar on the mantelshelf, Phoebe was confident that they could keep themselves in food until the family returned. The coin had felt hot in her hand and she hated being beholden to Rogue Paxman, but she did not think for a moment that he would keep his appointment. When Gino came home she would borrow the money from him and repay her debt to the man she wished she had never met. Or at least she wished that her mother had not allowed herself to fall in love with Ned. The two brothers were indivisible in her mind, and she blamed them both for the death of her parents. Quite suddenly she found herself missing Gino. He was the one person who knew and understood her present dilemma. He was kind, honourable and steady; the sort of man who would make an excellent husband and father. When she laid her head on the pillow that night she decided that she would give him his answer on his return. She would do her best to make him a good wife.

Going about her chores next morning with Teddy clasped in one arm, Phoebe balanced him on her hip while she dusted the heavily carved furniture in the front parlour. He had awakened several times in the night and Ivy had looked pale and exhausted at breakfast, prompting Phoebe to suggest that she ought to go back to bed for an hour or two and catch up on her sleep. She had agreed willingly, but Teddy had other ideas and instead of sleeping in the drawer that had been made into a makeshift crib he howled loudly every time Phoebe attempted to lie him down. She shifted him from one hip to the other, thinking proudly that he had doubled his birth weight and was thriving, despite showing signs of the Paxman temper and their undoubted stubborn streak. She flicked the duster over the pot dogs that glowered at each other from opposite ends of the mantelshelf, and only narrowly missed knocking the spill jar onto the floor when the sound of someone hammering on the front door startled her and awakened Teddy. He had been dropping off to sleep but he began to cry and was inconsolable as she hurried down the narrow hallway.

She opened the door and instantly realised her mistake as Rogue stared in amazement at the bawling infant. 'Well now, that's something I didn't expect.'

He stepped over the threshold without waiting to be invited, and taking off his top hat he hung it on the row of pegs behind the door. 'My appointment,' he said, eyeing Phoebe with a ghost of a smile. 'Had you forgotten?'

'Yes. I mean, no. I didn't think you were serious. Why would you want to contact the other side?'

'Call it curiosity. I've sent a few souls that way, although they were villains to the last one and are probably stoking the fires of hell if the truth were told.'

He stroked Teddy's downy head. 'He's a fine little chap. What's his name?'

'Teddy,' Phoebe said, cursing the fact that she had not been stricter and made her little brother accept the fact that he should be enjoying his morning nap.

Paxman took the squalling baby from her arms and as if to spite her, Teddy immediately stopped crying and he opened his eyes wide as he tried to focus on Paxman's face. She held her breath. They might have been father and son. She hoped that Rogue could not see the likeness. But he was smiling at Teddy and making ridiculous noises that seemed at odds with his reputation as a hardened criminal. Who would have imagined the tough gang leader cooing at a baby? She was tempted to snatch her brother away from him but she restrained herself. She knew what was coming even before Paxman raised his head to give her a questioning glance. 'Whose child is he?'

'Dolly's.' The lie was born of desperation. She could not tell him the truth and she knew that he was too astute to believe her if she said that Teddy was hers. She looked him in the eyes. 'He's Dolly's baby, and I'm looking after him until she's well enough to take over his care.'

'And where is Dolly? Surely she wouldn't want to be parted from her child?'

She was afraid that he had seen through her lies, but she had no alternative now but to carry on with the fiction. 'She caught – measles. She's quite poorly and we didn't want to expose the baby to the disease, so Dolly stayed in Brighton and I brought him back to London with a wet nurse. He'll be returned to his mother as soon as she regains her health and strength.'

'Really? Well, that's quite heroic of you if I may say so.' He laid the baby gently in her arms. 'I can see that you're busy. Perhaps we should put off the séance until another day. I'll call again when you have more time on your hands.' He headed for the front door.

'But your money. I have it here. I can give it back to you now.'

He took his hat from the peg and set it on his head as he opened the front door. 'Keep it. I'll hold you to our arrangement some other time.'

Then he was gone, leaving Phoebe feeling weak at the knees. She glanced at Teddy, shaking her head. 'I can see you think this is funny, but it's not. I'm not sure if he believed me, but I hope he did. You are a troublesome boy, Teddy Giamatti. Had you been sleeping he would not have known of your existence. Now see what you've done, you naughty baby.' She tempered her words with a smile and dropped a kiss on his forehead. 'But now I've got another problem. What on earth am I going to tell Nonna and Nonno? If I say you're Dolly's child they'll expect me to send you back to Brighton, and I can't do that. Cousin Judy wouldn't want you anyway, and Dolly is never going to be a responsible adult.'

Teddy opened his mouth, exposing two rows of pink gums, and yawned.

Phoebe sighed. 'You don't know what I'm saying, thank the Lord. But I'm in a terrible dilemma, Teddy, and I can't see any way out of it.' She returned to her chore of dusting the front parlour. The family would be arriving home in less than a fortnight and Nonna would be casting a critical eye over everything. Phoebe worked with renewed vigour.

Two weeks later, almost to the day, the house in Saffron Hill was filled with noise and seemed to grow smaller as Fabio, Lorenzo and Julio clattered into the hallway hefting bundles and battered suitcases that had survived countless sea crossings and railway journeys, ending up in their native village on the backs of hard-worked donkeys. Phoebe had been expecting them but had not known the exact date and time of their arrival, and it was fortunate that this coincided with Teddy's afternoon nap. Ivy had seized the opportunity to catch up on her sleep leaving Phoebe free to tidy the parlour after the morning session, which had earned her a florin. Her clients had been the well-to-do wife of a city merchant and her unmarried daughters, both extremely plain and fearful of being left on the shelf. They were more concerned about looking in the crystal ball for prospective suitors than with contacting their dear departed grandfather who had left them each a small annuity. They had gone away content in the knowledge that they would not end up as spinsters, but Phoebe had refrained from telling them that she had sensed tears and unhappiness for at least one of them in their marriage. People paid for good news and she rarely admitted to seeing anything else. Sometimes her flashes of intuition were frighteningly real but she refused to believe that she had any genuine psychic powers. If she had inherited her mother's somewhat doubtful gift in that direction, she reasoned that she would have foreseen the tragedy of Annie's death in childbirth and the responsibility that had subsequently been thrust upon her.

Phoebe had still not decided how to explain Teddy's existence to her family, and she prayed silently for inspiration as her grandfather entered the room, arms outstretched and a huge grin on his bearded face.

'My little princess. I've missed you, cara.'

She walked into his embrace struggling to hold back tears. His clothes were travel-stained and smelt of tobacco and garlic with the added and unmistakeable odour of railway stations, soot and maybe a tang of salt from their sea crossing. She laid her head on his shoulder and felt safe for the first time in months. 'I've missed you too, Nonno.'

He gave her a hug. 'I was sorry to hear about Annie,' he said gently. 'We never got on well but she was my son's wife and your mother; for that alone I respected her place in the family. What was it that took her from us? You didn't say in your letter.'

She had known that this question would arise sooner or later, but as she struggled to think of a suitable answer she had a temporary reprieve when Maria bustled into the room, taking off her bonnet and shawl and tossing them onto a chair. 'Don't bother the poor child with questions now, Fabio. Can't you see that she is still in mourning for her mother, you stupid fellow?' She wrested Phoebe from his arms, clasping her to her bosom and almost smothering her. 'You should have come with us, cara. It was a mistake leaving you here with Annie, God rest her soul. She was always a flighty piece and I daresay it was the drink that did for her in the end. But we won't talk about it now. Come and help me in the kitchen. The boys are starving, as usual.'

'Let the poor child catch her breath, Maria. You could talk the hind leg off a donkey.' Fabio chuckled, blowing a kiss to his wife who was visibly bristling with indignation. 'We'll speak later, Phoebe. As for me I'm going down to my cellar and check that everything is ready for the new season. With this pleasant spring weather I might even consider starting early. People love my hokey-pokey.'

In the kitchen, Maria started unpacking a parcel containing the herbs and spices she had brought from Italy. She went round opening cupboards and tut-tutting loudly when she discovered them bare. 'Didn't Fabio leave you enough money for food? Haven't you been carrying on with the séances?' Her expression softened as she turned to Phoebe and she held out her hand. 'I'm sorry, cara, I should not have said that. Of course you must have had a difficult time with Annie passing away so suddenly. Where is she buried? I would like to see her grave and say a prayer for her soul.'

Phoebe hesitated. If she admitted that her mother was buried in Brighton the whole sorry story would come out, but at that moment Julio burst into the kitchen, caught her round the waist and whirled her round. 'We missed you, little one. Mamma insisted on coming home early so that we could be with you in this sad time.' He kissed her on both cheeks, squeezing her hands with a sympathetic smile softening his dark eyes. 'But there is someone who missed you even more than us.' He jerked his head in the direction of the doorway.

Phoebe looked round to see Gino hovering on the threshold, looking a little nervous. Without stopping to think, she broke away from her uncle and ran to Gino, throwing her arms around his neck. 'I'm so glad to see you.' The words tumbled from her lips and were sincerely meant, but more from relief that someone was here who understood her predicament than from the joy of being reunited with the man she had decided to marry.

'There, you needn't have worried,' Julio said before Gino had a chance to catch his breath. 'I told you she was the faithful sort and would be pining for you.' He turned to his mother. 'What's for supper, Mamma? I'm starving.'

'You always are,' Maria said fondly. 'Go away and let me prepare it in peace or you won't get anything at all, and take Gino and Phoebe with you. I can't work with people looking on.'

Blowing her a kiss, Julio left the room calling to Lorenzo to hurry up with the rest of their things.

Left alone, apart from Maria who was busily sorting out the ingredients for their supper, Gino held Phoebe in his arms, looking deeply into her eyes. 'I missed you so much, my love, and I was very sorry to hear about your mamma. It must have been very hard for you on your own.'

She drew away, startled by the ardour of his expression and regretting her impulsive reaction on seeing him again. 'I'm all right, Gino, but I must talk to you in private.' She took him by the hand and was about to lead him from the room when Julio returned with Fabio close behind him. She could see by the expressions on their faces that something was wrong and her heart gave an uncomfortable thud against her ribs. 'What's the matter?'

'There's a baby in the house.' Julio said, pulling a face. 'It's yelling its head off upstairs.'

Fabio pushed past him. 'What is the meaning of this, Phoebe?'

She froze as she looked over his shoulder and saw Ivy coming down the passageway towards them holding a screaming Teddy in her arms. At a loss for words, she tried desperately to think of a plausible explanation, but Teddy's cries were growing louder and Ivy was cowering against the wall staring at Fabio as if he were the devil incarnate.

'Who is that woman?' Fabio demanded. 'What is she doing in my house? And whose baby is that? Answer me, girl.'

Chapter Thirteen

In a moment of panic Phoebe was tempted to lie and tell them that Teddy was Ivy's child. It would be so easy to fabricate a story casting Ivy as the abandoned wife left to raise her baby as best she could by a faithless husband. It was close to the truth except for one small detail – Teddy. She could not risk the possibility of losing her brother; neither could she place such an unfair burden on Ivy, who had already suffered so much. Phoebe met her grandfather's stern gaze with a steady look. 'Ivy is the baby's wet nurse.'

Fabio's bushy eyebrows knotted together in a puzzled frown. 'Whose child is it then? Are we taking in orphans now?'

'There are homes for such children,' Maria said, abandoning her preparations for the evening meal to peer over Phoebe's shoulder. 'We have enough mouths to feed as it is.'

Phoebe looked to Gino in desperation but he met her anxious gaze with a helpless gesture, which was not lost on Lorenzo who moved swiftly to his side. 'Has this anything to do with you, Gino?'

Julio clenched his fists but Fabio laid a restraining hand on his shoulder. 'Wait, son. Let Phoebe have her say.' He fixed her with a steady look. 'Whose baby is it? The truth now.'

She could not tell them of her mother's fall from grace or the true paternity of her tiny half-brother. All eyes were upon her and even Teddy had quietened as if he sensed that something momentous was about to happen. She took a deep breath. 'He is mine, Nonno.' She sent a pleading look to Gino. 'Mine and Gino's.' She flinched as her grandfather uttered a sound halfway between a gasp and a growl, adding hastily, 'But I didn't tell him about the baby before he left for Italy. I wasn't certain about my condition then, so I said nothing.' She bowed her head, unable to bear the disappointment she saw in her grandfather's eyes.

It was Gino who broke the shocked silence. He slipped his arm around Phoebe's shoulders. 'I am proud to be the father of Phoebe's baby. I've never wanted anything other than to marry her and take care of her for the rest of my life.'

There was a stunned silence, and it seemed to Phoebe that even the clock on the wall had stopped ticking. Her uncles were staring at her in disbelief and Ivy was gazing at her wide-eyed in astonishment.

'What?' Fabio's roar echoed round the house like thunder. 'You were in the family way when we left for Italy?'

Maria rushed at Phoebe and slapped her across the face. 'Whore,' she cried angrily. 'I thought better of you, but you're just like her. No wonder Annie died. It must have been of shame.'

Phoebe's hand flew to her afflicted cheek and hot

tears welled up in her eyes. She bit her lip to prevent herself from crying, but she could say nothing in her defence without giving away Teddy's true parentage.

'Hold on, Maria.' Fabio caught her by the wrist as she was about to strike Phoebe for a second time. 'This is not the way.' He glowered at Gino. 'You left her to bring a bastard child into the world.'

'He didn't know,' Phoebe protested. 'I didn't tell him.'

'I begged her to marry me before we left for Italy,' Gino said, taking Phoebe's hand in his. 'But she wanted to be sure of her feelings before she agreed to wed.'

'Her feelings.' Maria's voice rose to a crescendo. 'What about family honour? You've disgraced the Giamatti name, and you've brought a stranger into our house without our permission.' She pointed at Ivy who was cowering against the wall, her escape barred by Lorenzo who was somewhat sinisterly rolling up his sleeves as if ready for a fight.

Teddy began to howl dismally. 'Baby needs his feed, missis,' Ivy whispered, glancing nervously at Maria as if fearing she might be the next victim of her wrath. 'Shall I take him upstairs now?'

'You had to hire a woman in to feed your baby. You cannot even suckle your own child.' Maria curled her lip in scorn. 'What sort of woman are you, Phoebe? Your father would be turning in his grave if he could see you now.'

'Shall we take Gino outside and give him a good thrashing, Papa?' Lorenzo flexed his muscles, smacking a fist against his open hand.

Fabio shook his head as Julio prepared to follow his brother's example. 'There will be no violence. The deed is done. I want to know what he intends to do about it.'

'My wish has always been to marry Phoebe.' Gino gave Phoebe's hand a comforting squeeze. 'But it's up to her.'

'Not now it isn't,' Maria said angrily. 'She will wed you, like it or not.'

Fabio shot her a warning glance. 'I won't force my granddaughter to do anything she doesn't want to. It's your decision, Phoebe.'

Ignoring the others, and still clutching Phoebe's hand, Gino went down on one knee. 'I love you with all my heart. Will you marry me, and make me the happiest man in London?'

There was no doubting his sincerity, but she felt trapped. If she refused his offer of marriage she had no doubt that the baby would be taken from her. One look at Nonna's intractable expression was enough to convince her that Teddy would at best be sent to Italy to be raised by distant relations, or at worst sent to an orphanage. And Gino, who had bravely admitted fathering a child not his own, would share in her disgrace. He would be shunned by his family and his life would be ruined. She knew there was only one answer she could give him, but deep down she felt as though her world was crumbling about her ears. She had thought she could marry Gino and learn to love him as he undoubtedly loved her. She had been pleased to see him as she had demonstrated impulsively when she first saw him, but she had felt nothing deeper. His presence was comforting but did not make her pulses race. He was solid, dependable and everything she ought to want in a husband. He had lied to save her from blurting out the truth. So why could she not give him her heart? She jumped as her grandmother prodded her sharply in the ribs. 'Give him your answer, girl. Or do you want to shame your family?'

Fabio frowned. 'Let the girl speak for herself, Maria.'

'Will you be my wife, Phoebe?' Gino said softly. 'I will love you always and any other children we might be blessed with. What name did you give our son?'

'Edward,' Phoebe said automatically. 'I call him Teddy.' She took the baby from Ivy's arms and Teddy stopped crying. For a moment she thought that he gave her a gummy smile, but it was merely the onset of hiccups. Gino reached out to stroke the baby's downy head. 'He's a fine boy. I'm proud to have him for a son.'

Phoebe smothered a sigh. There was no way out for her now. Teddy's welfare must come first. 'I will marry you, Gino.'

'The sooner the better,' Maria said, turning her back on them. 'Now get out of my kitchen all of you or you won't get supper until midnight.'

Teddy's face crumpled and his mouth drooped at the corners. Recognising the warning signs, Phoebe handed him back to Ivy before he had gathered enough momentum to scream for his next feed. Ivy scuttled off in the direction of the staircase as Fabio shepherded his sons through the cellar door. 'We'll start cleaning up now and get a head start on tomorrow's work. Call us when supper is ready, Mamma.'

'Come outside,' Phoebe said, tucking her hand into the crook of Gino's arm. 'We must talk.'

'Yes,' Maria called as they left the kitchen. 'You must decide a date for the wedding.'

An April shower had just ceased as they left the house. The sun had struggled out from between grumpy grey clouds but its feeble rays barely managed to penetrate the squalor of Saffron Hill. It was not until they reached the river that it was possible to appreciate the full impact of sunlight reflected on the tea-coloured water. Gino led Phoebe to the spot on Pigs Quay where he had first proposed to her all those months ago. In the shadow of the gas works it was not the most romantic of places but it was quiet in the late afternoon. He took her gently in his arms. 'Now tell me everything, Phoebe.'

She stared down into the water as it swirled around the wooden structure of the quay wall, lapping and making sucking noises. The green weed growing on the stanchions waved rhythmically in the current creating the impression of mermaids' hair, and as she peered into the murky depths Phoebe could see pale faces staring back at her. It was like looking into a crystal ball, only now it was the muddy waters of the River Thames that were trying to tell her something. She closed her eyes. Suddenly she did not want to talk about what had happened in Brighton. She wanted to close the chapter on her mother's death and her difficulties with Caspar. What she desired most of all now was to forget the past and to move on towards the future. Opening her eyes, she met Gino's tender gaze with a smile. 'Thank you for standing by me, even though I told a dreadful lie to my family. It was wrong of me but I didn't know what else to say.'

He laid his finger on her lips. 'Hush now, Phoebe. I'd do anything for you, you know that, and as far as I'm concerned Teddy will be as much my son as any children of our own.'

'Even though he's part Paxman?' She had to be sure that he understood.

'Even so.' Taking her in a close embrace he devoured her lips in a hungry kiss. 'I want you so much, Phoebe. I can't wait to make you my wife, but I promised my mother that we would be married in Stresa. That means waiting until the autumn, although your grandparents want us to marry straight away. What do you think?'

A wave of relief almost took her breath away. 'I think it would be lovely to be married in the church by the lake.'

'And you don't mind waiting until the autumn?'

She detected a note of disappointment in his voice and she answered his doubts with a kiss. He held her close, whispering endearments in her ear in between kisses that excited her body but left a cold place in her heart. 'We will be married in Italy,' she said when he allowed her to draw breath, but it was more to convince herself that this was what she wanted than to answer Gino's question.

'And now,' he said, sitting down on an upturned crate that had been abandoned on the quay wall and drawing her onto his lap, 'tell me what happened in Brighton. Your last letter was very brief, little more than a note, when you told me that Annie had died.'

She related the facts simply and without embellishment, omitting any mention of Caspar's unwelcome advances. That was all in the past and to mention it would only upset Gino. Neither did she mention the fact that she had bumped into Rogue Paxman in Farringdon market. She omitted the fact that he had come to the house and had seen her with Teddy in her arms and that she had told him that he was Dolly's child. The web of lies and deceit seemed to be enfolding her in its silken mesh, but there were things that she felt Gino did not need to know.

Maria received the news that Phoebe and Gino were not to be married immediately with her customary fiery outburst of temper which was calmed by her less volatile husband. Fabio pointed out that the deed was already done. The child was born and thriving and it did not matter what the gossips said. Gino was prepared to make an honest woman of Phoebe, and, he added smiling, to wait several months would mean they could save for a bigger wedding at home and make their relations green with envy. Maria accepted this with the glimmer of a smile and Phoebe knew that her grandfather had won this particular battle. But she could see that Nonna was going to have the last word as usual and Maria did not disappoint. She fixed Phoebe with a gimlet eye. 'It will give you time to wean the boy before you get that way again. Me, I had Paulo nine months after our wedding day, and in less than a year Lorenzo arrived, followed eleven months later by Julio.' She stood arms akimbo. 'You see how they ruined my shape. I was a slip of a girl before my babies were born.'

Fabio slid his arms around her ample waist. 'But now I have more to hold on to, Mamma. And you were a little minx if my old memory isn't failing me.' He gave her a smacking kiss and she pushed him away, giggling like a girl and blushing.

'You silly old fool. We're past that sort of thing.' She wriggled free from his grasp, patting her hair in place. 'If you are half as happy with Gino as we have been all these years then you will be a fortunate woman, Phoebe. I suppose it doesn't matter if you wait until September to marry Gino. At least it gives me a chance to outshine Cousin Violetta, who has never stopped boasting about the wedding of her ugly daughter to that boring town clerk.'

'I'm glad you don't mind, both of you,' Phoebe said, smiling with relief. 'I thought you might want to talk it through with Gino's mother and that would end in a row.'

Lorenzo had come into the kitchen halfway through this conversation. 'Say the word, Papa, and I'll show Gino what I think of a chap who has dishonoured our little Phoebe.' He glanced at Ivy who was busy at the sink washing the last of the supper dishes. 'I would respect my woman, if I had one.'

Phoebe was quick to notice that Ivy paused, casting a furtive glance over her shoulder in Lorenzo's direction, before going back to her task with renewed vigour.

Phoebe slipped her hand through the crook of her uncle's arm. 'Any girl would be lucky to get you, Nenzo.'

He dropped a kiss on top of her head. 'Thank you, cara. But just say the word and I'll be glad to sort out young Gino. If he's refused to marry you . . .'

'No,' Phoebe said hastily. 'That's not it at all. We're going to be married in September, in Stresa. That's what his mother wants and if Nonno and Nonna don't mind then that's all there is to be said.'

Lorenzo looked to his parents for confirmation and they nodded in unison. 'Well,' he said grudgingly. 'If you're certain, but any man who dishonours a member of our family deserves to be treated like a cur. As it is, I will take Gino to the pub and buy him a drink.'

Fabio shook his head. 'We don't waste our money on cheap grog, Nenzo. We are saving now for the biggest wedding that Stresa has ever seen, and I expect you to contribute to it and Julio too, if only for the sake of Paulo who is not here to see his daughter married into a good, respectable family.'

Lorenzo shrugged his broad shoulders. 'One glass of beer is not going to break the bank, Papa.' With a last glance in Ivy's direction he sauntered out of the room calling for his brother to join him.

Phoebe could only be grateful that none of the male members of her family knew that Ned Paxman was Teddy's real father. If they were to discover the truth it would result in a terrible vendetta. There would be a blood feud such as never seen before in London. It did not bear thinking about. She went to the sink and picked up a drying cloth. 'I'll finish up here, Ivy. Go to bed. I'm sure you must be exhausted.'

Ivy shook the greasy water from her work-reddened hands. 'Ta, miss. I am a bit tired. Young Teddy wakes so often in the night.'

Maria opened the larder door and reached inside to pick up a jug of milk from the marble slab. She poured some into a cup and handed it to Ivy. 'Drink this. You're feeding my great-grandson and he needs proper nourishment if he's to thrive. I still say it's a crying shame that Phoebe can't make her own milk, but better luck next time. You probably didn't try hard enough, my girl. When you have your second child I'll be there to show you how it's done.' She replaced the jug and swept out of the room beckoning to Fabio. 'Come, it's time for bed. You have to be up at four o'clock if you're going to collect ice from the importer.'

Obediently he rose to his feet from his chair by the range. Winking at Phoebe he followed his wife out of the room.

During the next few months life slipped into an everyday routine where Phoebe did readings of the tarot cards and the crystal ball in the mornings, and conducted table tipping sessions and séances in the afternoons. With the return of the Italian community who had overwintered in their native land she found that she was increasingly busy. She employed none of the tricks that her mother had used but somehow, whether by luck or some power that she had failed to utilise in the past, she found that she could pass on messages to her eager audience from their loved ones. It must, she thought, be simply her vivid imagination and the fact that she knew most of her clients and their family histories, making it a matter of commonsense to relay good tidings from beyond the veil.

Teddy flourished and quickly became a favourite with his great-grandparents and his great-uncles. Watching them with him Phoebe could not help wondering how they would feel if they knew that he was the proverbial cuckoo in the nest, unrelated to them but being reared as one of their own. She had not seen Rogue Paxman again or his brother and she avoided going to places where their paths might cross. Gino came to call every evening after the day's work ended, but as spring turned into a hot summer and the days grew longer their time together shortened. They went for walks after supper when Teddy was asleep in the wooden crib that Lorenzo had made for him out of old packing cases. Maria had cut old sheets down to size and had spent her evenings crocheting a blanket, using wool she had bought from a market stall in Petticoat Lane. Lorenzo, Phoebe noticed, spent rather more time than she would have expected with Teddy, and when she saw him walking out one summer's evening with Ivy on his arm her suspicions were confirmed. She had seen from the start that they had a mutual attraction and she was pleased to think that her favourite uncle had at last found a woman who appealed to him. Ivy had changed almost out of all recognition from the half-starved, timid creature who had accompanied Phoebe and Teddy to London.

She had thrived on the diet of pasta and vegetables, and having lost the scrawny waif-like look she was almost pretty. Dressed in some of Annie's old clothes that Phoebe had not had the heart to sell to the dolly-shop, Ivy looked like a different woman. Her dark hair now glowed with auburn lights and Phoebe had shown her how to fashion it into a heavy chignon that complemented her heart-shaped face. She would never be a beauty, but her small features had a sweetness of expression that belied her unhappy past. Even more in her favour was the fact that she deferred respectfully to everything Maria said. She obeyed without question and never once offered an opinion of her own.

Gradually, as the summer wore on, Phoebe began to worry less about anyone discovering the truth about her small brother. He was thriving and beginning to sit up and take notice of his surroundings. He was a placid child with a happy temperament, quite unlike either of his parents, and had won hearts with his smiles and the delighted cooing noises he made when he recognised someone close to him.

Phoebe put aside her doubts about marrying Gino. His open adoration and tender kisses were a balm to her soul. She concentrated on returning his affection as best she could. What was love after all? She vowed that she would try her utmost to make him happy, but as the summer days began to shorten she knew that time was running out. Soon it would be September and the wedding in Stresa that her grandparents had spent the last few months planning and saving for. Tiny arrows of doubt pierced her heart and sometimes in the middle of the night she awakened in a panic, but with the dawn commonsense reasserted itself and she was calm again. There were no monsters. Her life would be safe and secure when she married Gino. She and her brother would never want for anything.

Phoebe was alone in the house. Maria had gone to market with Ivy, who was pushing Teddy in the perambulator that Fabio had bought from a pawn-shop around the corner in Charles Street. The men were out on their rounds selling hokey-pokey and Phoebe had no bookings that morning. She was washing some of Teddy's clothes in the stone sink when someone hammered on the front door. Thinking that it might be one of their neighbours wishing to borrow something, or perhaps a prospective client, she wiped her hands on her apron and hurried to open it. Shielding her eyes against the bright light, she stared in disbelief at the man who had his hand raised to knock again. 'Caspar.' She attempted to close the door but he stuck his foot over the threshold and with a mighty shove sent her stumbling back-wards into the hallway.

'It's taken me months to find you, Phoebe. Did you think you could get rid of me so easily? I told you that I wouldn't let you go and I meant it.'

'Go away,' she cried passionately. 'Leave me alone. I don't want anything to do with you.'

He pushed past her and strode into the front parlour as if he owned the place. She followed him, her heart thudding against her ribcage. She was as close to panic as she had ever been in her life. Caspar did not know the full story but he knew enough to make things very difficult. If he told her grandparents that Teddy was Annie's child the whole sorry tale would come out. She hesitated in the doorway, watching him as he strolled around the table, picking up the bell that she had placed in readiness for the séance that afternoon. He rang it once and the sound reverberated eerily through the silent house. 'What do you want, Caspar?' She made an effort to appear calm and in control of the situation, but inwardly she was quaking.

'You, my pet.' He replaced the bell on the table. 'I see you're carrying on where your slattern of a mother left off.'

'Get out of my house. I won't allow you to sully Ma's good name with your vicious words.'

'She's dead, and unless you can conjure up her spirit she's past caring what anyone says about her.'

Phoebe glanced nervously at the black marble clock on the mantelshelf. Nonna would be returning from market any minute now. She must get Caspar away from the house. 'Why did you come here? You must have found another assistant by now.'

'Yes, I have, but she's a silly girl with fewer brains than a fly. I want you back, Phoebe. I've got a booking at the Charing Cross theatre, and I must have a perfect act if I'm to make my mark in London.'

She shook her head. 'I can't help you, Caspar. I have responsibilities at home and I'm engaged to be married.'

He fixed her with the gaze that had always had the

power to mesmerise her. 'You don't love him, whoever he is, and you won't marry him.'

'You're talking nonsense. You know nothing of my life here.'

'But I know you, Phoebe. We worked closely together in Brighton. I understand the way you feel and think. Together we can make our fortune.'

She held the door open, motioning him to leave. 'I'm sure you will do quite well without me. I'm asking you to go now.'

'I'm not leaving until you agree to hear me out.'

The sound of the front door opening and Nonna's firm tread on the creaking floorboards made Phoebe move a little further into the room to avoid being seen by her grandmother. The squeaking wheels of the perambulator and Teddy's hungry whimpering made her glance anxiously at Caspar, hoping that by some miracle he had not heard.

He had cocked his head on one side, eyeing her like a blackbird that had spotted a juicy worm. 'Annie's little bastard. I didn't think you would have left him in Brighton with that simpleton Dolly.' He held up his hand as Phoebe opened her mouth to protest. 'It was through her that I traced your whereabouts. She couldn't tell me who fathered the boy, but she did know that your father died many years ago and that Annie had never remarried.'

Phoebe's nerves were stretched to breaking point. 'My grandmother has just come home,' she said in a low voice. 'I don't want her to see you.'

He gave her a smug smile. 'Then you will have

to listen to my proposition or I will introduce myself to the good lady. I'm sure she would be most interested to know that her daughter-in-law gave birth to an illegitimate child.' He chuckled mirthlessly. 'I just wonder how you explained the parentage of the child that you brought home from Brighton.'

She reached for her shawl. 'We'll discuss this some-where else.'

'That's the most sensible thing you've said so far.'

Tiptoeing along the hallway, Phoebe led him out of the house. She walked on ahead, fearing that one of their neighbours might see her with the tall stranger whose dandified appearance marked him out as a man of means. His charcoal-grey frock coat was impeccably cut and his pin-stripe trousers tailored to perfection. He walked with a swagger and carried a silver-topped ebony cane that must have cost a week's wage for an ordinary working man. Part of her hoped that the street arabs would mob him and steal his valuables, but they slunk away when he glared at them and hid in door-ways until he had passed by. There was something magnetic and yet menacing about Caspar Collins. She wished with all her heart that he had remained in Brighton or Bournemouth or wherever his last theatre booking had taken him.

'I could do with a glass of brandy,' Caspar said, stopping outside the pub frequented by the Paxmans.

This was the last thing that Phoebe wanted. She had intended to take him to a coffee house nearby. 'This isn't a nice place.'

'We won't stay long and I have other matters to

attend to today.' He opened the pub door and a gust of warm air wafted out laced with tobacco smoke and the odour of stale beer and sweat. She closed her eyes as memories flooded back of the times when as a small child she had been sent out looking for her mother, and had brought her home dead drunk. She was about to refuse but she caught sight of Ethel Fowler and Minnie Sykes heading their way. She knew that Ethel would neither have forgotten nor forgiven her for thwarting her plans for Dolly and she wanted at all costs to avoid a confrontation. The pub seemed the lesser of two evils.

'All right,' she said, slipping past him into the taproom. 'Just for a few minutes and then I must go.' She blinked as her eyes grew accustomed to the dim light and the smoky atmosphere. She made her way to a table as far away from the entrance as possible, where she could get a good view of anyone who came in after them, but she did not see Ned Paxman until she almost trod on his outstretched foot.

'By God, you're a stranger, young Phoebe.' His smile faded. 'Rogue told me about Annie. I was sorry to hear she'd passed away. You must miss her.'

Shooting a covert glance in Caspar's direction she was relieved to see that he was talking to the barman and not paying any attention to her. 'Yes, I do.' She made to move on but he caught her by the wrist.

'What was it that took her so suddenly? She was well enough when I last saw her.'

It was a question that she had been dreading, and when she did not answer straight away Ned eyed her curiously. 'Rogue told me she died of lung disease, but she was a tough little thing. I find it hard to believe that she could succumb so easily.'

'It was a chill,' Phoebe said, thinking quickly. 'She got wet one stormy night on the way to the theatre. The doctor said it was pneumonia that took her.'

'And my brother told me that young Dolly had a baby, and you are looking after it for her.'

'What was that you said, Ned Paxman?' Ethel Fowler's strident voice rang out behind them, causing all heads to turn and stare.

Phoebe backed into the corner as Ethel advanced on her like a warship in full sail. 'You took my little girl away from me, Phoebe Giamatti. What's this I hear you say about my Dolly?' She turned on Ned in a fury. 'Or was that just your filthy mouth, Paxman? I ain't afraid of you so don't you go scowling at me like that.'

Chapter Fourteen

'He's a bad 'un, Ethel,' Minnie said, standing well away from Ned. 'You don't want to fall foul of them Paxmans and their gang.'

'I wouldn't be surprised if you wasn't the one what seduced and ruined my little girl.' Ethel's voice rose an octave and she lunged at him, grabbing him by the collar. 'She wouldn't be the first one you've deflowered, you bastard.'

Ned leapt to his feet, shaking her off so that she stumbled against Minnie and they both fell to the floor in a flurry of dirty red petticoats, each of them exposing a large expanse of bare leg.

Caspar had been standing silently, listening to the exchange between Phoebe and Ned, but he was forced to leap out of the way as Ethel and Minnie struggled to their feet. His eyes met Phoebe's and she knew that he had overheard Ethel's accusation.

'Please don't say anything,' Phoebe said urgently.

'Sit down.' He waited until she was seated before setting a glass of port on the table in front of her. 'Drink that. You look as though you need it.' He righted Ned's chair, which had been knocked over in the fracas and sat on it, turning his back on Ned and Ethel who were now involved in a fierce row, with Minnie throwing in unhelpful comments. 'Well, Phoebe. What is your answer?'

'It's the same as before, Caspar. Nothing you could do or say would make me change my mind. I only agreed to come here because I didn't want you to meet my grandmother. You're no longer part of my life. In fact you never were. Working with you was simply a means of earning money. I didn't enjoy being your assistant and I wouldn't want to do it again.'

He downed his brandy in one greedy gulp. 'You weren't supposed to be having fun. Assisting me in my act is equivalent to helping a great artist create something wondrous and beautiful. You understood that, I think.'

'Perhaps I did, but I'm not free now, Caspar.' She tried to moderate her tone in order to placate him. She could tell by the dangerous glitter in his eyes that she was treading on quicksand.

'Then make yourself available.' He leaned across the table, breathing brandy fumes in her face. 'If you don't I'll tell those peasants behind me that it was Annie who gave birth to your brother, and judging by what I've just seen and heard it doesn't take a genius to work out who fathered the child.' He jerked his head in Ned's direction. 'I think he would be most interested to learn the truth.'

'You're mistaken,' Phoebe said urgently. 'And you don't want to get on the wrong side of Ned Paxman. He and his brother are the leaders of a notorious street gang.'

'Then you have more to fear from them than I. Give me your answer now, Phoebe, or I'll tell him your mother's shameful secret. Your life won't be worth living round here if these people discover the truth.'

She shook her head. 'I don't believe you'd do something so wicked, and I won't be bullied into working with you. Teddy needs me and I'm marrying Gino in September.'

Caspar rose to his feet. He tapped Ned on the shoulder. 'I've something to tell you, mister.'

Ned brushed his hand away. 'Who are you?'

'That doesn't matter, but I know that young Dolly isn't the mother of the child living in the Giamatti house.'

Ethel stared at him in astonishment. 'What's this cove saying?'

Phoebe stood up even though her knees were trembling violently. 'Don't take any notice of what he says. He's a madman.'

'Madman, am I?' Caspar rounded on her. 'You're the one who's been lying and duping people. Tell him whose baby it is that you're bringing up as your own.'

'Yours, Phoebe?' Ned stared at her, and his shocked expression might have been comical had the situation not been so dire. 'That's not what you told my brother.'

Ethel pushed past Caspar to grab Phoebe by the shoulders. She shook her mercilessly. 'What have you been up to? You stole my girl from me and now I hear that you're a wanton like your mother. I won't allow Dolly to live with someone like you. I want her back. D'you hear me?'

Ned pulled them apart. 'Shut up, Ethel.' He clamped his hands on Phoebe's arm, his strong fingers digging into her flesh. 'Whose baby is it? Answer me.'

246

She bowed her head and tears streamed from her eyes. 'Yours,' she whispered. 'Ma died in childbirth.'

He relaxed his hold and she sank back onto the chair, covering her eyes with her hand.

'Is this true? Are you telling me that Annie died giving birth to my son?'

She nodded. 'Please don't take my brother away from me, Ned. And for God's sake don't tell my grandfather or my uncles.'

'My son.' Ned brushed his fair hair back from his forehead in a gesture so like his brother's that for a moment it could have been Rogue staring at her as if he could not believe his ears. 'I have a son.' His hand shot out and he grabbed her by the wrist. 'Why wasn't I told of this? Why did you keep it from me?'

Phoebe wrenched her arm free, rubbing her flesh where bruises were already beginning to show. 'Because this is exactly how I thought you'd behave, Ned Paxman. Teddy is my half-brother and I wanted to protect him from you and your kind.'

'Teddy.' He shook his head. 'Who named him that?'

'My mother wanted him to be called Edward. It was her dying wish.'

'My name is Edward,' Ned said slowly. 'I was named after my father. He died many years ago, leaving Rogue and me to fend for ourselves.'

'My heart's breaking for you,' Ethel said with a sarcastic curl of her lip. 'Never mind about the Paxmans, Phoebe. Where's my daughter? I want her back where she belongs.'

'She's safe and happy and she doesn't want anything

to do with you, Mrs Fowler.' Phoebe picked up her shawl which had fallen to the floor. 'She doesn't want to come back to London. Who could blame her?'

'Slap the little trull, Ethel.' Minnie reached out to tug Phoebe's hair. 'You're a troublemaker just like Annie. You deserve a good walloping.' She dodged behind Ethel's back as Ned raised his hand to her.

'Get out of here, you harpies. If you've got a grievance against Phoebe sort it out somewhere else.' He took a swipe at Ethel but she dodged and he caught Minnie a glancing blow on the side of her head which sent her reeling.

'Very brave, hitting a woman,' Ethel hissed, backing away from him. 'I'll set me dog on you next time you come my way, Ned Paxman.' She hoisted a tearful Minnie to her feet. 'I'll get even with you.'

'Get out before I throw you out,' Ned roared, fisting his hands.

Phoebe rose from her seat to face Caspar, who had been watching with his arms folded across his chest and a smirk on his classic features. 'I hope you're satisfied, Caspar Collins. You've done your worst so don't you dare pester me any longer. I won't work for you and that's final.'

Ned turned on him, his teeth bared and his nostrils quivering. 'What have you been saying to Phoebe, mister? Her mother was my woman and I'll not stand by and see Annie's daughter bullied by a toff like you.'

Caspar's eyes opened wide in surprise. 'How dare you speak to me in that tone, my man? Do you know who I am?'

'I don't bloody care who you are, mate. If Phoebe says she don't want to go with you then that's enough for me.' Moving with the grace of a panther, he caught Caspar by the collar and the seat of his well-cut trousers and frogmarched him through the taproom, much to the amusement of the men drinking at the bar. Kicking the door open, Ned ejected Caspar from the pub with the toe of his boot. Wiping his hands together, he returned to Phoebe's side. 'Come on, ducks.'

'What?' She stared at him dumbfounded. 'Where are we going?'

'To see me son, of course. Did you think I'd turn me back on my own flesh and blood?'

Someone cheered and was instantly hushed by his companions as Ned shepherded Phoebe out of the pub without giving her a chance to protest. But outside in the street she came to a halt, refusing to move. 'You can't come to the house. My grandmother is there and she thinks that Teddy is mine. It was the only way I could explain his birth without giving Ma away.'

He studied her face, frowning. 'So you were going to keep my son's birth a secret from me forever?'

She nodded. 'You've heard of vendetta?'

'I'm not afraid of a parcel of hokey-pokey makers.'

'Perhaps you should be. It wouldn't just be my family who would come after you and your brother. There would be out and out war between them and their supporters and your gang. Do you really want that?'

He took her by the hand. 'Come with me.' He started off in the opposite direction to Saffron Hill.

'Where are we going?'

'To find Rogue. I'll not do anything without asking his opinion.'

'Please don't. Can't you just forget all about this? If it hadn't been for Caspar you would never have known.'

Still slightly breathless from the walk to the Paxmans' four-storey terraced house in Wilderness Row over-looking Charterhouse Green, Phoebe was astonished to find them living in a respectable area with a tailor's establishment on one side and a watchmaker's on the other. It was hardly the sort of dwelling that she might have expected to be inhabited by the leaders of a street gang. Visions of dingy rooms in old-fashioned rookeries would have seemed more appropriate to their nefarious calling. Even more surprising, a fresh-faced maidservant wearing a clean cotton print dress and spotless white mobcap opened the door and ushered them into the entrance hall. The gleaming oak floor-boards smelt of beeswax polish and wet dogs. This latter fact was confirmed by the sudden appearance of two springer spaniels who leapt at Ned, yelping ecstatically and bouncing about spraying droplets of water from their damp coats. At his command they came to heel. 'Follow me,' he said, beckoning to Phoebe. He strode into the front room and she was left with little option other than to comply. She could not help feeling that her place in the scheme of things was slightly lower than that of his dogs, and she might have refused such a curt order, but her curiosity was aroused.

The oak-panelled room more closely resembled a gentleman's study than the hub of a gang leader's operations. A charcoal portrait of a distinguished-looking gentleman caught her attention and his eyes seemed to follow her as she crossed the floor to where Rogue was seated behind a desk, poring over some kind of ledger. He closed it with a snap when he saw her, and rose to his feet, frowning. 'Ned. What's the meaning of this? Why did you bring her here?'

'I can explain,' Ned said, motioning the dogs to sit. They obeyed instantly, tongues lolling out of their mouths and their eyes shining as they looked up at him.

'Miss Giamatti, please take a seat.' Rogue waved his hand vaguely in the direction of two armchairs, upholstered in brown leather, set on either side of the fireplace.

Phoebe perched on the edge of the one nearest to her, feeling suddenly detached from the proceedings as if the whole matter had been taken off her hands. The truth had come out in the worst possible manner and there was very little she could do to limit the damage caused by Caspar's vindictive revelations. The brothers were talking in low voices and she found herself more interested in her surroundings than in listening to what they were saying. The ambience of the room was masculine but she could see a woman's touch here and there. Her attention was drawn in particular to four gilt-framed watercolours depicting country scenes which adorned the far wall, and the tasselled velvet curtains at the windows. 'Our mother executed those,' Rogue said, as if reading her thoughts. 'She was a lady of gentle birth and considerable talent.

Those are just a few of the paintings she did when she was a girl living in the country.'

'They're very pretty.' A vision of a blue-eyed young woman with soft nut-brown curls flashed into Phoebe's mind, but she banished it with difficulty. She must not start thinking of the Paxman brothers as being anything other than villains.

'The charcoal drawing on the far wall is a portrait of our father. A gentleman by birth and a farmer by nature, but he was no businessman.' Rogue hesitated, clearing his throat as if embarrassed by revealing too much. 'Anyway, that's not relevant to what's occurred today. I think you'd better tell us everything, Phoebe. I'm not here to judge your mother or Ned, or you for that matter, but you'd better start at the beginning and go on from there.'

Haltingly, Phoebe began once again with her mother's ill-advised visit to Snape's lodgings and their subsequent flight to Brighton. Visibly moved by her account of Annie's death, Ned paced the floor, but Rogue remained seated, his gaze never wavering from her face.

'What is this Collins fellow to you?' he demanded when she had finished her explanation. 'Why did he pursue you to London, and why did you lie to me about the boy? Why didn't you tell me that he is my brother's child?'

'I should have thought that was obvious,' Phoebe said stoutly. 'This is just the sort of situation I was trying to avoid.'

'He's my son.' Ned came to a halt in front of her. 'I have a child but you were never going to tell me.'

She looked him in the eyes and was surprised to see hurt, puzzlement and genuine distress in their blue-green depths. Teddy's eyes would be almost exactly that colour when he was older. 'What are you going to do?' she asked anxiously. 'You can't take him away from me.'

'Why shouldn't I? I'm his father. I've every right.' Ned turned to his brother. 'What do you say, Rogue?'

'That depends on you, but we can't look after an infant.'

Phoebe shot him a grateful glance. 'That's right. Teddy's just a baby. He needs proper care and attention.'

'But he's a Paxman,' Ned said stubbornly. 'I'm not having him brought up to be an Eyetie hokey-pokey maker, or worse still spirited off across the Channel never to be seen again.'

Phoebe leapt to her feet. 'You can't take him away from me. I've looked after him since he was born. I've been up at night, walking the floor with him when he's cutting a tooth. He's my flesh and blood too, and I love him.'

'But you'll marry Gino,' Rogue said evenly. 'And you'll have a baby every year. You won't have much time for my nephew. He would be better off with us.'

'Better off with two criminals? What happens when the law catches up with you? You could both end up dangling on the end of a hangman's rope. Who would take care of Teddy then?'

'It won't happen like that,' Ned said firmly. 'We keep the law sweet. The coppers won't get us.'

She turned on him in amazement. 'You mean that you bribe the police?'

Ned tapped the side of his nose. 'You never heard me say that, ducks. Now take me to that hovel you call home. I want to collect my boy.'

'No.' Phoebe faced him squarely. 'If you try to take Teddy from us you'll stir up a hornet's nest. You can't begin to imagine what vendetta does to a community. I've heard my grandfather speak of it, and it's terrible.'

Ned bared his teeth in a sarcastic grimace. 'If they want trouble, then that's what they'll get from us and it will be twice as bad as anything the Eyeties can hand out.'

'Shut up, Ned.' Rogue rose to his feet. 'This is getting us nowhere.'

'I'm not giving in to her just because she's got a pretty face, or because she's her mother's daughter.' Ned loosened his neckerchief, running his finger round the inside of his collar. 'I did care for Annie in my way.' He met Phoebe's curious gaze with a vague shrug of his shoulders. 'Yes, I know. There's no need to give me that look. I wouldn't have married a woman who was ten years older than me, but we had a good time together and I was genuinely fond of her. I may be a bad 'un but blood is blood, and I want my son.'

Phoebe turned her back on him, holding her hands out to Rogue. 'Please don't let him do this. At least wait until after I've married Gino. When we return to London next spring I'll make sure you see Teddy when-ever you want to, but please allow me to bring him

254

up in a respectable family. When he's old enough to choose I won't stop him if he wants to come and live with you.'

Rogue nodded his head slowly. 'That makes sense. I can see you're a woman of your word, Madonna. I trust you.'

'Madonna?' Ned spat the word out as if it left a bad taste in his mouth. 'What nonsense is that? Have you gone soft in your old age, brother?'

'No, I haven't. I'm using my brain, Ned. Try using yours for a change. We've got enough on our hands fending off the high mob. We can do without having the Camorra on our backs as well. If Phoebe is sincere and she'll let you see the child on a regular basis, then I say leave well alone.'

Phoebe smothered a sigh of relief. 'I will honour my promise, and Gino won't try to stop me. He knows you're the father, Ned. But he's the only one apart from us who's in possession of all the facts.'

'And Collins?' Rogue's tone was clipped and his eyes suddenly ice cold.

'I don't want anything to do with him. He'll have to find someone else to help him in his act, for it won't be me.'

Rogue met her earnest look with a hint of a smile. He turned to his brother. 'Then it's up to you, Ned. What do you say? Is it going to be war with the hokey-pokey makers or are you going to see sense?'

Reluctantly, Ned nodded. 'I suppose so. But I won't agree to anything until I've seen the boy. I want to be sure that she's telling the truth and that he is my son.'

'He's just a baby,' Rogue said impatiently. 'How will you know?'

'I'll feel it in my bones. And if he's got black hair and eyes then I'll know for sure that he's not mine. I'll take you home, Phoebe. Then you can show him to me.'

Once again, panic seized her. 'No, please don't do that. I don't want any of my family to see me with you. I'll meet you later and bring Teddy with me.'

'All right, but if you don't . . .'

'I will,' she said hastily. 'Cross my heart and hope to die.'

'That can be arranged too,' Ned said grimly. 'Bring the boy to the Charterhouse gardens then at four o'clock. I'll be there with the dogs. No one would suspect our meeting was anything but a coincidence.'

'I'll see you out.' Rogue crossed the floor and ushered her into the entrance hall. He hesitated at the front door, turning to give her a searching look. 'You meant what you said, I hope?'

'Of course. I don't lie and I don't cheat. I know that my mother really did love your brother, and I'm certain he's Teddy's father. He has a right to see him.'

Rogue opened the door. 'You're a remarkable young woman, Phoebe. I hope that Gino is worthy of you.' And to her intense surprise he took her hand and raised it to his lips. 'Goodbye, Madonna.'

Shocked by the sudden change in his attitude, Phoebe went slowly down the front steps. She started off in the direction of home and quickened her pace. She could only hope and pray that the Paxmans would keep their word, and that Ethel Fowler and her sister would be too drunk by now to remember the details of their encounter in the pub. She had reached the corner when someone grabbed her from behind and a hand clamped over her mouth as she opened it to scream.

What happened next was always a bit of a blur when Phoebe tried to recall the exact sequence of events. One minute she had been walking along, minding her own business, when suddenly she had almost been throttled by an unseen assailant. She had struggled, of course, but then everything had gone black and the next thing she knew she was lying on the pavement gasping for breath. All around her there were the sounds of scuffling, raised voices and running footsteps. Someone helped her to her feet and then, before she had completely recovered her senses, she was bundled into a hansom cab.

'You're all right now. You're safe. I'm taking you home.'

She opened her eyes and found herself leaning against Rogue Paxman. She inched away from him and leaned back against the stale-smelling leather squabs. 'What happened? Who attacked me?'

'I've never seen the cove before, but I've a feeling it might have been your magician friend.'

'Collins?' Phoebe stared at him in disbelief. 'No. It can't have been. Why would he do such a thing?'

'It's lucky that I didn't go indoors straight away or he might have succeeded in carrying you off. I assume that was his intention.'

'I can't believe he would do something like that,

especially not in broad daylight. And why were you watching me? Did you think to catch me out by spying on me?'

He shook his head, a ghost of a smile on his lips. 'Don't flatter yourself, Madonna. One of the dogs ran out into the road. He has a particular fondness for the duck pond in the gardens, and I was calling him back when I saw a tall fellow dressed in black from head to foot. It was obvious that he was following you and then he pounced.'

She frowned. None of this made sense. 'What could Caspar hope to gain by setting about me? It's not the way to win me over.'

'Perhaps he didn't care about anything other than having you for himself. I've known men do equally insane things for love of a woman.'

Phoebe recoiled at the thought. 'Don't say such things. He doesn't love me. He doesn't know the meaning of the word.'

'And you feel nothing for him?'

'Are you mad? I hate him.'

'He doesn't seem the sort who will give up easily. I can arrange to have him stopped, if that's what you want.'

'You'd have him killed on my say so?'

Rogue threw back his head and laughed. 'Nothing so dramatic. I'm not a violent man.'

'How can you say that? You're a gang leader. Your men are thugs and extort money by terrorising innocent citizens.'

'The only violence they are allowed to use is against

the high mob, who, believe me, are far more of a danger to the people we protect. I'm not defending myself, or the way I make a living, but there are others far worse than Ned and me.'

'And that makes it all right, does it? You rule by fear and you take what isn't yours.' She turned away, unable to look him in the eyes lest she weaken. There was something compelling about his personality that almost made her believe that he was doing a public service. She could not allow her defences to drop or she might be forced to acknowledge the fact that she was attracted to him, and had been from the moment they first met.

'This isn't a perfect world, Phoebe. I learned that a long time ago when my father died leaving nothing but debts. The disgrace sent my mother to an early grave.'

She turned on him angrily. 'If you're trying to make me feel sorry for you, you're failing dismally. You and your brother chose the path you've taken. You're not a stupid man; you could have done something better with your life.'

'You're probably right, but it's too late to change now. And we've strayed from the subject, which was how to protect you from Collins. I could make his life in London so uncomfortable that he would want to remove himself to a safer place.'

'Why would you do that for me?'

'I'm doing it for my nephew. I trust you to care for him like a mother, and no harm must come to you.'

'Oh!' She turned away, hoping he had not seen disappointment in her eyes. She had won her battle to keep her baby brother, but she could not help feeling that she had lost something deeper and more meaningful. In the last couple of hours the world seemed to have gone topsy-turvy. She stared out at the familiar streets packed with carts, drays and costermongers trading their wares from their barrows. Respectable house-wives brushed shoulders with prostitutes, and bankers hurried past the beggars who lolled on the pavements, holding out tin cups in the hope of attracting alms. Ragged children dodged in and out between horses' hooves and feral dogs and cats scavenged for scraps of food in the detritus piled high in the gutters. She reached up to bang on the roof. 'Stop here, cabby.'

'I want to see you to your door,' Rogue said sharply. 'Drive on, cabby.'

'No, stop, please.' Phoebe struggled to open the half-door which covered their knees. 'I don't want anyone to see us together. Everyone knows everyone else in Saffron Hill. Please, Rogue, let me go.'

His hand covered hers and he pushed the door open. 'All right, but I'll wait here until I see you safe in your house.' His fingers curled around hers for a brief moment. 'And before you question my motives yet again, just remember we're part of the same family now.'

She stared at him in surprise. 'I suppose we are. If Ned had married Ma he would be my stepfather.' She covered her mouth to suppress a chuckle. 'And you would be my uncle.'

His eyes lightened with a smile. 'I'd prefer it if we kept that between ourselves. It would ruin my reputation as a hard man if such a rumour were to get out.' He climbed down from the cab and helped her to alight, holding her round the waist for a little longer than was strictly necessary. 'You will keep your promise to Ned, won't you, Madonna?'

She was suddenly breathless. She could feel the warmth of his hands even through the layers of cotton shift, her linen and whalebone stays and the print gown she wore. Her heart was thudding against her ribcage and quite irrationally she found herself wondering what it would be like to be held even closer to him. She drew away from him on the pretext of smoothing her crumpled skirts. 'I'll be there at four o'clock, Rogue Paxman.' She lapsed into the safer area of formality, but he caught her by the hand as she started to walk off.

'I keep telling you that my name is Roger. If we're to be related I think you could call me that, Madonna.'

She shot him a glance beneath her lashes. 'I'll call you Rogue. It suits you better.' She pulled her hand free and walked on, quickening her step and lifting her skirts above her ankles as she trod through the piles of rubbish and dried mud. She knew that he was watching her but she did not look back. She let herself into the house, hoping that her grandmother had not noticed her absence.

'Phoebe, is that you?'

Sighing, she paused at the foot of the stairs. 'Yes, Nonna.'

'Come here at once, girl.'

Hanging her bonnet and shawl on the hallstand, Phoebe hurried into the front parlour where, to her horror, she saw Ethel Fowler and Minnie Sykes seated at the table where she held her séances.

Chapter Fifteen

'You wanted me, Nonna?' Phoebe struggled to maintain her calm, but she could see that Ethel and Minnie were out for trouble. The smell of strong drink and pipe tobacco clung to their persons and overpowered even the heady aroma of Nonna's lavender-scented furniture polish.

Maria rose slowly to her feet. 'We've been waiting for an hour or more for you to return. These persons have told me some bad things about you, cara. I want you to tell them they are not true.'

'I got a name, old woman,' Ethel said, bristling like an angry turkeycock. 'Me and Minnie have both got handles to go by, and we ain't telling no lies.' She pointed her finger at Phoebe. 'Ask her. She's the one who's been fibbing her head off.'

Maria fixed Phoebe with a stern look. 'What have you to say for yourself, my girl?'

Mustering every ounce of courage she possessed, Phoebe decided that attack was the only strategy left to her. 'What have you been saying, you old witch?'

Ethel stood up, puffing out her chest as if she were about to explode. 'You took me daughter away from me. You robbed me of the money old Snape was going to give me for her dowry.'

'You don't even know what that word means,' Phoebe said scornfully. 'You sold her to him so that he could use her as he wished.'

'That's as maybe, but she's still my kid. And you lied about the baby.'

Phoebe held her breath. It was all going to come out now. The family would never forgive her for her deception, let alone the disgrace that her mother had brought upon them. 'How did I lie?' she demanded.

'You told the Paxmans that Dolly was its mother.' Ethel leaned across the table, glaring at Phoebe. Her breath would have stunned an ox, but Phoebe was too relieved to allow the stench of alcohol and rotten teeth to upset her.

'Why did you say that, Phoebe?' Maria cried angrily.

'Yes, why indeed?' Minnie echoed. 'You're a wicked girl.'

'She wanted to hide her shame,' Ethel said, hiccuping. 'She didn't want Ned Paxman to know she had a nipper. I seen the way she looked at him in the pub. She wants to be his sweetheart, but he wouldn't want a trull like her. He's got more taste.'

Phoebe smothered a sigh of relief. It was becoming obvious that Ethel and Minnie had only heard part of Caspar's accusations.

'I knew it was all a pack of lies,' Maria said, moving swiftly round the table to give Ethel a hearty shove. 'Get out of here, you drunken old bitch. I won't have you and your ugly sister in my house a moment longer. Go now before I really lose my temper.'

'Don't push me, you Eyetie slut.' Ethel fisted her

hands, dancing about like a prize fighter at the start of a round, but Minnie caught her by the arm.

'Come on, Ethel. Leave them. They ain't worth the bother.'

'I ain't leaving until she tells me where to find my girl,' Ethel said, jerking her head in Phoebe's direction. 'I'm not budging from this spot.'

Maria made a move to push Ethel out of the door, but Phoebe stepped in between them. 'Dolly is safe and well. She doesn't want anything to do with you.'

'I'm her ma,' Ethel protested, working her mouth as though she was trying to summon up tears. 'I loves me girl.'

'In that case allow her to live her life as she chooses.'

Ethel recoiled like a snake about to strike. Her small eyes almost disappeared between folds of flesh as she screwed her face up in a snarl. 'You haven't heard the last of this, missis. You're a trollop just like your ma, so you can drop your airs and graces.'

'I told you to leave my house.' Maria picked up a wooden candlestick and brandished it above her head.

Minnie tugged at Ethel's arm. 'Come on. She means business.'

'All right, I'm going.' Ethel shook her fist at Phoebe. 'If I hear that you've spread spiteful rumours about Dolly, it'll be the worse for you. I got friends in the high mob and they ain't afraid of the Paxmans. Come to think of it, I wouldn't be surprised if one of them had fathered your brat.'

Maria rushed at her but Phoebe caught her grandmother round the waist before she managed to land a blow on Ethel's retreating form. 'Don't, Nonna. Let them go.'

'I'd have brained the evil woman,' Maria said, replacing the candlestick on the mantelshelf with a dull thud. Her bosom rose and fell, betraying the depth of her emotion. She gazed at Phoebe with a puckered brow. 'Was there any truth in what she said?'

'No!' Phoebe's emphatic denial reverberated round the room. She shook her head. 'Of course not, Nonna. I barely know the Paxman brothers.'

'Of course you don't, cara.' Maria wrapped her arms around her granddaughter. 'I know that, but I had to ask. You love Gino, and in September when we return home you will be married in the church of San Vittore on Isola Pescatori, just like me and Fabio were, and our parents before us.'

Momentarily diverted, Phoebe stared at her grandmother in surprise. 'But I thought the family came from Stresa.'

'Not all of us, cara. I was born on Isola Pescatori. My father and his forefathers were all fishermen. I met Fabio when I accompanied my eldest brother to Stresa to sell fish in the market there.' Maria clasped her hands to her bosom. 'I was just sixteen, and it was love at first sight.'

'How romantic,' Phoebe said, giving her a hug. 'Was it the same for both of you?'

Maria nodded, her eyes misting. She moved away to wipe her eyes on her apron. 'Yes. Fabio was so tall and handsome. After that first meeting he rowed out to the island every day to see me. We were married

265

that September, which is why I want the same for you.'

Phoebe closed her eyes and she could see the jewel-like island seeming to float on a lake of deep ultra-marine. It was a far cry from the stews of the East End, and suddenly she had a burning desire to be there beneath the benign Italian skies, with the sun on her face and the crystal clear air from the mountains in her lungs. 'I want that too, Nonna.' She wanted so much to believe that this was true. Surely all the problems that beset her in London would vanish like a puff of smoke once she was married to Gino. Neither the Paxmans nor Caspar could touch her when she was another man's wife. Teddy would have a father and she would be as good as a mother to him. They would all live happily ever after, like the characters in the penny dreadfuls that she had loved to read when she was growing up. Tales such as The Castle of Otranto, and The String of Pearls, still had the power to thrill and absorb her. All she wanted was a happy ending. Surely it was not too much to ask after the tragedy of losing both her parents and the trials that beset her now?

'Daydreaming again, Phoebe.' Maria patted her cheek as she walked past. 'I must get on with my work or there'll be no supper tonight. What time is the next séance booked for?'

Phoebe glanced at the clock on the mantelshelf. 'In ten minutes, Nonna. I must get everything ready.'

'You won't have to do this sort of thing once you're married to Gino,' Maria said with a worried frown.

266

'I don't like meddling with the spirit world. I wasn't happy with Annie doing it and I like it even less now. I'll be glad to rid my home of unwanted visitors from the other side.' She made the sign of the cross and hurried from the room as if expecting evil entities to chase after her.

Phoebe sighed. She was tired of the whole business. Sometimes she saw things that others apparently did not, but mostly she told people what they wanted to hear, just as her mother had done for as long as she could remember. This afternoon's clients were a newly bereaved widow and her sister-in-law who were squabbling over money. It was all very sordid and Phoebe could imagine the dead man turning in his grave if he could see the two women who were supposed to love him the most fighting for possession of his fortune. But where the lawyers had failed to appease both parties, perhaps a few well-timed words from beyond the grave might bring them to their senses. Phoebe sat down at the head of the table to compose her thoughts in preparation for the séance, but worries about how Ned might react when introduced to his son were still very much on her mind.

'He's a Paxman, all right.' Ned held the baby at arm's length, as if examining a thoroughbred pup. 'He's got the right colour eyes. Can't quite remember what colour Annie's were, but he's not an Eyetie, that's for sure.'

Teddy had been quiet until this point, but now he seemed to have had enough of being dangled in mid-air

267

and his mouth opened, his face reddened and he roared his disapproval. Ned chuckled delightedly as he deposited the screaming infant in Phoebe's arms. 'He's a chip off the old block. What a temper. He takes after me, of course.'

'I'm sure he does,' she said, smiling.

'I've changed my mind about letting you keep him. I don't know anything about little 'uns, but he's mine and I'm not giving him away to the Eyetie. You can marry Gino, but I'm damned if I'll allow him to bring up my son.'

Phoebe's heart lurched against her ribs. 'It won't be like that. Gino knows you're Teddy's father. He's a good man and he won't stop you seeing your son.'

Ned's attention had wandered as one of his dogs rushed off after a cat. He summoned it back with a sharp command. 'Damn dog.' He bent down to pat its head. 'Do that again and you'll get the strap.' He straightened up, meeting Phoebe's anxious gaze with a straight look. 'I want the boy. As soon as he's old enough I want him to come here and live with Rogue and me. I'll pay a woman to look after him, but I'm not going to have my kid brought up by anyone else, not even you, Phoebe. You're a good sort, but you're only his half-sister.'

Her heart sank. 'But, Ned. Think about it carefully. If the truth comes out about Teddy's birth, my family and their many supporters will pursue a vendetta against you.'

He stared at her and for a moment she thought that he had seen sense, but he shook his head. 'I ain't afraid of a pack of Eyeties, but I don't trust them either.'

Phoebe covered Teddy's head with her shawl as large spots of rain began to fall from a sudden accumulation of dark clouds. 'What do you mean?'

'They could take the boy abroad and I'd never see him again.'

'I wouldn't let that happen.'

'Marry that Gino chap and you won't have any choice in the matter, ducks.' Ned took her by the arm, propelling her out of the gardens in the direction of the house.

'I must go home,' Phoebe protested. 'Teddy will need feeding soon.'

'It's going to pour down any minute now. Come into the house and wait until the storm passes.' Ned's fingers closed into a tight band around her arm. Phoebe's first instinct was to break away from him, but it would have been impossible without disturbing Teddy who was sleeping peacefully in the crook of her arm.

The rain was coming down steadily and already she could feel the damp seeping through her cotton blouse. 'All right, but only for a few minutes. I'm leaving as soon as it stops.'

Ned opened the front door and stepped inside. 'It's just a shower. Come on in.' He held out his arms. 'Here, let me hold the boy while you take your bonnet off.'

A little reluctantly, Phoebe placed Teddy in his father's arms. She could hardly deny him a few intimate moments with his son, since they would be apart for the whole of the winter. She took off her bonnet and hung it on the hallstand. A shiver ran down her spine although it was warm in the house. She glanced anxiously at Ned but he was grinning. 'D'you know, I think I'd make a good father,' he said proudly. 'I'm beginning to think this domestic life might be just the thing for me.' He headed towards a door on the opposite side of the hall to the study. 'Come into the parlour and I'll ring for some tea. That's the right thing to do, isn't it?'

She followed him into the room on the opposite side of the entrance hall to Rogue's study, and once again was surprised by the homely atmosphere. Although the furnishings were slightly shabby and well worn, their faded elegance suggested that this must have been the domain of the lady of the house. Sun-bleached chintz curtains hung at the two tall windows overlooking Charterhouse gardens, and the sofa and armchairs were upholstered in what must once have been a deep shade of blue velvet, but were now a smoky grey with only the folds of the buttoned backs retaining the original rich hue. Ned motioned her to sit and he perched on the padded seat of the nursery fire guard. 'Ma never let anyone take this away,' he said, hitching Teddy over his shoulder as he started to cry. 'Even when we were quite old enough to know that toppling into the fire wasn't a good idea, she still insisted that it stayed. Rogue and I never had the heart to move it after she died.'

Phoebe sat on the sofa, spreading her damp skirts out around her. She sensed a genuine note of sadness in Ned's voice, and she found herself looking at him with different eyes. 'How long ago was that?'

'Ten years or so. Haven't kept a strict count.' He reached across the empty grate to tug at the bell pull. 'You'd like a cup of tea, I suppose?'

Phoebe glanced out of the window. It was still pouring with rain but she could see a break in the clouds. 'No, thank you,' she said politely. 'We really must go home as soon as it stops. Teddy will start bawling his little head off when he's hungry.'

'Can't you feed him on sops, or something?' Ned regarded her with a frown.

She sensed that there was something more than idle curiosity behind the question. He looked much more comfortable holding Teddy now than he had at first, and she felt suddenly apprehensive. 'No,' she said firmly. 'He needs a wet nurse for a while longer.'

'I'm sure there are plenty of women who would step up for the job if paid enough.'

'He's used to Ivy, and she's very fond of him. I have no reason to find anyone else.'

'But if you would stay here for a while with him, just until he's used to me and my brother, you could leave him then and not worry.'

Her initial anxiety proved to be justified and Phoebe leapt to her feet. 'Are you mad? Haven't you listened to a word I've said?'

He shrugged his shoulders. 'I told you that I ain't afraid of your family or their mates. Let them do what they like. Teddy is my boy and he's going to live here with me.'

'That's not what we agreed. You can't do this.'

He snorted with laughter. 'I'm a villain. Didn't your ma tell you that? She knew it all right and it excited her. She was a good 'un, was Annie.'

Fingers of fear clutched at Phoebe's heart. 'Yes, she was, and she loved you. Please don't do this. Think of what Ma would have wanted for her little boy.'

Ned's smile froze and he stood up, startling Teddy who began to whimper. 'She'd have wanted him to be brought up by his father. The boy won't want for nothing and you'll be well looked after too, as long as you behave yourself.'

'Me?' Phoebe backed towards the doorway. 'You must be joking. You can't mean to keep me here against my will.' She jumped as the door opened and the maidservant entered the room.

'You rang, sir?'

'Yes, Lizzie. The lady would like some tea, and cake if there is any. And send Judd out to find a wet nurse for my son.'

'No,' Phoebe cried. 'Stop this nonsense, Ned. You can't do this.'

He regarded her calmly. 'All right then, send Judd to Saffron Hill to fetch the woman called Ivy. Tell him to bring her here, but do it without alerting the rest of the household.'

Lizzie gazed at Teddy who was now crying in earnest and her eyes widened in astonishment. 'It's a baby.'

'Well done,' Ned said sarcastically. 'Now do as you're told and push off.'

'Wait.' Phoebe turned to the young servant in desperation. 'Stop, please. This is complete madness.'

Lizzie hesitated in the doorway. 'What shall I do, master?'

Phoebe took a step towards Ned, holding out her arms. 'Give him to me, please. Let me take him home now. You can't keep us here and it's unlikely that Ivy will go with a complete stranger. She knows nothing of all this.'

'But she knows who Teddy's real mother is, I'll warrant.' Ned lifted a now screaming Teddy above Phoebe's head and out of her reach. 'You can go if you like, but he stays here with me.'

'But what would Rogue say?' Phoebe saw a glimmer of doubt creeping into Ned's eyes, and she pushed home her advantage. 'He would be very angry, and he'd tell you to put Teddy's needs above your own.'

'Shall I go now, master?' Lizzie's bottom lip trembled as she shifted from one foot to the other. 'What shall I do?'

Ned thrust Teddy into Phoebe's arms. 'Good God, what a pair of lungs he has. Hold him, but stay where you are.' He waved his hand in Lizzie's direction. 'Forget what I said about Judd. Just bring tea and cake for the lady and a cup of milk for the baby. He'll drink it if he's hungry.'

Lizzie bolted from the room, slamming the door behind her.

'Bloody girl.' Ned took a small black cheroot from a box on the mantelshelf and struck a vesta. 'Maybe fatherhood ain't quite so easy as I first thought, but I'll get there in the end.'

Rocking Teddy in her arms, Phoebe made for the door but Ned was too quick for her and he moved swiftly to bar her exit. 'You're staying here, my girl. I told you, I ain't giving in to threats of vendetta.'

'They'll send out a search party,' Phoebe said, hoping she sounded more confident than she was feeling. She wished now that she had told Ivy where she was going and that she had not been stupid enough to trust a Paxman.

'This is the last place they'd think of looking, unless you told someone of your plans.' He tossed the smouldering cheroot into the grate. 'But I think you'd do anything to keep your family from finding out about Annie and me.'

'You can't keep me here indefinitely. Rogue would have something to say about that.'

Ned took her by the shoulders, looking deeply into her eyes. 'I've got the perfect solution to our problems. You're not the sort of girl I'd have chosen, and I doubt if you're half as much fun as your mother, but I'll marry you. I'll get a special licence and we'll do it all legal and above board. Your family won't be able to do a thing about it.'

Phoebe paced the floor in the attic room, trying in vain to pacify Teddy whose screams had reached an ear-splitting pitch. He was hungry, and there was nothing she could do about it. Ned had locked them in the sparsely furnished room, leaving with the promise that he would fetch Ivy from Saffron Hill. That had been over an hour ago and she was growing more desperate with each passing minute. She had been a fool to trust Ned Paxman, and soon the whole sorry story would come to light. Her grandparents would be shocked and mortified to learn that Annie had given herself to a villain and borne his child. She blamed herself for allowing sympathy for Ned to outweigh common sense. Gino would stand by her, she knew that, but even so he would be under immense pressure from his widowed mother. Phoebe had no doubt that Signora Argento would beg her son not to marry a woman whose mother had brought disgrace upon her whole family.

'Please stop crying, Teddy.' She crooned a half-remembered lullaby but, despite her efforts, he was inconsolable. Hitching him over her shoulders she went to the window and peered out. From the top floor of the house she had a good view of Wilderness Row and the gardens, but there was no sign of Ned or Ivy. In desperation she returned to the door and tried the handle again, rattling it and kicking at the lower panels in sheer frustration. The sound of approaching footsteps and the click of the key turning in the lock made her stop and take a step backwards. She hoped it was Ned who had seen sense and was about to release her, but to her consternation it was Rogue who entered the room.

'What the hell is going on?'

'Your mad brother locked me in.' She had so far kept her emotions in check but her voice broke on a sob as she clutched Teddy to her breast. 'He says he wants to marry me. I think he's lost his mind.'

'Why did he lock you in?' Rogue's tone was icy. He took the squalling baby from her. 'What's the matter with the little fellow?'

'He's hungry.' Phoebe dashed away tears of relief with the back of her hand.

'Come with me.' Rogue tucked Teddy under his arm and strode out into the narrow corridor, his booted feet clattering on the bare floorboards.

Phoebe ran after them, hardly daring to hope that this was the end of her ordeal. Teddy's cries echoed throughout the house and when they reached the ground floor they found Lizzie hovering anxiously at the foot of the stairs. Rogue thrust the howling baby into her arms. 'Take him to Mrs Warboys. She'll know what to do.' He turned to Phoebe with a grim smile. 'Cook has eleven children of her own, so I think she'll know how to deal with young Teddy.'

Phoebe opened her mouth to protest, but Lizzie had scuttled away carrying her noisy burden as if he were a valuable piece of porcelain and might shatter if dropped. 'Come into my study,' Rogue said gruffly. 'You look as though you could do with something stronger than tea.'

'How did you . . . ?' She broke off as he pointed in the direction of the parlour. Through the open door she saw the tea tray with the plate of fruitcake untouched. 'Oh, I see.'

'Your bonnet was hanging on the hallstand, for one thing.' Rogue opened the study door and ushered her inside, closing it behind her. 'And for another, Ned never touches tea and cake. Then I heard the baby crying.' He walked over to a side table and drew the cork from a brandy bottle, pouring two stiff measures. He handed one to Phoebe. 'Sit down and sip that. You've had a nasty experience and for that I blame my brother. I'm sorry.'

She sank down on the nearest chair, accepting the drink and taking a sip, which almost took her breath away. 'It's not your fault. But I'm afraid he's done something so ill-judged that it will be the ruin of us all.'

'Ned seems to have gone out. Have you any idea where he might have gone?'

'He went to fetch Ivy, Teddy's wet nurse. He's determined to keep him here at all costs, but it won't do. It just won't.'

'I'll speak to him. You mustn't worry.'

'You don't understand,' Phoebe said in desperation. 'If he's gone to my grandparents' home in Saffron Hill and demands to see Ivy, the truth is bound to come out. There'll be terrible trouble.'

'Then we'd best get you home as soon as possible.' He downed the brandy in one gulp. 'Get your bonnet and I'll fetch young Teddy from the kitchen. That's if Mrs Warboys will part with him.'

'I'll come with you. He might be scared with people he doesn't know.' Phoebe rose hastily to her feet, handing him the glass. 'I'm sorry. I don't like brandy or any strong spirits. The smell reminds me of the times when I had to help Ma home from the pub and she could hardly put one foot in front of the other.'

Rogue replaced the glass on the table. 'You've had a difficult life, Madonna. I'll try not to make it even harder for you.' He led the way out of the room and down the back stairs to the basement kitchen.

To Phoebe's surprise she found her baby brother sitting on Mrs Warboys' knee taking sops from a spoon. 'He's not weaned yet,' she said anxiously.

Mrs Warboys' plump face creased into a smile. 'No wonder he's hungry all the time. He's a fine boy and he's quite ready for a spoonful or two of sops. How old is he?'

'Six months or so. I've lost count.'

'There, then. That's what I thought. My boys were just the same and they're not much different now they're grown men. He still needs his ma's milk, of course.' She inclined her head towards Phoebe and her meaning was clear.

'Oh, no.' Phoebe said, feeling even more discomforted as the ready blush rose to her cheeks. 'I'm not his mother. I'm his sister.'

'An easy mistake, ducks. You've got the look of a little mother about you. I can see you with a brood of nippers afore you're very much older.'

Lizzie and a young girl who had emerged from the scullery with a cloth in her hands both giggled at this, but were silenced by a look from their master. The scullery maid scuttled back to her place at the sink, and the bell marked *Front Door* jangled on its spring, causing Lizzie to hurry up the stairs in response to its urgent summons.

Phoebe took Teddy from Mrs Warboys. He was

smacking his lips appreciatively having consumed at least half the contents of a bowl of bread and milk, and seemed no worse for the experience. 'Thank you, ma'am,' Phoebe said politely. 'I think you must be right.'

'I am, indeed.' As Mrs Warboys heaved herself off the chair, her stays creaked like the timbers on a sailing ship. 'You'll learn, my dear.'

Rogue was already halfway up the stairs. 'It sounds as if my brother has returned. You'd better come up and face him, Phoebe. We'll sort this matter out once and for all.'

She was trembling inwardly, but she followed him up the stairs and into the hall. It was obvious that Lizzie had forewarned Ned. He glared at Rogue as if ready for a fight. 'What's the matter, brother? Has she been telling tales?'

Rogue shook his head. 'What d'you think you're playing at, you damn fool?'

'None of your business, brother.'

'Yes, it is. What in hell's name did you think you were doing, locking Phoebe and the kid away in the attic?'

'I'm going to marry her.' Ned extracted a crumpled piece of paper from his pocket. 'Special licence. We can be married tomorrow, although I'd prefer to do it today and get it over with.'

'Give that to me.' Rogue snatched it from him. He scanned its contents, frowning. 'As I thought, Ned. You didn't have time to obtain the real thing. This is a forgery, and not even a good one. I'll bet you bought this off old Ezekiel in Five Foot Lane.'

'What if I did? No one would know the difference. Most clergymen are near-sighted from squinting at the small print in the Bible all their lives.' Ned made a grab for the document but in doing so the fragile sheet of paper was torn in two. He swore loudly. 'Now look what you've done.'

Phoebe could stand it no longer. She made for the door, snatching her bonnet from the peg as she went past the hallstand. 'You two are like a pair of hateful schoolboys,' she said bitterly. 'There's not much to choose between you, if you ask me.' She attempted to open the door but her bonnet strings had become tangled in the handle, and she was further hampered by Teddy, who was struggling with renewed vigour.

Lizzie rushed to her assistance. 'Let me, miss.'

'Stop where you are,' Ned commanded in stentorian tones. 'You're not going anywhere, Phoebe. Even if I have to tie you to a chair, you're staying here. We will be wed, and I'll get another licence in the morning.'

Chapter Sixteen

'Shut up, Ned.' Rogue stepped in between them. 'This has gone far enough. We must do what is right for the boy. From now on you'll see him when Phoebe says so, and you can forget this marriage nonsense. She won't consent to it and neither will I.'

'There you are, miss.' Lizzie had somehow managed to untangle the bonnet strings and was holding the front door wide open.

Phoebe shot her a grateful smile. 'Thank you, Lizzie.' She hurried out of the house, eager to escape from the clutches of both Paxman brothers. She could hear them shouting at each other as she ran down the street, but she did not look round. She could only hope that she would reach home before her grandfather and uncles returned from their day's trading, and that her absence had gone unnoticed by eagle-eyed Nonna.

Teddy was fast asleep by the time Phoebe let herself into the house. She paused in the hallway, holding her breath as she heard male voices emanating from the parlour. It was unusual for the Giamatti men to sit down and relax before supper as it was their habit to clean the equipment and make everything ready for their early morning start before they thought about satisfying their hunger. A trill of laughter from her grandmother aroused her curiosity even more, but she went first to the kitchen where she found Ivy deep in conversation with Lorenzo. They did not hear her at first and she was struck once again by the easy intimacy that seemed to have developed between them. It was good, she thought, to see Nenzo enjoying female company. Of her two uncles, she harboured a soft spot for kindly Lorenzo. Painfully shy with women, he seemed to have found his soulmate in Ivy. Phoebe certainly hoped so for both their sakes. She cleared her throat and they leapt apart with guilty looks that might have been comical if Phoebe had been in the mood to laugh. 'Sorry,' she murmured. 'I didn't mean to make you jump.'

'You shouldn't creep around like that, cara.' Lorenzo picked up a towel and made for the door leading into the back yard. 'I'm going to have a wash before dinner. That is if Mamma remembers to cook anything.' He strolled outside, humming a popular tune.

Phoebe handed Teddy to Ivy, taking care not to wake him. 'He's been fed,' she whispered. 'He took bread and milk and kept it down, so perhaps we should start giving him more solids now.'

'Where have you been?' Ivy asked anxiously. 'The missis was starting to fret, that is until the stranger came to the door.'

'What stranger?' Phoebe was suddenly alert, her pulses racing. 'What did he look like?'

'I dunno who he is, but he was tall and dressed all in black like an undertaker. He talked like a toff, but he had strange eyes and he scared me.'

'I'm sure my grandfather will deal with him,' Phoebe said, making an effort to appear calm. 'Take Teddy upstairs and put him in his cot, please, Ivy. He should sleep for a while.'

Ivy smiled at the sleeping baby in her arms. 'He's growing up fast. Soon he'll have no need of me.' She sighed. 'I suppose I'll have to find another place, or go back to Brighton. Not that there's anything there for me now.'

'We'll worry about that when the time comes.' Phoebe shooed her out of the kitchen. 'But don't let it bother you,' she called after her. 'I'm sure things will work out.' Alone in the kitchen, she leaned against the doorpost. Caspar. Ivy's brief description fitted him perfectly, but there could be only one reason for him to come to the house. He meant trouble. She took off her bonnet and patted her hair into place. There was little use procrastinating; she must face him sooner or later. Better go now and get it over with. If he had come to denounce her she needed to know. She squared her shoulders and headed for the parlour.

Her worst fears were confirmed when she entered the room. Caspar was sitting on the horsehair sofa next to her grandmother, who was beaming at him as if delighted by his company. Nonno was standing with his back to the empty grate, smoking his pipe and looking at ease with the stranger. He greeted Phoebe with a smile. 'There you are, cara. We were beginning to think you'd got lost. Or were you with Gino?' He gave a throaty chuckle. 'My little Phoebe is betrothed to a fine young man, Mr Collins. But I expect you know that already, as you were such good friends in Brighton.'

Caspar rose to his feet, holding his hands out to Phoebe. 'My dear, how nice to see you again. I was in the vicinity so I thought I would pay a courtesy call on you and your family.' He turned his head to smile at Maria. 'I've been royally entertained.'

Phoebe kept her arms clamped to her sides. She was not going to play his game, whatever that was. 'What do you want, Caspar?'

'Phoebe,' Maria said in a shocked tone. 'Where are your manners? Mr Collins is a guest in our house.'

'I've nothing to say to him, Nonna. We did not part on the best of terms.'

'A simple misunderstanding,' Caspar said, smiling and baring his teeth at the same time so that his expression held a hint of menace. 'I apologise profusely for anything I may have said that upset you, my dear. I am a perfectionist, as I told your excellent grand-parents. Perhaps I allow my artistic temperament to run away with me at times.'

'I think you'd better leave.' Phoebe held the door open.

'Whatever passed between you, I think you should give the man his due,' Fabio said sternly. 'You should at least listen to what he proposes, Phoebe.'

'Yes, cara. Think hard before turning down such a generous proposition.' Maria sent her a meaningful look, jerking her head towards Caspar, whose face seemed to have set in a rictus grin.

'What is it you have to say to me?' Phoebe demanded, refusing to respond with a smile.

Caspar held his hands palms upwards as if in supplication, his face frozen in the truly awful grimace. 'My dear, I need you to help me in my act. I've promised your grandparents that it is only for two weeks, which is the term of my contract at the theatre, but the young lady who was assisting me has had an unfortunate accident and cannot perform. I'll pay you well, Phoebe. Surely you can help an old friend in his hour of need?'

The warning glint in his eyes told her that a refusal would incur a swift reprisal. He did not have to put the threat into words. 'You want me to be your assistant for two weeks. Is that it?'

'You could give up these horrible séances and table tipping,' Maria said before Caspar had a chance to respond. 'You know how I hate having all that spooky business going on in the house, Phoebe. Heaven knows, I put up with it while Annie was dabbling in the occult, but it's not what I want for you, cara. And you won't be able to continue with it when you are married to Gino.'

'Well, Phoebe? What do you say, my dear?'

She glanced at her grandfather, hoping that he might disagree with Caspar's proposal, but Fabio shrugged his shoulders. 'It seems a reasonable request, Phoebe. I wouldn't approve of you going on the stage as a career, but I can have no objection to you helping out an old friend.'

'I'd like a few words in private.' Phoebe left the room, beckoning to Caspar who snatched up his top hat and followed her, pausing for a moment to offer a few words of apology to her grandparents. She waited until they were outside the house before turning on him. 'What are you playing at? I thought I made my position clear when we last met.'

'And I thought you understood that I want you to work with me. With your psychic powers and my genius we could top the bill in the most prestigious theatres in London and on the Continent. I can't do it alone, but with you at my side I could be one of the greats.'

'You're talking nonsense. I have no psychic powers. It's all a trick and I don't want to go on the stage. And I don't want to work with you.'

He set his top hat on his head. 'But you will none-theless. Or I will feel obliged to tell your charming grandparents that you are a liar and that your mother was a whore.'

Phoebe clenched her hands at her sides. Her fingers itched to wipe the smug smile off his face, but she managed to control herself. She knew now that his sanity was balanced on a knife edge. She had seen him change in a moment from the charming intelligent man he purported to be into a malignant entity who was completely beyond reason, and was more than capable of carrying out his threats. She must play for time. 'When do you want me to start?'

'That's a good girl. I knew you'd see sense. Come to Villiers Street tomorrow morning at ten o'clock. You will move into my lodgings for the duration of our contract, so bring whatever you need.'

Horrified by the overt proposition, Phoebe recoiled. 'That wasn't part of the bargain.'

'The only bargain I'm prepared to make is to keep my mouth shut in return for whatever service I require of you. Do I make myself plain?' He thrust his face close to hers, fixing her with a gaze that sapped her will. In the flicker of an eyelid she was turned into a puppet and he the puppet master. 'Do you understand, Phoebe?'

She nodded wordlessly and he kissed her on the lips before sauntering off down the street. She covered her mouth with her hand, and a shudder ran down her spine. His brief, passionless gesture of possession had felt like a threat rather than a lover-like embrace. She could scarcely believe that he wanted to own her body and soul, but she knew instinctively that to put herself in his power would be to lose everything she held dear. And he would not let her go. She knew that now. He was quite mad.

Picking up her skirts, she ran towards the house at the end of the street where Gino and his mother rented a couple of rooms. She arrived just as he was about to leave the building. His face lit up when he saw her and he held out his arms. 'Cara mia. I was on my way to see you.'

She rushed into his embrace. At least she felt safe and loved with Gino. She raised her face to receive his kiss. There was no doubting his sincerity or the depth of his emotions, but no matter how hard she tried she still could not respond in kind. When they drew apart he did not seem to have noticed anything amiss. His eyes shone and his lips curved in a tender smile. 'I've missed you too, Phoebe. I can't bear to be parted from you even for a day.'

She could not keep up the pretence that all was well, and her eyes filled with tears. 'I'm in terrible trouble, Gino. I don't know what to do.'

'My darling, what's wrong? Come in and tell me all about it.' He pushed the door open and led her into the dark and narrow hall. The smell of boiled cabbage and garlic almost overpowered the stench emanating from the communal privy in the back yard. The room that Gino and his mother rented was on the top floor of the three-storey building, and he shared a basement kitchen with another immigrant family in which they made their daily quota of ice cream. It was not, as he often said, a very satisfactory arrangement, but it meant that he and his mother could live cheaply and save money.

Phoebe followed him into the attic where Signora Argento was attempting to boil pasta over a desultory fire in the small grate. The room was hot and stuffy even though the roof window had been wedged open with an old boot. She straightened up when Gino entered and her curious expression dissolved into a pleased smile when she saw Phoebe. 'I haven't seen you for weeks, cara. This bad leg of mine makes it difficult for me to cope with the stairs these days.' She indicated her left hip, grimacing with pain as she made a move towards Phoebe. 'I can't wait to go home next month.'

'Phoebe is in trouble, Mamma,' Gino said softly. 'She needs our help.'

'Trouble!' Lalia Argento's voice rose to a squeak. 'Not another bambino on the way so soon?'

Phoebe shook her head vehemently. 'No, Signora Argento. It's not that.' She turned to Gino with a worried frown. 'Haven't you told your mother?'

'Told me what?' Lalia sank down on a three-legged stool, the only seating apart from a crude wooden bench placed beside a table in the middle of the room. 'What are you keeping from me, son?'

Gino pulled up the bench and motioned Phoebe to sit. 'Give her a chance to explain, Mamma.'

Phoebe looked from one to the other. She was fond of Lalia Argento, who never said a bad word about anyone. Lalia had always been kind to her when she was a child, and until the onset of the rheumatics in her hip she had been an active woman who had taken in washing as well as helping her son to make ice cream. They lived even more frugally than the rest of the Italian community in order to save enough money to purchase a boat for Gino, whose aim in life was to return home and become a fisherman. Making ice cream and living in the slums of East London was simply a means to an end. Phoebe knew that Lalia would make a kind and caring mother-in-law, but she could not allow her to be misled any longer. 'I thought Gino had told you the truth about Teddy,' she said, ignoring his attempts to attract her attention. 'He's not our baby. He's my brother.'

Lalia shook her head. 'I don't understand. Gino, why did you lie to me?'

'I didn't mean to, Mamma. I suppose I was afraid that once the truth was known, everyone would find out. Phoebe didn't want her mother's memory sullied by scandal.'

'So Teddy is Annie's child. Is that why you went away, Phoebe?'

'Yes, but it's even more complicated than that, Signora Argento. Teddy's father is Ned Paxman.'

'Not that dreadful gangster?'

'Yes. And he's found out that Teddy is his son. He wants to bring him up as his own, but he's not in a position to look after a baby. Anyway, I don't want my little brother to be brought up by criminals.'

'You must tell him so, cara. It is not for a man like him to have care of a tiny child.'

'I know that, and so does Ned, which is why he wants to marry me.'

Gino sank down on the bench beside Phoebe, holding her close. 'The man is mad. You're engaged to me.'

'He's aware of that, but he doesn't care. He needs someone to look after Teddy. It's not me he wants, but he knows that I love my brother and will do anything to keep him safe.'

Lalia threw her hands up in despair. 'This is terrible. What shall we do?'

'It's even worse than that,' Phoebe whispered. 'There's this man I worked with in Brighton. He's an illusionist and a magician. He knows about Teddy and he's threatening to tell my grandparents unless I do what he wants.'

Gino's fingers tightened on her shoulder and she felt his muscle tense. 'What is that, cara? You must tell me.'

Phoebe hung her head. 'He wants me to be his assistant and . . .' She broke off, unable to put Caspar's proposition into words.

'And what, cara?' Lalia asked gently. 'Tell us, please. Gino will protect you. He's a good man just like his father.' She crossed herself and her eyes filled with tears. 'My poor Antonio. He was a saint.'

'What did he say to you, Phoebe?' Gino demanded angrily. 'Tell me.'

'He wants me to be part of his stage act, and I must live with him or he'll tell my grandparents everything. I can't let these men destroy my family, Gino. What shall I do?'

'You must go away, Phoebe.' Lalia broke the silence. 'If you stay there will be open warfare between our countrymen and the Paxman gang. As to the magician, who knows what mischief he might do?'

'Mamma is right,' Gino said, nodding his head in agreement. 'I'll take you and Teddy somewhere safe. We'll go tonight.'

Phoebe rose to her feet. 'No. I can't do that. Ned wouldn't rest until he found us, and Caspar won't give up easily. He's convinced that I'm the only one who can help make his act great. He's wrong, of course.'

'And if you remain in London, what will happen then?' Lalia exchanged worried glances with her son. 'You must take her and the boy to a place of safety, Gino. One way or another, there's going to be trouble.'

Gino ran his hand through his abundant dark hair. His dark eyes were sombre. 'We should go home to Isola Pescatori. They can't touch us there.'

'But this is my home,' Phoebe said in desperation. 'I've only been to Italy a couple of times and I was very young then.'

Gino leapt to his feet and took her in his arms. 'I understand that you're scared, cara. But things will be different when we're married. I promise to look after you and I'll do everything in my power to make you happy.'

She relaxed just a little. 'I know you will, Gino.'

'Perhaps I can get a loan to purchase a boat and then we'll be set up for life. We need never return to England. You and the boy will be safe on my island, and your grandparents will retire soon. They will be close at hand in Stresa, so you won't feel like a stranger.'

Suddenly she could see her future mapped out for her, and she was even more afraid, but the doubts she harboured in her heart were something she could not share even with the man she had promised to marry. She managed a wobbly smile. 'You're a good chap, Gino. I'm a lucky girl to have someone like you.'

Lalia jumped up to embrace them both. 'You will make a lovely couple. I say we pack up and go now.'

'No, Mamma,' Gino said earnestly. 'I need you to stay here until the end of the season. You must make everyone believe that I am still here. There will be an even bigger scandal if Papa Giamatti thinks that Phoebe and I have eloped.'

'You can't leave me on my own, son. What will I do if Maria comes to my door and demands the truth? You know that I'm no good at lying.'

Phoebe moved away from them, attempting to clear her mind. Gino's plan was well intentioned, but it had flaws. They might not be planning an elopement but that is how her grandparents would see it. They would be mortified at first, and anger would follow swiftly. A rift would open up between the families, which would not augur well for a happy marriage. She turned slowly to face them. 'Mamma Argento is right. I must go away with Teddy, but you have to remain here, Gino. I'll tell my grandparents that I'm going to stay with Judy for a couple of weeks.'

'What excuse would you make for rushing off?'

'I'll think of something, but I must leave tonight.'

'Paxman isn't a man who will give up easily. Everyone knows that when he wants something he takes it, regardless of who gets hurt in the process.'

'I'm not afraid of the Paxmans,' Phoebe said firmly, but more in an effort to convince herself than to comfort Gino.

He moved to her side, taking her hand in his. 'Phoebe, think this through. It's not only Paxman, there's this other fellow, the magician. From what you say he's obsessed with you. If either of them discover where you've gone they might follow you to Brighton, and you'll have no one to protect you.'

She laid her finger on his lips. 'I don't intend to linger in Brighton. I'll move on to Dover and find a cheap place to lodge until you and Mamma Argento are able to join me. We'll travel to Italy together and by that time I hope both Ned and Caspar will have given up the search.'

'You make it sound so easy.' Gino did not look convinced.

Lalia laid her hand on his arm. 'Can you think of a better idea? Phoebe is talking sense. If you are seen to be here and you carry on as normal, everyone will assume that she plans to return soon.'

Phoebe nodded vigorously. 'Your mother is right, Gino. It's the only way, but there is still a problem.'

'What is that, cara? Tell me. I'll do anything to help.'

'I haven't any money.'

'Don't worry about that, Phoebe.' Lalia limped over to the truckle bed on the far wall. She slipped her hand under the straw-filled palliasse and brought out a leather pouch.

'My boat money, Mamma.' Gino stared at her in horror. 'I've saved every penny I could so that I could build up a business, and give us a better life.'

'And what future will you have if Phoebe is spirited away by the Paxman gang, or becomes embroiled with that magician fellow? How will you comfort her if her brother is taken from her to be raised by villains, and her disgraced family call for a vendetta?'

He held up his hands as if defeated by his mother's logic. 'Take it, Phoebe. Mamma's right, as usual.'

She hesitated. It was tempting but she had seen the look on his face, even if it was fleeting, and she knew how much the fishing boat meant to him. She shook her head. 'No. Keep it, please. You can't give up your dream because of me and my family.'

'I'm nothing without you, Phoebe.' He took the purse from his mother and thrust it into Phoebe's hands, closing her fingers over the soft leather. 'You are more important to me than anything. We'll manage somehow once we get home. I can work for my Uncle Marco. He's always wanted to take me on.'

Lalia wiped her eyes on her none-too-clean apron. 'Take it, cara. You have my blessing. You will be the daughter I never had, and little Teddy will be my first grandson. One of many, I hope.'

Phoebe gave her a hug. 'I'll be careful with the money, Mamma Argento.' She turned to Gino with a rueful smile. 'I must go now. I have to leave tonight.'

'Let me at least take you to the station, cara.'

'No. We mustn't draw attention to ourselves. I'll send word when we're settled in Dover.'

He followed her to the door. 'I'll see you home.'

'No, don't do that. You should stay here with your mother.' Phoebe kissed him on the cheek. 'I'll send word as soon as I can, I promise.'

He seized her in a passionate embrace. 'Be careful, my darling. I'll be thinking of you every minute of every day that we're apart.'

She broke away from him and hurried from the room. Tears flowed down her cheeks as she negotiated the steep staircase, but it was not the prospect of being parted from Gino that made her feel so wretched: it was something deeper than fear of vendetta or the machinations of Caspar Collins. She paused on the first floor landing, shuddering as a rat ran across her feet. She had seen many such vermin every day in Saffron Hill, but it was not that which made her suddenly breathless, nor was it the impending flight from London that terrified her. She closed her eyes and saw dark water and heard the sound of waves crashing on the shore. She felt a sharp pain in her chest as though someone had stabbed her through the heart, and she opened her eyes. There was nothing to see other than the dank stairway with plaster flaking from the walls and spiders' webs hanging from the blackened ceiling. She ran down the remaining stairs and burst out of the front door into the street.

Outside it was even hotter and the stench from the rubbish-filled gutters was appalling. The dilapidated buildings leaned on each other for support and grimy windows gazed blindly onto the street. Swarms of flies turned piles of horse dung into heaving masses and two mangy curs were fighting over a bone. She could hear the familiar metallic clatter of iron wheels on iron rails, and the screech of brakes accompanied by a burst of steam as trains pulled into the Metropolitan Railway terminus in Victoria Street. The smell of burning coal from the engines mingled with the acrid odour of soot and the stench of blocked drains was a familiar but unpleasant fact of life in Saffron Hill. Then the clock on St Peter's church in Cross Street struck seven and she knew she was late for supper.

All these sights, sounds and smells had been part of her existence for as long as she could remember. This was home. She stepped aside to avoid treading on the feet of a homeless person, male or female, it was impossible to tell which, who was slumped in a shop doorway snoring beneath a pile of old newspapers. She walked on, the gnawing pain in her heart growing fiercer with each step she took. Why was she feeling like this? What was it that made her so afraid? She paused, stopping to pick up the broken head of a flower that must have been discarded by a street seller. She plucked one white petal from the marguerite and let it fly away on the cool east wind that had come in with the tide. 'He loves me.' She pulled another and watched it flutter to the ground. 'He loves me not.' She could not stop until she held the sunny yellow centre of the flower in the palm of her hand. 'He loves me.' But it was not Gino's face she saw in her mind's eye. She tossed the remains of the daisy over her shoulder. This was the truth that she had denied until now. This was the dark secret she had hidden from herself for so many weeks. Now she was even more afraid. Everything was revealed to her in a split second of utter madness. It was Rogue Paxman who had claimed and now owned her heart. She had no choice in the matter. She loved him even though he had never shown anything but a passing interest in her, and despite the fact that his way of life repelled her. The Paxman gang had been the cause of her father's death, even if they had not actually fired the shot that killed him. Ma had died giving birth to Ned's son, and it was unthinkable that she, Phoebe Giamatti, would even consider giving herself to a man who had caused her family so much pain and distress.

She gazed up at the unbroken blue of the summer sky. 'Ma, if you're up there,' she whispered, 'please help me to do the right thing.' She broke into a run and did not stop until she reached home. Bracing her shoulders she went inside to prepare Ivy for an un-expected journey, and to tell her grandparents that she had received a telegram from Judy saying that she was unwell and needed someone to run the boarding house for a week or two. Phoebe knew she ought to feel guilty for lying to them yet again, but she was desperate.

Chapter Seventeen

It was almost midnight, and Phoebe had trodden this path before. With a sleeping child in her arms she climbed the front steps of Judy's house, followed by Ivy at a slower rate, burdened as she was with a portmanteau in each hand. A hunter's moon illuminated the scene around them, sending a silvery satin pathway across an inky velvet sea, but Phoebe was too exhausted to fully appreciate the ethereal beauty of the scene. She raised the doorknocker and let it fall.

'They're probably all asleep,' Ivy said pessimistically. 'I daresay Miss Judy won't be too pleased to see us at this time of night.'

Phoebe knocked again. This time she was rewarded by the sound of footsteps pitter-pattering along the tiled hallway. The door opened halfway to reveal Judy clutching her dressing robe with one hand and holding an oil lamp in the other. She was quite obviously ready for bed as her hair was tied up in rags. She did not look overjoyed to see them. 'We've been here before,' she said, opening the door wide. 'Come in, for goodness' sake. I don't want the neighbours to think I take in fallen women.'

'That was uncalled for,' Phoebe protested as she carried Teddy into the house. 'I'm sorry if we disturbed you, and I know it's an imposition, but could you put us up for a couple of days?'

Ivy staggered in after her, dropping the bags on the floor with a sigh of relief. 'I couldn't have carried them another step further.'

'Well you'll have to move them from there,' Judy said with a disdainful sniff. 'I can't have my hallway littered with luggage. My paying guests get up early in the morning. It's the summer season, you know. We're full. Even the attic rooms are taken, so you'll have to sleep on the sofa in the parlour. One of you will have to use a chair.'

Phoebe had not expected to be welcomed with open arms; that was not Judy's way, but she had hoped for a comfortable bed. 'Well, it's more important to find somewhere for Teddy to sleep. I'm sure Ivy and I can manage.'

'You'll have to, I'm afraid.' Judy led the way into the parlour. 'I can spare some blankets and a couple of pillows. You can empty a drawer for the baby.' She held the lantern above his head and peered at him. 'He's grown.'

'Babies have a habit of doing that,' Phoebe said wryly. 'But thank you for taking us in. We'll try not to get in the way.'

'Here, give the little 'un to me. I'll see to him.' Ivy took Teddy in her arms. 'I don't suppose there's any chance of a cup of tea, is there?'

Phoebe glanced anxiously at Judy. 'I could make some for all of us, and then I can explain why we've had to bother you like this.'

'I doubt if the water in the kettle is hot enough, but it'll do for cocoa. Help yourselves. As to the details, you can tell me those in the morning. I have to be up at six.' Judy left the room, returning moments later with an armful of blankets and two pillows. She picked up the lamp. 'I'll take this. You may light a candle but just one. I'm not made of money.'

'We can pay our way,' Phoebe said hastily. 'I don't expect charity.'

'Help yourself to some bread and cheese if you're hungry, but don't make a noise.' Judy closed the door behind her, leaving them to their own devices.

Phoebe lit a candle. 'I'll get us something to eat and drink.'

Teddy opened his eyes with a cry of protest as Ivy laid him down on the sofa. 'I'll give him a feed,' she said, slipping off her shawl and unbuttoning her blouse. 'But I won't be able to carry on much longer, Phoebe. My milk's drying up. You won't have need of me then.' She sat down on the sofa and put Teddy to her breast. Phoebe saw a tear run down Ivy's cheek and she felt suddenly guilty. She had not given any consideration to what Ivy might want for herself, despite the fact that she had known of the deepening relationship between her and Nenzo. She had commanded and Ivy had obeyed like a well-drilled foot soldier.

'You don't have to stay with us, Ivy,' Phoebe said slowly. 'I'll understand if you want to return to London. Uncle Nenzo will be very upset when he discovers that you've gone.'

'Do you really think so?' Ivy looked up at Phoebe, her eyes magnified by tears. 'I mean, I'm not the sort of woman your grandmother would want her son to marry.'

'Nonsense. Nenzo is a lucky man to have someone like you, and Nonna will want him to be happy. All I ask is that you stay for a few days until Teddy is fully weaned and can take cow's milk. Then you must return to London, or we'll have Nenzo on the doorstep looking for you.'

'Ta, Phoebe.' Ivy's sad expression melted into a smile. 'If I marry Nenzo, I'll be your auntie. How about that?'

'Shut up and feed the baby,' Phoebe said, chuckling. 'I'll go and make the cocoa.'

Next morning Phoebe was awakened by the door bursting open to admit Rose followed by Gussie and Dolly.

'Darling Phoebe. What a wonderful surprise.' Rose rushed over to her and gave her a hug. 'What are you doing back in Brighton?' She glanced over her shoulder at Ivy's sleeping form on the sofa with Teddy clutched in her arms. 'And look at Teddy. How he's grown.'

Ivy opened her eyes and sat up, still cradling Teddy as if he were the most precious thing in the whole world. 'What's all the fuss about?'

'We're just pleased to see you, Ivy,' Rose said, smiling. 'It's such a surprise to wake up and find you all here again.'

Dolly nudged her aside to cuddle up to Phoebe,

laying her head on her shoulder. 'I've missed you. It ain't the same here when you're gone from us.'

Phoebe suppressed a shudder as she recalled Ethel's vicious expression when she had demanded the return of her daughter. The thought of Dolly falling into her mother's clutches was enough to make her blood run cold. She gave her a hug. 'I've missed you too, but I thought you were happy here with Judy.'

Dolly raised her face and smiled. 'Yes, I am, and I love Miss Judy. She's been ever so kind to me. But that don't stop me wishing you was here too.'

'Well, I am now. So that's all right, isn't it?' Phoebe looked up to see Gussie, standing arms akimbo, staring at her with a puzzled frown.

'What's it all about, girl? Are you in trouble again?'

'It's a long story,' Phoebe said wearily. 'But it's good to be here again.'

'Tell us everything.' Rose's eyes shone with excitement. 'This is so wonderful. I thought we'd lost you forever.'

Gussie moved closer to the sofa, staring down at Teddy with a tender smile on her face. 'Look at the little lamb. Isn't he a picture? Those golden curls make him look like an angel.'

Ivy curled her lip. 'You won't think him such a cherub when he starts bawling his head off. This little gent has lungs like a town crier.'

Dolly left Phoebe's side. 'Can I hold him, Ivy? I'll be ever so careful.'

Phoebe stretched and rose stiffly to her feet. 'I'm sure you will, but let Ivy see to him first.'

Dolly knelt down, stroking Teddy's tiny hand. 'I think he's a poppet. I'd like one just like that.'

'You wait until you see him in one of his crabby moods,' Ivy said, shaking her head. 'You'll change your tune then, young lady.'

'I can't wait to tell the others that you're here.' Rose slipped her arm around Phoebe's waist. 'Poppa and I have to go out early to set up the booth on the beach, but we'll have plenty of time to talk later. How long are you here for, Phoebe?'

'Just a few days. I'll tell you all about it when we have time.'

'You weren't going to leave me out, I hope.' Madame Galina's huge bulk almost filled the doorway. She sailed across the floor to push Rose aside in order to clutch Phoebe to her bosom. 'Fred and Herbert are in the kitchen and they're dying to see you again. The wretched Chinese tumblers are moving out today so the attic room will be vacant. Good riddance to them I say, with their foreign food and chopsticks. Who but a heathen would eat with knitting needles?' She kissed Phoebe on both cheeks before plumping down on the sofa beside Ivy.

Disturbed, Teddy opened his eyes and stared up in wonder at Gussie who was still hovering close by. She snatched him up in her arms, cuddling him and laughing when he tugged at her gold earring. 'Come with Auntie Gussie, my little love. I'll get you some milk for your breakfast, and some bupper.'

'For God's sake use the proper terminology,' Madame Galina said crossly. 'Do you want the child to grow up talking rubbish?'

'He's just a baby.' Gussie rocked Teddy in her arms. 'Who's a beautiful little boy, then?'

'If you talk to him like that he'll turn into an idiot or a molly-boy.' Madame Galina struggled to her feet and attempted to wrest him from Gussie's arms, but was instantly repulsed.

'Go away. Let me hold him for a while. You think you know it all, but you don't. The little chap likes me. See how he smiles at me. You'd scare him, you old war horse.'

Ivy jumped up and for a moment it looked as though all three of them were going to have a tug-of-war over the unfortunate Teddy. Phoebe was amused but also a little alarmed. She did not want to see her brother pulled apart by three broody women, and she moved in swiftly when he started to cry. 'I think Ivy had better give him his first feed,' she said calmly. 'We're going to wean him but it should be done slowly, don't you think?'

There was a murmur of assent and reluctantly Madame and Gussie retreated to the kitchen, still arguing over who was the best qualified to look after a baby.

Rose burst out laughing. 'The house hasn't been the same without you, Phoebe. I've missed you so, and I can't wait to hear what's been going on in London. Have you seen the dreaded Caspar? He came here and unfortunately got hold of Dolly, who gave him your address. There was nothing we could do about it.'

Phoebe passed Teddy back to Ivy. 'Yes, I know. It's part of the reason why we're here.'

'Rose.' Hector's voice echoed round the hallway. 'Rose, come and get your breakfast or you'll go without. It's a fine day and I want an early start.'

'I have to go,' Rose said apologetically. 'Come to the beach by the south pier at midday. We have a short break then and you can tell me all. In the meantime, let's get something to eat. I'm ravenous. Come along, Dolly. I'm sure you must be hungry too.'

With a reluctant backwards glance at Teddy, who was now firmly latched on to Ivy's breast, Dolly followed Rose from the room. Phoebe smoothed her hair in place and shook out her crumpled skirts. She had been too tired to unpack her nightgown when they arrived and had fallen asleep in the armchair fully clothed. 'I'll bring you a cup of tea, Ivy,' she said, pausing in the doorway. 'Then I'll take care of Teddy while you get something to eat.'

Ivy pulled a face. 'He's got two teeth already. I'll not be sorry to see him weaned, although I love the little man like he was my own, dear dead child.'

'You'll have more babies,' Phoebe said gently. 'If you decide to marry Nenzo you'll probably have one a year.'

'I don't think your grandparents would like it if they found out that I was deserted by my common-law husband. I think Signora Giamatti would think ill of me if she found out that I'd had a child out of wedlock.'

'Nonsense. You're as good as any of us, and Nonna has been longing for more grandchildren. She'd be even more heartbroken if she discovered that Teddy is not a Giamatti.'

Ivy's lips trembled. 'Anyway, I told Lorenzo about

my past and he said he didn't care, but he hasn't asked me to marry him, and maybe he never will.'

'Then more fool him,' Phoebe said stoutly. 'But you must return to London as soon as possible. It was thoughtless of me to bring you here like this. I'm sorry, Ivy.'

'If he wants me, he can come and get me. I never had to chase after a man, and I ain't going to start now. I'll not leave you and Teddy in the lurch.'

'You're a brick,' Phoebe said with a grateful smile as she left the room. She hurried to the kitchen but came to a sudden halt when she saw Marcus White seated at the head of the long table. He rose to his feet as she entered the room. 'My dear, Phoebe. Judy told me that you'd arrived late last night.'

Judy bustled over to the table carrying the large black saucepan filled with porridge. She ladled some onto his plate. 'Hush, Marcus. There's no need to tell the whole world that you slept in my bed.'

He threw back his head and laughed. 'Why not? I intend to make an honest woman of you the moment you say yes. What d'you think of that, Phoebe?'

'I think it's marvellous. I couldn't be happier for you both.' Phoebe went to hug Judy but the steaming saucepan was in the way and she patted her on the shoulder instead. 'Why didn't you tell me before?'

'Are you hungry or not?' Judy slapped a ladleful of porridge onto a clean bowl. 'I'm all behind like the cow's tail this morning, thanks to those confounded Chinese tumblers. They insisted on cooking for themselves.' She wafted her hand in front of her face. 'I can't get rid of the smell of foreign food, no matter what I do.'

Marcus took the saucepan from her, pressing her down on the seat next to his place at table. 'Never mind them, my dear. You must eat something yourself. You spend far too much of your time looking after others. Now it's my turn to take care of you. Name the day, Judy, and we'll be married.'

Rose clapped her hands and Dolly almost choked on a mouthful of hot tea. Madame Galina and Gussie stared open-mouthed. Hector paused with a slice of toast halfway to his mouth, and Fred covered his face with his handkerchief, his shoulders shaking. Phoebe was not sure if he was laughing or crying. She had not realised that he too had feelings for Judy, who had always seemed to be a dedicated spinster. 'It's wonderful,' Phoebe said, patting Marcus on the shoulder. 'You were made for each other.'

'I'm a truly happy man,' Marcus said, beaming.

Judy glared at him. 'I haven't said I would. I don't call that a proper proposal either. Just because I allow you certain privileges, Marcus White, doesn't mean that I'm going to shackle myself to you for the rest of my life.'

Phoebe and Rose exchanged anxious glances, and it seemed that everyone else held their breath, but Marcus appeared to be unabashed. He went down on one knee, taking Judy's hand in his. 'My dearest, will you do me the honour of becoming my wife?'

The silence in the room was almost unbearable. Phoebe hardly dared breathe for fear of missing Judy's answer.

'Oh, get up, you silly man,' Judy said at last. 'Those wretched Chinamen dropped noodles on the floor. You'll ruin your trousers.'

'I want an answer, Judy. I'm not moving until you say yes.'

Judy's thin lips curved in a smile. 'All right, then. Yes, I suppose I'll have to marry you, if only to stop you making a complete fool of yourself.'

There was a sharp intake of breath all round and then everyone started clapping. Marcus rose from his knees and wrapped his arms around Judy, kissing her on the lips. She responded with a passion that surprised Phoebe, but then she pushed her new fiancé away and picked up her spoon. 'Eat your porridge before it gets cold, Marcus. I'm not making another batch.' She looked up at the smiling faces. 'What are you all staring at?'

Phoebe bent down to kiss her cheek. 'I'm so happy for you.' She turned to Marcus with a smile. 'Congratulations. I know you'll make a wonderful couple.'

He nodded in agreement. 'So do I, my dear Phoebe. Tonight we'll celebrate. I'm inviting you all to the pub which Madame Galina graces by her presence. We'll have a party that will be remembered for years to come. What d'you say to that, Herbert, old man? And you, of course, Fred.'

Herbert puffed out his chest. 'I say you're on.'

Fred mopped his eyes with his red and white spotted hanky. 'My loss is your gain, Marcus. The better man won the fair lady.'

'I wish someone would fight for my hand,' Gussie

murmured, bowing her head. 'I'm doomed to be an old maid.'

Madame Galina, who was seated beside Fred, nudged him hard in the ribs. 'Here's your chance, you old codger. You could do a lot worse than her.'

He leapt to his feet and rushed from the room, muttering something about being late for work, and Madame Galina doubled up with laughter that echoed round the room. 'Silly man,' she wheezed. 'I was only teasing him.'

'You don't know when to stop,' Gussie said crossly. 'You've upset him and I won't be able to look him in the eye again.'

'Why won't you?' Dolly asked innocently. 'I don't understand.'

Rose reached across the table to pat her hand. 'It's not important, dear. Why don't we ask Phoebe to tell us what's been happening to her in the big city? I'm sure we're all dying to know.'

A murmur of assent rippled round the table and Phoebe was left with no alternative but to begin her story from the time she left Brighton until the moment she returned.

'That Caspar is a wicked man,' Rose said with an exaggerated shudder. 'I can't think what I ever saw in him.'

Hector cleared his throat noisily. 'It sounds as though you've had a lucky escape, my dear girl. You did the right thing in returning to us, your true family.'

Judy rose to her feet, ignoring Marcus who begged her to relax and let someone else do the work for a change. 'Since you're going to be here for a while, Phoebe, I'll expect you to do your share of the chores, as before. You start by making sure that Dolly clears up the breakfast things and leaves the kitchen in its original state. I'm going to market.'

Marcus pushed back his chair and stood up. 'But, my love, we've just become engaged. I thought you would want to come with me to choose a ring.'

Judy's eyebrows shot up to her hairline. 'Waste of money. What would I do with a diamond ring? Getting married won't change anything. I'll still run the guest house and you'll go to the theatre every day. We will carry on just as before.'

'But, my dove, surely we could spend a few hours together. Even if you don't want a ring, we could go and see the vicar and arrange for the banns to be called.'

'You can do what you like,' Judy said calmly. 'But I'm going to market before it gets so hot that everything is on the turn.' Snatching her bonnet and shawl from the peg behind the door, she left the room, which seemed to be a signal for the others to depart and go about their daily business.

Leaving Dolly to clear the table, Phoebe took a bowl of porridge and a cup of tea into the front parlour for Ivy. She set the tray down on the small table in the bay window. 'I'll change him,' she said, pulling out a chair. 'Come and get your breakfast while it's still hot.'

Ivy hitched the baby over her shoulder, patting his back until he emitted a satisfactory burp. 'Ta, I won't say no. I'm starving.' She rose from the sofa and handed Teddy to Phoebe. 'He'll be hungry again soon. As I told you, me milk's drying up. You'll need to get a pap boat for him to sup from.' She sat down and began tucking into the porridge with a will.

'A pap boat? What's that?' Phoebe's knowledge of babies was limited and she was beginning to wish that she had asked more questions of her grandmother.

Ivy made a motion with her spoon which Phoebe thought must represent the mysterious pap boat. 'It's a china dish with a spout for feeding babies soft food. I expect Miss Judy has one tucked away in a cupboard somewhere. She must have had lodgers with infants staying here at one time or another. We'll manage somehow.'

Phoebe took a seat, setting Teddy on her knee. 'I don't know what I'd have done without you, Ivy, but you must return to London when you see fit.'

Ivy swallowed a mouthful of porridge. 'I'll stick with you and Teddy no matter what. Like I said before, if Lorenzo wants me, he can come looking. We'll see this thing through together.'

The next few days passed pleasantly enough, although nagging worries pursued Phoebe wherever she went. If she walked along the promenade and stopped to watch Herbert's Punch and Judy show, she would find herself looking over her shoulder and studying faces in the crowd. She did not know who she feared the most, Ned or Caspar, but she was certain that one of them would eventually come looking for her. She knew she must move on but she was loath to leave the people who had come to mean so much to her. She had been happier in Brighton than she had in London, but she knew that this period of respite would soon end. She must move on to Dover and wait for Gino to join her. It would be safer there, but she would miss everyone here and Rose in particular. They had picked up where they left off and it was such a relief to have someone who knew what Caspar was really like, and who understood the threat that he posed. Phoebe knew that the time was coming to depart, and yet she kept putting it off.

She was sitting in the parlour one evening with Rose. It had long been cleared of her personal belongings, which were now arranged neatly in the attic room vacated by the Chinese tumblers. Judy had gone to the theatre with Marcus and everyone else, except Dolly who was curled up in a chair sound asleep, had gone to Madame Galina's pub where a musical entertainment had been laid on. Phoebe had not felt in the mood for such gaiety and she had volunteered to stay behind and look after Teddy. Rose had also opted to remain, and they sat side by side on the sofa, drinking cocoa and chatting in soft voices so as not to disturb Dolly.

'Why do you have to go to Italy?' Rose whispered. 'You don't have to marry Gino. If you don't truly love him it would be unfair on both of you.'

'He loves me,' Phoebe said simply. 'He's been so good to me throughout this nightmare time, Rose. I couldn't break his heart, and he's told everyone that he's Teddy's father. When Gino and I are married Teddy will be safe from Ned Paxman. He won't be able to take him from me.'

'I wouldn't count on that,' Rose said, shaking her head. 'And think of the boy. Is it right to bring him up thinking he's more than half Italian when he's English through and through? One day he's sure to discover the truth, and he won't thank you for keeping it from him.'

'But I can't give him away to the Paxmans. I won't allow them to turn my little brother into a criminal.'

Rose angled her head. 'There's something you're not telling me. What is it? Every time the Paxmans' names come up you get that closed look on your face.'

'It's your imagination. If I appear unwilling to talk about them it's because I despise the way they live and what they stand for. I hate everything to do with the Paxman gang. They're educated men and they ought to know better.' She stood up, turning away from Rose in case she betrayed her innermost feelings. She thought she had conquered what must surely be a girlish crush on Rogue Paxman, but in her heart she knew that it was not so. She had read somewhere that women were always attracted to bad men, but she was determined to ignore the tender emotions he aroused in her breast. 'I'm going to make some more cocoa,' she said abruptly. 'Would you like some, Rose?'

The kitchen seemed oddly quiet and deserted as Phoebe set about her task. The long pine table where everyone ate their meals was scrubbed clean, and even in the light of a single candle it gleamed silvery-white like animal bones washed up on the Thames foreshore after a particularly high tide. The empty chairs seemed oddly creepy, as if occupied by invisible spirits of long

314

deceased inhabitants of the house that came out only at night to reclaim their old home. Phoebe shivered despite the fact that it was a warm night and there was heat radiating from the range. She poured hot milk onto the cocoa powder that she had already mixed to a paste and added a spoonful of sugar to each cup. She was about to carry them through to the parlour when the sound of someone tapping on the window made her spin round. She could just make out the shape of a male figure peering in from the side street. He rapped on the windowpane again, and with a cry of fright she dropped the mugs. They shattered into shards on the tiled floor.

Chapter Eighteen

For a moment she felt as though her heart had stopped beating. Her first instinct was to panic and scream for help, but there was something familiar about the shape of the man's head, and whoever it was had his finger to his lips as if begging her to remain silent. Stepping over the spreading pool of dark chocolate she moved closer to the window as if drawn by an invisible thread. This time her heart gave an uncomfortable jolt against her ribs, and her breath hitched in her throat. She raced through the scullery to open the back door. It led into a tiny back yard surrounded by a six foot brick wall. The moon had suddenly vanished behind a bank of clouds, and in her hurry to reach the side gate she stumbled over unseen objects left carelessly on the ground. Her fingers trembled as she lifted the latch and opened it a crack. 'Who's there?'

'It's Roger Paxman. Let me in, Phoebe.'

All thoughts of him as the enemy were dispelled by the sound of his voice. She wrenched the door open and stood aside to let him in. 'What d'you want?' She spoke brusquely in order to disguise the ridiculous sense of relief that threatened to overcome her, together with a guilty pleasure on seeing him again. 'How did you know where to find me?'

He entered the yard, closing the gate behind him. 'I need to talk to you urgently.'

His tone was harsh, and although she thought that she detected a note of anxiety in his voice, there was nothing about his manner to make her suppose that he was pleased to see her. She was both ashamed and embarrassed by her instinctive reaction. 'Come inside.' She led him into the scullery. Once indoors with the back door securely fastened, she felt much safer. 'Well, what is it you have to say to me?'

He glanced round at the whitewashed walls and the stone sink with its wooden draining board. The smell of rancid cooking fat mingled with the faint odour of mouse droppings. 'Might we go somewhere a little more comfortable?'

'I was just making some cocoa.' As soon as the words left her lips she realised that it was a rather silly thing to say to someone who might be about to kidnap her brother, but she was at a loss as to how to handle her unexpected visitor. She was not thinking clearly. Her pulses were racing and she could hear the blood drumming in her ears. She hurried into the kitchen, but his close proximity in the semi-darkness almost took her breath away.

In an attempt to cover her confusion she busied herself picking up the broken china and mopping the sticky mess off the floor. 'Judy hates a mess,' she said breathlessly. 'She's my cousin and she owns this house.'

Rogue took the mop from her and set it aside. 'Never mind that now. I'm sure it can wait until morning.'

She shivered as their hands touched briefly. 'Judy is very particular.' She knew she was talking nonsense but his sudden appearance had completely thrown her. 'Why are you here, Rogue?'

'Who else is in the house?'

'Everyone is out except Dolly and my friend Rose.'

'Can they be trusted?'

'Of course, but what's this all about?'

'You're in great danger. I came to warn you.' He pulled out a chair. 'Please sit down and listen to what I have to say.'

She could tell by his expression and his tone that he was in deadly earnest, and she sank down on the hard wooden seat. 'What's happened? Why have you come here? You still haven't told me how you knew where to find me.'

'I had you followed.'

'You what?'

'I did some checking on Collins. Believe it or not, I have friends in the police force. Although we operate on different sides of the law, sometimes it suits us both to cooperate, especially when it comes to the more dangerous members of the high mob.'

'You spied on Caspar?'

'I didn't need to. He's quite well known in police circles, but not by the name of Collins. He's used several aliases in the past when his crimes were petty, but everything has changed now, which is why I travelled from London to warn you.'

'Warn me about what?'

He took her hand in his. 'He's wanted for murder.

His assistant died on stage last night when part of their act went disastrously wrong.'

Phoebe wrenched her hand free to smother a cry of distress. 'No. I can't believe it. He was meticulous in planning everything down to the last detail. It must have been an accident.'

'Maybe, but the police don't seem to think so, and Collins has disappeared.'

'How did she die?' She hugged her arms around her body in an effort to stop herself trembling as she recalled part of their act which had involved a cabinet lined with metal spikes. 'Was it the iron maiden?'

He nodded. 'Are you all right?'

'Not really. But we performed that trick night after night. All I had to do was step inside and press a button which made the spikes retract as the door closed. It was foolproof.'

'Not last night. Someone had apparently tampered with the mechanism and the girl received multiple stab wounds. She died almost instantly, and now Collins is on the run. I was afraid he would come here.'

Phoebe's head was reeling. She knew that Caspar was ruthless but she could not believe that he would kill an innocent girl. 'Why would he do such a dreadful thing?'

'Who knows? I wouldn't pretend to know what went through a cold-blooded murderer's mind, but I suspect it had something to do with you.'

'No. Don't say things like that. It can't be true.'

'Phoebe. What's going on? Who is this?' Rose had entered the kitchen unnoticed. She rushed to Phoebe's side. 'You look as though you've seen a ghost. What has he said to you? What's wrong?'

'You must be Rose,' Rogue said calmly. 'Phoebe needs a friend right now.'

'And you must be one of the Paxman brothers.' Rose slipped her arm around Phoebe's shoulders. 'What have you said to upset her so?'

Phoebe shook her head, attempting a smile. 'It's all right, Rose. This is Roger Paxman, better known as Rogue. He came to warn me about Caspar. He's wanted for murder.'

Rose sank down on the chair next to her. 'My God. Who did he kill?' She looked up at Rogue. 'What has this to do with Phoebe?'

'I think the man is mad. Phoebe refused his advances and he's obsessed with her. Perhaps he thought she would take pity on him if his assistant died as a result of a terrible accident, but he reckoned without the theatre manager being well versed in magic tricks. He suspected foul play the moment he inspected the cabinet.'

Rose seized Phoebe's hand and held it to her cheek. 'My poor dear. It could have been you.'

'And might still be,' Rogue said drily. 'I've come to take you away from here, Phoebe. You're in danger every minute that he remains at large.'

'She's safe here with us,' Rose said fiercely. 'She doesn't need you or your criminal gang to protect her.'

'I'm afraid she does. Collins could be in Brighton now, just waiting his chance to get to Phoebe. Who knows what's going on in his sick mind?'

'And you might be making all this up so that you can kidnap her brother. Phoebe's told me all about you Paxmans. This could be a ploy to get to Teddy.'

Rogue went down on his knees beside Phoebe. 'Listen to me, I beg you. I'm not here to take the boy. I've tried to reason with Ned and make him see that Teddy is best left with you, but I'm here to see that you get to a place of safety. I have a house in the country just outside Dover and I want you to stay there until Collins is behind bars. There's no doubt the man will hang. He has nothing to lose and he's desperate. He won't rest until he has you in his power, and I'm begging you to think this through. We need to leave immediately.'

Phoebe stared at him in disbelief. 'Do you really expect me to abandon my friends and go with you?'

A grim smile curved his lips and he rose to his feet. 'It does sound odd, I grant you, but that's exactly what I'm saying. I'll take you to a place I know where you can stay until Collins is caught and arrested.'

'This could be a pack of lies,' Rose said anxiously. 'It might be an excuse to get you and Teddy back to London.'

Rogue put his hand inside his jacket pocket and pulled out a crumpled newspaper. He handed it to Phoebe. 'It's headline news.'

She took it from him and her heart sank as she realised that everything he had said was true. The murder of the magician's assistant was the leading story. There was even a daguerreotype of Caspar dressed in his stage costume. It had been taken some years previously but it was a creditable likeness. Phoebe read the first paragraph and then handed the paper to Rose. 'He's not lying. It's all true.'

Rogue nodded his head. 'I only want to help. This is the first place that Collins will look when he discovers that you've left London. You're in danger every minute you remain here.'

Rose looked up from reading the horrifying account of the girl's death. Her face was white and her eyes wide with fear. 'He's right, Phoebe. Caspar must have gone mad to do such a wicked thing.'

'The man is undoubtedly out of his head,' Rogue said grimly. 'It's obvious that he'll stop at nothing to get what he wants. If you refuse his advances he might well vent his anger and frustration on you, or Teddy.'

The mention of her brother's name brought Phoebe quickly back to reality. Looking into Rogue's eyes, which in the semi-darkness were the colour of jade, she knew instinctively that she could safely put her life in his hands. She nodded slowly. 'I'll come with you, but I won't go without Teddy.'

He shook his head. 'We can't travel with an infant. Anyway, he would be safer here with Rose and the rest of your friends. I know that Ivy accompanied you here. She'll take care of him until you're able to return.' He stood up, helping Phoebe to her feet. 'We must go quickly. I've a hired carriage waiting in the side street.'

She drew away from him. 'I can't leave Teddy.'

'It may be for the best,' Rose said tentatively. 'He'll be well looked after here. You know we all love him and Caspar isn't interested in the child.'

Phoebe shot a sideways glance at Rogue. 'No, but Ned won't have changed his mind. How do I know that he won't come here and take Teddy the moment I leave with his brother? For all I know Ned could be outside waiting to snatch him.'

'You have to trust me,' Rogue said firmly. 'I give you my word that Ned knows nothing of this. I left on the excuse of doing business in Manchester. Come with me, Phoebe. I swear I'll take good care of you.'

'I won't leave without Teddy. I'm supposed to be meeting Gino in Dover quite soon. We'll be going to Italy where we'll be far away from Caspar and from Ned. I wouldn't rest easy if I left Teddy here.'

Rose leapt to her feet. 'You're right, Phoebe. But to make sure that he's telling the truth, I'm coming with you.'

'This is ridiculous,' Rogue said angrily. 'I'm not traipsing about the countryside with three women and a baby. I assume that Ivy would have to come too.'

Phoebe faced him with a determined lift of her chin. 'I won't leave without my brother and Ivy.' She turned to Rose. 'But you should stay here with your father. I can't ask you to give everything up just to keep me company for a few days.'

'You're not asking me to do anything. I'm coming and that's that.' Rose threw her arms around Phoebe and held her tightly. 'I won't let you do this thing on your own.' She shot a sideways glance at Rogue. 'After all, I know Caspar and I can be with Phoebe night and day, which you can't.'

Rogue threw up his hands. 'All right. I can't fight

both of you. Get the boy and his nurse and pack a few necessities for yourselves. I want to leave here as soon as humanly possible.'

'I haven't said I'll go,' Phoebe said in a low voice. 'I need time to think, and there's Dolly to consider. I can't just abandon her without saying goodbye.'

'She'll be better off here with your cousin, and I'm quite prepared to throw you over my shoulder and carry you out to the cab.' Rogue folded his arms across his chest. 'Either way, we're leaving in five minutes.'

Phoebe opened her mouth to argue, but this time it was Rose who shook her head. 'Don't waste time, dear. I hate to admit it but I think he's right. I remember how Caspar treated me when I was foolish enough to go with him that evening. I saw a flash of something in his eyes that frightened me. I think we should go now, before he comes looking for you.'

It was cramped inside the ancient barouche and it lumbered across cobblestones and along country lanes like a rheumaticky old gentleman. The leather squabs were worn and greasy from years of contact with pomaded heads and unwashed hands. It smelt of stale tobacco and bay rum with overtones of the stable. Ominous creaks and grinding noises from beneath the bodywork made Phoebe fear that the whole equipage was going to disintegrate each time the wheels hit a rut. Even so, Teddy slept throughout the long journey, cuddled up in Ivy's arms. She refused all offers to take him from her and soon both she and Rose were asleep and snoring softly. Rogue had chosen to ride on the

324

box beside the coachman and Phoebe had a whole seat to herself, but she was too anxious to sleep. She had agreed to this mad venture under duress, and then only because she was able to keep Teddy at her side. Rose had finally persuaded her with all the conviction of a convert to the Paxman way of doing things. Without blinking an eyelid, she had written a note to her father explaining why she had decided to accompany Phoebe on her journey, and had stressed the need for secrecy. Phoebe was grateful to her friend, but she suspected that for Rose this journey was a golden chance to get away from her father, if only temporarily. She could only sympathise with her and be grateful for her company.

The carriage rumbled on through the night, stopping several times to change horses, but Rogue would not allow them to alight and take refreshment in the coaching inns along the way. He had tea and cake brought out to them, explaining that he did not want to leave a trail that Collins might follow. On the first of these stops, Phoebe took the opportunity to question him about the house he was said to own near Dover. She was not sure whether or not to believe him, as it seemed an unlikely coincidence, but he told her that he had inherited the property from his mother's side of the family who had farmed in the area for centuries. He spoke with obvious fondness of his boyhood home, but she found it hard to imagine either of the Paxman brothers tilling the soil or rearing livestock. Still slightly sceptical, she supposed that a place in the country would come in quite handy as a means of escaping from the law. In the end she was too tired to think or feel anything, and she must have drifted off to sleep in the early hours, as she was awakened by a sudden jolt as the carriage came to a stop and the door was wrenched open.

Outside the sky was an opalescent shade of green merging with crimson at the horizon as the sun struggled to rise. Rogue put the steps down and helped her to alight. 'Welcome to Windy Bank Farm,' he said, grinning.

Phoebe gazed at the black and white half-timbered building with its lattice windows and thatched roof. It must have been built in the time of Good Queen Bess but had been added on to several times. It was not the archetypal farmhouse sitting in a muddy yard and surrounded by tumbledown barns and brick outhouses, but more the residence of a gentleman farmer with a neat garden at the front and possibly at the rear of the house as well; she could not see from this angle. The outbuildings, barns and stables were set back from the road at a respectful distance from the farmhouse, and behind them stretched green fields enclosed by neat hedgerows. Beyond that Phoebe could just make out a glimpse of the sea with a purple line at the horizon.

'You'd better wake your companions,' Rogue said softly. 'I'll go into the house and warn the Merrydews that we have guests.'

Alarmed, Phoebe caught him by the sleeve. 'Who are they?'

He smiled. 'Don't worry. They're completely trustworthy. Old Merrydew worked for the family for years, and now he and his wife take care of the place for me. I come down to Kent when the way of life in London gets too much to bear.'

'Why do you live as you do when you could have all this?' She encompassed the house and the land with a sweep of her hand.

'Because my grandfather was tricked into signing away the deeds, and I've been buying it back brick by brick and timber by timber. It's taken me ten years, but after a few more payments the debt will be repaid.' He smiled. 'Don't look so worried. The bailiffs won't come in and take everything while you're here.' He strode off before she could think of a suitable answer, leaving her standing on the road, staring after him. He was a man full surprises and this was perhaps the most astonishing of all. From the beginning she had had him down as a cold-hearted villain, terrorising the weak and exploiting their defencelessness in order to make a huge profit, but she had gradually begun to revise her opinion of him. To see him in a different light, as a man trying to right the wrongs done to his family, was both confusing and strangely endearing. She peered into the carriage, where everyone was still fast asleep. She was tempted to climb back inside and instruct the coachman to drive on. If she could reach Dover before Rogue had a chance to follow them she could book into a small boarding house and lie low until Gino came for her. She hesitated with one foot on the bottom step, but she was tired and at a low ebb. She leaned into the carriage and shook Rose by the arm. 'Wake up.'

Rose opened her eyes, gazing sleepily at Phoebe. 'Are we there?'

At the sound of her voice Teddy began to whimper, and Ivy awakened with a start. 'What's the matter? Why have we stopped?'

'We're here,' Phoebe said, suppressing a sigh. In a moment of weakness she had given in, allowing Rogue to take control of the situation. The die was cast and now she would have to go along with whatever he suggested. She took Teddy in her arms. 'Come along, sweetheart. Let's get you indoors.'

Rose climbed stiffly from the vehicle. 'Where are we?'

'I don't know exactly,' Phoebe said truthfully. 'And I don't much care. I can't imagine that Caspar would find us in a million years. This place seems to be quite isolated.'

Ivy clambered down the steps, staring at the black and white building with the first rays of the sun kissing its golden thatch. 'Who lives there?'

'It belongs to the Paxmans,' Phoebe said shortly. 'Let's go inside and see if Mrs Merrydew has put the kettle on.'

'Mrs Merrydew?' Rose hurried along beside her. 'Have you been here before? Is there something you haven't told me, Phoebe?'

'No, of course not. It's just that Rogue, I mean Paxman, mentioned the fact that this couple look after the house while he's away in London. It's a long story, it seems, and I've only heard a tiny bit of it.'

'Well, blow me down,' Ivy said breathlessly. 'It looks

328

like a palace to me. He must be a rich man to own all this.'

Rogue met them at the front door. 'Come in. The main part of the house is still under dust sheets, so we'll go straight to the kitchen.' He led the way through the wainscoted entrance hall, and Phoebe could not help noticing the thick coating of dust on the ancient floorboards and the wide oak staircase, leading to a galleried landing. She wondered vaguely what it was that Mrs Merrydew did with her time; dusting and polishing did not seem to be a priority.

The hallway narrowed to a passage with closed doors on either side, and at the far end they came to a room which, Phoebe thought, must have been the hub of the home in its heyday. The smoke-blackened ceiling beams were studded with large hooks from which strings of onions, bunches of herbs and joints of ham would once have hung. Phoebe could imagine the room filled with the aroma of frying bacon and freshly baked bread, with the farmer's wife feeding an army of itinerant workers at harvest time, but now it was a quite different scene that met her eyes. The flagstone floor was barely discernible beneath a coating of sawdust and caked mud. There was a chill in the air despite the fact that a fire burned in the range, and a pervading smell of rotten vegetables and rancid fat made her wrinkle her nose. A burly man wearing a tattered shirt and nankeen breeches slouched in a chair by the rusty range, which was in desperate need of a good clean and a coat of blacklead. 'Get up, Merrydew,' Rogue said angrily. 'I don't expect to find you lazing around at this time of day.'

Merrydew heaved his bulk from the chair. 'Sorry, master. We wasn't expecting you.'

'That's obvious. This room is a disgrace.' Rogue glanced around with an expression of disgust. 'What have you to say for yourself, Mrs Merrydew?'

Merrydew's wife had been standing quite still as if turned to stone by the shock of seeing her employer so early in the day. Her mobcap was tilted to one side revealing strands of lank, greasy brown hair, and her clothes including her pinafore were all filthy. She attempted a gap-toothed smile. 'I weren't expecting you, master,' she whined. 'I got nothing in fit for the young ladies to eat. We live simply when you're away.'

Rogue stared pointedly at the debris that littered the pine table. Dirty plates, used cutlery and empty beer bottles were scattered over it together with the remains of what looked liked several past meals. 'You don't seem to have done much work, Mrs Merrydew. I'll swear that piece of pork pie was in the exact same position six weeks ago.'

She uttered a cackle of laughter. 'Oh, sir. You are a one.'

Teddy began to fidget in Phoebe's arms and his mouth turned down; a sure sign that he was about to voice his disapproval at being kept waiting for sustenance. Ivy held her arms out. 'Let me take him, miss. I think I can probably manage to give him something myself, but he'll need fresh milk and some sops.' She gazed at the general mess and clutter in the room with a frown. 'Don't look like we'll get much to eat here.'

'Oy, you.' Mrs Merrydew took a step towards her.

'That kind of talk ain't called for. We wasn't to know we'd got visitors arriving at the crack of dawn.'

'There should be milk at least,' Rogue said firmly. 'I pay a cowherd's wage. Where is the fellow?'

Merrydew licked his lips, casting a warning glance at his wife. 'Had to sack him, master. He were a lazy good-for-nothing.'

'So who tends the animals now?'

'I do it meself, master.' Merrydew backed towards the door. 'I was just having a cup of tea afore going about me business.'

Rogue gave him a withering look. 'You've let the place go to rack and ruin, Merrydew. We'll talk about this later.'

'Yes, master. But you don't understand . . .'

'One more word from you and you'll be looking for another job.'

Merrydew shambled out into the scullery and a gust of fresh air wafted into the kitchen as he opened the back door. Phoebe was beginning to regret her decision to allow Rogue to bring them to this dire place, but he seemed to sense her distress. 'It's not usually like this,' he said with an apologetic smile. 'Mrs Merrydew will go now to collect the eggs and then she'll make breakfast.'

'Yes, master. Anything you say.' Mrs Merrydew bobbed a curtsey and was about to follow her husband when Rogue called her back.

'I expect this mess to be cleared up and the rest of the house made habitable. Call in some help from the village, but get it done. The ladies will be staying for a week or two, and I want them to be made as comfortable as possible.' He put his hand in his pocket and took out a handful of coins. 'Merrydew can take you to market later. Get whatever you need.'

'Yes, master.' She scuttled from the room, following her husband out into the back yard.

'I'm sorry,' Rogue said apologetically. 'I haven't been down here for some months, and things seem to have got out of hand.'

Phoebe picked up a none-too-clean cloth and dusted a chair so that Ivy could sit down. 'Perhaps there's some bread,' she suggested tentatively. 'The Merrydews must eat something other than pie.'

'There might be a loaf in the larder.' Rogue went to investigate but as he opened the cupboard door a cloud of bluebottles flew out and buzzed angrily around his head. He covered his mouth and nose with his hand. 'Good God. Something must have died in there.' He shut the door quickly. 'This isn't good enough. I'll sack the pair of them.'

'Please don't do anything rash,' Phoebe said anxiously. 'They know we're here and if you send them away they'll spread the news, and soon everyone in the area will be aware that you've brought three women and a small child to the farmhouse. If Caspar does come looking for us this is the first place he'll look.'

For the first time since she had met him Rogue looked genuinely discomforted. 'You're right, of course. I'll sort the Merrydews out later, but now the main thing is to see you all settled.'

'We'll look after ourselves,' Phoebe said, glancing at

Rose and receiving a nod of approval. 'If you could just show us where we can sleep tonight, we can do the rest.'

'I don't think we can trust Mrs Merrydew to make us comfortable,' Rose said, giggling.

Ivy had been attempting to keep Teddy quiet, but he was obviously working up to a loud howl. 'He's hungry,' she said apologetically. 'He's teething too. No wonder the poor little chap's miserable.'

Rogue frowned thoughtfully. 'Give me a few minutes while I investigate the rooms upstairs. I want to make sure they're habitable, and I might have something to help the boy. After all, he is my nephew.' He left the room hastily, as if half expecting Phoebe to argue the point.

She shrugged her shoulders. 'Strange as it seems, he's right. He's as closely related to Teddy as I am. I'm not sure I'll ever get used to that.'

Ivy unbuttoned her blouse and put Teddy to her breast. 'I thought he'd never go.'

Rose laid her shawl on a chair and began untying her bonnet strings. 'I don't trust that Merrydew hag to clean this place properly. We'll be poisoned if she's allowed to cook for us in this midden.'

'I couldn't agree more,' Phoebe said wholeheartedly. 'It looks as though we're going to be stuck here for a few days, so we'll start as we mean to go on. We'll need lots of hot water, soda crystals and lye soap.' She rolled up her sleeves. 'Where do we start?'

'I'll brave the larder,' Rose said, pulling a face.

Phoebe picked up an empty sack that had been left

on a heap of what appeared to be discarded clothes. 'I'll clear the table. Anything that's rotten or too dirty to wash goes in here.'

'I'll help when Teddy's had his fill,' Ivy said, shifting to a more comfortable position on the hard wooden seat. 'But if someone could make a pot of tea I'd be more than grateful.'

Rose uttered a cry of triumph. 'Consider it done, Ivy. I've found a caddy filled with tea, although we'll have to wait for the milk. But there's something in the back of the larder that might interest you.' She backed out of the cupboard, clutching the tin caddy and brushing a cobweb from her hair.

Phoebe swept an armful of rubbish into the sack. 'What is it?'

'Right at the back,' Rose said breathlessly. 'It's too dark to count how many, but there are several kegs and I'd know that smell anywhere; it's Pa's favourite tipple.'

'Brandy.' Phoebe and Ivy spoke as one.

'Yes. Brandy. What does that suggest to you?'

Phoebe's breath caught in her throat. 'Contraband.'

Rose laid her finger on her lips. 'Hush, keep your voice down.'

'You don't think that the Paxmans are smugglers as well, do you?' Phoebe's breath hitched in her throat. Just as she had begun to think more kindly of Rogue, something came up to make him appear even more of a villain.

'Why not?' Rose picked up a chipped brown teapot and warmed it with water from the kettle. 'They're crooks, Phoebe. Why shouldn't they be into smuggling as well?'

'It makes sense,' Ivy said, nodding her head. 'That's probably what Merrydew does for them while they're up in London. He and that slut of a wife of his organise the contraband and store it here on the farm.'

'I can hear him coming,' Rose said, tipping the hot water into a slop bowl. 'Don't let him see that we know anything. Act normally.'

Chapter Nineteen

Rogue strolled into the room, and Phoebe bowed her head, not wanting him to see the look of suspicion in her eyes. Everything made sense to her now. It explained why he had kept the farmhouse. It was in an ideal position for such nefarious goings-on, and everything he had told her must have been a pack of lies. He must think her a simpleton to fall for such a tale.

'See what I found.'

The triumphant note in Rogue's voice forced Phoebe to look up. He was holding a silver rattle set with a strip of red coral. 'For teething,' he said, smiling. 'This was given to me by my maternal grandfather and it's been passed down through the family for a good few generations. I know that Ned would want his son to have it.'

Ivy took it from him. 'Ta, ever so.'

Phoebe looked away, concentrating on the task in hand. She had almost managed to convince herself that the relationship between her half-brother and the Paxmans did not exist, but being here, in the family home, it was impossible to ignore the fact that Teddy was one of them. It made her even more determined to take him away from this den of iniquity. He would be brought up by a God-fearing Italian family who would teach him the difference between right and wrong.

Rogue tapped her on the shoulder. 'Phoebe.'

'What do you want? I'm busy.'

'I can see that, but I've found two rooms that are reasonably clean, although the bedding needs airing. I'll leave it to you to sort that out, but you really mustn't do all this.' He encompassed her attempts to tidy the kitchen with a sweep of his hand. 'This is Maggie's job, and I'll see that she does it.'

Ivy held the silver rattle in front of Teddy and he made a grab for it, shoving the coral into his mouth and gnawing on it like a dog with a bone. 'See this, Phoebe,' she said, smiling. 'It's just what the little fellow needed.'

Rogue nodded in approval. 'I'm glad to see it in use again after all these years.'

'It belongs to you,' Phoebe said coldly. 'You will want it one day for your own children.'

He regarded her with a quizzical smile. 'Until then I'm sure it's in safe hands. I want to keep it in the family.'

Phoebe covered her ears with her hands. 'Stop it. Stop saying these things. Teddy is a Giamatti. I won't let you turn him into a criminal like you and your brother.' She broke off, realising that they were all staring at her as though she had gone mad. Stifling a sob, she made for the back door. She needed to get out of this disgusting rats' nest. She needed fresh air. She vaguely heard Rose calling out to her and the footsteps that followed her, but she ignored both of them as she ran from the house. She found herself in a stable yard where the cobblestones were covered in green lichen and littered with straw. A horse whinnied at her as she passed its stall but she raced on, heading towards the double gates and the open expanse of green fields beyond. She would have continued until she was as far away from the Paxmans' dwelling as her legs would carry her, but a painful stitch in her side forced her to stop suddenly. She bent double, gasping for breath.

'Phoebe!'

She stiffened at the sound of Rogue's voice. 'Go away.'

'Are you all right?'

'Leave me alone. I wish to God I'd never met you or your hateful brother.'

'Many people say that.'

She straightened up, turning to face him. 'You think this is funny?'

He shook his head, his expression suddenly serious. 'No, of course not. I'm genuinely sorry that my brother's inexcusable treatment of your mother has caused you so much distress.'

'You're just saying that.'

'No. I mean it, although looking at Teddy I can't help feeling that some good has come out of this.'

'He's still a baby but one day he'll be a man, and I don't want him to grow up like you and your brother. I want him to be a decent human being and have a proper job.'

'Like making ice cream?'

Phoebe clenched her hands at her sides. If she had been a man she would have punched him. That would wipe the smile off his smug face. 'Making ice cream is a respectable trade. It's better than terrorising the neighbourhood with threats of violence and worse in order to extract money from innocent people.'

His smile faded. 'Is that how you see me?'

'You're not exactly Robin Hood, are you? You don't take from the rich and give to the poor. You take from the poor and make yourself rich.'

'If you hate me so much, why did you come with me last night?'

'I've been asking myself that question and the answer is simple. I was more scared of Caspar than I am of you, but I wasn't thinking straight. Now I've brought my good friends here to your den of thieves, and I've delivered Teddy into your hands. I hate myself for being so weak, and I hate you for bringing me here.' She ended on an involuntary sob, glaring at him with tears of anger and frustration running down her cheeks.

He was silent for a moment and then he moved closer, taking her in his arms and devouring her lips in a kiss that almost robbed her of her senses. Suddenly her knees weakened and her whole body melted against his as if they were one being. She slid her arms around his neck but only to stop herself from falling. Her mouth opened beneath the pressure of his lips and despite her pain and anger she found herself kissing him back with a passion she could not have imagined. This was another world; she was another being. She was not Phoebe Giamatti who allowed Gino to kiss her gently and sweetly as if bestowing a favour upon him; she was not the Madonna-like creature that Rogue had imagined. In his close embrace she was a woman with fire in her blood; she was an elemental. There was nothing in heaven or earth that equalled the desire that welled up and threatened to overpower her. Horrified at herself, she broke away from him. 'Go away,' she breathed. 'I loathe you, Rogue Paxman. I detest you and everything you stand for.'

Visibly shaken, he remained motionless, staring at her as if seeing her for the first time. 'I don't believe you, Madonna.' He turned on his heel and went striding off in the direction of the house.

Left alone on the edge of the field, Phoebe sank down onto her knees covering her face with her hands. How long she remained in that position she did not know, but eventually she clambered to her feet and walked slowly back to the farmhouse. She could not believe that she had allowed him to hold her in his arms and that she had returned his kisses with equal fervour. Was she now a fallen woman, just like Ma? She could not answer her own question. Her feelings were a jumbled maelstrom of emotions that mixed anger, passion, desire and disgust in equal quantities. She must ensure that such a despicable act could never be repeated. They might be compelled to take shelter in this terrible place, but she would never again allow him to put her in such a position.

She walked into the kitchen to find Rose mopping

the floor and Ivy standing at the range stirring something in a pan that smelt appetisingly like scrambled eggs. A fragrant aroma of tea mingled with the strong smell of carbolic soap. Rose paused, leaning on the mop, her face creased with concern. 'Are you all right, Phoebe?'

'Yes. I'm sorry about earlier.'

'He had it coming to him,' Ivy said, heaping a pile of golden egg onto a plate. 'You're just in time for breakfast. Teddy's having a nap and we've just about finished in here. We're going to tackle the bedrooms when we've eaten.'

Phoebe sat down at the table, which had been scrubbed clean. 'Where are the Merrydews?'

Ivy set the plate before her, passing her a knife and fork from a pile of newly washed cutlery. 'They went off to market.'

Phoebe felt her throat constrict. If Rogue entered the room now she knew she would get up and run. She could not face him after what had just occurred. 'Where is Paxman?'

Rose bent down to wring out the mop. 'He's gone back to London. He said he had urgent business there, but we're to stay here and make ourselves as comfortable as possible. He may be a villain, Phoebe, but the man's got manners. He's a bit of a mystery, if you ask me.'

'I didn't,' Phoebe said shortly. 'And there's nothing mysterious about the Paxman brothers; they're criminals through and through. I'd leave here right now if it wasn't for Caspar.'

She looked up and saw Ivy and Rose exchanging knowing glances. 'What's the matter with you two?'

Ivy put two more plates of food on the table and she sat down beside Phoebe. 'Nothing.'

Phoebe sighed and pushed her plate away. 'I'm not hungry.'

Rose emerged from the scullery, wiping her hands on a towel. She took a seat beside Phoebe. 'What's wrong? What did Rogue say to you while you were outside together? He came in looking like thunder and left for London barely saying a word, and you're acting most oddly. What went on out there?'

'It was nothing.' Phoebe rose to her feet. 'I think I hear Teddy crying. I'm going to check on him.' She left the room before either of them could continue the cross-examination. How could she explain things to them when she did not understand her own feelings?

She paused in the narrow passageway, overcome with curiosity. She could not resist looking behind the closed doors in order to discover what lay on the other side, but apart from the usual domestic offices such as a broom cupboard, a dry store and a linen room, there was nothing that she might not expect to find in any house of this size. She discovered a small parlour that might once have been the domain of the mistress of the house, a dining room and a drawing room where all the furnishings were concealed beneath white holland covers, and another parlour with a distinctly masculine feel about it. The shelves were stacked with books mainly devoted to agriculture and animal care, and a desk in the corner had obviously been used fairly recently as it was piled with account books and ledgers, and a bill hook filled with receipts for payment for animal foodstuffs, seed and household necessities. It seemed a homely, well-organised place and totally at odds with how she imagined a den of smugglers might be run.

She left the room, feeling more confused than ever by the conflicting evidence she was discovering about the private life of the Paxmans. She closed the door behind her and made her way upstairs to investigate the upper floor. She found Teddy sound asleep in the middle of a large four-poster bed. The tester and curtains were made of heavy tapestry that must have cost a small fortune when new, but were now faded and falling rapidly into a state of disrepair. The curtains at the leaded casement windows were much the same, and although the room might once have benefited from a woman's touch there was little evidence of such niceties now. A willow-pattern washbowl and jug stood on a stand beneath the window, but the mahogany dressing table was bare and dusty. The clothes press was empty, as were the drawers in the tallboy. The carpet too had seen better days, and the surrounding floorboards were in sad need of a good polish. Phoebe went on to inspect the rest of the six bedrooms on the first floor.

The largest, overlooking the front of the building, bore traces of recent use, and the bed was still unmade. She felt a shiver run down her spine as she fingered the rumpled sheet. The experience of Rogue's kiss was disturbingly fresh in her mind. She could still taste him and feel his breath warm on her neck. She was certain that his hands must have left indelible marks on her breasts where they had lingered for a few brief and tantalising seconds. Just thinking of that close embrace made her tremble with desire. Touching the bedclothes and imagining herself lying in his arms was enough to make her feel sick with longing, followed immediately by pangs of conscience and self-loathing. She was engaged to Gino. She had promised to marry him. He was a good man and true, but Rogue lived up to his nickname. She abandoned her inspection of the room, closing the door behind her, and she was about to ascend the attic stairs when she heard the sound of a horse's hooves and the rumble of wheels. For a moment she thought that he had returned, but a quick look through the landing window revealed the Merrydews clambering from a dog cart laden with provisions. It looked as though they were expecting their guests to stay for a very long time.

That night, sleeping in the big four-poster beside Rose with Teddy slumbering in a crib that Merrydew had brought down from the attic, Phoebe was awakened by the sound of subdued voices and what sounded like barrels being rolled over cobblestones. She lay still for a moment, gazing into the semi-darkness as the moonlight filtered through the grimy glass window-panes. She held her breath, hardly daring to move. Perhaps she had been dreaming. Maybe it was an overactive imagination that made her think she was hearing things.

She slid her legs over the edge of the bed, sitting up

slowly so as not to disturb Rose, and tiptoed over to the window which overlooked the stable yard. Her breath caught in her throat as she saw figures moving about. She could not distinguish one from the other, but they were unloading the dog cart and their cargo appeared to be kegs, just like the ones that Rose had discovered hidden at the back of the larder. She was so intent on watching the scene below that she almost fainted with fright when Rose touched her on the shoulder.

'What's the matter?' Rose demanded. 'What are you looking at?'

Phoebe clutched her hand to her breast in an attempt to steady her heart, which was hammering against her ribcage. 'You scared the life out of me, Rose.'

'Sorry, but what is it? You look as though you've seen a ghost.'

The moon emerged from behind a bank of clouds just long enough to illuminate the scene below. Phoebe's suspicions were confirmed as she identified Merrydew who, with the aid of two other men, was unloading kegs and carrying them into the house.

'So we were right,' Rose whispered. 'That can't be anything legal. What will we do?'

Recovering a little, Phoebe steadied herself, leaning against the windowsill. 'I need proof before I report any of this to the police. I'm going downstairs to see if I can catch their names or something that will incriminate them in a court of law. I want to see Rogue and Ned Paxman behind bars where they belong.'

Rose's face was a pale oval in the dim light. 'Don't do anything silly. They're dangerous men.'

'I'll be careful. Go back to bed, Rose.'

She shook her head. 'Not I. I'm coming with you. This is the most exciting thing that's ever happened to me. Just wait till I tell the others. They'll never believe it.'

Phoebe laid her finger on her lips. 'Hush. Come if you like but keep quiet.' She crept over to the door and opened it slowly so as not to allow the rusting hinges to creak and give them away. Tiptoeing downstairs, it was anger that fuelled Phoebe's determination to put an end to the Paxmans' illegal activities. She paid scant attention to Rose, other than to repeat her warning to keep quiet at all costs. They stopped outside the kitchen, where the door had been left ajar.

Maggie Merrydew's shrill voice exhorted the men to hurry up and get everything stowed away. 'We don't want them stupid trulls poking their noses into our business. It's all I can do to keep them from rearranging me kitchen. If they find the brandy they'll go straight to the master, and then there'll be ructions.'

'Shut up, Maggie.' Merrydew raised his voice. 'Those stupid whores wouldn't know a keg of brandy from a barrel of molasses. Anyway, Haggerty will have the biggest part of this consignment sold afore the master returns from London. He won't know nothing about it. The best part is that he'll take the blame should our little business venture be found out. Who'd believe that Paxman wasn't the brains behind it all?'

A murmur of assent greeted this statement.

'Well I'm going to me bed,' Maggie said irritably.

346

'Keep the noise down. That means you as well, Haggerty, and you, Bollom. I know what you lot are like when you get into the liquor. We don't want Miss High and Mighty from London peaching on us to the master, or even worse, the coppers.'

'Quick,' Phoebe whispered. 'I think she's coming this way. Let's get out of here.'

Rose needed no second bidding and she raced towards the staircase, her bare feet pitter-pattering on the flagstones in the passageway and padding softly on the floorboards when she reached the entrance hall. Phoebe was close behind her and they did not stop until they were safely in their bedroom with the door locked.

Phoebe slumped down on the bed, fighting to catch her breath. 'That was close. I think the Merrydews must sleep in a room downstairs somewhere.'

Rose sat down beside her. 'Well, one thing's clear. Rogue isn't in on the smuggling, and I'm glad. I know he's a villain but I can't help liking him. There's something about him that makes me think he can't be all bad.'

'That's how he and his wretched brother have got away with it all these years,' Phoebe said bitterly. 'Ned wormed his way into Ma's affections with his handsome face and smooth tongue. Rogue may not be into smuggling but that doesn't alter the fact that he's a criminal. My pa was killed by the street gangs, and Ma would be alive today if she hadn't got involved with Ned.'

Rose slipped her arm around Phoebe's shoulders. 'I

know, and I'm truly sorry, but you wouldn't wish that Teddy hadn't been born. I'm sure that Annie would have loved him dearly if she . . .' she paused, biting her lip. 'I'm sorry. I'm saying all the wrong things.'

'No, you're right, Rose. I'm the one who's all mixed up. I was quite willing to believe the worst of Rogue even though he's gone out of his way to help me.'

'But you do like him, don't you?' Rose said softly. 'You can't fool me, Phoebe. And I think he's in love with you. Why else would he go to all this trouble?'

'No.' Phoebe jumped to her feet. 'Don't say such things. I love Gino and I'm going to marry him.' She paced the floor, clasping and unclasping her hands. 'It's just a matter of a week or so until my family pack up in London and set out on the return journey to Italy. Gino and I will be going with them, Rose. I'll marry him and that will be an end to all this.'

'And are you going to allow the Merrydews to get away with their business venture as they call it? Would you be happy letting Rogue take the blame when he knows nothing about their criminal acts?'

Phoebe shrugged her shoulders. 'He'd probably turn a blind eye and take a cut from their profits. I'm not going to worry myself over a man like him. I'm just counting the days until I can leave here and go to Dover.'

'And our adventure will end,' Rose said, sighing. 'I've never been happier. It may sound silly, but my whole life so far has revolved around Poppa. We've moved from town to town and one lodging house to

348

another. I think our time with Judy has been the longest we've ever been in one place.'

Phoebe came to a halt, staring at her. 'How selfish I've been, Rose. I've only been thinking about Teddy and me, even though I knew you had a difficult time with your pa. I've seen him when he's swipey and gets nasty with it, but you've always seemed to cope so well.'

'I've had to, and don't get me wrong. I love my pa, but sometimes I could kill him, if that makes sense. I'd like to have a normal life with a proper home and a nice husband. I don't think I'd mind if he wasn't perfect, just so long as he loved me and was good to me. You can't have everything, after all.'

Phoebe was to mull over Rose's words during the days that followed. Perhaps she had been too judge-mental when it came to the Paxmans. They were certainly no worse than most of the men who governed the ungovernable in London's East End. In fact they were better than the majority of gang leaders, and Rogue had astonished her when he had admitted that they occasionally worked in conjunction with the police. She had been quick to believe that he knew what was going on in this house, but as time went on she was growing ever more suspicious of the Merrydews. There was nothing she could put a finger on, but she had noticed the sly looks that passed between husband and wife, and their attitude was not one of servitude. It was as if Merrydew considered himself to be the head of the household with his wife running a close second. Phoebe made up her mind to keep a closer eye on them.

The days passed pleasantly enough so long as they kept out of the Merrydews' way. Phoebe spent much of her time exploring the countryside. Most of her life until now had been spent in the filth and squalor of Saffron Hill and the surrounding area, with a couple of winters spent on the banks of Lake Maggiore. But nothing compared to the verdant woodland or the neat fields bounded by green hedgerows where the placid cows munched the sweet grass. The cornfields were filled with ripe golden wheat studded with scarlet poppies and blue cornflowers, and the warm late summer air was filled with the scent of wild flowers and the heavenly song of the skylark. Here she found peace and inner serenity. She wondered what made anyone want to leave such an idyllic place and move into the city. She was beginning to understand why Rogue had gone to such lengths to hold on to his birthright. If the farmhouse and land had been hers she knew she would fight tooth and claw in order to keep it in her family.

Exactly a week after their arrival, Phoebe noticed an air of tension in the house. Merrydew was even worse tempered than usual and Maggie was extra strident in her responses. By the end of the day, when the heat had built up to a sultry threat of thunderstorms, Phoebe was beginning to suspect that there might be another consignment of contraband on its way. She had slept very little since the first night of their arrival, and even when she dozed off she would awaken at the slightest sound. It was usually just the old floorboards creaking or mice running around behind the skirting boards, but she was convinced that tonight something was going to happen.

She refused to get into bed despite a reasoned argument from Rose and the suggestion that they should leave well alone. 'After all,' Rose said, yawning as she cuddled down beneath the blankets, 'in a few days you'll be heading off for Dover and I'll return to Brighton with Ivy, as Teddy seems happy with cow's milk and sops and can do without a wet nurse. Pa will have packed up the booth now that summer's over. I suppose we'll be back at the theatre, unless he decides that it's time to move on again.'

'You're right, as usual,' Phoebe said, pulling a chair up to the window and sitting down. She wrapped her shawl around her shoulders as a draught whistled through the ill-fitting casement. 'But I'm not sleepy. I think I'll sit up for a bit longer, just in case something happens.'

She realised that she must have nodded off when she woke up suddenly at the sound of hooves on the cobblestones and the telltale rumble of wooden wheels. It was as she had thought: Haggerty and Bollom had brought another load of kegs as well as a few large wooden crates. Merrydew emerged from the scullery to help them heft their cargo of contraband into the house. Not wanting to wake Rose, Phoebe left the room and crept downstairs, hoping that she would not bump into Maggie on the way. As luck would have it she reached the kitchen without seeing a soul, and she

351

opened the door a crack so that she could peer inside without being noticed.

Maggie was in her chair by the range, smoking a clay pipe and drinking something out of a stone bottle. Judging by the pungent smell, Phoebe decided that it must be Hollands, and it looked as though Maggie had imbibed more than her fill of the strong gin. Merrydew was grumbling at her as he staggered past with a keg. 'Get up and do something useful, you drunken bitch.'

'Go to hell,' Maggie mumbled, her words slurring. 'I done me fair share today, looking after them upstairs. I'll be glad when they're gone.'

'Hey, Merrydew. Where d'you want these crates?' A deep male voice from the far side of the room made Phoebe's skin prickle with apprehension.

'Put them down for now, Haggerty,' Merrydew said, dumping his load on the flagstone floor. 'We'll stow the tobacco in the linen cupboard. There's not much in there since Maggie decided to hawk the master's bedding round the market.'

'Well, he won't be master for much longer.'

It was another man who had spoken this time and Phoebe held her breath, waiting for someone to qualify this statement. She heard Maggie's loud cackle of laughter and Merrydew's muttered response.

'Bollom's right,' Haggerty said, chuckling. 'I'd like to see Paxman's face when the magistrate summons him to appear on charges of receiving smuggled contraband. The coppers will have him dead to rights, and the Boss will get the farm and all the land that goes with it.'

'Shouldn't be surprised if that don't go for the house in London too,' Merrydew said grimly. 'Maggie and me will be in for a nice little nest egg to live on for the rest of our lives. I say we wait for the consignment of silk to be landed in two days' time and then we alert the revenue men. They'll nab him and that brother of his too.'

Chapter Twenty

Phoebe stifled a gasp of dismay. So that was their plan. She had sensed that something was brewing and she had been right. She turned and tiptoed until she was out of earshot and then she ran. She raced upstairs to the bedroom where Rose was sleeping peacefully, and Phoebe shook her until she awakened with a start. 'What's the matter? Is the house on fire?'

'No, but almost as bad,' Phoebe said in a hoarse whisper. 'I've just overheard Merrydew and his gang plotting to have the Paxmans arrested for smuggling. They're working for someone they call the Boss, and he's the one that Rogue has been paying off for years in order to keep the farm.'

Rose sat up straight. 'How do you know all this?'

'He mentioned it when he was showing me the house. I didn't pay too much attention to it then, but now it all makes sense. Whoever this man is he's going to see to it that the brothers are sent to jail for something they haven't done. It might be funny if it weren't so serious.'

'You do care for him, Phoebe. You're in love with Rogue Paxman. You must be, or you wouldn't care what happens to him.'

Phoebe hesitated for a moment, but suddenly she

had to confess the feelings that she had hardly dared acknowledge. 'You're right, but I wouldn't say that to anyone other than you.'

'I knew it.' Rose raised Phoebe's hand to her cheek. 'You must tell him how you feel. You can't marry Gino when you're in love with another man.'

Phoebe withdrew her hand gently. 'What I want isn't important now. The main thing is we have to warn Rogue, and we mustn't let the Merrydews know that we suspect anything.'

'What will you do?'

'I should go to London and warn Rogue, but I can't do that because of Caspar. He might have given up, but on the other hand he might still be searching for me. He's certainly mad enough to do anything.'

'Then I must go,' Rose said firmly. 'Ivy has to stay here and look after Teddy. You can't go in case you run into Caspar, so that just leaves me. We'll have to think up a good excuse so that the Merrydews don't suspect anything.'

'Would you really do that for the Paxmans?'

Rose smiled. 'Probably not, but I'd do anything for you, Phoebe. I can't allow you to suffer a broken heart without trying to do something to prevent it happening in the first place. Besides which, it will be exciting. I've never travelled on my own before, and I've never been to London. It will be a whole lot of firsts crammed into one.'

Phoebe angled her head. 'It's a lot to ask of you, Rose. But we'd have to pretend that you're going home to Brighton. We mustn't let the Merrydews know that

355

you're travelling to London. Stupid as they are, I'm sure they'd smell a rat and would try to stop you.'

'It's like being the heroine in a penny dreadful,' Rose said, cupping her chin in her hands. 'I could pretend to fall out with you and demand to be taken to the station. I don't suppose that Merrydew would wait to see me safely on board the train.'

'We could stage an argument,' Phoebe said, allowing herself to be carried away by Rose's enthusiasm. 'But not in front of Teddy, of course. And perhaps we ought not to tell Ivy until you're away from here. She's a good sort but she might get nervous and spoil the whole thing. We can't afford to make mistakes.'

'And if you say there's only two days until they plan to do this thing, I must leave first thing tomorrow morning.' Rose hesitated, frowning. 'There's just one problem. I haven't any money.'

Phoebe delved beneath the mattress and extracted a leather pouch. 'There's enough here to get you to London and pay your cab fare to Wilderness Row. Don't, on any account, walk those streets alone. You'll be set upon and robbed before you know what's happening. I don't mean to scare you, but it's not like Brighton.'

Rose took the purse from her, weighing it in her hand. She looked up at Phoebe wide-eyed. 'But this is the money you've been saving to pay for lodgings in Dover. How will you manage without it?'

'Don't worry about that now. The main thing is to warn Rogue about the Merrydews' plan.'

'You'd do this for him?'

Phoebe turned her head away. 'I'd do it for anyone who was in a similar position.'

'And when I bring him back here, will you promise to tell him how you feel?'

'It's not that simple, Rose.'

'But you love him, Phoebe.'

'I love my family too. Their honour is at stake here. I don't expect you to understand that, but it's everything to them.'

Rose sighed heavily. 'I hope you're doing the right thing. I really do.'

'Go to sleep now,' Phoebe said gently. 'You've got a long journey ahead of you tomorrow.'

Rose slid down beneath the covers, closing her eyes. 'And a great adventure too.'

It was surprisingly simple. Perhaps working in the theatre and watching actors perform had made it easy for Rose and Phoebe to stage their carefully choreographed quarrel, but enacted in front of the astonished Merrydews and a tearful Ivy, it was enough to convince their audience that the rift between them was irreparable. With genuine tears running down her cheeks, Rose demanded that Merrydew take her to the railway station in Dover. Surprisingly, he offered no resistance and immediately went outside to harness the horse and hitch it to the cart.

Phoebe waited until they had left and Maggie had gone out to collect eggs from the henhouse before she confided in Ivy, who was seated at the table feeding Teddy with bread and milk. 'So you see,' Phoebe concluded, 'all we can do is hope that Rogue gets here by tomorrow at the latest, or he'll face serious charges that will certainly land him and his brother in prison.'

Ivy stared at her with a puzzled frown. 'Why should you care? I thought you hated the Paxmans.'

'I hate what they stand for, but I won't see them punished for the one thing they haven't done.'

'Seems to me they deserve to go to jail, no matter what.'

'Perhaps, but the Merrydews are just as bad, or even worse.'

'What if the revenue men think that we're all part of the plot? We could all be in trouble for aiding and abetting criminals.'

Phoebe felt a cold shiver run down her spine. This was something that had simply not occurred to her, but she realised with a pang of dismay that Ivy might have a point. 'Surely not,' she said doubtfully.

'I think we ought to leave right now, before things start to turn nasty.'

'We can't go anywhere at the moment. I gave all my money to Rose. We'll just have to stay here and hope that she finds Rogue. He deserves a chance to save his home.'

'I don't like it. You can't trust men. They walk out on you in your time of need.' Ivy wiped Teddy's face on a scrap of towelling. 'I should know if anyone does.'

Phoebe rose from the table. Things had seemed so clear last night. She had not thought any further than the need to save Rogue from disaster and disgrace. Now she questioned her own motives. Perhaps she had been blinded by her foolish infatuation for a man who could never be anything to her, and she had put him and his interests before the safety of her brother and her friends. 'Best get our things together, Ivy. If they haven't returned by tomorrow morning we'll leave for Dover.' She fingered Gino's heavy gold signet which she had concealed by hanging it around her neck on a length of ribbon. 'I'll pawn this and it will keep us for a few days. I've asked Rose to get a message to Gino to tell him where we are, so I'm sure it won't be long before he arrives in Dover, and then all our troubles will be over.'

Ivy picked Teddy up and hitched him over her shoulder. 'Yours will just be starting, if you ask me. I don't know how I'm going to face Lorenzo after all this.'

Smitten by a further attack of guilt, Phoebe laid her hand on Ivy's arm. 'I'm so sorry that I dragged you into this, but Nenzo is too good a man to think ill of you. He'll know that I'm the one who brought us to this state.'

Ivy's plain face creased into a smile. 'I came along willingly enough, and if it hadn't been for you I'd never have met Lorenzo.' She chuckled as Teddy planted a kiss on her cheek. 'As for this young man, I love him almost as much as if he was my own dear dead baby. So I'm not complaining, Phoebe. We'll get through this somehow. You'll see.'

The sound of Maggie's heavy tread and the slamming of the outside door made them both jump. Ivy scuttled from the room taking Teddy with her and

Phoebe picked up her bonnet, assuming a casual manner that was at odds with the turmoil raging inside her. She was fastening the ribbons as Maggie stamped into the room carrying a basket of eggs.

'So you're off somewhere, are you? After that performance this morning I wonder you've got the nerve to stand there bold as brass, dressing up with no one to see you. The master might have said he'll return soon but I wouldn't count on it, love.' She set the basket down on the table. 'Now get out of me way. Some of us have got work to do. This ain't a hotel.'

'I'm well aware of that, Mrs Merrydew,' Phoebe said icily. She snatched up her shawl and draped it around her shoulders. 'I'm going out.'

'Hoity-toity,' Maggie called after her. 'Stuck-up bitch.'

Phoebe set off with a purpose. This was not simply a stroll along the country lanes. Having arrived in the middle of the night she had no idea which route they had taken, but she decided that by heading east they would be going in the right direction for Dover, and she wanted to find the quickest and easiest path for them to take. She followed the narrow twisting lanes between dusty hedgerows laden with scarlet hawthorn berries and brambles bowed down with juicy blackberries, but she ignored autumn's bounty and continued walking until she reached a crossroads where a signpost pointed its wooden finger in the direction of Dover. She retraced her steps. Now she knew which way to go if they were forced to flee, and all she could do for the rest of the day was to wait and try to appear as though nothing untoward had happened.

Night came and there was no sign of Rose. Having eaten the meagre supper of bread and cheese provided by a grudging Maggie, Phoebe and Ivy went upstairs. Teddy was already fast asleep in Ivy's arms, and Phoebe dropped a kiss on his round cheek. 'I think you'd better have him in your room tonight, Ivy. I don't think I'm going to get much sleep as it is.'

Ivy rocked him gently in her arms. 'I don't mind in the least.'

'What would I do without you?' Phoebe leaned over to brush Ivy's cheek with a kiss. 'We must carry on as normal in the morning, but if Rose hasn't returned by noon we'll leave as quietly as possible.'

'It can't be soon enough for me,' Ivy said with feeling. 'I hope you manage to get some rest, Phoebe.' She carried Teddy into her room and closed the door.

Phoebe was suddenly nervous as she entered her bedroom, locking the door behind her. Perhaps it was her over-active imagination but she had noticed Merrydew giving her sly looks all through the evening meal. Perhaps he had intended all along that she would be implicated in the plot to incriminate the Paxmans. She did not undress. Her bag was packed and she was ready for flight. She lay on the bed, but even when she drifted off to sleep she was plagued with bad dreams and awakened at dawn with a headache. She raised herself from the bed and went to the washstand to splash cold water on her face. She glanced out of the window half expecting to see the stable yard crawling with revenue men, but the only living thing she could see was the old horse sticking its head out of its stall.

Realising that she was dripping water all over the floor, she picked up the huckaback towel and patted her face dry. The coarse material was harsh against her cheek and she remembered hearing Merrydew accusing his wife of selling the best linen at market. Both of them, she thought wryly, would have a lot to explain when Rogue arrived home. She could only hope that it would be soon. Although it was still early, she decided to brave Maggie's disapproval by going downstairs and making a pot of tea. Since Rogue left for London their position in the house had been difficult, they were neither guests nor paying lodgers, and the Merrydews had taken every opportunity to make them feel unwanted. Phoebe was about to leave the room when she heard the sound of a horse-drawn vehicle entering the stable yard. Her heart gave a great leap of delight. She could not wait to see him and pretending otherwise was simply not an option. She unlocked the door and ran downstairs.

In the kitchen she was met by a stony-faced Merrydew. 'You got a visitor, miss.' He stood aside, ushering the man into the room.

Phoebe froze at the sight of him. She could neither speak nor move.

'Phoebe. At last I've found you.' Caspar glided across the flagstone floor as if skating on ice. His smile was fixed and his eyes glittered with triumph. He held out his arms. 'My dear girl. You've led me a merry dance.'

'Get away from me,' Phoebe cried, suddenly finding her voice. 'What are you doing here?'

He laid his hand on his heart in a theatrical gesture. 'How can you be so cruel? You know that my act is nothing without you. I've been searching for you night and day. I'd almost given up when I happened to run into that pretty little daughter of the drunken puppeteer.'

Merrydew cleared his throat noisily. 'Never mind all that, mate. You want the girl, you take her away now, afore the other one comes down and starts carrying on.'

Caspar turned on him with a look that made Merrydew recoil. 'Be silent, you peasant. Do you know who I am?'

Recovering himself, Merrydew thrust out his chin. 'No, and I don't care, mister. I want you and her out of here afore my missis comes in from milking the cows.'

'I'm not going anywhere with him,' Phoebe said, backing towards the inner door. 'Leave me alone, Caspar. I don't want anything to do with you.'

He took a step forward and then stopped, dropping his hands to his sides. 'My dear, how cruel you are, considering what I did for you in Brighton.'

'Go with him for Gawd's sake,' Merrydew growled. 'I've had enough of you city folk coming here and disturbing us. Take her, mister.'

'No,' Phoebe cried in alarm. 'You don't understand, Merrydew. This man is a murderer. He's on the run from the police.'

Merrydew blinked, but he shook his head. 'It's none of my business. I don't want no trouble.'

With her hands behind her back, Phoebe felt for the door handle. If she could just get upstairs to Ivy's room they could lock and barricade the door, and they would be safe for a while at least. 'Where's Rose?' she demanded. 'You said you'd seen her. What have you done to her?'

'Nothing, my sweet. On my honour, I happened to be strolling along Saffron Hill when I saw her going into your grandparents' hovel.'

'You were spying on my family. That's low even for you, Caspar.'

He shrugged his shoulders. 'I still can't believe that you lived in a place like that. It's not the sort of house that I would pick for a young woman of your outstanding beauty and talent.'

'If you've hurt my family . . .' Phoebe heard her voice rise to a screech. She was trembling and her mouth was so dry that she could hardly swallow.

He raised his hands. 'Don't be so melodramatic, my dear. Save that for our stage act. I made discreet enquiries amongst the hokey-pokey people, and on one occasion I called at the house. I merely wanted to ascertain whether or not you were at home, but a big burly brute of a fellow came out onto the pavement, rolling up his sleeves. I retreated to the shadows, of course, but I have him marked.'

'You're evil,' Phoebe whispered. 'Rose is the only one who knew I was here. What did you do to make her tell you? Where is she now?'

'I've no idea. She was unwilling to part with the information as to your whereabouts at first, but with a little persuasion she came round to my way of thinking. I let her go then. She was no further use to me.'

Merrydew tapped Caspar on the shoulder. 'Look here, mate. I like your style, but what I said still goes. I got unfinished business to attend to and it don't concern you.'

Caspar turned on him with a reptilian hiss. 'Take your hands off me, my man. I won't hesitate to use the dark arts on you, so leave me alone.'

'All right, cully.' Merrydew backed away. 'No need to get shirty with me.'

Seizing the opportunity to escape, Phoebe wrenched the door open and tore along the passageway, heading for the stairs. She did not look back but she could hear Caspar calling her name and the pounding of his footsteps getting closer every second. She managed to get to Ivy's room but found it locked. She hammered on the door. 'Ivy, let me in.' She could hear movement inside and then the door opened just as Caspar reached the top of the stairs. She pushed past Ivy, slamming the door behind her and turning the key in the lock.

'What's going on?' Ivy demanded. 'You look like the devil himself was after you.'

'It might as well be,' Phoebe said breathlessly. 'It's Caspar.'

'No. It can't be. How did he find us?'

Phoebe was too busy dragging a chair to the door and wedging it beneath the handle to answer straight away. Outside Caspar was shouting and banging on the wooden panels. 'He was watching my house and he saw Rose go in. Heaven knows what she was doing in Saffron Hill but somehow he got hold of her and bullied her into telling him where to find us.'

'Come out, you little fool.' Caspar's voice accompanied loud thumps on the door. 'I've got all day,' he added in a slightly calmer tone. 'You can't stay in there forever.'

Teddy had begun to whimper in fright and Ivy rushed over to lift him from the bed. 'There, there, sweetheart. Ivy's here. It's all right.' She glanced anxiously at Phoebe. 'What will we do? I don't suppose that oaf downstairs will help us.'

'He's desperate to get rid of us,' Phoebe said in a low voice. 'I think his accomplices must be arriving soon with the remainder of the contraband, and then they're going to tip off the revenue men.'

'Merrydew isn't likely to do anything while Caspar's here,' Ivy said thoughtfully. 'I wonder if there's a reward for turning him in.'

Phoebe shrugged her shoulders. 'I don't know if Merrydew is bright enough to think of that. Anyway, Caspar has frightened the life out of him by claiming to be able to do black magic. It seems that country folk are very superstitious.'

Ivy sighed heavily. 'I wish that Nenzo would come and save us, or even the Paxmans. I think that Satan might look good in comparison to him out there.' She jerked her head in the direction of the din that Caspar was making, but suddenly he was quiet.

Phoebe stiffened, putting her ear to the door and

listening. 'I think he's given up. I can hear his footsteps getting fainter and fainter.'

Teddy was sobbing in earnest now and waving his small fists. Ivy unbuttoned her blouse and put him to her breast. 'We can't stay up here all day. This won't keep him quiet for long, and I could do with a cup of tea.'

'So could I, but that's the least of our troubles. I wonder what Caspar is up to. I don't think he'll give up easily.' Phoebe hurried over to the window. 'I can hear someone moving about in the stable yard. If it's the revenue men I'm going to call for help.'

'Be careful. It might be the smugglers.'

Peering through the tiny diamond-shaped window-panes, Phoebe could hardly believe her eyes when she saw Caspar and Merrydew emerge from the coach house carrying a wooden stepladder. 'I can't believe he's doing this.'

'What's the matter?' Ivy asked nervously. 'What can you see?'

'They've found a ladder. I think Caspar is going to try and get in through the window.'

'What will we do?' Ivy's voice rose in panic. 'We must hide.'

'I'll push it away,' Phoebe said more in hope than certainty. 'I won't let him get to us.'

'Be careful. He might grab hold of you. It's a long way to fall.'

Phoebe turned her head to give Ivy a wry smile. 'It's him or me, and I'm not giving in without a fight.' She opened the window and leaned out. 'Don't try it,

Caspar.' Ignoring her warning Caspar and Merrydew heaved the ladder into place. 'Don't say I didn't warn you,' she added, reaching for the water jug. Lifting it from the washstand, she waited until Casper was about halfway up before tipping its contents over his head. 'Don't come any closer.'

Coughing and spluttering, he almost lost his footing but somehow he managed to cling on. He looked up, his customary mask of indifference giving way to white-faced fury. 'Just wait until I get my hands on you. You'll be sorry for what you just did, my lady.'

Phoebe threw the jug at him but it merely caught him a glancing blow on the shoulder and fell to the ground where it shattered into shards. Caspar continued his steady ascendance. Panicking, Phoebe attempted to lean out further and made a grab for the top rung, but the wooden ladder was heavy and with Caspar's added weight it clung to the wall like a limpet. She had not enough strength to move it even an inch. In desperation she tossed the soap dish at him, but missed. She hurled the washbasin but it too plummeted to the ground. He was almost at the top when the sound of approaching horses' hooves caused Merrydew to release his hold on the ladder. He hurried towards the gateway but was forced to leap aside as three horsemen rode into the yard.

'Rogue.' Phoebe uttered his name on a sob of relief. 'He came, Ivy,' she cried joyously. 'He's come to rescue us.' Shielding her eyes against the sun, she saw all three men dismount. 'Nenzo's with him, and so is Ned. Come and see, Ivy.'

'I can't come to the window with the baby at me breast. It wouldn't be decent. Tell me what's happening.'

'They've taken hold of the ladder.' Phoebe leaned out further, shouting words of encouragement as Rogue, Ned and Lorenzo exerted their combined strength to pull it away from the wall. 'Caspar is dangling from it like a trapeze artist at the circus,' she added excitedly. 'Just listen to him.'

'Put me down,' Caspar roared. 'It'll be the worse for you if you don't.'

'Do as he asks, boys,' Rogue said calmly.

Phoebe held her breath as they stood back, taking their hands off the rungs. For a moment, the ladder teetered in mid-air, and then it crashed to the ground, flinging Caspar onto the cobblestones with a sickening thud.

Phoebe clapped her hands. 'Serves you right,' she murmured. She waved to Rogue, blowing him a kiss despite the fact that his brother was looking on and grinning. Caspar lay on the ground, but he was clearly not dead, judging by the noise he was making. Merrydew was standing by the stable door watching the proceedings with his mouth hanging open.

Maggie had come hurrying into the yard, slopping milk from her bucket as she came to a sudden halt. 'What's going on, Merrydew.'

His response was lost in the general hubbub. Phoebe turned to Ivy with a dazed smile. 'They came just in time. I'd almost given up hope.'

Ivy set Teddy down on the floor. 'Sit there, like a good boy.' Buttoning her blouse, she joined Phoebe at the window. 'Lorenzo,' she shouted. 'You came to save me.'

He looked up, smiling as he swept her a courtly bow. 'Of course I did. We caught the first train this morning from Victoria, and hired these nags at the local livery stable. Gino and Rose are following on.'

At the mention of Gino's name, Phoebe's world began to crumble about her ears. The sheer joy she had felt on seeing Rogue and the realisation that he had come to her rescue was dashed to smithereens. Nothing had changed. All the problems that had beset her in the past were even more relevant now that Ned had arrived on the scene. He was smiling now, but perhaps that was because he had come to claim his son. She hoped that he had thought better of his plan to force her into marriage. Perhaps Rogue had managed to talk sense into his younger brother's thick head. She looked down at the two of them, so alike in looks but so unalike in character. She was about to move away from the window when there was a further disturbance below. Merrydew was shouting a warning to his accomplices but they had already driven their cart into the yard. Lorenzo seized the horse's reins while Rogue and Ned leapt forward to drag Haggerty and Bollom from the driver's seat. At that moment, as if on cue, the revenue men put in an appearance. There seemed to be a small army of them, but Phoebe did not stop to count. 'I'm going downstairs, Ivy. I have to make sure that the revenue men don't arrest Rogue.'

'I'm coming too.' Ivy swooped on Teddy and lifted

him from the floor. 'I can't wait to see Lorenzo. Did you see the way he smiled at me?'

Phoebe murmured something by way of assent as she struggled with the chair which was firmly wedged beneath the door handle. It came free after a brief tussle and she ran from the room oblivious to anything other than the desperate need to save Rogue. She was both flustered and breathless by the time she reached the stable yard. The scene that met her eyes was one of chaos and confusion. Haggerty and Bollom were trussed up like chickens ready to be put on a spit, but Merrydew and Rogue were being interrogated by one of the officers, while the others stood guard over the captives. Maggie was shouting and storming hysterically, making little sense other than demanding for her husband to be set free.

Phoebe hesitated in the doorway, not knowing quite what to do. Caspar lay on the ground screaming that he had broken his leg and demanding the services of a doctor, until one of the revenue men threatened him with dire consequences if he did not stop his noise. This had the effect of subduing Caspar a little, but he continued to groan and mutter beneath his breath, pointing an accusing finger at Rogue.

Ned was standing apart from the main group and on seeing Phoebe he came towards her. His expression was inscrutable and her heart sank. Hardly daring to breathe, she waited for him to speak.

Chapter Twenty-One

'Why did you run away from me?' he demanded in a low voice. 'I offered you marriage and a home for you and my boy. What more could I do?'

'I don't have any feelings for you,' Phoebe said urgently. 'I'm engaged to Gino. I told you that, but you wouldn't listen.'

'And do you love him?'

She could not lie. 'I'm very fond of Gino. He's a good man.'

'Ha! I knew it. You're too much like your mother to fall in love with a good man.'

Somehow he made the words sound more like an insult than a compliment. Phoebe shook her head. 'It doesn't matter what you say, Ned. My family would never forgive me if I married you, and it wouldn't stop at that. They value their honour more than life itself, and you deserve a wife who really cares for you.'

His expression changed subtly as Ivy emerged from the scullery carrying Teddy in her arms. 'There's my son. He's my flesh and blood, Phoebe. Nothing you can say will alter that fact. His place is with me, and if you want to be close to him while he's growing up, you know the answer. You're either for me, or against me. It's your choice.'

'I'm not against you, Ned.' She grasped him by the sleeve. 'And I must tell you something really important.'

He angled his head. 'I'm listening.'

She took a deep breath. 'Rose came to London to tell you that I'd overheard Merrydew plotting to tell the revenue men that you and Rogue are in charge of the smuggling ring. He's working for someone he calls the Boss, and this man intends to ruin you and take everything you own.'

Ned stiffened. 'Did he now? Well, we'll see about that.' He strode off to stand beside his brother.

'What's going on?' Ivy demanded. 'Why haven't they arrested Merrydew?'

Phoebe took Teddy from her. 'Never mind that now. Go to Nenzo. Tell him you love him, and let some good come out of this terrible mess.'

Ivy needed no second bidding. She ran to Lorenzo, who was standing quietly minding the horses. He swept her into an ardent embrace, and Phoebe could not help feeling slightly envious. She did not begrudge Ivy her happiness, but Gino would be arriving at any moment, and the fact that Rogue had brought him here was all the confirmation she needed that their brief moment of passion had faded from his memory. If he loved her he would not stand aside and allow her to marry someone else. She needed to look no further for the answer to her dilemma. She would do her duty by her family and she would honour her pledge to Gino. But her resolve faltered a little as a fully laden cart was driven into the already crowded stable yard. Rose and Gino were squashed together in the back of the vehicle, which was loaded with what looked like the contents of someone's home.

Gino leapt down and lifted Rose to the ground. Phoebe braced herself to face him, hoping that her innermost feelings did not show on her face, but to her relief he was waylaid by the carter who appeared to be demanding money. It was Rose who ran across the cobblestones to hug her. 'Are you all right? I've been so worried about you.' Teddy seized Rose's bonnet strings, tugging at them and chortling with delight. She kissed him on the cheek. 'Bad baby,' she murmured, smiling and patting his head, but her expression changed as she glanced anxiously at Phoebe. 'Did Caspar hurt you? We came as quickly as we could.'

'No, I'm all right.' Phoebe managed a watery smile. 'I'm so glad to see you, Rose. I was beginning to give up hope earlier on, but then help arrived just as Caspar was about to climb in through my window.'

Rose eyed him dispassionately as he lay on the ground, still complaining vociferously. 'I'm not at all sorry for the brute. He frightened me half to death in London.'

Phoebe drew her to a quieter spot away from the turmoil in the yard. 'What happened, Rose?'

'When I got off the train I took a cab to Wilderness Row, as you instructed, but a housemaid told me that both the brothers were out on business. I was at a bit of a loss then. It was past midday and I didn't know what to do, so I hailed another cab and went to the address you'd given me in Saffron Hill. Lorenzo had just arrived home and he gave me coffee and cake and listened to what I had to say, even though it must have sounded like the ravings of a madwoman. I was tired and upset and I must admit I was scared to be all alone in London. It's a terrifying place.'

'You were very brave to go there. It didn't occur to me that Caspar might be spying on my grandparents' house.'

Rose shuddered. 'Your grandparents were out, but Lorenzo said that he would go and look for the Paxmans. He said he knew where he was likely to find them, and he told me to stay indoors and wait for him to return. Then someone started hammering on the front door. It sounded urgent so I opened it and Caspar forced his way in. He held me at knife point until I told him where you were. I'm so sorry.'

Phoebe shook her head. 'Don't be. It wasn't your fault. He's a maniac.'

'I know, and I was so scared, Phoebe. I think I must have fainted from sheer fright because when I came to your grandmother was splashing water on my face. I wanted to come straight back here but I had to wait for Lorenzo and it took him ages to find Ned and even longer to find Rogue. By that time we had missed the last train, so there was nothing for it but to wait until morning.'

'Did you tell my grandparents about Teddy?'

'No, of course not. They think you were running away from Caspar and that's why Rogue brought you here, which is the truth after all. They were concerned for you, of course, and they sent for Gino, saying that he should be the one to bring you home. I couldn't stop them.'

Phoebe laid her hand on Rose's shoulder. 'Of course not. You did your best and I'm truly grateful.'

'You are pleased to see him, aren't you? Oh, heavens! He's coming over to speak to you. Let me take Teddy.'

Rose held out her arms, and somewhat reluctantly Phoebe relinquished him to her. This was the moment that she had been dreading, but could not be put off any longer. She submitted to Gino's fond embrace. His kiss tasted of garlic and coffee. His clothes were travel-stained and smelt of railway stations and dust. She could not help comparing his boyish enthusiasm with the measured passion of Rogue's kisses, which had melted her into a quivering mass of desire. She drew away from him. 'Not now, Gino. Everyone's looking.' She regretted her words the instant they left her lips. His hurt expression made him look like a whipped puppy. She kissed him briefly on the cheek. 'I'm sorry. I didn't mean to snap, it's just that my nerves are in a state.'

His smile returned and he tightened his arms around her. 'My darling, of course you must have been scared out of your wits. Rose told me everything.' He glanced at Caspar. 'He's a cold-blooded killer. I was so afraid for you.'

She could see Ned striding towards them, and she closed her eyes, offering her lips to be kissed again. Gino was quick to oblige, but he released her when Ned tapped him on the shoulder. Phoebe met Ned's stern gaze with a mute plea but he ignored her. 'I suppose you know that the boy is mine, Argento?'

Gino slipped his arm around Phoebe's waist. He was a good head shorter than Ned but he raised his chin and met his gaze squarely. 'Yes, I know everything.'

'I want my son.' Ned tucked his thumbs in his wide leather belt, standing feet apart as if squaring up for a fight. 'I'm not allowing you to turn him into an Eyetie.'

'I'd say that it's Phoebe's decision. She'll do what her mother would want, and what's best for the boy.'

'But I'm his father and that gives me every right to claim him. I'm not wasting my breath arguing with you. I don't care if you threaten me with vendetta and your damned secret societies; you aren't in Italy now, mate. In our part of London it's what we say that goes. So you can take Phoebe if you must, although I've made her a better offer which she'd be mad to refuse, but whatever her decision, Teddy stays with me. D'you understand?'

'We'll talk about this later,' Gino said with dignity. He nodded in Rogue's direction. 'It doesn't look as though your brother is winning this particular battle. I suggest you sort out the business with the revenue men before you start laying down the law to me.'

'Gino's right, Ned.' Phoebe said firmly. 'You've got more important things to think about at the moment.'

He hesitated, frowning, but Rogue was deep in conversation with the more senior revenue officer, and the Merrydews were protesting loudly and casting blame for everything on the Paxmans. The carter had also become involved in the fracas and he was arguing violently with one of the officers, who was insisting that he had to take Caspar to the police station. 'Look here, guv,' the carter said angrily. 'I got to deliver all this furniture to Fox Cottage by noon. I can't go traipsing back to the village with a violent maniac.'

The revenue officer jerked his head in Caspar's direction. 'The man's got a broken leg. He's not likely to give you any trouble.'

Caspar uttered a loud groan. 'I need a doctor. For pity's sake, take me to a bonesetter or I'll be crippled for life.'

'You'll be facing the drop, mate, if what these men say about you is true.' The officer prodded Caspar with the toe of his boot. 'I suggest you keep quiet and let this good man go about his business.' He put his hand in his pocket and thrust some coins into the carter's palm. 'This will recompense you for any delay you suffer on his account. Come on, men; let's get the murderer onto the wagon. We'll let the local constable deal with him.'

On a count of three they lifted Caspar and flung him none too gently onto the cart. He was silent, and Phoebe could only suppose that he had fainted from the pain. She felt almost sorry for him, but then she remembered his unfortunate assistant and her agonising death. She jumped as Gino laid his hand on her shoulder. 'I know this has all been a terrible experience for you, but we must go now and take the child before Paxman gets his hands on him. That is what you want, isn't it, my love?'

His dark eyes were like brown velvet caressing her with such tenderness that she knew what course she must take, even if it broke her heart.

'It's your choice, Phoebe,' Gino said, holding her hand to his cheek. 'I will love and protect you for the rest of my life and raise the boy as my own son. Come with me now. No one will notice if we slip away.'

She glanced anxiously at Rogue, who was deep in conversation with the revenue officer. It was frustrating that she could only catch snatches of what passed between them. Ned was at his side and was supporting his brother wholeheartedly. She looked across the yard to where Ivy and Lorenzo were standing, arms entwined, lost in a world of their own. Would she ever experience that kind of happiness with Gino? Phoebe raised her eyes to his face and she knew that the fault would be hers if their relationship failed. Her decision now would affect the lives of all those who were dear to her. He was waiting for her answer.

'Is it such a hard choice to make, cara?'

Phoebe twisted her lips into a reassuring smile. 'Of course not, Gino. You're right, we must get away before Ned realises what's happening.'

He held her hand in a firm grasp. 'But only if you're certain of your feelings, Phoebe. I don't want you to marry me and then regret it.'

'How could I be sorry that I'd married a man like you?' She reached up to brush his lips with hers. 'I need to go upstairs and get our things.'

He shook his head. 'No, cara. We must leave right away. There's no time to pack and we have to travel light. I think that Paxman will come after us, providing the revenue men don't turn the whole lot of them over to the police.'

'Do you think they will?'

'Do you care?'

'I don't want Teddy to grow up knowing that his father was hanged like a common criminal.'

Gino pulled a face. 'But that is what he is, and the law must take its course. I will be Teddy's father. There is no need for him to know any different.' He squeezed her hand and then released it. 'Wait here. I'll go and tell Nenzo to meet us in the lane outside. We'll have to walk to the village and hope that we can hire some kind of vehicle to take us to Dover.'

Panic seized her. She struggled to find an excuse to linger. 'But I need clothes for Teddy and food.'

'We'll get what we need on the way.' Gino hesitated, looking deeply into her eyes. 'Are you sure this is what you want?'

She could hear the chief revenue officer's stern tone as he interrogated Rogue and Ned, with Merrydew's whining assertions of innocence in the background. 'Yes, Gino. I'm very sure.'

He nodded his head wordlessly and walked slowly across the yard to where Lorenzo and Ivy were standing by the open stable door.

They travelled on foot for the rest of the day, their progress hindered by the need for frequent stops. Gino's plan to hire some sort of conveyance from the village had been discussed and dismissed. He was convinced that there was no danger of the Paxmans pursuing them as they would have been taken into custody by the local police, but Lorenzo and Phoebe were not so certain. In the end they took the cliff path, stopping at an isolated farmhouse to purchase milk, bread and cheese, and that night they slept beneath a hayrick.

It was noon on the following day when they reached Dover. Lorenzo led the way to an inn on the waterfront where he had arranged to meet the family, and to Phoebe's intense relief they found Fabio, Maria, Julio and Gino's mother waiting for them.

They sailed for Calais on the evening tide, and next morning they were travelling southwards by train, along with several other Italian families from Saffron Hill. Phoebe found herself the centre of attention, and was forced to regale friends and relatives with the story of her virtual imprisonment in the Paxmans' farm whilst hiding from Collins, the brutal murderer. Gino and Lorenzo had taken the credit for her rescue, and she was embarrassed to discover that she had become a heroine in the eyes of her grandparents' compatriots, and that Nonna was busy making plans for the wedding. The guest list was growing by the minute and Fabio complained that they would be bankrupted if his Maria had her way, but he winked at Phoebe as he spoke the words and slapped Gino on the back. 'I couldn't wish for a better husband for my little Phoebe.'

When Lorenzo and Ivy announced that they too wanted to be married in the little church on the island of the fishermen, Maria was ecstatic. She gathered together her female friends and they spent the rest of the journey making even more lists and planning menus for the wedding feasts. Phoebe was relieved when at last they arrived in Stresa on the banks of the magnificent Lake Maggiore. If only Ma was here, she thought, as she stood at water's edge one evening, watching the lake absorb the fiery sunset.

It was two weeks since they arrived in Stresa and she had done her best to settle into their way of life. She had struggled to put aside her feelings for Rogue, but he haunted her dreams and was never far from her thoughts. The pain of leaving him without a word was like a knife to her heart, and she could only hope that he did not think too badly of her. She missed Rose, in whom she could have confided her innermost thoughts, but if Gino had his way she would never see any of them again. He had told her that he had no intention of returning to England, and it had come as a bitter blow. It was at times like these that she would have given anything to be able to talk honestly to her mother and ask for her advice. Annie might not have been the wisest woman when in love, but she was never judge-mental. Phoebe knew that she could have unburdened her heavy heart to Ma and she would have understood. But then a small voice of reason in her head prompted her to remember that it was her mother's folly that had put her in this situation in the first place. Annie's legacy to her daughter was a lifetime of deception and a half-brother to raise as her own child.

Phoebe retraced her steps to the cottage owned by her grandparents. Gino and his mother were staying with relatives on Isola Pescatori. Gino's uncle, Marco, owned a fishing boat, and, having no children of his own, had offered him a half share as a wedding present, providing Gino took over the thriving business and allowed Uncle Marco to enjoy a well-earned retirement. Gino had accepted gladly. It was, he told Phoebe, an answer to all his prayers. His life-long ambition had been to earn his living as a fisherman and now, by the grace of God and thanks to his uncle, he could support a wife. 'We will bring up our children here, where we belong,' Gino had said, and although she had attempted to reason with him, Phoebe could tell by the look in his eyes that he had made up his mind, and nothing she said would make any difference.

His words echoed in her head as she trudged home-wards along the dusty road. The night air was warm and heavy with the scents of marjoram, wild thyme and garlic. Someone in a cottage nearby was singing in a clear soprano, her voice equal to any that Phoebe had heard in the music halls in London. A dog barked in the distance and birds coming home to roost swooped above her head in the darkening sky. It was all beautiful and sensuous, but although Gino might think of this lovely place as home, she felt out of place and desperately lonely. Used as she was to roaming the narrow streets of Clerkenwell, she felt exposed and vulnerable in the countryside, and the fact that her family was even more well known here than in Saffron Hill was unnerving and confusing. There were aunts and uncles, cousins and second cousins all eager to congratulate the happy couple. It seemed to Phoebe that half the population of the small town were in some way related to the Giamattis or the Argentos.

She glanced up at the mountains, and the serrated peaks were jagged against the blue velvet sky. A wind sprang from nowhere, bringing the taste of snow from the mountain tops and flecking the surface of the lake with tiny white horses. She shivered with apprehension as the old forebodings threatened to engulf her. Then, just as suddenly as they had come, the clouds split apart and the mountains were bathed in moonlight. The silver lake was as placid as a millpond. She quickened her pace. She had thought she had left the sudden flashes of intuition behind her in London, and it was unsettling to learn that they had followed her here.

She reached the cottage, pausing to calm herself before she went inside. Her grandparents' dwelling was modest. The scene that met her eyes was homely and comforting. Nonna was stirring a large pan over the fire and Nonno was polishing his precious fowling piece. Ivy was seated at the small round table in the middle of the room with Teddy on her knee. She looked up as Phoebe entered and smiled. 'Not long now, love.'

Phoebe smiled and nodded. 'Has Teddy been a good boy?'

'He's an angel,' Ivy said cheerfully. 'Are you getting nervous?'

Maria looked up, red-faced from the heat. 'Of course she's nervous. Every bride feels the same the night before her wedding.'

Fabio rose from his chair. 'I can see this is going to be women's talk. I'm going out to join the boys for a glass of wine.' He left the house before Maria had time to voice an objection.

'Men!' she said as the door closed on him. 'Always absent when there is work to be done. But thanks to Cousin Violetta we are all organised for the celebrations tomorrow.' She gave Phoebe a searching look. 'You should go to bed early, cara. Gino doesn't want to see his bride with dark shadows beneath her eyes. That's the trouble with having a fair complexion.' She resumed stirring the savoury-smelling game stew. 'Have something to eat first. You'll need all your strength for tomorrow night.'

'Mamma Giamatti,' Ivy said, giggling. 'That's not like you.'

Maria shrugged her ample shoulders. 'I was young once. I remember my wedding night, but at least I waited until I was married to lie with my Fabio.'

Phoebe and Ivy exchanged amused glances.

'I don't know what you're talking about, Mamma,' Ivy said, spooning broth into Teddy's eager mouth.

'I am not deaf, child. I hear the sounds in the night, but I suppose that is the way with you modern girls, and your nuptials are next week, so if there is a little one already conceived it won't look too obvious. Although my family will be counting the months and the days, and the whole town will know if it's a seven-month baby.'

Ivy collapsed in a fit of helpless laughter and Teddy joined in. Phoebe smiled, but she felt suddenly quite sick and extremely tired. 'I think I'll go to bed,' she murmured. 'Would you see to Teddy for me, Ivy?'

'Of course, love.' Ivy jiggled him up and down on her knee, making him laugh even louder. 'I'd best get in practice since Mamma has decided that I'm already in the family way. You'll be next though, Phoebe.'

'Everyone thinks she's a mother already,' Maria said, shaking her head. 'The wedding is long overdue, but once the ring is on your finger people will forget that Teddy was born out of wedlock. Now off to bed with you, girl. Gino won't leave the island tonight.'

Phoebe hardly slept, and when she did doze off in the early hours of the morning she dreamed of Rogue. She awakened in a cold sweat with tears coursing down her cheeks, but she stifled her sobs so that she did not disturb Ivy or Teddy who shared the small room beneath the eaves. She sat up in bed, staring at the cream muslin gown that was laid over a chair, and the straw bonnet with a lace veil that hung from a peg on the wall. The time had come to put her old self aside and begin a new life in Italy with the man who adored her and put her first, ahead of everyone and everything. Gino had quite literally worked his hands to the bone, enduring deep blisters caused by rowing the boat when there was no wind to fill the sails. He had promised to earn enough to rent a cottage of their own before the year was out, but for the present they would have to live with Uncle Marco and Aunt Cosima in the small terraced house with white stucco walls and a red-tiled roof that was situated on the waterfront and overlooked Stresa on the opposite bank.

The ceremony was to be at noon in the chapel of San Vittore on Isola Superiore dei Pescatori where Maria and Fabio had been married all those years ago.

The party afterwards was expected to go on well into the night. Maria and her cousin Violetta, whose plain daughter had done well for herself and married the town clerk, had treated the catering like a military operation, conscripting every able-bodied woman of their acquaintance to cook something for the feast. Fabio and his sons had organised the wine and there was unlikely to be a sober adult left standing by the time the last bottle had been consumed.

Phoebe spent the morning in a haze. She was surrounded by female relatives clucking over her like hens as they helped her to dress and put up her hair. They talked incessantly, but that was to her advantage as no one noticed that the bride-to-be was unusually silent. At last it was time to set off for the landing stage, where a small armada of boats was waiting to take the bridal party to the island. Clutching a posy of white roses, Phoebe leaned on her grandfather's arm as they left the cottage and followed the track to the water's edge. The lake was so blue that it almost hurt her eyes to look at it. The sky was a paler shade but innocent of the smallest cloud and the purple mountains were a perfect frame for the view of the jewel-like islands. Phoebe thought that she had never seen anything so beautiful, but inside her heart was like a lump of snow taken from the highest peak. As she stepped into a boat garlanded with flowers, she glanced over her shoulder half hoping to see Rogue's handsome face amongst the crowd of well-wishers from the town. Just one look would have given her the courage to go on, but it was a forlorn hope and she

387

knew now that there was no escape. She had chosen her future and she must face it head on.

She scarcely heard the words of the ceremony. She had been raised as a Catholic, although her mother was nominally an Anglican but rarely saw the inside of a church. Phoebe had always done what her family had asked of her and today was no exception. She left the chapel a married woman.

It was dark by the time the party sailed away from the island, crossing the choppy expanse of water to the landing stage where they staggered ashore in varying stages of intoxication. Phoebe had eaten almost nothing and drunk very little. Her throat had constricted each time she tried to swallow and her face ached from being set in what she hoped was a happy smile. Gino was in a high state of excitement. She did not think that he had imbibed much wine, but he was drunk with delight and delirious with happiness. He had hardly left her side since they were proclaimed man and wife and his pride in her would have touched the hardest heart, although she was certain that hers would never thaw. It felt like a lump of lead inside her breast, but she was determined that he would never know. He handed her onto the wooden staging and led her into the lantern-lit square where a small band was playing and people were already dancing.

The night air was like warm baby's breath, freshened by a breeze scented with wine and the bowls of roses that had been placed on the tables. The lights flickered like fireflies and the sound of laughter filled her ears. She danced with her husband until her feet were sore and eventually she excused herself, saying that she must rest a while. Reluctantly Gino left her and went to make sure that his mother was comfortable and well cared for. Phoebe breathed a sigh of relief as she moved away from the swirling dancers, intending to sit at a table beneath a tree strung with paper lanterns.

'Phoebe.'

Out of the darkness a man came striding towards her. She would have known him anywhere by the way he walked, the timbre of his voice, and as he drew closer the familiar scent of him filled her nostrils.

Chapter Twenty-Two

'Rogue.' His name was like music on her lips. Her knees buckled and he slipped his arm around her waist, supporting her, holding her. His breath was warm on her neck and his lips caressed her skin, causing her pulses to race.

'Phoebe, my Phoebe. I got here as soon as I could. I pray to God that I'm in time.'

She raised her hand to show him her wedding band. The gold gleamed palely in the moonlight. 'Oh, Rogue. I thought I'd never see you again.'

'This is your wedding party?'

The words ripped into her soul. She broke away from him. 'Yes. I married Gino. It was the only way.'

He seized her in his arms. 'I would have been here sooner but the fools arrested me for smuggling. We were thrown into the local jail and it took my lawyer a long time to convince them that Ned and I had nothing to do with the gang. By the time I reached London I found that you'd all left for Italy. I set off immediately.'

'But too late,' she whispered as he took her mouth in a kiss that made the stars explode and caused the lump of ice in her breast to shatter into shards.

'I love you, Phoebe,' he murmured into her hair,

which had come loose from its combs and hung freely around her shoulders. 'I won't let him have you.'

'It's too late,' she repeated sadly. 'It can never be.'

He kissed her again, crushing her to him so that their hearts beat to the same rhythm. For a few blissful moments she felt that they were one and the same person.

'It can be annulled,' he said in a low voice. 'You haven't consummated the union yet. Tell me that you haven't lain with him, Phoebe?'

'I haven't, but that doesn't change anything.' She pushed him gently away. 'Let me go, Rogue. I can't think straight when you touch me.'

He stood facing her, his arms hanging limply at his sides. 'You will come away with me, Phoebe. I'm not leaving you here. I love you. D'you hear what I'm saying?'

She held up her hand. 'Don't say these things. There's no hope for us. Perhaps there never was.'

He reached out and grasped both her hands in his. 'Look around you, Phoebe. Are you really a part of all this? Do you want to spend the rest of your life tied to a man you don't love? And what about the boy?'

She wanted to tear herself away from him but her small fingers closed around his like those of a drowning woman clutching a spar. 'I'm doing this for Teddy. He'll be brought up to be a decent, law-abiding man, which is something that wouldn't happen if I let you take him away from me.'

'I don't want to take him away from you, my darling.' Rogue dropped his voice to a caressing murmur. 'But he hasn't a drop of Italian blood in his tiny veins. He's an Englishman and he belongs with his family. That's you, me and Ned. We should be together forever, my dearest girl. Don't destroy all our lives by your misplaced loyalty. Come away with me now. I'll get my lawyer to fix everything.'

She closed her eyes, swaying on her feet. Every breath was painful. She wanted nothing more than to give in and allow herself to be swept away by a will stronger than her own. She knew that what he said made sense, and that her mother would have wanted the man she had loved to raise her child, but that did not alter the fact that both the brothers were involved in a life of crime. Would Ma really have wanted her baby boy to be raised amongst criminals and in all likelihood travel that path himself? Phoebe knew the answer to that, even as she knew that she could not dishonour her family. She opened her eyes and turned her head to look through the trees to the party being held in honour of her wedding. She twisted the gold ring on her finger. 'I can't,' she said simply.

He tightened his grip so that it was impossible for her to break free. 'Can't, or won't?'

'I promised in church,' she said slowly, each word more painful than the last. 'In front of my family and their friends, I promised to love and honour Gino. He's a good man and he doesn't deserve to be treated like this.'

Rogue let her go with a loud epithet that made her glance round anxiously to see if anyone had heard, but the music and singing had apparently drowned out all other sounds. She met his angry gaze, holding herself together with an effort. She must not give in, even if it tore her heart from her breast. 'Nothing has changed. It would start a war between your people and mine. We couldn't build a life together in those circumstances. We couldn't bring our children into a world of vendetta and violence.'

He regarded her steadily. 'And that's your last word, is it? I'll not force you to come with me, Phoebe. I want you for my wife, but obviously you don't love me enough to risk causing upset to others.'

'That's not true and it's not fair.'

'None of this is fair. D'you think I wanted to fall in love with a woman who insists on putting the needs of everyone else before her own? I'm concerned with you and me, and the boy, of course, although he's Ned's problem, not mine.'

'Teddy isn't a problem. He's a little boy who needs love and a proper family to care for him. He'll get that here, but what would happen to him in London? Any moment you might fall foul of the law, even if you do have the police force in your pocket now. What would we do if you and Ned ended up dangling on the end of a noose? I don't want that sort of life and it's not for Teddy either.'

Rogue's expression was unreadable. 'So you don't love me.'

'I do.' The words tumbled from her lips and she immediately wished them unsaid as she saw a glimmer of hope flicker in his eyes. 'But I hate the way you live, and I won't break Gino's heart or bring disgrace on my family. Go away, please. Leave me alone.' Without waiting for his response, she picked up her skirts and fled blindly in the direction of the revellers, but she came to a sudden halt as she barged into someone who was standing on the edge of the circle of dancers.

'Phoebe. What's the matter?'

'Julio. Thank God it's you.' She leaned against her uncle, gasping for breath.

'What happened? Who's upset you like this?'

She looked up into his solid, dependable face and she knew that she had done the right thing. Julio was the quiet one in the family, but there was no one upon whom she would rather depend for quiet commonsense and good judgement. 'I'm all right,' she said softly.

He glanced over his shoulder and his dark brows drew together in a frown. 'Is that who I think it is?'

'Yes, but he's leaving. I've sent him away.' Her voice broke on a sob. 'I made him go.'

'Why did he follow you here?'

She could scarcely answer him. Her teeth were chattering, and even though the night was warm she was shivering violently. 'Please don't make a fuss, Julio. It was nothing.'

He slipped his arm around her shoulders, holding her close. 'I don't call it nothing. Nenzo told me that Paxman had kept you prisoner in Kent. If he's dishonoured you in any way you must tell me now and we'll settle this once and for all. We'll go after him and make sure that he doesn't bother you again.'

'It wasn't like that. He saved me from Caspar.'

'Phoebe, I'm not stupid. A man doesn't do all these

things for a woman unless he wants her for himself. Is there something you're not telling me? I can keep a secret as well as any man, and I hate to see you upset like this.'

'It's all over between us,' Phoebe said, choking back a sob. 'I'm married to Gino.'

'And you have a child to bring up,' Julio said softly. 'Teddy is a fine boy and soon he will have brothers and sisters to keep him company.'

Phoebe had never been so close to blurting out the truth, but she managed to suppress the impulse to tell him everything. 'I'll make Gino a good wife,' she murmured. 'I swear it on my mother's grave, Julio.'

She was rewarded with a hug.

'You did the right thing, cara. He's gone now, and you'll never see him again.'

'I'll never see him again,' Phoebe repeated dully.

'Dry your eyes,' Julio said urgently. 'Gino's coming. Don't let him see that you've been crying. This is best kept between you and me, cara.'

Phoebe turned her head to watch her new husband as he threaded his way through the swirling couples. His face was pale in the moonlight but his look of consternation dissolved into a rapturous smile when he spotted her. He held out his arms. 'I thought I'd lost you, cara mia. Where have you been hiding?'

Suddenly panic seized her and she could not keep up the charade. She glanced over her shoulder in the hope of catching a glimpse of the man she truly loved. She broke away from Julio. This was her last chance. If she ran like the wind she could catch up with Rogue.

But Gino was too quick for her and he enveloped her in a fond embrace. 'I'm so happy, Phoebe. I can't believe that you're mine at last.'

Somehow she faced her new husband with a smile. He must never know how sorely she had been tempted to leave him on their wedding day and escape back to England with Rogue Paxman. Gazing up into the canopy of leaves above her, illuminated by paper lanterns swaying in the gentle breeze, she made a silent pledge to honour her wedding vows and put the past behind her. She had married a man who was superior to Rogue in every way, and she was determined to make him a good and loving wife. She owed him so much and she knew that he would cherish her for the rest of his life. Nothing in the world would make her do anything that would hurt him.

She laid her hand in his and allowed him to lead her once more into the dance. The party went on late into the night and they toasted each other with wine, but no matter how good her intentions Phoebe was there in body only. Her heart and soul had flown away to join Rogue on his perilous journey through life. What remained of her was just a husk, a pleasant, well-mannered and affectionate woman who in the early hours of the morning lay on the marriage bed wide-eyed and unable to sleep after her husband had made love to her for the first time. She had responded as best she could to his passionate lovemaking but it had left her as untouched as a virgin. She might be a wife in name and in fact, but fond as she was of Gino she knew that he would never reach the innermost place in her heart. It was a sad truth, but one she must keep to herself.

In the darkness, listening to the soft sound of Gino's rhythmic breathing, she gazed out of the small window at the stars. Despite her promise to herself that she would put him out of her mind, she allowed herself a few moments to think of Rogue. She had meant it to be a last goodbye, but she could not forget the way his kisses had set her body aflame with desire. The longing to hear his voice, and to see the tender curve of his lips when he smiled just for her, cut into her heart like a physical pain. She lay beside her husband, rigid with despair but determined to survive, and with the dawn she put all her memories away in a secret compartment of her mind. They might be taken out when she was alone and remembered like the words and melody of a much-loved song, but then they would be tucked away again until they faded into an old woman's dream.

Gino awakened early, opening his eyes and turning to her with a loving smile. She wrapped her arms around him and he took her more slowly than he had previously. This time there was no pain other than the ache in her heart. She kissed him tenderly but it was more from pity than from passion. He deserved better, she thought, as he rolled away sighing with satisfaction. He would never know that she had cheated him of the love that he thought he had earned. She would stand by him through thick and thin and she would bear his children. Teddy would be raised as their own son, but one day, when he was old enough to understand, she might tell him the truth about his parentage, although that was a long way off. She had to live with the here and now. She must raise herself from the marriage bed and face the world like a happy young bride. Gino was already out of bed, pulling on his trousers, and he leaned over to kiss her on the lips. 'My wife,' he murmured, smiling into her eyes. 'My beautiful wife. I can hardly believe that you're mine forever, my darling.'

She pulled the sheet up to cover her nakedness and she knew she was blushing, but she was saved from answering by Teddy stirring in the wooden cot that Uncle Marco had brought over from the mainland. 'I must see to the baby,' she said quickly as Gino's eyes darkened with desire.

He straightened up, turning away to fasten his breeches. 'Of course.' He glanced over his shoulder, his lips twisting into a wry smile. 'Maybe we will have one of our own by next summer.'

The thought appalled her and she was shocked by her reaction to his perfectly natural wish for a child. She slid out of bed, wrapping the cotton sheet around her. 'Not too soon, Gino.' She tempered her words by kissing him on the cheek. 'We need time together, and we should have a house of our own before we start a family.' She glanced round at the tiny room beneath the rafters, which was only just large enough to house the bed, a single chest of drawers and Teddy's cot.

Gino took her in his arms, ignoring Teddy's cries. He held her close, running his hand down her back and tracing the curve of her buttocks with obvious pleasure. 'You're right, as ever, my love. But I'll have to start earning good money before we can afford to rent even the smallest cottage.' He released her as Teddy's cries evolved into a full-blown howl. 'He has the Paxman blood in him, that's for certain. Me, I am much more easy-going. Our babies will be little angels.' He sat down on the bed to pull on his boots, and Phoebe went to lift Teddy from his cot. He stopped crying immediately and nestled against her shoulder, sucking his thumb.

'I can smell coffee,' Gino said, rising to his feet. 'I'll bring you some, cara.' He paused in the doorway, smiling at her. 'Madonna and child. What a beautiful sight.'

As he left the room Phoebe buried her face in Teddy's soft brown curls with a groan of pain. Madonna had been Rogue's name for her, and hearing it on Gino's lips was yet another painful reminder of love lost and beyond recall. Teddy tugged at her hair and she raised her face, smiling at him through her tears. 'You must be hungry, poor little boy.' She sat him on the bed while she dressed quickly before Gino could return and see her naked. Last night she had been thankful for the darkness when he had helped her disrobe. She had felt his hot breath on her neck and the way his fingers trembled as they unlaced her stays. Her cheeks flamed at the memory and she struggled with feelings of guilt. Although Gino was her husband in the sight of the church and in law, she felt that she had somehow betrayed the true husband of her heart. Rogue would be well on his way to England by now, and she was in Marco Argento's tiny house on a small island set in a vast lake. She was in another world and here she must stay for the rest of her life. When Gino returned to the room bringing her a cup of coffee, she walked into his arms and wept on his shoulder.

'My darling, what's the matter? Have I hurt you in any way?' Gino set the cup down carefully on the chest of drawers. 'Why are you crying?'

She wiped her eyes on her sleeve. 'It must be happiness, Gino dear. Or perhaps I'm a bit tired after everything.'

He lifted her in his arms and laid her on the bed. 'How thoughtless of me, cara. Of course you must be worn out after all the excitement yesterday, and then I kept you awake half the night.' He paused, chuckling to himself. 'Anyway, you must rest. Aunt Cosima will take care of the boy this morning. You get some sleep.' He picked Teddy up and carried him from the room.

Downstairs, Phoebe could hear Aunt Cosima's loud protests. 'Isn't it bad enough that you wait hand and foot on the girl, Gino? Now you want me to look after the baby. Is she too much of a lady to look after her own child? I'm not a servant, you know. Send for that other Englishwoman if you need a nursemaid for your son.'

Phoebe curled up in a ball and gave way to the flood of tears that she had been holding back since she had sent Rogue away. At last, spent with grief, she slept. When she awakened the sun was high in the sky and she could smell the savoury aroma of garlic, herbs and tomatoes wafting up the wooden staircase. She rose from the bed, dressed in her simple cotton print gown and brushed her hair, securing it in a knot at the back of her head before descending to the one room which served as living room, kitchen and sleeping quarters for Marco and Cosima.

'Well, my lady. This is a fine time to get up. I've done all my chores and taken care of your son. I hope you don't think this is going to happen every day.' Cosima stood arms akimbo, glaring at Phoebe with overt animosity. She had treated her quite differently when her husband and Gino were present, but now she was showing her true feelings and it was not pleasant.

'I'm sorry,' Phoebe murmured, bending down to snatch Teddy from the floor and stop him from putting a large black beetle in his mouth. 'It won't happen again.'

'Quite right it won't,' Cosima said angrily. 'You will get up before Gino and make sure he has some food inside him before he goes out on the water. You will take over the cleaning as I am reaching the age when I should take things easy and you are young. And you will look after your child.' She stared pointedly at Phoebe's chest. 'Gino should have married a good, study peasant girl who could have suckled her own babies. You look too puny to bear him the children he wants. That's what comes of marrying a foreigner.' She thrust a broom into Phoebe's spare hand. 'Go outside and sweep the street. Take the boy with you and make sure he doesn't stray into the water. Or else take him to his grandmother. Lalia may be a cripple but she can watch the child.' She went to sit by the fire and began stirring the pot containing the delicious-smelling fish stew.

Phoebe was only too glad to go outside into the warm September sunshine. She found Lalia sitting on a wooden bench set against the whitewashed wall of the adjoining house, where she rented a tiny room on the ground floor. 'I heard it all,' Lalia said, shaking her head. 'That Cosima has always been a bitch. She used to make my life a misery when I was younger, but now I am too old to care what she says.' She held out her arms. 'Let me hold my grandson. I may not be very good on my feet, but I can keep an eye on him for you.'

Phoebe set Teddy on her lap. 'He's very strong now, Lalia. He wants to get down and crawl.' She glanced at the water's edge which was just yards away. 'I hope we won't be here too long. It's a dangerous place to bring up a child.'

Lalia nodded in agreement. 'But it will be some time before Gino can afford to pay the rent they demand these days. That aside, he was raised here and he didn't come to grief in the lake.'

'I'm probably making too much of it.' Despite her brave words, Phoebe felt a shiver run down her spine. 'Anyway, I'll watch Teddy like a hawk.'

'I don't see much work being done.' Cosima appeared in the doorway, holding an earthenware bowl in her hand. She stepped out of the house and set it down beside Lalia. 'There's your food. I'll add the cost of feeding you onto your son's rent. I'm not a charity.'

'Thank you, Cosima,' Lalia said meekly. 'I'm very grateful to you.'

'Well, if your husband had made provisions for his widow you wouldn't be in this sorry state.' Cosima eyed her coldly. 'My Marco has seen to it that if anything happens to him I will be taken care of, and my daughters know their duty. It's a pity your son hasn't saved more from the money he makes in London. By now he should be able to support his old mother and a wife.' Cosima was about to re-enter the house, but she hesitated, turning her attention once again to Phoebe. 'You can eat later, when you've finished your chores. Best get on with it, my girl.' She went inside and slammed the door.

Lalia pulled a face. 'Let's hope Gino gets a good catch today. He's gone out with Marco, who's showing him the best fishing grounds.'

Phoebe gazed over the calm and silky water. In the distance she could see small fishing boats and she wondered which one was Marco's. Despite the fact that she had spent winters here as a young child, things had been different then and Ma had always encouraged her to think of London as her real home. She had known that when spring came they would return to Saffron Hill, and for all its squalor, disease and poverty, the East End was where she had been raised. She was a Londoner through and through, and despite the majestic grandeur of the snow-capped mountains and the picturesque beauty of the lake, Phoebe had always been afraid of the water. Even now, beneath the glassy surface, so still and serene on a fine autumn day, she could feel danger lurking.

An impatient rapping on the window made her

jump. Cosima was glaring at her and Phoebe set to work sweeping the cobblestones. Life here might appear idyllic in comparison to the harsh world of the East End, but there were different kinds of hardship to conquer. There was little else she could do other than try to keep Cosima happy until such time as they could move into a place of their own. Lalia was breaking off bits of bread and dipping them into the bowl before feeding them to Teddy who consumed them greedily, opening his mouth for more like a baby bird.

'He will grow big and strong,' Lalia said, smiling. 'He's a fine boy but he takes more after your side of the family, Phoebe. Those eyes are the colour of the lake in spring. He is more of an Englishman than an Italian, I think.'

Phoebe swept the dust and dead leaves into the water. 'My mother was fair-haired and she had blue eyes.'

'I remember her well.' Lalia set her empty bowl down on the bench. 'The boy is very like his grand-mother. A pity she didn't live to see him.'

Phoebe dropped the broom and ran to snatch Teddy back from the water's edge. 'No,' she scolded. 'Naughty boy. Stay with Nonna.' She gave him a shake, but more from fear than anger, and she cuddled him against her when he started to cry. 'It's not safe here,' she said angrily. 'We can't remain in this place.'

She repeated the same words to Gino as they lay in bed that night. All day she had been on edge, unable to relax until Teddy was safely asleep in his cot. Cosima stubbornly insisted on propping the cottage door open, saying that it was too hot to keep it closed. Teddy had reached the crawling stage and could move with surprising speed, which made it impossible for Phoebe to take her eyes off him for a moment, hampering her in her efforts to carry out the tasks set for her by Cosima. Lalia promised to watch him that afternoon, but she had a habit of dozing off in the warm autumn sunshine and Phoebe had only just prevented Teddy from falling into the water on several occasions.

'He'll learn, cara,' Gino said, drawing her to him. 'You mustn't worry so much. I'm sure that Mamma and Aunt Cosima will help to look after him.'

She moved away as far as she could in the narrow wooden bed. 'You don't understand, Gino. I love your mother, but she's an old lady, and your aunt doesn't like me. We must find somewhere else to live. I can't bear it here.'

He stroked her hair back from her forehead with gentle fingers. 'Cara mia, I understand that it's difficult for you. You must miss your family, and Ivy too.'

'Teddy misses her most. You must find us somewhere to live in Stresa, as far away from the water's edge as possible.'

'We can't leave here until Uncle Marco thinks I'm competent to go out on my own to fish the lake. It's his boat, after all.'

'That's another thing, Gino. I keep getting terrible visions of a storm, and the lake looking more like the sea with giant waves. Teddy is in mortal danger; I feel it in my bones.'

He took her in his arms, holding her so that she could not escape from his embrace without a fight. She could feel his body hard against hers and she realised that their first real disagreement had inflamed his desire. 'Please, Gino. Not now. I'm tired. I've been working hard all day.' She broke off as his mouth sought hers and his hands caressed her body.

'My darling,' he whispered into her hair. 'I love you. All I want to do is to make you happy.' He seemed to sense her lack of response and he pulled away just far enough to study her face. 'You do love me, don't you, Phoebe?'

Chapter Twenty-Three

Phoebe could see frustration and disappointment in his eyes. She knew she was being unreasonable and that he was doing his best to provide for his ready-made family, and she wished with all her heart that she could return his love threefold. She slid her arms around his neck. 'I'm sorry, Gino. Of course I love you.'

He kissed her with mounting passion and took her with a degree of urgency that came as a shock after his usual gentle, almost respectful love-making. 'I adore you, cara,' he whispered. 'I promise you that I'll find us a home on the mainland before Christmas, if it's the last thing I do.'

But things did not go quite as planned and Uncle Marco proved reluctant to allow Gino to take the boat out on his own. The bad weather was coming, he said, and Gino was still inexperienced in the ways of the lake. He needed more knowledge of the conditions and areas where he would catch the most fish before he could be allowed to sail the craft single-handed. Perhaps another year, and then Gino might be competent to take over the vessel.

Phoebe had accepted the news with a sinking heart. Each day was a battle of wills between her and Aunt Cosima, who grumbled, bullied and took spiteful digs at Phoebe, but never when the men were within earshot. When her husband or Gino was present, Cosima was all smiles and could not praise Phoebe highly enough. Cleverly she turned the tables and made it appear that it was Phoebe who was at fault. She was the transgressor, the ungrateful foreign woman who had little respect for their home or their customs. Phoebe could have screamed with frustration, but she knew that if she challenged Cosima openly her accusations would be met with denial, followed by tears and then hysterics. Cosima would be the centre of attention and Phoebe would find herself accused of everything from ingratitude to malice. She learned very early that she could not win. Cosima was a past mistress at getting her own way, and she had Uncle Marco wrapped around her little finger.

Phoebe had to tread lightly and keep her thoughts to herself. She adopted a passive attitude, doing her best to keep out of Cosima's way and taking Teddy to the mainland at every possible opportunity. She lived for the visits to her grandparents' home, where she was assured of a warm welcome. She could unburden herself to Ivy, who although newly married to Lorenzo was always ready to lend a sympathetic ear to Phoebe's troubles.

'I'd strangle the old cow,' Ivy said, pouring wine into a glass and handing it to Phoebe. 'Drink up and forget her for a while.'

Phoebe stretched her bare feet out in front of her, feeling the warm dust trickle between her toes as they sat outside the Giamattis' cottage one sunny afternoon at the end of October. The days were getting shorter and the mornings and evenings were cool to the point of being chilly, but there were still leaves on the trees and a gentle heat at midday. Ivy and Lorenzo were living with Phoebe's grandparents, but Nonna was quite different from Cosima and had welcomed Ivy into the home. 'You're so lucky,' Phoebe said, sighing. 'If only we could find a place to rent nearby. It would be such a relief to be away from Cosima, and I worry constantly about Teddy.' She smiled as she watched him attempting to walk by holding on to the wooden fence which enclosed the tiny garden. 'I hate living so close to the water.'

Ivy sipped her wine. 'It won't be for long. I'm sure Gino's doing his best.'

'He is,' Phoebe said quickly. 'He's working so hard to convince Uncle Marco that he can manage the boat and sell the catch successfully. I feel guilty, but sometimes I can't help nagging him and begging him to stand up to his uncle. I've tried to convince him that he can cope very well on his own, but he's still unsure of himself.'

Ivy reached for the wine bottle and topped up Phoebe's glass. 'Never mind, ducks. Drink that and it'll make things look a bit rosier.' She glanced over her shoulder. 'It sounds like Mamma is starting to prepare the evening meal.' She refilled her own glass and hid the empty bottle behind a pile of empty plant pots. 'She doesn't approve of me having a drink in the day. I suppose it's because of your ma, God rest her

409

soul, but all due respect to Annie's memory, I ain't going to go down the same path. It's just nice to sit here in the sun and listen to the birds singing in the trees and sip this lovely red wine. I love it here and I never want to go back to gloomy old England.'

'I wish I was like you,' Phoebe said enviously. 'I know it's beautiful here, and the sun shines a lot more than at home, but I miss London.'

'And what about Rogue Paxman?' Slightly tipsy, Ivy eyed her with a knowing grin. 'Oh, come on, Phoebe love. I ain't stupid. I know there was something going on between the two of you, and it weren't just on his side.'

Phoebe downed her wine in one gulp. Suddenly the truth had to come out. She could keep it to herself not a moment longer. 'I love him, Ivy. I don't know how it happened or when it first started, but I can't get him out of my mind. I try to forget him but I can't, and then I feel terrible. Gino is a good man and I want to love him in the same way, but it just doesn't happen.'

Ivy reached out to pat her on the shoulder, and her eyes were brimming with sympathy. 'I guessed as much, and I feel for you, I really do.'

Phoebe wiped her eyes on the back of her hand. 'Sorry, I shouldn't have burdened you with my guilt. Forget what I said.'

'It will get easier,' Ivy said softly. 'Gino adores you, that's obvious for all to see. You'll settle down if you give yourself time, and when you have a baby of your own it will bring you closer together.' She patted her belly, smiling. 'I get the feeling that I might be in the

410

family way. It's too early to tell for sure, but I hope I'm right.'

Phoebe set down her empty glass and leaned over to give Ivy a hug. 'I'm really happy for you.'

'What about you?' Ivy cocked her head on one side like an inquisitive robin. 'I know it's early days, and you waited until you were legally wed, unlike Nenzo and me.' She winked and nudged Phoebe in the ribs. 'Once we'd realised that we wanted each other there was no stopping us.'

A bank of clouds blotted out the sun and a cool breeze from the mountains rippled the glassy surface of the lake. Phoebe rose to her feet. 'It's getting late. I'd better get back to the island or Cosima will tell Gino I've been out all day and left her to do all the work.'

'Tell the old bitch to go to hell.' Ivy stood up, smoothing down her skirts. 'I'll give her what for, if you like. I ain't afraid of Cosima Argento.'

From their elevated position Phoebe could see a small craft preparing to leave the jetty with supplies for the island. 'I must go or I'll miss the ferry.' She picked Teddy up in her arms, ignoring his protests. The sky seemed to darken suddenly and she could hear waves crashing on the shore. The sails of the small boat disappeared in the darkness and above the howling of the wind she could hear cries for help.

'What's the matter, Phoebe? You're white as a sheet.'

The sound of Ivy's voice brought Phoebe out of the living nightmare that had suddenly blotted out every-thing but fear itself. The sun was still shining and the deep blue waters of the lake mirrored the sky. The white sails of the boat were flapping idly in a gentle breeze and she could see the ferryman hefting boxes on board. Teddy wound his small fingers in her hair, giving her a smacking and very moist kiss on the cheek, and everything was normal again.

'Are you all right?' Ivy asked anxiously. 'You had a funny turn, ducks.'

'I'm fine,' Phoebe said, struggling to hold Teddy, who was now wriggling in an attempt to get down on the ground and continue his exploration of the insect life in the garden. 'It was just an odd fancy.'

Ivy grinned. 'That happens sometimes when you're in what they call a delicate condition. Maybe we'll both have babies next year. Wouldn't that be lovely?'

Glancing over Ivy's shoulder, Phoebe saw her grandmother coming towards them. She frowned. 'Don't say anything to Nonna. It was nothing.'

'I won't say a word.' Ivy smiled, tapping the side of her nose. She kissed Teddy, laughing as he wound his arms around her neck. 'No, little man. You can't stay here, much as I'd love to keep you for myself. Go with Phoebe like a good boy.'

Maria thrust a bag of apples into Phoebe's hand. 'You look pale, cara. Are you feeling poorly?'

Phoebe kissed her wrinkled cheek. 'No, I'm quite well, but I have to go now. I really hate living so far from you.'

Maria frowned. 'You're a married woman now, Phoebe. You have to go wherever your husband takes you. I didn't want to live in London, but I made the best of it, and that's what you must do.'

'I try, but Cosima is a difficult woman.'

'I know that well enough, and to be honest I've never liked her, but on the other hand it was good of her to take you all in.'

Phoebe could see that this conversation was going nowhere. She could not expect her grandparents to save her from the situation that she had created for herself. 'Yes, you're right, of course, Nonna.'

'Maybe you should rest a bit more,' Maria suggested, exchanging knowing glances with Ivy.

Phoebe knew exactly what they were thinking. She smiled vaguely, and nodded her head. 'I'll try, but now I must take Teddy and catch the ferry before it sails.' She kissed them both again and tucking a protesting Teddy under her arm she left the garden and set off for the jetty.

During the next few weeks Phoebe made an effort to keep Cosima happy. She held her tongue when she might otherwise have retaliated, and she forced herself to smile when she felt that she could scream with frustration. She lay in her husband's arms each night and prayed silently that she would not conceive a child, at least not until they had a home of their own.

Each day was more or less the same as the last. The weeks passed and autumn gave way to winter. The comparatively mild climate allowed Gino to continue fishing, but Phoebe found herself trapped in the tiny house or bound by the confines of a small island. Despite her attempts to keep the peace, the tension between her and Cosima reached danger level.

413

Sometimes, when Cosima pushed her to the limit of her patience, Phoebe could do little other than take Teddy to the tiny bedchamber beneath the eaves, which was unheated and bitterly cold. They would huddle together in the bed while she attempted to keep him amused by telling him stories. She would have given anything for a picture book or some toys to keep him amused, but apart from some wooden bricks that Julio had made, he had nothing to play with. Sometimes she took him for walks around the island, but the lake with its ever changing temperament still terrified her and she kept tight hold of his hand, scolding him if he ventured too near the water's edge. Her nerves were in a constant state of agitation and late one afternoon, when she returned from such a walk, she found Cosima waiting for her with a look on her face that meant trouble.

The row that ensued was based on the fact that Phoebe had not scrubbed the stone step outside the house; a chore that she was forced to undertake every day whether or not it was strictly necessary. It had rained in the night, washing away the dust and fallen leaves, but that was not good enough for house-proud Cosima, or at least that was the objection she raised now. Phoebe had gone off gallivanting without a thought for the woman who had taken her in, despite the fact that it put her to great inconvenience. Looking into Cosima's narrowed eyes, glinting with malice, something inside Phoebe snapped and she lost her temper. She told Gino's aunt exactly what she thought of her, collected her few belongings and stormed out of the cottage with Teddy in her arms. She stood on the jetty in the sleet-spiked rain and waited for an hour until the ferryboat arrived. Lalia had seen her through the window where she sat daily, watching the changing colours of the lake, and she came hobbling towards her in an obvious state of distress. When Phoebe told her that she would never put a foot in Cosima's house again as long as she lived, Lalia begged her to reconsider.

'Please, Phoebe. Think about Gino. What will he do if his uncle refuses to allow him to use his boat?'

'He won't,' Phoebe said shortly. 'Gino invested all his money in that vessel. Uncle Marco can't continue working alone. It's too hard for an old man.'

Lalia wrung her hands. 'Don't leave like this.' She glanced over her shoulder at the cottage. 'Cosima is watching us now. Make your peace with her, please. I'm begging you to swallow your pride. Think of the boy.'

'I am thinking about Teddy and he deserves a better start in life.' She turned round, squinting into the storm as she heard the plashing of the water on a wooden hull and the flapping of the sail. 'I'm sorry, Mamma,' she said firmly. 'But I'm going to my grandparents' house. Gino knows where to find me.' She kissed Lalia on the cheek but Teddy turned his head away when Lalia tried to embrace him.

'He's forgotten me already,' she said tearfully. 'How will I live on this island without my family?'

Phoebe picked up the bundle containing her possessions. 'Goodbye, Mamma. We'll visit you often, but you must see that I can't stay with that woman.'

'I have to put up with her,' Lalia muttered beneath her breath as she turned and limped away.

With the aid of the ferryman, Phoebe climbed aboard the small craft and settled down with Teddy on her knee. When they set sail she closed her eyes, hugging Teddy to her so tightly that he could scarcely move. She was not a good sailor and she hated boats, but she managed to keep calm even when they hit squally patches of water.

She received a mixed reception when she reached the Giamattis' cottage. It was her grandfather who welcomed her with open arms, but Maria was angry with both her and Cosima, and she did not dissemble. 'You were at fault,' she said, folding her arms across her bosom. 'You should have shown more respect for someone who has put a roof over your head.'

'Come now, Maria,' Fabio said mildly. 'The girl put up with a lot from Cosima. You know what she's like.'

Maria turned on him, her dark eyes flashing angrily. 'Of course I know what she's like, but she was good enough to take them in and she deserves to be respected. Phoebe must go back immediately and tell her she's sorry.'

'No,' Phoebe said, shaking her head. 'I won't do it. I've been an unpaid servant to that woman right from the start. I've done everything she asked of me and more. I've kept my mouth shut when she said hurtful things to me, and I've done my best to fit in, but I'd rather sleep in the vegetable patch than go back to the island.'

Ivy took Phoebe's hand and squeezed it. 'You poor

thing.' She turned to her mother-in-law. 'Please, Mamma. Don't make Phoebe go back to that awful place.'

Maria pursed her lips, frowning. 'Well, she can't stay here. We're crowded enough as it is, and she's a married woman now with a child of her own.'

'Have a heart, cara,' Fabio said, stroking his chin as he did whenever he was agitated. 'Phoebe is a good girl. There must have been something bad going on there for her to leave in such a hurry. We can't send her away.'

'And where will they sleep?' Maria spun round to face him. 'Gino will come running after her and we've only the two small bedrooms. Julio is forced to lie on the kitchen floor at night as it is.'

Phoebe was wet, cold and shivering from nervous exhaustion but anger roiled in her stomach at the unfairness of it all, and she took Teddy by the hand. 'We won't stay where we're not wanted. I'll find somewhere in the town.'

'Go then,' Maria said with a stubborn set to her jaw. 'You must learn to be a responsible adult, Phoebe. You aren't a child who can come running home because you've fallen out with Gino's relations. I had to live with my mother-in-law for many years before we had a home of our own.'

Ivy uttered a murmur of protest but was silenced by a look from Maria. Phoebe could hardly believe that her grandmother was taking sides with Cosima, but she was too proud to argue the point any further. She left the house, walking out into the rain, but her grandfather followed her and caught her by the hand. 'Wait, cara. Don't take too much notice of your grand-mother; she's upset. She only wants the best for you.'

Phoebe gazed up into his anxious face and she felt a surge of love for the old man who could be strict, but had always been kind and fair. 'I know that, Nonno. But things have gone too far with Cosima. She really hates me. I can't go back there.'

He shook his head, his brow furrowed. 'There's only the shed where we keep the goat. It's rough, but it's warm and dry. If you're really that desperate you can sleep there for tonight.'

'Thank you, Nonno.' She reached up and kissed his leathery cheek. 'Anywhere would be better than living on that island with a witch.'

His lips twitched. 'I've always thought that Marco deserved better.' He took her bundle from her and held out his hand. 'Come with me, Phoebe. We'll go and ask the goat if she would like some company.' He squeezed her hand, smiling. 'Don't worry, cara. Your grandmother will come round in time.'

The outbuilding was constructed of stone with red roof tiles and a small window set high in one wall. The nanny goat occupied most of the ground floor, but a ladder led to a platform above where the straw was stored. Fabio lit a lantern and hung it from a nail protruding from the wall. 'It's not a palace, but it will do for tonight. It's warm and dry and the straw is clean.'

'It's fine, Nonno,' Phoebe said sincerely. Anywhere away from Cosima would seem like paradise. She could still hear her tormentor's whining voice carping endlessly. The sound reverberated in her head, and with it visions of her vindictive face. She might once have been quite handsome but Cosima's character was now etched on her features for all to see.

Fabio moved towards the doorway. 'I'll fetch you some bedding from the house, and some food. Can you remember how to milk the goat, Phoebe? I taught you when you were a little girl, but that seems a long time ago now.'

'Yes, I think so. I'll try anyway.' She set Teddy down and he made a beeline for the goat. Phoebe started forward with an anxious cry but her grandfather caught her by the sleeve.

'Let him go. She won't hurt him.'

Reluctantly, Phoebe watched her baby brother as he heaved himself up by hanging on to the animal's tail. The goat munched a mouthful of hay, ignoring Teddy as he clung to her, stroking her pelt and gabbling excitedly.

'A goatherd in the making,' Fabio said, laughing. 'You mustn't worry about him, cara. That boy is a true Giamatti.'

She could not look him in the eye. The lies she had told regarding Teddy's birth had been meant to save the family from disgrace, but she was finding it increasingly hard to live with the deceit. 'Yes,' she murmured. 'He's not afraid of anything, which is what scared me when we lived so close to the water.'

Fabio patted her on the shoulder. 'You worry too much. He's a boy and he needs to learn how to survive.'

'He's a baby, and I have to protect him.'

Fabio dropped a kiss on her forehead. 'And what about Gino? It seems to me that you pay more attention to the child than to your husband. That's not the way, cara.'

Her hand flew to her mouth. She had forgotten all about Gino. He would return to the island after landing his catch and taking it for market in Stresa, and he would find her gone. 'He won't know where we are. Cosima will say awful things about me.'

Fabio patted her hand. 'I'm sure he'll have a fair idea where to find you.'

'That woman will blame me for everything.'

'Gino knows you well enough. I'm sure he won't believe her lies.'

'She's cunning, Nonno. She twists everything.'

'I'll go to the jetty as soon as I've seen you settled in, and I'll try to catch him before he sets sail for home.'

Phoebe threw her arms around his neck. 'I'm sorry to bring my troubles to your door, but I'm truly grateful.'

'Hush now, child. What else would I do for my dead son's daughter?' He kissed her on the cheek and extricated himself gently from her grasp. 'I won't be long.'

She watched him as he bent almost double to avoid hitting his head on the low doorway. She could still feel the tickle of his whiskers on her cheek even after he had gone. She could do nothing other than try to make a comfortable place to sit and wait for Gino.

He arrived an hour later, wet and cold, and it was the first time that Phoebe had seen him really angry. He burst into the shed, gazing around in disgust. The goat backed away from him, obviously sensing that here was danger.

'What the hell is going on?' Gino demanded, looking up at Phoebe as she hesitated at the top of the ladder not knowing what to say.

Her own temper was frayed. She had spent time endeavouring to make a semblance of a home, sweeping the hay into the corner of the floor and covering it with the blankets provided by her grandfather. He had also brought a basket containing bread, cheese and a bottle of wine, which he left saying that Gino would need something stronger than milk when he realised that this was where they were to spend the night. After a few failed attempts Phoebe had managed to milk the goat, but now her nerves were stretched to breaking point. Everything that had happened that day had conspired to make her anxious and jumpy, and with the added effort of keeping Teddy away from the edge of the platform she was on the verge of hysteria. She glared down at her husband, seeing an angry stranger staring back at her. 'Your hateful aunt is the person who has caused this,' she said icily. 'I've taken as much as I can stand from that woman, and I'd rather live in this shed forever than go back to the island.'

Gino threw off his wet jacket and negotiated the steep ladder with the speed of a steeplejack. He took Phoebe by the shoulders, his cold fingers pressing into her soft flesh. 'What have you brought us to?' His eyes were dark with rage and water dripped down his face from his sodden hair. He shook it back from his forehead with an angry toss of his head. 'I've worked all the hours God sends trying to provide for you and the boy, and this is how you repay me?'

She pulled away from him, shocked by his tone as much as his words. 'He's got a name. He's supposed to be our son and you promised you'd treat him like your own.'

Gino let his hands fall to his side. 'You're trying to put the blame for this on me. I've done everything that you wanted of me. I've lived a lie for your sake and all I asked was that you got along with my aunt. I know she's a difficult woman, but surely you could have kept a civil tongue in your head for a while longer?'

'You make it sound as though I forced you to marry me.' She backed away from him, bending down to pick up Teddy who was clinging to her skirts. She cuddled him to her in an attempt to calm his fears. 'You begged me to marry you, Gino Argento. You said you would do anything in the world to make me happy, and yet you allowed Cosima to make my life a misery.'

He flinched as if she had struck him a blow across the face. 'She's an old woman and she took us in. You were the one who insisted that we lie about Teddy's birth to protect your mother's memory. She was a slut, Phoebe. She was a drunkard and a cheat who pretended to speak to the dead in order to take money from grieving relations.'

'How dare you say such awful things about my mother? She's not here to defend herself, but I know she loved Ned and I think he might have had genuine feelings for her. I lied about Teddy's birth to stop our families declaring a vendetta against the Paxmans, and you were only too eager to go along with it. You'd have done anything to marry me, so don't pretend that I forced you into it.' Her knees buckled suddenly as exhaustion and emotion combined to overcome her. She sank to the floor, bowing her head and rocking Teddy in her arms.

Gino took a faltering step towards her. 'Phoebe, I didn't mean it.'

She raised her head to glare at him through a veil of tears. 'Yes, you did. You meant every word. Perhaps Cosima was right. You should have married a local girl who would bear your children and allow herself to be bullied, and never complain.'

Gino knelt beside her, placing his arms gently around her so that he did not crush Teddy, who was sobbing quietly into her shoulder. 'I'm sorry, cara. I didn't mean to hurt you. It wasn't supposed to be like this.'

Her spine was rigid and she could not forgive him so easily. She wiped her eyes on her sleeve. 'You can't unsay what's been said, Gino.' She made a huge effort to sound calm when inside she was still inwardly raging. 'You shouldn't have married me if you didn't want Teddy. I never deceived you, and you know very well that there would have been open warfare between the Italian families and the Paxman gang if the truth came out. No one would be safe. I don't make the rules and I don't hold with vengeance, but I'll do anything to protect Teddy.'

Gino sat back on his haunches, eyeing her speculatively. 'Including marrying me?'

'That's not fair.'

'But is it true?' He took her cold hand in his. 'Answer me, Phoebe. Do you love me?'

She snatched it away. 'What sort of question is that?'

'It's simple enough and I deserve an honest answer.'

'Of course I care about you, Gino. I pledged myself to you and I'll honour that promise until the day I die.'

He shook his head. 'I know you did, and I believe that you meant it, but you still haven't answered my question. Do you love me?'

She scrambled to her feet, laying Teddy down on the blankets as his eyelids drooped and he sucked his thumb, a sure sign that he was falling asleep. She faced Gino, who had also risen and was looking at her with desperation written all over his pale countenance.

'Answer me honestly. Do you love me as I love you?'

'Why are you doing this to me? I've told you that I do.'

'No, you haven't. I want you to say those words and mean them. Sometimes, when we make love, I feel that your heart is somewhere else.' He raised his hand as she opened her mouth to object. 'I know I possess your body, but that's not enough for me. I want to hear you tell me that you love me, and only me. Otherwise we're living a double lie.'

Chapter Twenty-Four

It would be so easy to utter the words that he was desperate to hear, but Phoebe could not deceive him any longer. The guilt that she had felt on her wedding day threatened to engulf her and she had to tell him the truth. She took a deep breath. 'I have strong feelings for you, Gino. I love you for who you are and what you've done for me, but I'm not in love with you.'

'And you never were?'

The pain in his eyes made her wince as if it were her own. She shook her head, unable to frame the words that spoke of treachery and deceit.

His lips were white and his eyes bleak. 'I was too blindly in love with you to see it,' he said slowly. 'It's that villain you really love, isn't it?'

She held her head high. 'I'm sorry, Gino. But I'll never see him again. I sent him away when he wanted me to leave you on our wedding day.'

'He was here then?'

'I sent him away.' She repeated the words like a mantra. 'I chose you, Gino.'

'You chose me?' For a moment she thought that he was going to strike her, but he clenched his fists at his side. 'What went on between the two of you in Kent? Were you lovers? Are you a whore like your mother?'

'No,' she said in a low voice, not wanting to wake Teddy. 'How dare you even suggest such a thing?'

'But you love him nonetheless?'

'Stop it, Gino. Stop tormenting yourself. Nothing happened between Rogue Paxman and me. I swear it on Teddy's life.'

'Why should I believe you?'

His voice was harsh and his livid expression chilled her to the bone. This was not the man she had known all her life. This was a stranger, seemingly hell bent on wrecking their marriage, if she had not already done so by the admission he had forced from her. She drew herself up to her full height. 'Don't believe me then. Go away and leave me alone. I don't think I can bear the sight of you when you're like this.' She turned her back on him and went to sit beside Teddy.

There was a sudden silence, broken only by the sound of the wind howling round outside and the slap of the rain as it beat on the roof. Phoebe was forced to look up and found that Gino was watching her with an inscrutable expression. He might have been carved from marble like the effigies in church. She was filled with a sudden rush of pity for him. She had never intended to hurt him. She held out her hand. 'Gino, come and sit by me. We can talk this out. We can start again.'

'No. I'm going back to the island. It's where I belong. You can do what you like, Phoebe.'

She rose swiftly to her feet. 'Gino, don't go like this. At least stay here for tonight. Perhaps things will look different in the morning. I'm sorry.'

His lips curved in a humourless smile. 'And that's supposed to make things all right between us, is it? You're sorry. What are you sorry for, Phoebe? That you've taken my heart and wrung it out until it's dry? Or are you sorry that you admitted to being in love with another man when you made your promise to me in church?'

'I'm sorry that I hurt you. I do love you. You're a good, kind, man and . . .'

He took a step towards the ladder. 'Stop there. Don't say another word. I know that you believe what you say, but that's not good enough. I'm going and I won't return.' He descended the ladder, barely touching the rungs with his feet as he slid to the ground below. He snatched up his jacket and putting his hand in the pocket he pulled out a leather purse which he threw so that it landed at her feet. 'There's the money from my last catch. It will keep you for a while. I'll send more when I can.'

'I don't want your money,' Phoebe called after him, but he had opened the door and a gust of wind sent dry earth and straw up in a wild vortex, almost choking her. When it cleared she realised that he had gone. 'He'll be back,' she murmured. 'Everything will look better in the morning.'

There was nothing she could do. She could hardly go chasing out into the stormy night and leave Teddy on his own. Even if she caught up with Gino she knew that in his present mood she would be wasting her time. She sank down onto the straw and sat with her arms wrapped around her knees, trying to think.

Tomorrow she would go to the island. She would apologise to Cosima and she would make things right with Gino. He was hurt and angry now, but she knew that he still loved her. Maybe he could never completely forgive her, but there was something she had not told him. There was another life to consider now. Ivy and Nonna had been right. She had not wanted to tell anyone until she was absolutely certain. It was something that she had been dreading, but now it was becoming a reality she was feeling quite different. She laid her hand on her belly. Tomorrow she would tell Gino that he was going to be a father.

She lay down beside Teddy and tried to sleep, but the straw was prickly even through the thick blanket and the storm was growing in intensity. The wind howled around the building like a soul in distress, and the rain lashed at the windowpanes. When Phoebe closed her eyes she had yet another vision of the dark waters whipped into great waves as if the lake had become a wild sea. She snapped upright, gasping with fear. All her visions and dreams had led to this fateful night. It was not her baby brother who was in danger but Gino.

Stricken with panic, she wrapped Teddy in a blanket and descended the ladder with great care. She ran out into the night, heading for the cottage. She rapped on the door until Julio opened it. He was tousle-haired and bleary-eyed with sleep. 'Phoebe, what's the matter? Has the goat kept you awake?'

She thrust Teddy into his arms. 'The lake,' she screamed. 'The lake. Gino is going to take the boat to the island. I must stop him.'

Shaking his head and blinking, Julio caught her by the sleeve. 'Are you mad? You shouldn't be out alone on a night like this.'

She jerked her arm free. 'He'll be drowned. I've foreseen it many times. I've got to save him.' Ignoring his protests, she raced down the path, stumbling over stones and slipping in the mud as she headed for the jetty. Blinded by the rain, she tried to call Gino's name but the wind whipped the words from her mouth, battering her thin body until she could scarcely draw a breath. She fell several times and her skirts were sodden and caked with mud, making it even more difficult to move, but when she came in sight of the jetty she realised that the boat had sailed. She cupped her hands around her mouth, calling Gino's name. She could just make out a white sail flapping wildly as if out of control, and suddenly it was gone, swallowed up by a huge wave that caused the small vessel to breach and capsize. Her screams rent the night air.

Voices came and went. Sometimes she managed to open her eyes but then they closed again and she was overcome by the fever that racked her body. She was in a strange world, half waking, half sleeping. It was hot and her mouth was dry. She was vaguely aware of being lifted and cool liquid being trickled into her mouth. Swallowing was difficult. She wanted to speak but she was sinking once again into the dreamless depths of pain and heat.

When she opened her eyes she realised that she was

lying between cotton sheets on a proper bed. The white walls were bathed in pale winter sunshine and she could see the familiar crucifix on the wall opposite. She realised dimly that this was the room in her grandparents' cottage that she had shared with her mother many years ago. In her dazed state the past seemed more relevant than what was happening to her body now. She smiled as she remembered her mother taking down the symbol of Catholicism and stowing it in a drawer amongst her clothes. No matter how much Nonna tried to persuade Annie to convert to the Giamattis' faith, Phoebe had realised even as a young child that it only made Ma more determined to remain a nominal Anglican. Not that Ma was in any way religious, but perhaps that was due to the fire and brimstone teachings of her own father. Phoebe remembered the tiny house in Hoxton where her widowed grandfather had lived. His evangelical preaching came back to her now. He would have said that she was being punished for her wickedness. She closed her eyes again, only to be woken seconds later by a cool hand on her forehead.

'The fever's gone, Mamma.'

The familiar sound of Ivy's voice brought Phoebe back to full consciousness. She opened her eyes and this time she could focus more clearly on her surroundings. 'What happened? Why am I here?' She could see her grandmother hovering by the door and there were tears running down her cheeks.

Maria crossed herself. 'Thank the Lord. I'll make her some tea. I brought some from London especially for her, knowing that she isn't too fond of coffee. I always spoilt that girl.' She left the room, mopping her eyes with a corner of her apron.

'Why is Nonna crying?' Phoebe attempted to sit up but found she was too weak even to raise herself on one elbow. 'Have I been ill?'

Ivy took her hand and clasped it to her bosom. 'Don't you remember anything?'

Phoebe studied her face as she struggled to regain her memory. Suddenly she was very cold and she shivered convulsively. 'Gino.'

'I'm so sorry, ducks.' Ivy's dark eyes sparkled with unshed tears. 'The men went out straight away. Julio raised the alarm and the fishermen went out on the lake but all they found was the half-submerged boat.'

'No. Not Gino. Tell me he's alive, Ivy.'

She shook her head. 'I wish I could.'

'Maybe he swam ashore further along the lake?'

Ivy's face crumpled and she swallowed convulsively. 'They found his body next morning, Phoebe.'

'It's all my fault. I killed him, Ivy.'

'It was a tragic accident. You mustn't think about it, love. You've been very ill and you've got to concentrate on getting well again.'

'He would still be alive if it wasn't for me. I'm to blame.'

Ivy squeezed her fingers. 'That's nonsense.'

'He forced me to tell him the truth. He was so angry.'

Ivy released Phoebe's hand and tucked it beneath the coverlet. 'Stop this now. It's the weakness talking and nothing else. All married couples have rows. Me and

431

Nenzo shout at each other all the time and then we kiss and make up. It was your condition that made you speak out when you shouldn't.'

Phoebe's hand flew to her stomach. It was flat to the point of being concave. 'My baby,' she murmured. 'Tell me that my baby is all right, please.'

Ivy turned her head away. 'I'm so sorry.'

'No.' Phoebe covered her face with her hands; she was too weak even to cry. 'It's a punishment. I didn't want it at first, but then when I was certain . . .' She broke off on a dry sob.

·Ivy leaned over to envelop Phoebe in a hug. 'I wish I could tell you different, love. You miscarried shortly after they brought you home in such a state we thought you might lose your mind. Then the fever set in and we feared we might lose you as well.'

'I wish I had died. I brought all this on myself by lying to my family and allowing Gino to think I was in love with him. I should never have married him. I deserve to go to hell.'

Ivy sat upright. 'That's wild talk and it's all nonsense. You did what you thought was right, and if anyone's to blame it was your ma.'

'Where's Teddy?' Phoebe raised her head but a wave of dizziness forced her to sink back on the pillows. 'Is he all right?'

'He's being spoilt by everyone. He's just started to walk without clinging on to anything. He follows your grandfather everywhere.'

'How long have I been like this?'

'Long enough, and the main thing you need now is

rest.' Ivy rose to her feet as Maria entered the room carrying a cup of tea.

'Here you are, cara,' Maria said, smiling. 'A nice cup of split pea as your mamma would say. Prop her up, Ivy.'

Ivy lifted Phoebe as easily as if she weighed little more than the feather pillows that she plumped up and placed behind her. She eased her into a semi-sitting position. 'There you are, ducks. We'll soon get you better.'

'Thank you,' Phoebe murmured dully.

Despite her grandmother's and Ivy's best efforts, Phoebe's recovery was slow. She mourned for Gino and for the baby she would never be able to hold in her arms. She could not shake off the guilt that swamped her each night when sleep evaded her, and even Teddy's affectionate cuddles could not dispel the sadness that had invaded her soul.

Christmas came and went and the family feasted on game shot by Fabio and Nenzo. Julio was not a hunter but he provided them with fish from the lake and in the long winter evenings he carved wood into toys for Teddy. The true facts of his birth had emerged during Phoebe's long illness. Ivy admitted telling Maria during one long night vigil at Phoebe's bedside when the doctor had given them little hope of her recovery. The family had been shocked, she said, but not particularly surprised that Annie had given birth to an illegitimate child. They had been a little hurt that Phoebe had not trusted them with the truth, but after some consideration they had understood her motives. In the face of the recent tragedy it seemed that all was forgiven, and that a vendetta against the Paxmans was the last thing on their minds. In her weakened state Phoebe could not help being relieved, but their seemingly calm acceptance of the facts left her wondering if she had chosen the right course in the first place. Commonsense told her that matters might have been quite different had the truth been known while the family were in London, but it was difficult to think clearly during her spells of deep depression. She was still convinced that she was to blame for Gino's death, and that she would not have lost her baby had she behaved more rationally. When the grief became too much to bear, it was Ivy who comforted and consoled her.

Gradually Phoebe's health improved, but although she regained her physical strength her spirits were still low. She was able to leave the house and walk into the town, but everything reminded her of Gino, and she felt that people were pointing their fingers at her. Julio had overheard rumours, spread about by Cosima, that Phoebe had sent her young husband to his watery end. Cosima's two daughters were only too pleased to add to the tittle-tattle, and Phoebe found herself portrayed as a mean-spirited foreigner who had taken advantage of the Argentos' good nature and had made Gino's life a misery. Although her family stuck by her, defending her name and attempting to put the record straight, Phoebe was uncomfortably aware that Cosima's spiteful remarks would stick to her like burrs and were never likely to be forgotten. With the passing of the weeks there was another painful reminder of what she had lost as Ivy's waistline began to expand more rapidly, and her condition became obvious to all. People stopped in the street to congratulate her and then their eyes would slide to Phoebe's face and they would turn away. Her miscarriage had become public knowledge, but there was little sympathy for her. It seemed that she had been judged and found guilty without the benefit of a trial. She was the evil woman who had driven her husband to his death and if she had lost her baby that was rough justice.

Her grandfather did his best to comfort her by telling her that it was just a matter of weeks until they were due to travel to England, and by the time they returned to Stresa the gossips would have found someone else to talk about. Phoebe knew that he was trying to be kind, but she suspected that their collective memories were longer than that. Matters came to a head when she learned that another even more spiteful rumour was being broadcast, hinting that Gino was not Teddy's father and she had given birth to some other man's bastard. She knew then that she could not live with the poisonous lies being spread about by Cosima and her daughters, and she decided that it was time to go home.

Despite pleas from her family to stay and outface the gossips, she set off for England at the end of January, taking Teddy with her. They travelled by train to Calais where they boarded the packet boat for Dover. Phoebe still had the money that Gino had tossed at her on that last fateful night. She had tried to give it to Lalia, but she had refused, saying that as Gino's widow Phoebe was entitled to that and more. Lalia

435

had heard the rumours spread about by her sister-in-law and nieces, and she had repudiated them in public. She gave Phoebe her blessing and thanked her for the happiness that she had given her son. Her only deep regret was the loss of his baby and they had clung together, weeping for the child that would never be. It had been a tearful parting, but Phoebe had taken comfort from her mother-in-law's sympathy and understanding. Perhaps the burden of guilt was a little lighter as she stepped ashore on her native soil. There was only one place now where she could go and be certain of a genuine welcome. She set off once again, but this time she was headed for Brighton.

It was Rose who opened the door and she uttered a shriek of delight, throwing her arms around Phoebe's neck and hugging her until she could scarcely breathe. She drew away as Teddy uttered a squeak of protest at being ignored. She bent down and scooped him up in a fond embrace. 'How you've grown. I can't believe you're walking, little man.'

Phoebe picked up her battered leather portmanteau. 'I couldn't stand it there any longer, Rose. I've come home.'

Rose hitched Teddy onto her hip. 'Come in out of the cold. Judy will be so pleased to see you. We were all devastated when we received Ivy's letter. I'm so sorry about Gino and . . .' Her voice trailed off miserably. 'You know.'

'Yes,' Phoebe said quickly. 'It was awful. It still is, but I'd rather not talk about it.'

'I understand.' Rose led the way into the house. It was just the same as it had been when Phoebe departed in such a rush, but it seemed more like years than a matter of months since she was last here. The yellowed wallpaper in the entrance hall was still peeling in patches and as Rose opened the kitchen door Phoebe was greeted with a rush of warm air, scented with the aroma of baking.

Judy was up to her elbows in flour as she pummelled bread dough. 'Who was it, Rose?' she asked without looking up. 'If it was someone looking for a room, we're full.'

'I hope you've got room for one more,' Phoebe said, smiling. 'And a little one too.'

Judy looked up, her eyes widening and her jaw dropping in astonishment. A slow smile almost split her face in two. 'Phoebe.' She hurried towards her, shedding a fine mist of flour in her wake. She stopped short of hugging her, which Phoebe knew would have been too great a show of outward affection for a woman of Judy's nature and temperament.

'I hope you don't mind us turning up on your door-step yet again, Judy.' Phoebe held out her hand, and Judy took it in a grip that made her wince.

'Of course I don't mind. We've all missed you and the boy. The others will think it's Christmas all over again.' Her smile faded. 'We heard, you know. I'm sorry for your loss.'

'Thank you.' The words came automatically to Phoebe now. She looked round, realising that someone was missing. 'Where's Dolly?'

Judy placed the bread dough in a bowl and covered it with a damp cloth. 'I found her the ideal employer. One of the travelling repertory companies needed a wardrobe mistress and a general runabout. Marcus introduced them to Dolly and they loved her. She's currently touring the country with the theatricals and the last I heard of her she was well and happy. That dreadful mother of hers will never find her in a million years.'

'I'll miss her, but I'm glad she's doing what she wants to do.' Phoebe said, sighing. 'I hope they treat her well.'

'We wouldn't have let her go if we thought otherwise,' Rose said, setting Teddy down on the floor. He toddled over to Judy, stumbling on his last step and clutching at her apron.

Judy patted him on the head, leaving a dusting of flour on his damp curls. 'Well now, what a fine boy you are, Teddy. I expect you'd like some cake and milk. It's lucky that today is my baking day.' She whisked him off his feet and set him down on a chair. 'Rose, fetch milk from the larder. The boy needs feeding up.' She shot a critical glance at Phoebe. 'And you look like a wraith. Hang your cloak and bonnet on the peg and sit down. You look exhausted.'

Too tired to argue, Phoebe did as she was told. She sipped tea and ate a slice of warm seed cake not long out of the oven while Rose and Judy ministered to Teddy. He opened his mouth obediently accepting tiny pieces of cake, washed down with sips of milk. No one mentioned Gino by name and for that Phoebe was truly grateful. The conspiracy of silence continued even later that afternoon when Madame Galina and Gussie returned home. Fred arrived an hour later and he embraced Phoebe as if she were a long lost friend. He smelt of the outdoors and his sleeves were cold and damp after a day spent washing windows, but his welcome was warm. When Herbert and Marcus returned from the theatre in between the matinee and evening performances, their greeting was equally passionate. Phoebe felt that she had truly come home. The large kitchen was the beating heart of the shabby old house, and she was surrounded by friends. No one here would say cruel things to her. For the first time in weeks she felt easier in her mind. It was as if a huge burden had been lifted from her shoulders.

That night in her old room at the top of the house she had the comfort of knowing that Teddy was safe from the malicious tongues of the people who believed the worst of her, and she had the added comfort of Rose's presence to keep her company through the long hours of darkness.

Rose secured the last rag in her hair and climbed into bed, blowing out the candle. 'Are you really all right, Phoebe?'

'As well as can be expected. That's what they say, isn't it?'

'Yes, it is, and I understand if you don't want to speak about what happened in Italy.'

'I will one day, but not now. It's all too raw and I just want to forget.'

'There's just one thing I must tell you before you find out for yourself.'

Rose sounded hesitant, almost embarrassed. Phoebe wished that she could see her face, but the room was in almost complete darkness apart from a fractured beam of moonlight that struggled to penetrate the dirty panes of the window set in the sloping roof. 'Go on,' she said, suddenly nervous. 'You're not ill or anything, are you?'

'No, nothing like that. There's no way to make this easy so I'll tell you straight out. We've never had secrets from each other, have we?'

'Not that I know of. Please tell me – I'm dying of curiosity.'

'It's me and Ned. We're stepping out together. I'm sorry, Phoebe. I know it must seem like treachery but it just happened.'

Phoebe raised herself on her elbow. 'You and Ned!'

'I love him and he says he loves me.'

'Oh, Rose. Be careful. You know his reputation with women.'

'I do, and he's told me all about his murky past, but he's a reformed character now. He's put all that crime and violence behind him.'

'How can you be sure? I don't want to be cruel, but my mother must have thought much the same as you. He's a charmer, but once he gets his own way with a woman he loses interest.'

'We're getting married in the spring,' Rose said with a nervous giggle. 'You'll think it's sudden and that I don't know my own mind. I've had all those lectures from my pa and Judy, and even from Madame and

Gussie, but I truly believe he's changed and that he loves me.'

Phoebe shivered and slid back beneath the covers. It was cold in the room under the eaves but the real chill was in her heart. She had convinced herself that she had put the past behind her, but now memories came flooding back and with them came the pain. 'And what does Rogue say to all this?' Just speaking his name hurt her more than she could have thought possible.

'He seemed pleased that Ned means to start a new life in the country.' Rose paused, as if choosing her words carefully. 'I'm so sorry, Phoebe. I'd rather cut my right hand off than do anything to hurt you. I know you had feelings for Rogue.'

'He followed us to Italy, but he arrived too late. Gino and I were already married. Rogue wanted me to run away with him then, but I refused. I sent him away, Rose. I tried to be a good wife to Gino, but in the end I destroyed him.'

'No. I'm sure that's not true.' Rose's voice shook with suppressed emotion. 'He was a good man but he wanted you above anything else in the world, and he was prepared to take you no matter what. If he couldn't live with the consequences then that was his failing, not yours.'

'I let him think that I loved him, and I did after a fashion, but it wasn't enough. I cheated him. I let him down.'

'I know you better than that, Phoebe. You would have stood by him no matter what. He lost his life

441

because of a moment of madness. If he'd stayed with you that night instead of rushing out into the storm he would be alive now.'

'If I hadn't lost my temper,' Phoebe murmured. 'If I'd told him about the baby, perhaps he would have behaved differently.'

'Oh, Phoebe. I cried all night when I heard that you'd lost your baby. I can only imagine how you must have felt.'

'It was my punishment.' Tears slid down Phoebe's cheeks. 'I didn't want it at first. I didn't want anything that tied me to Gino for life, but when they told me that both my husband and my baby were dead, I wanted to die too. I blame myself, Rose.'

'That's nonsense, love. Gino was a grown man. He must have known it was a stupid thing to do, setting off in such dreadful conditions. You can't spend the rest of your life punishing yourself.'

'Do you really love Ned?' Exhausted from travelling and the emotions that had been stirred within her, Phoebe forced herself to relax. She knew that Rose was talking sense, and that she must not allow her personal tragedy to cast a shadow over her friend's happiness.

'I do,' Rose said simply. 'And there's another thing, Phoebe. Ned is living in the farmhouse and he isn't ever going back to London. He says he's quite keen to work the land, which is wonderful.'

'I suppose they convinced the excise men that they had nothing to do with the smugglers or Rogue wouldn't have been free to follow me to Italy.'

'Exactly so. Merrydew and his wife and the others were arrested and sent for trial. The last I heard they were in Dover jail and will be for quite some time. Rogue's contacts in the City of London police cleared them of all suspicion.'

'I don't see how the police could turn a blind eye to their criminal activities.'

'They were collaborating with the police for years, so Ned told me. You know the old saying about taking a thief to catch a thief; well that's what they've been doing.'

'But they had a reputation for being one of the worst mobs in the East End.'

'Which is why the leaders of the high mobs never suspected anything until it was too late. They were either caught or fled south of the river.'

'If only he'd told me,' Phoebe said softly. 'I always thought that he was responsible for my pa's death. I wish he'd trusted me enough to tell me the truth.'

'Maybe you ought to see him and ask him to explain.'

'I doubt if he'll ever speak to me again, or that he'd have the slightest interest in me now. I'm not the same person I was before I married Gino.'

'Of course you are. You're just tired and unhappy, but it will pass. Everything does in time.' Rose yawned and the bedstead creaked as she turned on her side. 'Go to sleep, love. Everything will seem better in the morning.'

Phoebe stared into the darkness. It seemed to stretch into infinity, and nothing would ever be the same again.

Chapter Twenty-Five

It took Phoebe a week to get over her travel fatigue, and in that time Rose had taken Teddy under her wing, her fondness for the little boy growing deeper as she saw traits in him that reminded her of his father. His eyes, she said, were the same shape and colour as Ned's. He was a miniature version of his parent, and that made her love him even more.

At first Phoebe was simply grateful to be relieved of the responsibility for an energetic toddler, but as the days went by and she regained her full strength, she began to resent Teddy's growing dependence on Rose. Sitting by the fire in the front parlour one evening she confided her worries to Judy.

'You'll have to face the fact that when Rose marries Ned she'll be Teddy's stepmother,' Judy said, looking up from darning a man's sock. 'If Ned still wants to raise his son there won't be anything you can do about it.'

'But Teddy is my responsibility,' Phoebe said in horror. 'He's my baby brother and Ma would want him to stay with me.'

'You don't know that for certain.' Judy eyed her speculatively. 'Ned is his father, and as far as I can see he's determined to put his old life behind him. Rose loves Teddy and she'd care for him as if he were her own.'

Phoebe bit her lip. She had expected Judy to be on her side. 'But I was planning for us to live here with you. I'll get a job somewhere, or I'll go back to doing what I know best and set up as a medium or a fortune teller. I can work in the theatre or a tent on the beach.'

'I speak as I find, Phoebe. You must do what's best for the boy, and perhaps that means giving him up.'

Phoebe was shocked by Judy's words. 'But I love him too. I don't see why you and I can't bring Teddy up together.'

'It's not as simple as that.' Judy moved the work candle a little closer. 'I must get Marcus to have a gas mantle put in this room. I'm straining my eyes in this poor light.'

Momentarily diverted, Phoebe stared at her in surprise. 'What has Marcus to do with it?'

Judy held up the sock. 'This isn't mine, ducks. I may be a spinster but I haven't taken to wearing men's hose, and as a matter of fact I won't qualify for that title much longer.'

'You and Marcus are getting married?'

'Don't look so surprised. I may have turned forty but I'm not in my dotage and you knew that Marcus proposed to me before you left for Italy.'

'I'm sorry, Judy. I've been so wrapped up in my own problems that I hadn't given it a thought.'

'I know that, which is why I didn't mention the fact that we're getting married in the register office tomorrow. I would have told you sooner, but you've been in such a poorly state since you came home that Marcus and I thought it best to wait until you were yourself again.'

'I'm really happy for you,' Phoebe said, staring into the fire. She knew she ought to show more enthusiasm, but Judy's news had come as a shock, and it changed everything.

'But what?' Judy prodded her with her bony finger. 'Spit it out, girl. Something's bothering you.'

'You won't want me here when you're married, and anyway you might sell this house. You'll want to go and live with your husband.'

'Stuff and nonsense. Marcus owns a poky little cottage at the other end of town, and I'm not giving up my independence for any man. He'll move in here permanently tomorrow and I'll continue to earn my own living just as before.'

'And he doesn't mind?'

'He dotes on me,' Judy said with a smug smile. 'He'll do anything I say, and I wouldn't have it any different.' She put the darning down. 'I could do with an early night. We're having a little party at Madame's pub after the ceremony tomorrow.'

Phoebe raised her hand to her forehead. 'I've missed so much. I feel I've come back to a completely different place. Everything has changed.'

'Nothing stays the same forever, ducks.' Judy rose to her feet. 'Put the guard round the fire before you go up. We don't want the house to burn down round us, and make sure that whoever comes in last locks the front door. We don't want to invite burglars in either.' She left the room, closing the door behind her, and the candle flames flickered in the sudden breeze.

Phoebe curled up in the wingback chair by the fire. She felt small and suddenly very much alone. She had forgotten that Marcus had proposed to Judy, who had always seemed to be a confirmed spinster. Nor could she have foreseen that Rose would fall in love with Ned Paxman. A more unlikely pair would be hard to envisage. Madame Galina and Herbert were talking about opening a bar together, although theirs was a purely professional arrangement. Gussie and Fred were also keeping company in a lukewarm romance that had a hint of desperation about it rather than blind passion, but still they had each other, and that was better than facing life unwanted and alone.

Phoebe had to come to terms with the fact that Teddy would eventually live with his father and Rose. She herself would slip into the part of the childless widowed relation whom everyone pitied and invited to their homes at Christmas, or when someone was sick and in need of a nurse or an unpaid nursery maid. The lot of single women without a profession or a private income was likely to be one of servitude and loneliness.

A loud knock on the front door brought her back to the present and she leapt to her feet. As she hurried from the room she hoped it might be Rose, returning early from the theatre. The thought of a chat over a cup of hot cocoa was a pleasing one and she was smiling as she opened the door, but the smile froze on

447

her face as she looked up into a pair of sea-green eyes that were so like Teddy's.

'Ned.' Phoebe glanced behind him in the vain hope that Rogue had accompanied him, but he was alone. She felt strangely cheated as she stood aside to let him in. 'I didn't expect to see you.'

He stepped over the threshold, pausing in the hallway to take off his top hat and damp greatcoat. 'It's good to see you again, Phoebe. I thought that Rose might have told you I'd been invited to Judy's wedding.'

Phoebe shook her head, at a loss for words. He was so like his brother in looks, if not in nature and temperament, that his unexpected arrival threw her into a state of renewed agitation.

He gave her a searching look, holding out his hand. 'I hope we can put the past behind us and be friends.'

She stared at his hand, the broad palm and spatulate fingers worthy of a farmer, and his once pale skin tanned by exposure to the elements. 'For Rose's sake,' she murmured, laying her hand in his.

'Thank you, Phoebe. I know that can't have been easy.'

She met his anxious gaze with an attempt at a smile. 'I love Rose, and if you hurt her . . .'

'I love her too. She's a wonderful girl and I don't deserve her.'

There was no doubting his sincerity, but Phoebe could still hear her mother telling her how much she loved Ned Paxman, and their love-child was sleeping in the room at the top of the house. Phoebe had not forgotten that Ned had attempted to gain control of his son by forcing her to marry him. His careless actions had started a chain of events that had led to her own personal tragedy, and now he was asking for her forgiveness and her blessing on his forthcoming nuptials to a dear friend. She wanted to hate him, but she felt suddenly drained of all emotion. 'Come into the front parlour,' she said, hoping that she sounded calmer than she was feeling. 'Rose will be home soon.' She led the way, although it was obvious that he knew the layout of the house as well as she did.

He stood with his back to the fire. 'It's all quite proper.' His lips twitched. 'I've booked into a boarding house nearby.'

Phoebe faced him squarely. 'Are you laughing at me, Ned?'

He was suddenly serious. 'No. On my honour, although you probably think I have none. I want you to forgive me, and to believe that I will do everything in my power to make Rose happy.'

'I think I do,' she said, sitting down on the chair she had recently vacated. The shock of seeing him again was wearing off a little, but his presence was a painful reminder of what she had lost. 'How is Rogue?' She stared down at her hands clasped tightly in her lap. 'Is he well?'

'He is in the best of health.'

She looked up. 'Does he ever speak of me?'

He answered with an almost imperceptible shake of his head. 'He doesn't confide in me. He never has. We might be brothers but we are as unalike as two men could be who are so closely related.'

'Does he know that I'm back in England?'

'I can't say. I'm no letter writer, although I might have mentioned it when he visited last week. Rose writes every day, bless her.'

'You saw him last week?' Phoebe's heart missed a beat. So Rogue knew that she was home and he had not made any effort to see her. It was hardly surprising but it still hurt.

'He comes down to the farm every few weeks to go over the books with me,' Ned carried on, seemingly oblivious to her distress. 'I'm no bookkeeper either. In fact, as you've probably already decided, I'm a fairly useless sort of fellow, but I've discovered one talent.'

'And what's that?' Phoebe sensed that he was eager to talk about himself and it was easier to listen than to talk as she struggled with the knowledge that Rogue wanted nothing more to do with her.

'I'm a good practical farmer. I like working outdoors and I have an affinity with animals.' He chuckled. 'You might think I learned that by mixing with the lowest of the low in London, and you'd probably be right. But at the very least I can make a good living for myself and my family, and an honest one too. I never thought I'd hear myself say those words.' He stopped short at the sound of someone rapping on the door knocker. 'I'll go, Phoebe. It might be Rose. I can't wait to see her again.'

He left the room with the haste of a man desperate to hold the woman he loved in his arms. Phoebe bent her head as she struggled to control her raw emotions. Outside in the hallway she could hear Rose's excited cries followed by Herbert's deeper tones, and a buzz of conversation as Madame, Gussie and Fred arrived close on their heels. She fumbled in her skirt pocket for a hanky and blew her nose. No one must know that her heart was breaking all over again.

It was a quiet ceremony at the register office with just Phoebe, Rose, Ned, Herbert and Gussie to act as witnesses and support the bride and groom. Madame Galina was on duty in the pub and had been given the task of organising a simple wedding breakfast, and Fred had remained at the house to keep an eye on Judy's cleaning woman who was supposed to be looking after Teddy. Gussie had warned Phoebe that, when she thought no one was looking, Mrs Wagg had a tendency to take nips from Judy's bottle of medicinal brandy. Phoebe had been loath to leave her in charge, preferring to look after Teddy herself, but Fred had volunteered to stay behind in order to keep an eye on Mrs Wagg.

When she arrived at the pub Phoebe was dismayed to find him ensconced in a seat by the bar drinking a glass of porter. She hurried over to him. 'You haven't left Teddy with Mrs Wagg, have you?'

He gave her a tipsy grin. 'She's promised to stay sober, love. Hasn't touched a drop all afternoon, I saw to that.'

Phoebe remained unconvinced. She nibbled at the food set out on a table in a private room at the rear of the building, and drank a glass of mulled wine to toast the bride and groom, but despite Gussie's assurance

451

that Mrs Wagg was perfectly capable of giving Teddy his tea and putting him to bed, Phoebe continued to worry. It had been difficult enough when Ned turned up soon after breakfast, ostensibly to see Rose, but it was obvious that he had also come to see his son. Teddy had been shy at first but Ned had exhibited a surprising amount of patience when dealing with a small child. He had let Teddy come to him, and Phoebe had grudgingly had to admit that he was good with the boy. There did seem to be a natural bond between father and son, and although it hurt at first, Phoebe knew in her heart that this was where Teddy's future lay. Rose adored him, and Ned seemed determined to prove that he could be a good husband and father.

Phoebe sat looking at the feast that Madame Galina had laid out for them. There was an array of cold meats, a raised pork pie and a selection of jellies, shimmering and quivering with every slight movement of the slightly rickety table. Madame had obviously gone to a great deal of trouble, not to mention expense, although she had been quick to explain that it was Marcus who had paid for the whole thing. Everyone seemed to be enjoying themselves, except Phoebe. She was even more conscious of being the only one there who was not in some kind of partnership. Madame and Herbert were engrossed in a discussion about their proposed business venture. They hoped to become the proprietors of an ancient coaching inn on the outskirts of the town. It was reputed to have been a haunt of smugglers, but was now respectable, if slightly run down. 'A good business opportunity', Herbert was fond of saying. 'We'll make it the best hostelry in the area.' Gussie planned to leave her job at the milliner's shop and was going to help Madame in the kitchen, and Fred was talking about abandoning his window cleaning round to become a potman and ostler. He had decided that his summer occupation of sword swallowing was a profession for younger men, and he was ready to give up the theatre and settle down.

Phoebe had listened to all their hopes and dreams and her heart swelled with pride for her adopted family, but she was still the odd one out. She was painfully aware that she was going to lose Teddy, and although Judy and Marcus had told her that she was welcome to live with them, she did not want to impose on their hospitality. There was, she decided, only one course open to her. She would return to London in the spring. She would endeavour to pick up the threads of her old life. There was always the table tipping, which was still the vogue amongst the middle and upper classes. The séances had provided a steady source of income, and telling the fortunes of young ladies eager to know when, where and whom they were to marry was always popular. She would go back to Saffron Hill, her grandparents and the ice cream trade. It would be a safer place now that the gangs had been broken up or moved on. She would make a life for herself. She would never marry.

Rose came to sit beside her. 'Are you all right, love? You look sad.'

Faced with Rose's glowing happiness, Phoebe felt her throat constrict. She made a huge effort to smile.

'I'm delighted to see Judy and Marcus so well suited to each other.'

'But you're not happy, darling.'

'I'm just a bit tired. It's been a long day, and seeing Ned . . .'

Rose clasped her hand. 'I know it must seem selfish of me to invite him here, but I want you to get used to seeing us together. Ned is desperate to have Teddy come and live with us when we're married. I promise you I'll look after him and love him as if he was my own little boy. You can come and stay with us as often as you like.' Her eyes brightened. 'You could live with us, Phoebe. You know how large the house is, and we could be a proper family.'

'I'll think about it,' Phoebe said, not wanting to hurt Rose's feelings by an outright refusal. She did not want to admit that witnessing their happiness would only add to her misery. She did not relish the idea of withering into a vinegar-faced widow with a great void where once she had had a heart. She rose to her feet. 'I think I should go and check on Teddy. I don't trust Mrs Wagg to stay sober all evening.'

Rose glanced anxiously at Ned, who was chatting amicably to his future father-in-law. 'Perhaps we ought to go and leave you to enjoy the party.'

Phoebe bent down to kiss her on the cheek. 'I'm not really in the mood for all this. You'll understand that, I'm sure. I'll slip out and no one will notice. This is Judy's day and I don't want to spoil it.'

Ignoring Rose's protests, Phoebe left the room quietly. She collected her cloak and bonnet and edged her way through the crowded taproom, which was filled with tobacco smoke and the babble of men's voices, interspersed with shouts of laughter. Outside the night air was bitterly cold and the pavements shone with frost. The waves pounded on the pebbles, sucking them out to sea and then spilling them back on the shore in a thunderous clatter. It was a short walk to the house and Phoebe's cheeks were tingling as she rattled the doorknocker. Her breath plumed about her head in clouds as she waited for Mrs Wagg to admit her.

The door opened. 'Phoebe. I was hoping it was you.'

She stood frozen to the spot. She could neither move nor speak. The shock had turned her to stone. He was silhouetted in the doorway. His back was to the light, but she would have known him anywhere.

'Come inside. You look chilled to the marrow.'

Rogue's hand was warm and his grip firm as he helped her over the threshold. He released her almost immediately but she could still feel the impression of his fingers on hers. She was struck dumb by the unexpected emotion that threatened to choke her. She held her hand to her breast, struggling to regain her breath. She hoped vaguely that he would put her lack of speech down to exertion or the extreme cold.

Closing the door, he turned to her and for the first time she could see his features clearly. His expression was inscrutable. If there had been a glimmer of a smile in his eyes, or the hint of a welcome, she would have fallen into his arms; but there was nothing. She might as well have been looking into the face of a stranger.

'Let me take your things. You must come and sit by the fire.' He was so calm, so polite and so practical. He might have been speaking to an aged aunt. Once again his touch sent shivers down her spine. He was standing so close to her that she could feel his warm breath on her cheek, but he moved away to hang her cloak and bonnet on the hall stand. Without giving her a second glance he walked towards the kitchen, and like an automaton she followed him.

The warmth from the range enveloped her as she entered the room. She looked around expecting to see Mrs Wagg, but they were alone. She found her voice. 'Where is Mrs Wagg? She was supposed to be looking after Teddy.'

'The woman was drunk. I sent her home.' He went to the range. The kettle was boiling and the teapot was at the ready as if he had been disturbed in the process of making tea. Phoebe pulled up a chair and sat down, resting her elbow on the table. Suddenly she wanted to laugh. A hysterical bubble rose in her throat but she swallowed hard. 'I never thought to see the leader of the Paxman gang doing something as mundane as making tea.' Even to her own ears her voice sounded high-pitched and strained.

'There is no gang now. Didn't Rose tell you that we'd disbanded it some months ago?'

'She said something about Ned taking up farming.'

Rogue filled the teapot with boiling water and set the kettle back on the hob. 'You look as though you could do with a hot drink. What possessed you to walk home alone? Why didn't you get a cab?' There was an

456

angry edge to his voice that was anything but loverlike.

She raised her chin, meeting his gaze squarely. 'Why are you here?'

'I came to wish the bride and groom well.'

'But you scarcely know them.'

'That's not quite true. I've met them both on several occasions since Ned and Rose have been walking out.'

'And do you think that your brother is in love with Rose? Or will he tire of her as he did my mother?'

Rogue stared at her for a moment, as if weighing her words carefully before he responded. 'Why so bitter, Phoebe? Don't you believe that a man can change?'

She knew that she had hurt him even though his expression was guarded, and once again she struggled against the impulse to hold him and kiss away the frown that furrowed his forehead. 'I don't know. You tell me.'

He poured the tea, adding milk and a dash of sugar to her cup before handing it to her. It seemed to Phoebe that he was playing for time. She wished that he would fight back. She wanted him to tell her that of course he could change; that he was a different man from the gangster she had known. That he loved her still. Her hand trembled as she took the cup from him and she covered her confusion by sipping the scalding brew. 'Well,' she said shakily when he did not answer. 'Do you think your brother will treat Rose well? Or will he abandon her?'

'I heard what happened to Gino,' he said slowly. 'And that you lost your child. I'm truly sorry.'

457

She could not look him in the face. 'It's in the past. I have to move on.'

'What will you do now? Will you return to London in the spring?'

The sound of the wedding party arriving home saved her from replying. She rose hastily to her feet, setting the cup down on the table. 'I must check on Teddy. They'll wake him up if they don't stop that noise.' She did not look back as she hurried from the room. She could not bear to be so close to him and yet feel that they were a hundred miles apart. It seemed a cruel irony that he had chosen to visit the house in the full knowledge that she would be present, but without any intention of making his peace with her. She had sensed his inner anger and it hurt more than she could bear.

She had to push past the revellers as they took off their outer garments. Rose was the only one who noticed her and she followed her to the foot of the stairs. 'What's the matter, Phoebe? You look as though you've seen a ghost.'

'Perhaps I have,' Phoebe said tersely. 'I'm going to make sure that all the noise hasn't woken Teddy.' She picked up her skirts and ran upstairs to her room. Teddy was sleeping peacefully and she lay down on her bed, still fully dressed. If she had thought her heart was broken when she parted from Rogue on her wedding day, she realised that it had merely been badly bruised. Now she could feel a physical pain and she was certain that if anyone could look inside her body they would see nothing but tiny shards where once there had been a beating heart. He was unforgiving.

It was quite obvious that he felt nothing for her, except perhaps disdain for a woman who thought that she had done everything for the best but had only succeeded in wrecking the lives of those she was supposed to love most.

Chapter Twenty-Six

Teddy whimpered in his sleep and she leapt up, rushing over to his cot to make sure that he had not kicked off his coverlet. She tucked it up around his chin, gently stroking his tumbled curls back from his forehead. 'I've been a selfish woman, Teddy,' she whispered. 'I'm not the best person to bring you up. I love you with all my heart, little man, but I know now that you belong with Ned and Rose. I'll always be there for you, but I'm only your sister. You need a mother and a father to raise you to be a good and honest man.' She dropped a kiss on his forehead and walked slowly back to her own bed.

Next morning she discovered that Ned and Rogue had returned to London on the first train out of Brighton station. Judy and Marcus left later that day for a short wedding trip to Eastbourne, where Marcus was combining business with pleasure as he negotiated a contract with a touring repertory company. Madame Galina and Herbert went off to sign the lease on their new premises and Gussie hastened to her place of employment to hand in her notice. Fred was suffering from a hangover but had loaded his ladder onto a handcart and was preparing to go out on his round. Rose scolded him and told him that it would be his own fault if he fell off and broke his neck. He answered with a stoic shrug of his shoulders and lit a cigarette which he held between his teeth as he staggered off down the road. Left alone with Rose and Teddy, Phoebe was about to put on her cloak and bonnet and take him for a walk along the promenade, but Rose waylaid her. 'What was all that about last night? Why did you run away?'

'I went to bed because I was tired.'

Rose's eyes flashed with anger. 'No. You had a row with Rogue and you went off like a petulant schoolgirl instead of staying and making things right with him.'

'You don't know what you're talking about.' Phoebe was about to walk away but Rose caught her by the sleeve.

'Don't try and fob me off with that nonsense. I know you too well. You're still in love with him, so why don't you admit it?'

'He made it quite clear that he despises me. I thought I was doing the right thing when I married Gino, but everything went wrong. I don't blame him for hating me. I hate myself for what I did.'

'That's utter nonsense. Of course he doesn't hate you. If he felt like that about you he wouldn't have come all the way from London especially to see you.'

'He came to wish Judy and Marcus well. He told me so himself.'

'And you believed him.' Rose threw up her hands. 'You are a stupid pair of idiots. You deserve each other.'

Phoebe shook her head. Suddenly she was too tired even to think. 'I'm going home to Saffron Hill, Rose.

I'll get the house ready for my grandparents. They'll be returning in a month or so, and I need to find new clients. I can't expect them to support me for the rest of my life.'

'If you do that you're just running away again. You're not facing up to the truth, Phoebe.'

'I don't know what that is any more. All I know is that I can't stay here, and I must be practical.'

'And what about Teddy? Surely you aren't going to drag him back to that awful place?'

Phoebe laid her hand on Rose's arm. 'No. I've realised that I was wrong there too. Teddy belongs with his father, and you'll make him a wonderful step-mother. You'll have babies and he'll be part of a proper family.'

Rose's eyes brimmed with tears and she flung her arms around Phoebe's neck. 'That's wonderful. You won't regret your decision. I'll love him and take great care of him.'

Phoebe extracted herself from Rose's affectionate hug. 'I know you will, and I'll be a loving big sister. It will be best for everyone.'

'And you're still determined to return to London?'

'Yes, but I want you to promise that you won't tell Rogue. It's better for both of us if we don't see each other again. He was so angry with me, Rose. I can't begin to tell you how much that hurt. I'm not going through that again, ever.'

A week later, amidst tears and fond farewells, Phoebe left Brighton and returned to London. It was the middle of March and winter was just losing its icy grip on the city. She spent her time cleaning the house in Saffron Hill and making it ready to receive her family when they returned from Stresa. She put cards in shop windows advertising the fact that she was ready to recommence séances and available for telling fortunes. She put a small advertisement in *The Times* in an attempt to encourage a more upper class clientele to brave the squalor of the East End, which some of them might consider an adventure akin to a safari where they could view wild species in their natural habitat. She had few takers, but she had the comfort of knowing that she had tried. Some of her old clients began to trickle back, and just as her money from Gino ran out she began to earn enough to keep herself in food and candles. She had nothing left to spend on coal or kindling, but she managed to combat the chill in the old house by putting on extra layers of clothes. She had written to her grandparents and informed them of her decision to return to London, and she had explained her reasons for leaving Teddy in Brighton. Fond as they were of the little boy, she knew that they would respect her wishes that he be raised by his father. They might even forgive Ned Paxman now that he was a reformed character and intent on setting up home with Rose and his son. There would be no question of vendetta.

She settled down to await their return and soon fell into a daily routine of getting up early and going out to market before the crowds had time to congregate. She avoided going to places where she might come across Rogue, although she occasionally gave way to temptation and paid a visit to Wilderness Row, convincing herself that it was simply to discover whether or not he was still in London. Without his gang to organise she could not imagine how he would keep himself occupied or how he would earn his living. She wondered if he had opted to join his brother in Kent and become a gentleman farmer. Somehow she did not see him in that particular role. She told herself that she did not care what happened to him and that it did not matter what he thought of her, but in her heart she knew she was lying. She did care very much. She hated the idea that he had a bad opinion of her, if he even thought of her at all.

The weeks passed and Phoebe received a letter from Ivy telling her that the family would be returning at the beginning of May, although she and Nenzo would remain in Stresa until after the birth of their baby. Rose and Ned were to be married at the end of April and Phoebe had promised faithfully to return to Brighton to attend their wedding. She had trimmed an old bonnet and altered one of her gowns so that it fitted her slender frame. Although she knew she was painfully thin, she had little or no appetite, but it did not seem to matter. Nothing much mattered now. She struggled through each day, a mere shadow of her former self. Her one pleasure was to walk to Charterhouse gardens and sit on a bench beneath the trees as they burst into leaf. Golden daffodils waved their trumpets in the breeze and she could almost imagine she was back in the country. She could see the houses in Wilderness Row clearly from her vantage point, and although she told herself she had just come to this green oasis in the city for a breath of fresh air, she knew that she was deceiving herself. Her reason for coming was simple: she hoped to catch a glimpse of Rogue Paxman. She had no intention of making herself known to him, but she needed to know that he was alive and well. Such information would make it easier for her to sleep at night, and put a stop to the nightmares in which she saw him walking out with a beautiful woman on his arm, or even worse confined in a small, dark prison cell living on bread and water.

She promised herself that this would be her last such visit to the gardens. She was due to travel to Brighton next day, and if Rogue was there, as he almost certainly would be, she would behave impeccably. No one would guess that beneath her serene exterior there was a maelstrom of emotion that threatened to choke the life from her.

She put aside her black mourning clothes and dressed in the gown that she intended to wear to the wedding. She put on the bonnet that she had renovated with such care and tied the blue ribbon at a jaunty angle. If, by chance, she should happen to meet Rogue, she did not want to look like a downtrodden drab. She walked to the park and took her usual seat, shooing away a few importunate pigeons. She sat for an hour or perhaps more; she had lost track of time. The sun had been shining but it disappeared suddenly behind a bank of clouds and it began to rain. She rose hastily and hurried towards a large plane tree for shelter, but before she reached it her attention was drawn to a commotion outside Rogue's house. She stopped, disregarding the rain that soaked through her thin shawl and dripped off the brim of her straw bonnet. A small noisy crowd had gathered and she could hear a man's voice raised in anger. Two police constables were in the middle of the fracas and one of them climbed the steps to knock on the door, which was opened almost immediately. Phoebe's hand flew to her mouth as she saw Rogue standing on the threshold. She moved closer, leaving the gardens and stopping on the opposite side of the street where she could get a better view of the house.

She recognised the man who was causing the disturbance, and the hairs prickled on the back of her neck. Snape was shouting accusations and a torrent of abuse aimed at Rogue, who seemed to be in imminent danger of arrest. She ran blindly across the road, narrowly avoiding being trampled by a drayman's horse.

'Stop,' she cried, as one of the constables laid his hand on Rogue's arm. 'Stop. You don't know what you're doing. Snape is a liar.'

There was a moment of silence as the crowd parted to let her through, and Snape stared at her with his eyes bulging and a vein throbbing at his temple. He shook his fist at her. 'Don't listen to that trollop. She's his woman and she'll say anything to protect her lover.'

Before Phoebe had a chance to retaliate, Rogue had taken the steps in one great leap and grasped Snape by the throat, shaking him like a terrier with a rat. 'You lying little worm,' he hissed. 'You'll take back that slur on a lady's reputation.'

'A lady.' Snape spat the word in his face. 'She's no lady. Her ma was a whore and she's one of a kind.' He turned purple as Rogue's fingers closed around his windpipe. 'Stop him, constable. He's trying to kill me.'

The more senior of the two police officers moved swiftly to tap Rogue on the shoulder. 'It's all right, guv. We'll take it from here.'

Phoebe leaned against the area railings for support as her knees buckled. She had thought that Rogue was about to be arrested, but it seemed that she had made a terrible mistake. It was Snape whom the police were after and not Rogue. She could tell by the amused glances of the passers-by that she had made a complete fool of herself, and she wished that the ground would open up and swallow her.

'All right, ladies and gents,' the younger constable said, opening his arms and shooing the crowd away. 'The show's over.' He turned to Rogue, tipping his helmet. 'Sorry to have bothered you, sir. This chap's well known to us. He'll be up before the beak in the morning.'

'Thank you, constable. I'll be prepared to give evidence if required. You know where to find me.' Rogue took off his jacket and slipped it around Phoebe's shoulders. 'Come inside. You're soaked to the skin.'

Her teeth were chattering with shock. The dampness seeped through her clothes to chill her skin and there was little she could do except allow him to help her up the steps into the house. She leaned on him, trying to keep her mind on anything other than the familiar scent of his body and the thrill of his touch. The young housemaid who had been in attendance the last time Phoebe was in the house bobbed a curtsey, her face puckered with concern.

'Can I do anything, master? Is the young lady ill?'

'She's had a shock. A cup of tea would probably be just the thing, Lizzie. And perhaps something to eat.'

'Yes, master. Poor lady, she looks done in.'

She hurried off to do his bidding and Rogue led Phoebe into the front parlour. 'You're as thin as a sparrow, Madonna,' he said, setting her down on the sofa. 'I could pick you up with one hand. What have you been doing to yourself?'

His face was close to hers and his eyes were warm with genuine concern. Phoebe choked back tears. It was easier to cope with her emotions when he was angry with her. His kindness would be her undoing. 'I thought they were arresting you,' she murmured.

He grasped her hands, chafing them gently. 'As you can see it was all a mistake. Snape has been trying to make trouble for me for a long time, but he's gone too far now. He won't be bothering either of us again.'

'I don't understand. What could he have against you?'

Rogue sat down beside her. She could feel the warmth of his body leaching into hers, and she did not protest when he slipped his arm around her waist. 'He was an informer. He hung around the pubs where the gangs met and then passed on information to the police, but he became greedy and tried to blackmail me. I would have none of it, and he didn't understand that I was already working with the police and had been for many years.'

She laid her head on his shoulder. It seemed the natural thing to do. 'So Rose was right. You really have reformed.'

His smile caressed her face like warm sunshine. 'It had to look as though Ned and I were hard men. We did run the gang, but our main aim was genuine protection of those terrorised by the mobs, and sometimes it led to violence. I'm no knight in shining armour, Phoebe. I've done many things of which I'm bitterly ashamed.'

She raised her hand to touch his cheek. 'I don't care. I would love you even if you were the worst villain in Christendom.'

His smile faded and he turned her to face him fully. 'Say that again, Madonna. Did I hear you right?'

His eyes were alert and filled with hope. He looked suddenly young and defenceless as he waited for her to form the words. She slid her hands around his neck, pulling his head down until their lips met in a kiss. His arms tightened around her and she was lost in his passionate embrace, but they drew apart at the sound of the maid knocking on the door and Rogue rose to his feet. 'Enter.' He straightened his tie, smiling ruefully down at Phoebe as Lizzie bustled into the room and set the tray on a small table in the window.

'Will there be anything else, sir?'

'I think I can manage from now on, thank you. I'll ring if we need anything further.'

Lizzie shot Phoebe a shy smile as she bobbed a curtsey and left the room. Rogue ran his hand through his hair. 'Are you all right, my love? I didn't mean it to happen like that, but I couldn't keep my feelings hidden for a moment longer.' He moved swiftly to kneel at her feet, taking both her hands and kissing them. 'I love you too, Phoebe. I think I fell in love with you right at the start, but you were always several steps ahead of me. I thought you despised me.'

'I tried to hate you, but I couldn't.' Tears coursed down her cheeks, but this time they were tears of joy and not sorrow. 'I can't remember the exact moment when I knew that you were the only man I would ever truly love, but the gap between us seemed too great to overcome. There were so many people whose needs had to come first.'

He drew her into his arms, claiming her mouth in a kiss that she wished would last forever. When they finally drew apart he rose to his feet, smiling down at her. 'That's all over now, my darling. From now on it will be just you and me.' He went to a side table and poured a tot of brandy into a glass. He pressed it into her cold hands. 'Sip this, darling. I don't want to lose you to pneumonia so soon after claiming you for my own.'

The fiery spirit warmed her body but his tender words set her soul aflame. 'You really want me?'

He poured himself a drink and raised his glass in a toast. 'I'll never let you go again, my dearest Madonna. I'm not asking you to marry me; I'm telling you that is what we are going to do at the earliest opportunity. You don't mind, do you?'

His laugh was infectious and she smiled happily. 'Not at all, Roger.'

He put his glass down and taking hers from her, he set it back on the table. He raised her to her feet, holding her so close that she could feel their hearts beating in perfect rhythm. 'No longer a rogue, my love?'

'I'll never call you that again. I love you with all my heart, Roger Paxman.'

'And will you marry me, Phoebe?'

'Yes,' she said simply. 'I will.'

He regarded her steadily, his expression suddenly serious. 'Do you want a big wedding, or shall we do it quietly by special licence? I'll do anything you ask, but I can't wait much longer to make you my wife.'

She traced the outline of his face with her fingertips. 'I just want you. Nothing else matters to me. We've waited so long, I don't think I could bear to wait a day longer than necessary.'

He gave a whoop of pleasure, so unlike his dignified persona that they both dissolved into fits of laughter. 'You've answered my question, my sweet,' he said, holding her round the waist and twirling her round the room. 'We'll get the ring now before the jewellers close. I'm not letting my younger brother steal a march on me. We'll attend their wedding next week as an old married couple. We'll give them all the surprise of their lives.'

Their arrival at Judy's house on the day of Rose and Ned's wedding caused exactly the effect that Rogue had desired. Their news was met with delight and not a little consternation, but it did not take long for everyone to see how happy Phoebe was, and that Rogue was genuinely devoted to her. Rose laughed and cried at the same time, declaring that it was mean of Phoebe to steal the limelight from her on her wedding day, and then she hugged her. 'I couldn't be happier for you, darling,' she said, wiping her eyes. 'I just wish we could have danced at yours. It must have been a very quiet affair.'

Phoebe kissed her on the cheek and adjusted the lace veil on Rose's bonnet. 'It was exactly what we wanted. We've waited a long time to be together, and I really didn't think it would happen.'

Rose glanced anxiously at her reflection in the mirror. Judy had generously allowed her to use her own bedchamber, which possessed a tall cheval mirror, and a dressing table. 'Well, it has, and you deserve to be happy, after everything you've been through.' She smoothed her silk skirts. 'How do I look? Will Ned think I'm worth all the trouble?'

'He's a lucky dog,' Phoebe said, smiling. 'He doesn't deserve you, but now I'm his sister-in-law I can tell him that with a clear conscience and without fear of being told to mind my own business.'

'As if you would,' Rose leaned over to kiss her. 'You will be the best sister-in-law anyone could wish for, and the sweetest sister to Teddy. Madame and Gussie are dressing him in his best sailor suit. He'll look so adorable. I wish he could come with us on our honeymoon.'

'No you don't,' Phoebe said firmly. 'He'll be spoilt to death here with Judy and the others.'

Rose picked up her posy of spring flowers. 'And will you and Rogue – I mean Roger; I must get used to calling him that now. Will you two be going away somewhere nice?'

Phoebe smiled dreamily. 'He's taking me to Paris. We're leaving first thing in the morning for Dover.'

'That's funny. So are we.'

Phoebe linked her hand through Rose's arm. 'How wonderful. We'll have a glorious time.'

They both turned with a start as Judy burst into the room. She was dressed in the latest fashion with a confection of flowers and feathers on her head. 'Come along, you two. The rest of the guests left ages ago for the church and the carriage is waiting to take the bride and the matron of honour.'

'It's all right, Judy,' Rose said serenely. 'I believe it's fashionable for the bride to arrive late.'

Judy frowned. 'Young girls these days. I don't know what the world is coming to. I was on time for my wedding.' She beckoned to Phoebe. 'And your husband refuses to leave without you. He doesn't seem to want to let you out of his sight. I'd make the most of it if I were you. It never lasts.'

Phoebe hurried Rose from the room. She paused in the doorway to pat Judy on the shoulder. 'You don't mean that, I know. You might pretend to be a cynic, but I know you love Marcus and he worships you.'

Judy had the grace to blush, but she shooed them out of the room. 'Get along with you both.'

Rose was already in the hall by the time Phoebe negotiated the steep bend in the staircase. She looked down and saw that her husband was staring up at her with a look that made her heart leap for joy. He held out his hand, and his smile enveloped her like a warm embrace. Her feet barely touched the ground as she descended the stairs to walk into his arms. She had come home at last.